For Jack Fields,
a remarkable teacher,
who taught me, above all things,
to write about what I know.

I am indebted to Howard Schage, Sally Sondheim, Susan Klein, Joyce Valentine, Betta Ferrendelli, and Linda Stenn—my supporters, my contributors, my friends. For only friends are required to tell the truth. And to Fredy-Jo Grafman, Mona Kunen, and Kasey Todd Ingram for their pinpoint research, and their willingness to participate in the creative process.

I must also thank Chief of Police John Sutton and Detectives Loretta Faust and Steve Cain of the Bainbridge Island Police Department for their patience, their wisdom, and their good humor. I hope I got at least most of it right.

I am grateful to Becky Fox Marshall, editor of the *Central Kitsap Reporter*, for sharing with me her experiences and her insight.

Finally, I wish to express my appreciation to the DNA experts at the Washington State Crime Laboratory, and the good people in the Kitsap County Prosecutor's Office for taking the time to answer all my questions, no matter how silly they sounded.

Without such help, this work would never have been accomplished.

PART ONE

The Crime

"Murder, though it have no tongue, will speak."
—*William Shakespeare*

1

Death came without warning. She saw the knife in the moonlight, grasped in his hand, but she thought he meant it only as a threat, and never dreamed he would actually use it. Then it plunged through the fabric of her skirt, somewhere just below the waistband. That was how she thought of it, in the split second she had to think, that he had ripped her skirt—not that he had driven the blade deep into her flesh.

Surprised, she peered down through the darkness, curious about the damage he had done to her skirt. Then her hands, following her eyes to the spot where the knife had been, met a rush of warm stickiness. The surprise turned to disbelief.

Still, she didn't fully realize his purpose until he came at her again, and looking up, she saw his eyes, devoid of all expression, all charity. Then she understood, and the disbelief turned to absolute terror.

Her instinct was to run, of course, to try and get away from him, to survive. But he must have guessed that and was ready for her, reaching out and grasping her by the hair, holding her easily within arm's reach. Then she felt the third thrust of the knife, inches from the first two, and then the fourth and the fifth and the sixth. After that, she lost count.

She felt herself growing weak and then dizzy, and then her vision began to blur. Finally, she no longer stood by her own will, only by his, as he continued to hold her erect with one hand, and carve her up with the other. A roar like the sound of sea surf pounded in her ears, yet she heard him clearly when he spoke.

"I'm sorry," he said, his voice like his eyes, "but I just can't let you do it. I can't let you ruin my life."

She thought of her own barely lived life, of all the things she had planned to do and would now never do. The places she would go, the people she would meet. Far from here, in a land of sunlight and forgiveness. She had wanted to be good, to do good. It seemed so unfair.

The warm stickiness was oozing from too many places now. She knew she could no longer hold it in. It would leak out of her until there was nothing left, and then she would be dead. Yet she didn't struggle. It was almost as though she accepted what was happening to her as God's will.

From her earliest moments, she had sat in church and listened, mesmerized, as Father Paul spoke about the better life that awaited the faithful, about the preservation of the soul, about the rewards of heaven. He had always sounded so reassuring and she wanted so much to believe. But in the last seconds of consciousness, she couldn't help herself—she wondered what death would really be.

When she felt a white hot explosion in her chest, she knew her heart was breaking. Summoning one final spurt of energy, she opened her mouth and screamed. It didn't matter that there was no one to hear her, to save her. It wasn't meant for that, but as her only remaining protest—an excruciating sound, made all the more unbearable because it was born not of pain, but of betrayal.

2

It was usually with great reluctance that the Pacific Northwest let go its gentle grip on summer and made the sharp turn into autumn. The season could be weeks old before the air began to crackle with burning leaves, hum with fresh sea breezes, and catch up with the chatter of schoolchildren. Before the pleasant odor of wood smoke returned to banish the evening chill. Before the endless rains came to soak the spirit as well as the earth.

This year was no exception. It was already the middle of October and morning skies were still blue, night skies still starry, and temperatures still mild, even as the days grew short.

At six-thirty on the second Sunday of the month, Tom Hildress drove his Dodge pickup through the entrance of Madrona Point Park, turned to his right, and followed his headlights through the predawn darkness toward a blue Dumpster that sat against the far edge of the large gravel parking lot.

This was the designated weekend for Seward Island's annual fall cleanup, and Dumpsters had been placed at a number of strategic points for the disposal of bulky items that could not fit into regular household garbage containers. Although Madrona Point, the densely forested area that sprawled across much of the northwest end of the Island, was the most remote of the designated drop-offs, it was the most convenient for the Hildresses, whose home was less than a mile away.

Tom had spent yesterday cleaning out the garage, and he was getting an early start this morning because he had two more loads to dump, and he had promised his wife that he would be finished in time to shower and dress and go to church with the family.

He backed his truck to within six feet of the Dumpster and killed the engine. "You go on top and I'll pass stuff up to you," he suggested to the tow-headed nine-year-old sitting beside him.

"Okay," Billy Hildress agreed, jumping down from the cab and darting up a makeshift set of steps that had been pushed against the front of the big container. "Yuck," he said, wrinkling his nose as he reached the top. "Something in here really stinks."

He squinted over the edge. Dawn would not be breaking for another hour yet, but in the grayness of not quite night, he could see that the Dumpster was already half filled with everything from bald tires to broken-down refrigerators. A dilapidated sofa lay in one corner, a thick roll of rug had been flung against another.

"Jeez, Dad," he called down to his father. "I bet you could just about furnish a whole house with the junk that's in here."

Tom Hildress was well known around the Island for the many patient hours he spent sifting through other people's castoffs in search of unrecognized treasures that he could restore, with loving patience, to their original glory. The Eagle Rock Methodist Church's annual Christmas bazaar was always a huge success thanks to his keen eye and clever hand. Any other morning, he would have bounded up beside Billy, eager to have a look.

"No time," he replied with a sigh, passing an armful of flattened cardboard boxes up to the boy. "Mom gave us strict orders."

Billy heaved the boxes toward the far corner of the Dumpster and reached for more. Turning back to toss the next armful in the same direction, he suddenly froze.

The first load of cardboard had hit against the rolled-up rug, causing it to come open at one end, and revealing what looked, in the dimness, like a head of blond curls and part of a shoulder that were much too big to belong to a discarded doll.

"Say, Dad," Billy said in a strange voice, "I think there's someone up here."

"Who's that?" asked Tom, who had little time to waste and was concentrating on a third stack of cardboard.

"A person," the nine-year-old replied. "A real person. I think maybe there's a body up here."

Tom frowned in the direction of his son. "What are you talking about? Is someone going through the trash?"

Billy shook his head. "Come look," he said, backing slowly down the stairs.

Controlling his impatience, Tom climbed past the boy to peer into the Dumpster. At once, the same fetid odor that Billy had smelled assaulted his nose. His eyes searched the pile of refuse from left to right until, coming to rest on the rug in the far corner, he saw what Billy had seen.

"Oh, my God," he gasped.

He vaulted over the side of the Dumpster and waded into the rubbish. Regardless that Tom was a tall, spare man in excellent physical condition, the going was slow—in places, the trash reached above his knees—and his heart pounded painfully with every step. By the time he reached the spot, he was telling himself that life-sized dolls were not unheard of, even as the stench of waste grew stronger and he knew, just as Billy had known, that he wasn't going to find a doll.

The first thing he saw clearly was the blood. The rug seemed to be soaked with it. Then he saw the girl. She was young, in her teens, and had apparently been wrapped inside the bit of carpet and then tossed onto the garbage heap. Tom couldn't help himself, his stomach heaved, and he turned away and vomited until there was nothing left inside of him.

"What is it, Dad?" Billy called from below.

"Don't come up here, son," Tom told the boy as soon as he could catch his breath. "Go wait for me in the truck. I'll be there in a minute."

Swallowing hard, he reached down and carefully unrolled the rest of the rug, exposing the body. Pieces of denim that might have been a skirt were stuck to parts of her; denim that had probably been blue, but now appeared dark red. A blood-drenched T-shirt fanned around her in shreds. Although Tom was no expert, it didn't take one to realize that she had been stabbed repeatedly. He could almost feel the fury of the attack just by looking at her, and he wondered what kind of maniac, loose on Seward Island, could have done such a thing.

He bent down and made himself touch one of the wounds. The blood was still sticky, telling him it was only a matter of hours since her life had oozed out of those grisly gashes. He was close enough to her so that, despite the lack of daylight, he could see she wore a small gold cross around her neck. Avoiding it, he pressed his fingers against her throat, just to confirm what he already knew. She was quite dead.

The bile began to rise in him again. He didn't want to move her or touch anything else—he was already thinking ahead to finding a telephone and calling the police. But several deep breaths later, he leaned forward and gently pushed the blond curls aside.

An eye stared up at him, wide and glassy and fixed in fear so palpable that Tom stumbled backward onto his heels. Her mouth gaped—grotesque, distorted, and frozen in a silent, agonizing accusation.

3

Ginger Earley had called Seward Island home from the time she was three years old. In fact, it was the day after her birthday that her family had moved from Pomeroy, a small city in the southeast corner of Washington State, so that her father could assume the job of bailiff at the Puget County Courthouse.

In part because it may well have been true, but mostly because of an acute sense of insecurity, Ginger's mother had always harbored the belief that the locals, a great majority of whom had lived on Seward for generations, looked down on her. As a result, it became her life's work, almost to the point of obsession, to see to it that her children were the neatest, the cleanest, the best spoken, and the best behaved on the Island.

Her efforts were reasonably successful as far as the three Earley boys were concerned, but Ginger was another story. The youngest, and by far most stubborn, was more than a match for her mother.

From her earliest days, and perhaps to some extent to frustrate her mother, Ginger declined to go by her given name, Virginia, insisting instead that she be allowed to use the pet name her father had bestowed upon her. She rejected dresses and patent leather shoes in favor of blue jeans and bare feet. She skipped dance classes to participate in touch football games, and practiced tree climbing instead of the piano. She knew nothing about the proper way to pour tea, but she knew everything about gentling a horse. She couldn't stand more than ten minutes in the company of her mother's gossipy friends, but she could spend hours in the woods where deer and chipmunks ate from her hand.

Ginger was taller than average, having achieved her full height of five feet nine inches by the time she was twelve years old. Along with her stature went a head of unruly red hair that her mother always claimed must have come from her father's side of the family, a face full of freckles, and large eyes that were brown and green and gold all at the same time. She wasn't beautiful, although someone once called her looks "arresting," which proved to be a source of private amusement to her later on, and she was far too athletic to arouse much romantic interest in the opposite sex during her growing-up years. But Ginger didn't seem to care. She was the only girl ever invited to play on the boys' varsity soccer and softball teams, and she more than held her own on both. She could fly a kite with the best of them, sit a horse better than anyone on the Island, and she held the Seward High School track record at 500 and 1,000 meters for three consecutive years.

There finally came a point where her mother threw up her hands in disgust. "Go ahead and be a tomboy then, be a total embarrassment to us," she cried one day, when Ginger was sixteen years old and chose a basketball game over a ballet.

"Don't blame *me* for what I am," the fiery redhead shot back. "It's *your* genes that made me this way." It became the last word on the issue.

Despite her mother's discomfort over the people of Seward Island, Ginger loved the place. In the days of her childhood, barely four thousand independent souls laid claim to the twenty-one square miles of rolling hills, lush valleys, thick woods, and sandy beaches. That left plenty of room for a free spirit to kick up her heels.

As much as was possible in the Earley household, Ginger thought her own thoughts and did her own thing. She was loyal to her friends, bright enough to be admired by her peers, and she would not back down from a just fight. Being tall and strong for a girl, she could beat up most of the boys her own age. When she couldn't, she would call on her big brothers to help make her point.

She became notorious for one incident. When the neighborhood bully doused the Earley cat with gasoline and set her on fire, Ginger promptly doused the bully with gasoline and set *him* on fire. Although the boy was more scared than hurt, it caused an uproar.

"Why didn't you just beat him up?" her father, a gentle bear of a man, asked in exasperation when the boy's parents threatened to sue.

"Because I wanted him to know exactly how Mittens felt when he did that to her," replied the eight-year-old. "Now he does, and I bet he'll never do it again."

The police conducted an investigation. The Islanders were divided right down the middle on the issue. After some negotiation, the matter was dropped.

The tomboy image suited Ginger. More than the freedom it gave her to be herself, it allowed her to conceal the fact that she was highly competitive. She discovered early in life that being as good as her brothers was not good enough—she had to be better to be equal. Despite the fact that she was the brightest of the four, and clearly the apple of her father's eye, she saw it was to the boys that he turned for what he called "man talk." It was their perspectives he sought and their opinions he considered, not hers. As much as Ginger resented that, she had to concede that it was to her father that *she* went with her problems and questions and doubts, not to her mother. She decided there had to be a way for her to be accepted by men as an equal, and still be respected as a woman.

When she graduated from high school near the top of her class, her friends and family expected that she would enter college and then go on to become either a veterinarian or an attorney. She surprised them all.

It was not her outward toughness that led her into the police academy and a career as a law enforcement officer. It was more a combination of her loyalty and her intelligence, an overwhelming sense of what was right, and at least the hope of a level playing field. And, too, there was her pride in her father as a dedicated civil servant.

"Tell me what you think, Dad," she said. "Tell me what you really think."

"I think you could do just about anything you set out to do," Jack Earley replied, because he could deny her nothing, and besides, none of his sons had chosen to go into his line of work. "But to join the force—well, I can't think of anything that would make me prouder."

"I thought you were going to be a lawyer," her mother said, thinking how nice it would be to have a professional in the family. Her three boys were all fine young men, but one had chosen the Navy, another worked for Boeing, and the third had a wife and a child by the time he was twenty, and a steady job with the telephone company.

"It was *your* idea for me to be a lawyer," Ginger told her mother, "not mine."

Ironically enough, her first job after the academy was in a small city in eastern Washington, less than thirty miles from Pomeroy where she had been born. She lived with an aunt and uncle while she was there. They introduced her to a tall young man who was in the farm equipment business with his father, and she promptly fell in love. The two of them dated exclusively for almost a year and a half, but when it came right down to it, he apparently couldn't handle the idea of having a policewoman for a wife. She was devastated, six months later, when he married someone else.

Her second job brought her back to western Washington, too far away to live at home, but close enough to visit on her off-duty weekends. For the next five years, she worked hard and learned well, and deserved her promotion to the rank of detective. Occasionally, she would date, but there was no one serious; or perhaps there was no one she was willing to let become serious.

When the opening on Seward Island was posted, she was one of the first to apply. It was no coincidence—she had always intended to come back. There were sixteen other candidates who interviewed for the position, all of them men. Despite the fact that some had more experience and some had handled more responsibility, Ginger never doubted the job would be hers; not necessarily because she was smarter or more intuitive than anyone else, but because she had the one asset the rest of them lacked—she had been raised here, and she understood the Island and its people better than all sixteen of the others put together.

Which explained why she knew, within minutes of arriving at Madrona Point Park, that what Tom and Billy Hildress had discovered in the blue Dumpster was going to destroy her home.

4

Seward Island sat in the middle of Puget Sound like a diamond on a bed of blue velvet—radiant and rare.

It had originally been claimed by a Commodore Nathaniel Seward, who, sailing in the wake of George Vancouver at the end of the eighteenth century, was said to have been so taken by the beauty of his discovery that he promptly came ashore, dispatched his ship back to Portsmouth for his family, and proceeded to live the life of a landed English gentleman well into his eighties.

In its way, Seward Island was as exquisite as any of the tropical paradises the Commodore had encountered in his travels. Towering evergreens graced the hills, clover-rich grass carpeted the valleys, and a breathtaking panorama greeted the eyes from almost any vantage point, sweeping from the jagged Olympic Mountains in the west to the rippling Cascades in the east, and highlighted by craggy Mount Baker to the north and the sky-scraping Mount Rainier to the south.

By the middle of the nineteenth century, however, the Commodore's descendants had grown tired of the isolation of island living, paradise though it may have been, and many began to sell off their holdings and move on.

Anxious for a new beginning, Englishmen from the mills of Manchester and the mines of Newcastle came seeking land of their own. Norwegians emigrated in droves to the Pacific Northwest, bringing with them long traditions of fishing and shipbuilding. Germans fled the farms of Alsace-Lorraine and Schleswig-Holstein in the face of war. And the Irish came, escaping the potato famine, looking to put down new roots.

The warm summer sun, mild winter rains, and rich soil made the tranquil island perfect for growing almost anything. From North Point to South Cove, flowers bloomed and fruits and vegetables flourished. Chickens were brought over from the mainland, and fresh eggs found their way to the local market. Horses grazed the meadows of Cedar Valley, and cows dotted the slopes that led up to Eagle Rock. Salmon filled fishing nets, clams littered the beaches, and crab pots overflowed. Businesses sprang up to service the residents, and a small shipyard began operation.

Eventually, Seward incorporated and became the seat of Puget County—a string of little islands bound together by geography and a lack of imagination as to what else to do with them. The citizens elected a mayor and a city council. Soon thereafter, a tax structure was set up, the roads were paved, electricity was brought across the water, police and fire departments were organized, a medical clinic was established, and a limited amount of light industry was encouraged.

Nonetheless, the Island managed to retain much of its rural charm in the midst of the great Pacific Northwest expansion, due in large part to the fact that it was accessible to the mainland only by boat. A marina on the south side of Gull Harbor provided mooring for one hundred and fifty private yachts, and Washington State operated a daily ferry service.

By the last decade of the twentieth century, the peaceful paradise boasted a population of just under twelve thousand, and the town, perched atop the harbor's central slope, was a little corner of old England that had been carefully constructed by the Commodore and his descendants, and lovingly preserved by those who came after.

Almost a third of the residents took the forty-five-minute water commute to Seattle and back every weekday, and tourists flocked to the Island on weekends. Not as many as crowded onto nearby Bainbridge and Whidbey, perhaps, but enough to browse in the quaint shops along Commodore Street, fill the charming tearooms that accented Seward Way, purchase the homemade jams, jellies, and lemon curd, and even sample the select vintages of the local Corkscrew Winery.

"Welcome to Seward Island," one of the resident artisans had carved into a rustic sign that greeted visitors coming off the ferry. "A good place to visit—a great place to raise a family."

The local newspaper had once observed that the sign said everything that needed to be said. The air was the cleanest in the Puget Sound area, the crime rate was among the lowest in the entire state, and the population was ninety-three percent Anglo-Saxon, Celtic, Teutonic, and Scandinavian, with a sprinkling of other Europeans, a handful of Middle Easterners, and a small community of Asian-Americans making up the remaining seven percent.

In this mostly homogeneous environment, Chief of Police Ruben Martinez was an anomaly. Smuggled over the Mexican border when he was two months old, and shuttled from one stoop-labor farm to another up and down the valleys of California until, at the age of twelve, he was sent to an uncle in East Los Angeles, Ruben was lucky to have survived his teens. He grew up lean and hard and hungry.

It was sheer strength of will that got him out of the barrio, and the belief that his parents had more in mind for him than a repetition of their own miserable lives. He took a keen intellect, a sharp eye, and the cunning of a street fighter to the Los Angeles Police Academy, where he graduated third in his class.

Ruben's intention was to stay in southern California and work with the barrio gangs he knew so well, but an errant bullet lodged too near his spine cut his days on the street short.

"It's a crapshoot, Sergeant," a Los Angeles doctor told him bluntly. "If we leave the bullet where it is, you'll have some level of pain and some reduction in mobility, but you'll still be able to function. If we try to remove it—well, the chances are fifty-fifty that you could end up paralyzed."

The bullet stayed where it was. Ruben was fitted with a back brace to help ease the strain, and a prescription for painkillers that made him fuzzy. He tossed the pills down the toilet after the first week.

For a while, he took a desk job, but it bothered his back to sit around all day, and his feet itched for action. He left Los Angeles for a smaller city in central California where police life was considerably less demanding. Then came a string of other small cities in which he gained valuable experience and honed his skills. Along the way, he married. His wife gave him a daughter before she died. After that, he chose his jobs with a different eye, basing his decisions more on the quality of a town's environment and the caliber of its school system than on the degree of its commitment to law enforcement.

It was a circuitous route that brought Ruben Martinez to Seward Island, but he came with impressive credentials, and a solid reputation for honesty and efficiency. The mayor and the majority of the city council were convinced that they could not have made a better choice for their new chief of police.

"He's certainly the best qualified," said one.

"Probably overqualified," agreed another.

"It'll look good on the record," suggested a third.

"He's an outsider," cautioned a fourth.

"He's exactly what we want," Albert Hoch, the giant pear-shaped mayor, declared.

The terms of Ruben's contract included a tidy, two-bedroom frame house on the outskirts of town, a three-minute drive from the police station and five blocks from Seward High School where his daughter was now a sophomore.

Fifteen-year-old Stacey Martinez was the linchpin in her father's life—a slip of a thing that combined her mother's pale hair and delicate features with his own tawny skin and dark eyes. He had cared for her all by himself from the time she was two until she was ten, when she had begun to take care of him. The arrangement may have gone a long way toward explaining why he had never remarried. As he saw it, he and Stacey were a team; they didn't seem to need anyone else.

Of course, he knew it wouldn't last forever. She was growing up so fast. Soon enough it would be time for her to leave him for a life of her own; time for him to reevaluate his situation. But there was no point in his dwelling on that until it happened, and for now he was quite content with things as they were.

In the three years since Ruben had been chief of the Seward Island police, the department had dealt with numerous outbreaks of petty vandalism, an alarmingly steady increase in teenage drug-related incidents, an occasional drunk and disorderly, a number of traffic violations, frequent minor injuries, some domestic violence, several burglaries, one armed robbery, two rapes, and three accidental deaths. To the best of anyone's recollection, there had never been a homicide.

Although Ruben was technically on call twenty-four hours a day, seven days a week, he generally worked Mondays through Fridays, stayed within hailing distance on Saturdays, in case of an emergency, and took Sundays off to spend with Stacey. Which was why, when the telephone awakened him at seven-thirty-five in the morning on the second Sunday of October, he was surprised to hear Detective Ginger Earley at the other end.

"Sorry to spoil your Sunday, Chief," she said in a voice that was clearly strained. "But I'm at Madrona Point, and I think you'd better get out here right away."

Going more by the urgency of her tone than by her actual words, Ruben didn't take time to shower. He pulled on his clothes, took three gulps of orange juice from a glass Stacey poured for him, and headed for the garage. Fifteen minutes later, he swung his black police-issue Blazer into the Madrona Point parking lot and pulled up next to Ginger's black-and-white.

"What have you got?" he asked, climbing out.

"I've never seen anything like it," the twenty-eight-year-old redhead, who in nine years on the job had seen her share of gruesome bodies, replied with a shudder. "I swear, this is awful."

Her fresh, freckled face had a greenish tinge to it that was more than familiar to Ruben from his days on the streets of East Los Angeles. She motioned him toward the Dumpster, and then led him up the makeshift steps. Dawn had broken and there was now no mistaking what lay mutilated on the bloodstained rug. Ruben got as close as he dared and then hunched over for a better view.

Although it was difficult to tell, due to the excessive amount of blood, there appeared to be somewhere around a dozen sharp-force injuries to the body. He looked at the color of the blood, then dipped the tip of his little finger in it to check the consistency. Next, he noted the bluish color of her skin, which in this warm weather, was more likely to be indicative of blood loss than hypothermia. Finally, he lifted an arm to gauge the extent of rigor mortis. Based on the kind of experience that someone in his line of work rarely forgets, he estimated that she had been dead for at least six hours.

"Did you touch her?" he asked the detective.

"No, I didn't have to—Dirksen was here," she said, referring to the young uniformed officer who had taken Tom Hildress's call and then summoned her. "He said he went in and touched her, but only to confirm she was dead."

"Did anyone else disturb anything around her?"

Ginger shrugged. "I was careful, but the call came in from a local who was dumping trash with his son. I haven't interviewed him yet, so I don't know what he did."

"Well, get on the horn," Ruben instructed almost by rote. "Get the whole park cordoned off. I don't want anyone within a hundred yards of this place until we're finished with it. And get someone down to the ferry to check things out. Hell, get the whole department out of bed, if you have to. I want this whole island crawling with uniforms, looking into every corner, questioning anything that moves. Then, of course, you'd better put in a call to Doc Coop and get hold of Charlie."

Magnus Coop was the town physician who doubled as the county medical examiner, and Charlie Pricker was the police department's other detective, in charge of gathering physical evidence.

"Dirksen is securing the site," Ginger replied. "Two uniforms are already at the ferry and a half dozen more should be out cruising by now. I had to leave a message for Magnus; he was busy delivering twins. And Charlie's on his way."

"Good," Ruben acknowledged, allowing himself a small smile because, as usual, she was way ahead of him.

"You know who this is, don't you?" she asked.

The police chief squinted down at the teenager. "She looks familiar," he murmured, but he was unable to place her.

"Tara Breckenridge," Ginger told him.

The name clicked. He knew who she was now. He looked at the brutalized body. "Jesus," he breathed.

She was the same age as Stacey, even, he thought, in a couple of the same classes at school. He knew that, with just a different toss of the dice, he could as easily have been looking at his own daughter.

"This is going to turn the whole island upside down," Ginger predicted.

Ruben struggled to his feet and climbed out of the Dumpster, feeling a sharp stab across his back because, in his haste, he had neglected to put on his brace. It was years since his last murder case, at least a decade since he'd had to deal with anything like this. He was a month short of his forty-sixth birthday, but at this moment, he felt closer to sixty-six.

He sighed an unhappy sigh. "I guess it was bound to happen someday," he said.

"What?" Ginger asked.

"Seward Island's first homicide."

5

Church services had barely begun before word of the murder had spread to every corner of the little island, leaving residents in a state of total shock. In the entire history of the peaceful community, nothing like this, nothing even remotely approaching this, had ever happened before. Almost everyone had either known the victim or knew her family, but even those few who didn't were outraged by the brutal and senseless death. The entire population felt violated.

"If something like this can happen to Tara," they whispered to one another over the telephone, across picket fences, at street corners, "it can happen to anyone."

To be sure, Tara wasn't just anyone. She was the daughter of the most prominent family on the Island. Her father, Kyle Breckenridge, was president and CEO of the Puget Sound Savings and Loan, and her mother, the former Mary Seward, was a direct descendant of the old Commodore himself.

In addition, Kyle was on the board of the chamber of commerce, a deacon in the Episcopal church, past president of the PTA, and a respected member of Rotary, the Elks, and the Hunt Club. It was generally known that he held the mortgages on at least half the Island's homes, and had never seen fit to foreclose on any of them.

Mary was a member of the Garden Club, worked tirelessly in behalf of Children in Need, a local Christian charity, and just recently had been instrumental in helping to establish the first halfway house in the county to shelter battered women.

Fifteen-year-old Tara was the Breckenridges' firstborn. There was also another daughter, Tori, just turned twelve. Blond and blue-eyed, Tara was the image of her father, and generally considered one of the prettiest girls on the Island. Along with her good looks and her sweet, if somewhat shy, personality went a true concern for those less fortunate than herself, a trait she had inherited from her mother, and that had always made her a community favorite. Just three days ago, she had been elected Harvest Festival Princess by an overwhelming majority of the population.

The housekeeper opened the huge front door at Southwynd, formerly the Seward estate, now known as the Breckenridge estate. The home sat on twenty prime acres in the southeast corner of the Island. It had been built of local cedar and stone by the Commodore's only surviving son in 1830, and added onto by each succeeding generation until the original house was lost in a sprawling architectural amalgam.

Crowning a gentle rise of lush green grass punctuated by blue spruce and maple trees, it afforded a splendid view across Puget Sound to Seattle and Mount Rainier beyond. It was the kind of place that, despite how far he had come in life, still made Ruben feel he ought to look for the service entrance.

"Mr. and Mrs. Breckenridge are not at home," Irma Poole replied to the police chief's question. "They went to Seattle for a christening."

"And the girls?" Ginger asked.

"They're here, of course," she said, and then stopped herself. "No, wait a minute. Just Miss Tori is here. I don't think Miss Tara's come back yet."

"Where did she go?" Ruben inquired obliquely.

"I don't know. Out somewhere, visiting a friend, I think."

"Did she spend the night with this friend?"

"Oh no, she doesn't spend nights out of the house."

"You mean, she went to a friend's house this morning?" Ginger prompted.

"I guess. And early, too. She wasn't at breakfast, and I made apple pancakes."

"Why do you think she's visiting a friend?" Ruben asked.

The housekeeper shrugged.

"Because that's what her father said, when she wasn't here," she told them. "He said that's probably where she went."

Ginger glanced at Ruben. "What time do you expect them back, Mrs. Poole?"

The woman shrugged again. "They didn't say."

"Does Mr. Breckenridge carry a cellular phone with him?" Ruben asked.

"Yes," the housekeeper replied.

"May we have the number, please?"

"I'm not supposed to give that out," the woman said. "Can't it wait until they come home?"

"No," the police chief said gently. "I'm afraid it can't."

Kyle Breckenridge looked much more like a movie star than a bank president. Nearing fifty, he was over six feet tall, with ice blue eyes and blond hair that was turning gray in just the right places. He kept himself in excellent physical condition, and cultivated a year-round tan that was regularly enhanced during the winter months at a local tanning salon. By contrast, his wife, Mary, was a frail, pale thing wearing an unflattering shade of brown.

There was always an air of purpose to Kyle's movements, a

trait that he had cultivated in his youth because he thought it made him look important. It was particularly evident at two o'clock on Sunday afternoon when he strode into the white clapboard building that housed the Puget County Medical Center, his wife almost a shadow in his wake.

The clinic interior was a pleasant surprise. Decorated in soft colors, with flowery wallpapers and comfortable furniture, it resembled the gracious home it had once been far more than the institution it had become. Magnus Coop, the Seward family physician for close to forty years, waited in the foyer with Ruben Martinez.

"All right, what's going on?" Kyle demanded as soon as he was through the front door. "You tell us to get on the next ferry back, but you won't say why."

"I'm afraid we have some bad news, Mr. Breckenridge," replied Ruben. "I didn't think it was something you'd want to discuss on the phone."

Mary Breckenridge gasped. "Is it Tara?" she whispered. "Did something happen to Tara?"

"Why would you think that, Mary?" Coop asked. Barely as tall as she, the doctor closely resembled a gnome. He had a shock of white hair and his small brown eyes, which peered through steel-rimmed spectacles perched halfway down his nose, missed very little.

"Because," she replied, darting a look at her husband, "she wasn't home this morning when we left to go to the christening."

"Do you know where she was, Mrs. Breckenridge?" Ruben asked.

"We thought she might have gone to visit a friend," Kyle answered for his wife.

"A specific friend?"

"I don't know, a girlfriend, a classmate," he said. "But never mind that. Please tell us what this is all about."

Coop cleared his throat. "I'm sorry," he said gently. "There's no easy way to say this . . . Tara is dead."

Mary Breckenridge began to wail, an eerie sort of sound that rose to an unearthly shriek as she stared first at her husband, then at the police chief, and finally at the medical examiner. "Tara . . . dead? Did you say Tara was dead?"

Her husband assisted her into the nearest chair, and Coop deftly administered a hypodermic he had been wise enough to prepare in advance.

"What do you mean Tara is dead?" Kyle then demanded, turning on Ruben, his face ashen. "How do you know she's dead?"

"She was found early this morning," the police chief told him.

"Found?" Kyle repeated, not comprehending. "What are you talking about?"

"An Island resident discovered her body at Madrona Point," Ruben said carefully. "It appears she was stabbed to death."

"Of course, we don't know all the circumstances yet," the medical examiner added. "We just brought her in."

"Stabbed?" Kyle said slowly, as though it were a word with which he was unfamiliar. He stared at the police chief. "You mean, it wasn't some kind of accident? She wasn't hit by a car? She didn't fall or drown? You're saying that someone actually . . . murdered her?"

Ruben nodded. "I'm afraid so," he murmured.

"It appears that way," Coop concurred.

The starch seemed to drain from the bank president's body. He clutched at the high back of Mary's chair to keep himself upright. "How could this have happened?" he managed to cry. "Why?"

"We don't know yet," Ruben said with a leaden sigh.

"But we intend to find out," Magnus declared. He glanced down at Mary. The fast-acting sedative was already taking effect;

the woman was slumped in the chair, the eerie shriek subsiding into a tuneless lament. She was no longer paying any attention to the conversation. "We need you to sign some papers, Kyle."

"What kind of papers?"

"For the autopsy."

Breckenridge gave the medical examiner an agonized look. "Autopsy?" he rasped. "No—no autopsy. I can't let you cut her up." He glanced down at his wife. "What do you want to do—kill Mary, too?"

"I'm afraid it's necessary, sir," Ruben told him. "An autopsy is essential to our investigation. Whether we like it or not, a crime has been committed. In order to find out who did this awful thing, we have to be allowed to collect every possible piece of evidence."

"I can appreciate your position, Chief Martinez," Kyle replied, "but I hardly think that anything essential will be gained from disemboweling my daughter."

Ruben barely knew the banker, but Magnus Coop had known Kyle Breckenridge for twenty years, ever since the man had arrived on Seward Island and won the hand of the town's wealthiest young woman.

"Well, the thing is, you see, we don't really need your permission," the doctor said kindly but firmly. "Signing the papers is just a formality. In homicide cases, an autopsy is mandatory."

Breckenridge's face froze in anguish. "Then go ahead and do whatever it is you have to do," came the abrupt reply.

"I want to see my baby," Mary wailed suddenly. "Take me to see my baby. Maybe it isn't Tara. Maybe you've made a horrible mistake."

Out of her line of vision, Coop shook his head at Kyle, thinking of the mangled body he had brought in from Madrona Point less than an hour ago, and that now lay on a table in the back room that served as the morgue, covered with a sheet.

"If Magnus says it's Tara," Breckenridge told his wife, his expression ragged, "then you can believe it's Tara. Do you really think that he'd put us through this if he weren't sure?"

"I need to examine her first, Mary," Coop said gently. "And find out what happened to her. After that, of course you can see her."

"That's exactly what you always say when she gets sick," Mary murmured.

"Yes, I guess it is."

"Well, that's all right then, Magnus," she conceded with a pathetic smile. "You take all the time you need to make her well again."

Deborah Frankel spent her Sundays doing the laundry. In an overcommitted life, it was the only time she had. During the week, she took the ferry to Seattle and her job as a vice president of a major investment firm. Saturday mornings, she did the marketing, and whatever other shopping was necessary. Saturday afternoons, she allotted to her husband, Jerry, and their eight-year-old son, Matthew.

This Saturday, they had spent their time together bicycling around Madrona Point, and as usual Matthew had tried too hard to keep up with his father, and ended up falling, scraping his knees and getting blood all over his brand-new jeans. Deborah had taken the pants from the boy immediately after they got back home, making far more of a fuss than the incident probably warranted, and deposited them in the sink to soak overnight.

As a result, when she finished folding the clean sheets and towels, and set about sorting the clothes, separating the whites from the colors and the lights from the darks, she was confused to find, buried in the pile, the light gray sweatshirt with the Seward Island emblem on it that Jerry had worn yesterday, also splattered with blood.

She located him in the library—an alcove, really, off the living room in the Northwest-style cedar and glass house, where they had put his books and papers and his antique rolltop desk so that she could have the spare bedroom for her high-tech home office. He was sprawled in a soft leather recliner they had managed to squeeze between the desk and the window, scowling over the *Sunday Times* crossword puzzle. It was almost nine months since they had left Scarsdale, but he still insisted on keeping his subscription to the New York newspaper.

"How did your sweatshirt get all bloody?" she asked, holding it out at him.

Jerry Frankel looked up in surprise. He had a nice face with even features that seemed to light up from within when he smiled. Dark hair fell across his forehead in boyish fashion. His warm brown eyes focused on something just past her shoulder.

"I cut myself," he replied after a blank second or two, and held up a bandaged thumb.

"All that blood from one little cut?"

He shrugged. "It was a deep cut."

"Why didn't you say something about it?" she persisted irritably.

"I did it last night," her husband replied, "working in the shop. It was after you went to bed. I didn't want to wake you."

"Couldn't you have washed the shirt out? Or at the very least put it in the sink with Matthew's jeans?"

He shrugged again. "I didn't think of it," he told her. "What's the big deal? I knew you were doing laundry today."

Deborah sighed and took the shirt to the sink in the utility room. She removed Matthew's jeans, filled the basin with fresh water, and added a good measure of Clorox. If the bloodstains had not yet had time to set, she thought, there was a chance they might come out.

6

Gail Brown was a third-generation Islander who left after high school for a bachelor's degree in English from Wellesley College in Massachusetts, a master's in journalism from Columbia University in New York, and a series of jobs on half a dozen Eastern newspapers before coming home to assume the editorship of the *Seward Sentinel*.

For decades, the publication had enjoyed a comfortable reputation as a commentary on the community's social life. Gail signaled her return by throwing a rather large wrench into the well-greased works.

"It's no longer enough to report that the Garden Club held its annual meeting," the anorexic brunette with a bushy ponytail and thick eyeglasses told her staff, "or that Susie Sweetpea celebrated her sixteenth birthday with a luncheon at Gull House. That kind of stuff just doesn't do it for the majority of our residents anymore—or advertisers, in case you haven't been noticing."

There were some nods and shrugs and a couple of sighs from those who had crammed themselves into the editor's office.

"If we wish to maintain our exorbitant salaries," Gail continued, pausing for the little titter she knew would come, "we quite simply have to increase revenue. To do that, we need to increase circulation. So from now on, the *Seward Sentinel* is going to become Puget County's newspaper of record. We're going to start dealing with the real issues—the serious issues that confront us, on the Island and around the whole county—politics, religion, education, land use, taxes, corruption—all the things people need to know to make informed decisions about the future of the place where they live. No one will be exempt from our legitimate scrutiny, and no topic will be off limits."

"Don't we risk losing the current subscribers who like the paper the way it is?" someone asked.

"If there are some who don't cotton to the new concept, let's invite them to write and tell us about it," the editor suggested with a mischievous grin. "We'll print their comments."

In six months, the newspaper's circulation had tripled. Within a year, advertising was up by forty percent. And before the end of Gail's second year at the helm, "Letters to the Editor" had grown from a lackluster weekly column to two full pages of often vigorous debate in almost every issue.

"If you really want to know what's happening on Seward Island," it came to be said, "just read the letters."

It was true.

"The character of a community is not defined by what happens there," Gail shrewdly observed. "It's defined by people's reactions to what happens there."

The day after Tara Breckenridge's death, the editor was at her desk by dawn, composing a suitably sympathetic, yet uplifting editorial. Engrossed as she may have been in her task, she was nonetheless aware of the steady stream of locals who were hand-delivering their written statements to the front counter just beyond her office.

The *Sentinel* operated out of a pretty gray building with white gingerbread trim that sat off by itself on Johansen Street, at the southernmost end of town. As the story went, the place, known as Curtis House, had originally been built in 1915 by one Adelaide Curtis, the town's most infamous madam, who had the audacity to erect it right at the juncture of Commodore Street and Seward Way. The city leaders were in an uproar, apparently caused not so much by moral outrage as by their desire not to be seen frequenting the establishment. They literally had it moved, at the taxpayers' expense, of course, to its present, somewhat less conspicuous location. Gail was never able to document the truth of the tale, but just the idea gave the little house a delicious dash of character.

At eight-ten, Iris Tanaka, the *Sentinel*'s diminutive editorial assistant, poked her head into Gail's office. "This is unbelievable," she exclaimed. "We've already got over two hundred letters about Tara Breckenridge, and they're still pouring in."

"Everyone wants his fifteen lines of fame," the editor said with a sigh, removing her glasses to rub the bridge of her nose.

"But what are we going to do with them all?"

"Sort through them," Gail told her. "Deep-six the ones that are obviously just about currying favor with the Breckenridge family. Then pick half a dozen of the more eloquent ones that genuinely mourn Tara for all the right reasons, and two or three of those that, despite the tragedy, just can't resist blaming the victim."

Iris wrinkled her nose in distaste. "At a time like this, do you really want to open that can of worms?"

The editor replaced her glasses. "Healthy debate is good for a community," she replied, turning back to her computer. "And it sells."

Jerry Frankel swung his maroon Taurus wagon into the space assigned to him in the teachers' section of the Seward High School parking lot. Climbing out, he buttoned his brown tweed jacket over his tan checked shirt, brushed the hair out of his eyes, grabbed his briefcase, and hurried up the covered walk to the north entrance of the building that had grown from a one-room schoolhouse, constructed in 1865, into a sprawling brick complex that included a gymnasium, an indoor swimming pool, a theater, and a science laboratory that were the envy of the Pacific Northwest and a testament to the generosity of the Island's residents when it came to the well-being of their children.

It was eight-twenty. Deborah had taken the early ferry into Seattle, leaving Jerry with the task of getting Matthew up, dressed and fed, and delivering him to his elementary school. Now the history teacher had barely enough time to get to his classroom.

The early ferry wasn't the only reason he was late. He had overslept because of a toothache that had begun to nag at him on Sunday afternoon, and by evening had progressed to a throbbing pain that kept him tossing and turning most of the night until Deborah had finally gotten up and given him a sleeping pill.

Jerry reached his second-floor classroom a scant two minutes before the bell. Fortunately, he reflected, as he began to pull an assortment of books and papers out of his briefcase and set them on his desk, Matthew had inherited his mother's teeth.

His lower jaw was throbbing unmercifully. Picking up a piece of chalk and beginning to scribble the lesson for this period on the blackboard, Jerry tried to calculate how long he had to wait before he could safely take another dose of aspirin. So absorbed was he by his own discomfort that it was a full five minutes past the bell before he realized that half the seats in the room were still empty.

"What's going on?" he asked. "Where is everybody this morning?"

"In shock," Hank Kriedler, a clean-cut blond sophomore, replied from the back.

"Haven't you heard?" a teary-eyed Jeannie Gemmetta said from her seat in the first row. "Gosh, I thought everybody would've heard by now. Tara's dead."

"Dead?" The teacher turned startled brown eyes on the chubby teen. "What do you mean Tara's dead?"

"She was murdered Saturday night."

Murdered? Jerry sagged against the corner of his desk. He had missed the weekly staff coffee, and hadn't had time to stop at the office, or even check the message board. He looked at the empty desk in the middle of the third aisle and felt weak. "I'm sorry," he said to no one in particular. "Does anyone know what happened?"

"She was stabbed," Jack Tannauer said.

"At least two dozen times," Melissa Senn amplified from her seat near the door, a raven-haired beauty who had come in second to Tara in the Harvest Princess election.

"And then dumped in a Dumpster," Jeannie finished, thinking that the history teacher was suddenly looking quite pale.

Jerry swallowed hard. "Do they have any idea who did it?" he managed to ask.

The students craned their necks in the direction of Stacey Martinez, who sat by the window.

The police chief's daughter did not appreciate the scrutiny. "I don't think so," she replied. "But then, I really don't know anything about it."

The Seward Island Police Department was housed in a square cinder block building at the eastern end of Commodore Street. It was affectionately called Graham Hall, after the Island's beloved first police chief.

Designed in 1949, when the population was less than three thousand and the department employed only six people, it was totally inadequate for the present complement of seventeen. The walls were badly in need of paint, the desks were battered gray metal, the floors were scarred gray linoleum, and the uniformed officers worked practically one on top of another in the cramped space. For five years in a row, ballot initiatives that would have allowed for the renovation and enlargement of the building had been voted down by the citizenry.

At exactly nine o'clock, Albert Hoch, the broad-beamed mayor of the city, sometimes referred to behind his back as the Bald Eagle because of his prominent nose and shiny pate, barged unannounced into the police chief's closet-sized office.

"Talk to me, Ruben," he bellowed, his voice carrying easily throughout the building. "We don't have violent crime on this island. Nobody's ever been murdered here."

"Well, somebody certainly has now," the chief responded mildly.

"Kyle Breckenridge is one of my closest friends," Hoch snapped. "And that 'somebody' was my goddaughter, goddammit. Now, I want to know whatever it is you know so far, and I expect to be updated every single day until this case is solved."

Ruben sighed. It wasn't that he disliked the pompous official. It was that Albert Hoch possessed very little acumen for police work.

"So far, all we know is that she was stabbed to death sometime late Saturday night or early Sunday morning, and then tossed into a Dumpster out at Madrona Point," Ruben told him. "Of course, we should know more once the autopsy is completed, and the investigation of the crime scene is finished."

"Do you have any clues?" Hoch persisted. "Do you have any idea who could have done it?"

"Nothing concrete as of this moment," Ruben said. "But then, we're just beginning."

The city official was not known for his discretion any more than his acumen, and Ruben had long ago learned that it was unwise to tell the mayor anything the police didn't want immediately spread all over the Island.

"Who are you going to put in charge of the case?" Hoch asked.

"I'm in charge," the police chief replied. "Ginger Earley will be running the investigation. Charlie Pricker will be responsible for the evidence. Before this is over, I expect everyone will be involved, one way or another."

In a department as small as this, it was always how they worked. It seemed absurd to Ruben to be sitting here, reassuring the mayor of what he already knew. After all, the Seward Island police force employed only two detectives: Ginger, whom he had hired himself a little less than two years ago, and Charlie, whom he had inherited, and just last year promoted out of the uniform ranks.

"Jesus," Hoch breathed, wagging his bald head back and forth. "What was Tara doing out at that hour? How did she get all the way to Madrona Point? How did she end up in a Dumpster, for God's sake? Why the hell would anyone do such a thing?"

All good questions, Ruben thought. None of which had an answer. Yet.

"I think Mr. Frankel was really shook up," Melissa Senn said during lunch period.

"Yeah," Jeannie Gemmetta agreed. "Did you see his face? It went so white, for a moment there it looked like he was going to pass out or something."

"I saw that," Melissa confirmed. "He looked totally tragic—almost like he'd lost his best friend."

"Well, Tara was a real looker," Jack Tannauer said. "Who knows—maybe they were getting it on together."

"Don't be ridiculous," Jeannie scoffed. Jack's father managed the Island's movie theater, and some of his son's ideas seemed to come right out of Hollywood. "I think he's just that kind of person. You know, someone who cares about other people." A smile spread across her round, homely face. "I wouldn't mind too much if he cared about me," she said recklessly. "You have to admit, he's awfully cute."

"You think so?" asked Melissa.

"Sure," Jeannie replied. "Those dreamy eyes of his—when they fix on me, it's like he's seeing right into my soul."

"Come on, he's gotta be old enough to be your father," said Bill Graham, a gangly sixteen-year-old with an unhealthy pallor that his friends decided was the result of spending too many hours in the back room of the mortuary where his father worked.

"So what?" Jeannie retorted. "He doesn't look it. In fact, I think he looks a little like Brad Pitt."

"Well, now that you mention it, I guess he *is* pretty cute," Melissa conceded with a giggle.

"Except for his nose," Hank Kriedler said.

"What's wrong with his nose?"

"It's kinda big, don't you think?" the big blond teen replied with a sneer.

"I never noticed," Jeannie admitted.

"It's because he's a Jew," Hank told her.

"He is?" Jeannie exclaimed. "I didn't know that. How do you know that?"

Hank shrugged. "What world have *you* been living in? I thought everybody knew."

"There isn't very much to go on yet," Albert Hoch reported, having been summoned to Kyle Breckenridge's spacious office on the corner of Commodore Street and Seward Way shortly before the end of the day.

The president and CEO of the Puget Sound Savings and Loan sat behind a sleek rosewood desk that seemed to float on a sea of aquamarine carpeting, and fixed hollow eyes on the portly mayor.

"I want to know whatever there is," he said.

"Well, Ruben's got everyone working on the case, of course. It's got top priority. The autopsy is in progress, and so is the crime scene investigation. Magnus should be giving Ruben his report in a couple of days, and Charlie Pricker will probably be done at the crime scene sometime tomorrow. Of course, you know it could be weeks, if not months, before anything comes back from the labs. Ginger Earley's already out talking to people—you know, people who knew Tara."

"I suppose that means someone will be coming out to Southwynd," Breckenridge said with a heavy sigh. "To be honest with you, Albert, I don't know how much more of this Mary can take right now."

Hoch nodded. Mary Breckenridge was not a strong woman, he knew. "Anything Phoebe and I can do, you know . . ." he murmured.

"Yes, of course, I certainly appreciate that," Kyle acknowledged, aware that the mayor's wife was at least as big a gossip as the mayor himself. "You two have already been more than kind." He blinked several times and then sat up a little straighter in his chair. "Do you know if there are any viable suspects yet?" he asked. "Has Martinez come up with any possible motive? Does he at least have a theory?"

Hoch twisted his big frame in his seat. Actually, the chief of police was not as forthcoming as the mayor would have preferred, apparently determined to keep whatever speculations he might have to himself, and Hoch had not really pressed him.

"I don't think so," he told Breckenridge. "I know there are situations where the evidence is so overwhelming, and the motive so obvious, that the killer can be identified almost immediately. But that doesn't seem to be the case here. Suspects aren't exactly crawling out of the woodwork. Ruben is going to have to go out and find the bastard. But then, that's what we hired him for, isn't it?"

"One of my students died over the weekend," Jerry Frankel told his wife during dinner Monday evening.

"That's too bad," Deborah murmured, her concentration

split pretty evenly between a plate of linguini and a hefty report that had to be read before breakfast the next morning.

"No, I mean, she was murdered."

Deborah looked up. "Somebody was murdered—here on Seward Island?" Her husband nodded. "My goodness, what a shock," she said. "I didn't think folks did anything more exciting around this place than watch the cedars grow."

They were alone in the soft gray dining room. Jerry routinely fed Matthew at six, then got him bathed and into bed. Deborah rarely got home before eight, but she was usually in time to kiss the boy good night. Jerry would have dinner on the table when she came down—he had become a fairly decent cook—and if anything worth discussing had happened that day, they would discuss it while they ate. Unless, of course, she had brought work home with her. It was one of the compromises they made when they agreed that Deborah would ask for the transfer to her company's Seattle office, and the only teaching job Jerry could find in the middle of a school year was on an isolated island with an inflexible ferry schedule.

"The kids were all talking about it," he told her now. "Matthew even mentioned it when he came home from school."

"Did you know her well?"

"I knew her, but not all that well," he said, casually winding his linguini inside a large spoon. "Her name was Tara Breckenridge. She was one of the students I taught in summer school, and she was in one of my sophomore classes this semester."

A shadow flickered across Deborah Frankel's light eyes. "What happened to her?" she asked.

Jerry frowned at the pasta coiled inside his spoon as though he were unsure whether he wanted to put it into his mouth. "According to what the kids say, she was stabbed to death, and then somehow ended up in the Dumpster at Madrona Point."

Deborah didn't know anything about Tara Breckenridge,

but the Frankels had been at Madrona Point just two days ago. A little shiver ran down her spine.

"How dreadful," she murmured as she forked up a mouthful of her linguini and turned to the next page of her report.

"Everyone at school is real upset about Tara," Stacey reported to her father that evening. "It's all they could talk about. Every single period, they kept asking me if I knew anything. I hate it when they do that, like I'm really going to tell them anything you tell me."

"I don't suppose you *do* know anything, do you?" Ruben asked with a sigh.

"Not really," Stacey said thoughtfully. "It's funny, you know. Everybody liked Tara. But when you listen to what they say, not that many kids actually knew her. They kind of just knew *about* her. She wasn't spoiled. In fact, I think her parents were pretty strict with her. She wasn't a snob or anything like that, either. She never lorded her money or her looks or her social position over any of us—she always went out of her way to be real nice to everyone—but she sort of, I don't know, kept to herself most of the time."

"What did you think of her?"

Along with his eyes and complexion, Stacey had inherited Ruben's keen mind, and he had learned that he could trust her instincts about people.

"I really hardly knew her—even though she was in two of my classes in eighth grade, three of my classes last year, and two again this year. You see, that's exactly what I mean—she would never let you get too close. I always thought she was a pretty decent student, but I guess maybe her grades had slipped or something because somebody said her parents made her go to summer school. The longest conversation we ever had was over some algebra notes."

"Who were her friends?"

"Let's see . . . the only girls I ever saw her with on a regular basis were Melissa Senn and Jeannie Gemmetta."

"Any boyfriends?"

Stacey shook her head. "She and Melissa and Jeannie ran with Hank Kriedler and his crowd sometimes, but I'm pretty certain it was just a group thing."

"Are you sure you never saw her alone with any of them? With anyone?"

The teenager considered that for a moment because there was something that seemed to hover around the edge of her memory, just out of reach. But then she shrugged and shook her head.

"If I did, I guess I've forgotten," she said.

7

"Tara Breckenridge wasn't just dumped at Madrona Point," Charlie Pricker declared first thing Tuesday morning. "She was killed there, too."

He was seated in Ruben's tiny office, the spare chair tipped back against the wall. His rimless glasses rested on top of his curly brown hair. The police chief sat at his desk, which left Ginger with a small square of standing space by the door.

"How do you know that?" she asked.

Pricker grinned. "We found the spot where he did her," he said. "It was about twenty yards from the Dumpster. Lots of blood. Looks like he tried to sop it up with something—maybe that rug he rolled her into because it was soaked and I found pieces of gravel in it. When that didn't work, I guess he figured to cover it up by moving the gravel around. I don't think he could really see too well in the dark." The detective wagged his head. "Here's hoping that these people don't learn that you can never get rid of all the blood."

"Why didn't he just leave her where she fell?" Ginger wondered aloud.

Pricker shrugged. "He's a meticulous man, our perp; a regular clean freak. Didn't want to leave a mess, I guess. Or maybe he put her in the Dumpster because he thought no one would find her there. You know, he actually went into the park bathroom after he did her and washed up. We found blood in there, too."

"Hers or his?" Ruben asked.

"Don't know," Pricker said. "All I can tell you is that she was type A and so was some of the blood we found in the bathroom. But we also found some type AB and some O, which may or may not be related. And I'd say at least a hundred fingerprints, which again may or may not be related."

"Public park? After a busy weekend?" Ruben mused. "A long shot at best. Any of them bloody?"

"No, none of them," Charlie replied. "But we got a partial print from the cross Tara was wearing."

At that, both Ruben and Ginger leaned forward.

"Bloody?" the police chief asked.

The detective shook his head. "Sorry."

"Well, it's something anyway," Ginger said. "It doesn't guarantee it got put there at the time of the murder, but we might be able to use it."

Ruben rubbed his back against his chair. "The first forty-eight hours in a homicide case are the most important," he told the two detectives. "That's when you expect to find the bulk of the evidence that will eventually connect the crime to the killer."

"So what do we have?" Ginger queried.

The Breckenridge case was forty-nine hours old. Ruben sighed. "Not enough," he replied.

They had an approximate time of death. They were pretty certain the autopsy would show that Tara Breckenridge had died of multiple stab wounds. They had eliminated both Tom and Billy Hildress from any suspicion. They knew the killer had removed the rug in which Tara had been rolled from the Dumpster, because sixty-six-year-old Island resident Egon Doyle had come forward to identify it as having belonged to his recently deceased mother. He told the police that he had personally deposited the rug in the Dumpster sometime around five o'clock on Saturday afternoon. They had eliminated Egon Doyle from any suspicion. And now they knew for certain that Madrona Point was the scene of the actual crime. Other than that, they had no eyewitnesses, no murder weapon, no apparent motive, no suspects.

"People around here desperately want to believe that this was done by some psychotic transient, you know," Ginger said. "The idea that Tara could have been brutally murdered by one of their own is just too frightening for them to contemplate."

"I can understand how they feel," Ruben conceded. "I don't blame them."

Ginger looked at him shrewdly. "You don't think it's a transient, do you?"

The police chief shook his head. "No," he admitted. "But I could be wrong. It's just a feeling I have, a hunch, about the nature of the crime."

"Well, I think we can rule out anything drug-related," Ginger said. "According to everyone I've spoken to, Tara was so straight she never even took aspirin. And nobody ever saw her anywhere near the junk druggies."

Marijuana, crank, and crystal meth were the current drugs of choice among teenagers, and police records showed that Island usage was more than double the national average.

"Charlie, can we rule out drugs?" Ruben asked.

The detective nodded. "Yup," he replied. "According to Magnus, she tested clean for both drugs and alcohol—and aspirin."

"If this was a random attack by some lunatic, either on or off the Island," observed Ginger, "it could be just the beginning."

"If this was random," Ruben said, "I'm going to lock my daughter in her room forever."

"Unless we come up with a motive," Ginger persisted, "what else can we assume?"

Ruben stood up and stretched his back. "Obviously, it isn't going to do us much good to sit around and assume anything at this point," he declared. "Charlie, go find us a smoking gun—or at the very least, a bloody knife. Ginger, go talk to everyone who knew her." He paused, remembering what Stacey had told him. "Talk to everyone who knew anything about her."

"I'm gone," said Charlie. "If you need me, I'll be at Madrona Point."

"I'm gone, too," Ginger told him. "If you need me, I'll be at the high school."

Ruben nodded. "If you need me, I'll be at Southwynd."

He rang the front doorbell at exactly ten o'clock.

"Come in, Chief Martinez," Mary Breckenridge invited, answering the door herself. "My husband is expecting you."

She was very pale. Her eyes were red, and there were dark circles around them, giving her a rather ghoulish look. Her light brown hair looked uncombed. Her black dress was obviously expensive but not flattering.

"I'm sorry to have to bother you in your time of grief," Ruben murmured.

She led him down a pale green marble corridor, enhanced by ancestral busts on graceful pedestals and huge vases of flowers, to a paneled library with gleaming leather furniture and thick red carpeting. Books of every conceivable size and category were crammed into floor-to-ceiling shelves. Among them, Ruben caught a quick glimpse of what were most likely first editions of works by Stevenson, Kipling, Hardy, and Maugham.

Slivers of morning sun slanted through windows covered with narrow wooden blinds. A small fire burned in a huge stone fireplace. This was clearly not a room that children played in. It was exclusively a man's room, and it was immaculate. As far as

Ruben could tell, there was not a speck of dust on any surface, nor a single item out of place.

"I'm more than happy to tell you whatever you want to know," Kyle Breckenridge said. "But I don't think I know anything that will help."

He was dressed in a dark gray business suit, with a crisp white shirt and charcoal tie. His normally tan skin had a definite gray tinge to it.

"Well, it sometimes happens," Ruben told him, "that a seemingly unimportant piece of information can turn out to be the key to a whole case."

Breckenridge gestured to two wing chairs that faced each other in front of the fire. His wife started to back out the library door.

"Please don't go, Mrs. Breckenridge," Ruben forestalled her. "If it would be all right, I'd like this conversation to be with both of you."

She looked at her husband and he shrugged, so she pulled up a side chair and sat down on the edge of it. This was obviously not a room in which she spent a great deal of time, Ruben guessed. He extracted a pad and a pen from his jacket pocket.

"Suppose we start with last Saturday," he suggested in a gentle, low-key tone. "When was the last time you saw Tara that evening?"

"I think it was about ten o'clock," Kyle replied. "We had dinner at seven-thirty. Then we watched some television. At nine o'clock, our younger daughter went up to bed. Then at ten, my wife retired with a headache, and I came in here to read for a while."

"And Tara?"

"When my wife went upstairs, Tara went to her room to do her homework."

"Was that customary?"

"What?"

"For Tara to spend Saturday evenings in her room doing homework?"

"I don't know if I'd call it customary, but it was something she often did, especially when she had an exam to study for, or a project due."

"Did she have an exam or a project?"

Breckenridge glanced at his wife. "I don't really know," he replied.

"Do you know, Mrs. Breckenridge?" Ruben asked politely.

"No, I don't," Mary Breckenridge almost whispered. "But I guess she must have."

"What did Tara generally do on those weekends when there were no exams or projects?" The question was directed to the mother, but the father replied.

"If my wife and I had plans to go out, she would stay home with her sister."

"And if not?"

"Sometimes we would all go out to dinner or to the movies," Breckenridge said. "Occasionally, we would go into Seattle for a concert or a play."

"Did Tara ever go out with friends on Saturday nights?"

"Once in a while," Breckenridge responded.

"Did she have a boyfriend?"

"No," the father said flatly. "We didn't allow her to date. She was only fourteen years old."

"Fifteen," the mother murmured.

Ruben glanced briefly from one to the other. "Where was Tara on Saturday during the day?" he asked.

"She went into town with her sister," Mary replied. "I dropped them off myself a little before eleven. They had lunch and they went shopping, and then I picked them up. We were home by three." The mother's gaze wandered toward the fire. "They were very close."

"And from three o'clock on, Tara was here?"

"Yes."

"Did she get any phone calls? Or make any that you know of?"

Kyle shook his head. "I wouldn't know. I was in a golf tour-nament on Saturday. I didn't get home until shortly after six."

"Do you know, Mrs. Breckenridge?" Ruben inquired.

Mary shook her head. "I didn't hear her make any calls. But there's a telephone in her room, so she could have."

"All right now," Ruben said as kindly as he could, "based on our current information, we believe that Tara's death occurred between midnight and two o'clock on Sunday morning. Which means that she had to have left the house sometime after ten, when you last saw her, and probably before midnight. Do you know why she would have gone out that late?"

Kyle shrugged. "No, I don't."

"And she said nothing to either of you before she went out?"

"As I've already told you, I was here in the library, reading. I didn't see her after she went upstairs, and I didn't hear her go out."

Ruben turned to the mother.

"I was in my room," she replied to the unasked question. "My headache."

"But you know it was after ten o'clock?"

"Yes," the father said.

"Did Tara often do that kind of thing?" Ruben asked.

"What kind of thing?"

"Go out late at night?"

"No, of course not," Breckenridge replied. "She was a good girl, very well behaved. She was always in bed by eleven o'clock on Saturday nights. Unless, of course, we were out."

"But that wasn't the case this Saturday night, was it?"

Kyle shifted in his seat. "No, I guess not."

"And she left the house without telling you."

"Apparently."

"And in the morning, when she wasn't here, you assumed she was at a friend's house."

"Yes."

"Why?" Ruben asked.

"It seemed the most reasonable assumption," Breckenridge admitted. "She had said something at dinner about needing to return some chemistry notes."

"But when she wasn't here for breakfast, you weren't concerned?"

Breckenridge frowned. "I was surprised, and I admit even a little annoyed because she hadn't bothered to tell anyone she was going out, but I wasn't concerned," he said. "This has always been such a safe island. Besides, we didn't know she'd been out all night, so we didn't think we had any reason to be concerned."

"Did anyone look to see if Tara had slept in her bed?"

"I did," Mary said. "The sheets seemed wrinkled. It looked as though she'd slept in them."

"It never occurred to us that anything could have happened to her," Breckenridge said. He sighed deeply. "How I wish I'd checked on her before I went to bed."

"You couldn't have known," Ruben told him.

Kyle closed his eyes. "No," he said. "I suppose not."

"By the way, what time *did* you go to bed?"

"About eleven-thirty, I think," Breckenridge replied. "Maybe a little later." He looked at his wife. "What time was it when I came up, do you remember?"

Mary Breckenridge blinked several times. "About eleven-thirty," she said.

"You're sure of that?" Ruben prodded gently.

She nodded wordlessly.

"The housekeeper can tell you," Breckenridge said suddenly. "Now that I think of it, she was in the front hallway, turning out the lights, when I went upstairs."

"Was there any kind of an argument during the evening that you recall?" Ruben asked. "Was Tara upset about anything? Were either of you angry at her for any reason?"

"No," Breckenridge replied. "There was no argument. No one was angry."

"Could there possibly have been something personal that was bothering her?"

"What do you mean?"

"Well, I've got a fifteen-year-old at home," Ruben said with a wry smile, "and I know she occasionally has problems that seem insurmountable to her at the time. Often, at that age, kids find it hard to discuss personal things with their parents."

"Why are you asking all these questions?" Breckenridge asked with a groan.

"I know how terribly painful this must be for you," Ruben said. "But the only way we're going to find out how and why this terrible thing happened to Tara is to learn all we can about her and her habits."

Breckenridge sighed. "Well, Chief Martinez, if she had a personal problem that she didn't feel she could discuss with us, then we wouldn't know about it, would we?"

"How about you, Mrs. Breckenridge?" Ruben asked. "Did you notice if there was anything that seemed to be troubling her?"

"No," the woman whispered, tears filling her eyes.

"How about her sister? You said they were close. Would Tara have talked to *her*?"

"Tori is barely twelve years old," Breckenridge said. "If Tara did talk to her, it couldn't have been about anything more important than dolls and hair ribbons. As I told you before, Tori went to bed at nine o'clock on Saturday night. She knows nothing—we've asked her. She's very upset by the death of her sister, and I would beg you not to make things worse right now by interrogating her about it. Perhaps in a week or two, when it's not so—so painful."

"Of course," Ruben conceded. "I certainly understand. All right then, you said something about chemistry notes. If Tara had decided she needed to return those notes that night, where

would she have gone? To a classmate? A friend? Do you know
who that might have been?"

"I guess I wouldn't know," Breckenridge admitted after a
few seconds. "I didn't really know much about her classmates or
her friends."

"Would you know, Mrs. Breckenridge?" Ruben inquired.

"Melissa, perhaps, or Jeannie," she ventured, dabbing at her
cheeks with a sodden handkerchief. "I think they had chemistry
together."

"Assuming she was on foot, do both of these girls live within
walking distance?"

There was a momentary pause.

"Jeannie lives on the other side of the Island," Mary Breckenridge replied. "Melissa lives about half a mile away. There may
be other classmates who live nearer. I don't know."

"You know, it's possible that all she did was go out for a
walk," Kyle said suddenly. "I mean, not to go anywhere specific,
just to get some fresh air. It could be that simple."

"Fresh air?" Ruben repeated politely.

Breckenridge nodded. "The weather was beautiful on Saturday, quite warm for the season. Maybe she just went out walking, and some psycho came cruising by, and for some terrible
reason, she let him pick her up. Not anyone from Seward Island,
of course," he added hastily. "I mean a stranger, out for his own
sick kind of fun."

"You could be right," Ruben conceded and veered onto another subject. "Does your housekeeper live in?"

"Yes, she does," Breckenridge confirmed.

"Anyone else?"

"No."

"Does she have visitors?"

"No. Mrs. Poole is a widow. She has no children, no visitors.
We're probably the closest thing she has to any family. She's been
with us for more than twenty years."

"Perhaps I might have a word with her," Ruben suggested. "Just to get everything straight in my head."

Breckenridge reached over and pulled on a thick silk cord that hung beside the fireplace. The three of them sat in silence until Irma Poole knocked softly on the door and entered the room.

"Chief Martinez is here about Tara's death," Kyle told her. "He's looking to confirm our whereabouts on Saturday night. I've already told him that I saw you turning off the lights as I was going up to bed. Mrs. Breckenridge and I believe it was around eleven-thirty. What do you remember?"

Irma Poole looked at her employer and nodded. "It was just eleven-thirty," she said.

"You're sure of that?" Ruben asked.

"Quite sure," the housekeeper replied.

"How do you come to remember the time so exactly?"

"Because I always turn off the lights and lock up at eleven-thirty," Irma Poole said.

"Did you see or hear anything out of the ordinary that night? Anything at all that you might not have thought important at the time, but now strikes you as unusual?"

There was a slight pause. "No," she said finally, and this time she looked straight at Ruben, her eyes filled with sorrow. "I didn't see anything and I didn't hear anything."

"Thank you, Mrs. Poole," Kyle said, and the housekeeper withdrew.

"She loved Tara," Mary said with a pathetic attempt at a smile. "Everyone loved Tara."

Ruben glanced at Breckenridge; the man was staring into the fire, his face drawn and gray. He hated putting them through this, but he had to do it.

"If it became necessary, Mr. Breckenridge, would you be willing to take a lie detector test and give us a sample of your blood?"

Mary gasped openly at that, and Kyle fixed the police chief with a glacial stare.

"Are you serious?" he demanded. "Do you really think I could have done such a thing to my own child?"

Ruben shrugged. "I'm sorry," he apologized. "But I wouldn't be doing my job if I didn't investigate even the most unlikely of possibilities."

"Then, at the point when you find sufficient reason to believe that I am implicated in this case in any way," came the stiff retort, "I will present myself at Graham Hall for whatever tests you wish to perform—given my attorney's consent, of course."

"Thank you," Ruben said smoothly and moved on. "Can either of you think of anyone who might have had a reason to harm your daughter?"

At that, Mary, already too close to the edge, dissolved into tears, burying her face in her handkerchief to muffle her sobs.

Kyle Breckenridge shook his head. "As my wife has already said, Chief Martinez, everyone loved Tara. She didn't have an enemy in the world."

"Well then, how about someone who might have wanted to get to *you* through her?"

"Me?" Breckenridge asked in genuine surprise. "But I have no enemies, either. My whole life has been about helping people. There couldn't possibly be anyone who could hate me so much that he would take it out on that beautiful girl."

His voice faltered on the last few words, and the composure he had tried so hard to maintain finally cracked. He turned away from the police chief.

One of the things Ruben had learned over the years was to know when enough was enough.

"Thank you both for your time," he murmured. "I can see myself out." He stuffed his pad and pen back into his jacket and got up to leave. But when he reached the door to the library, he stopped, wanting to say something relevant to these devastated people. "My daughter means more to me than my life," he said. "I know how I would feel if anything like this happened to her. Please accept my condolences."

At that, Kyle Breckenridge gathered himself together and stood up. "I know you have an investigation to conduct, Chief Martinez," he said in a leaden voice, "and I don't want to hamper you in any way. But we need to bury our daughter and do our grieving. I think the whole island needs that. So please, if you could expedite things so we can do what we have to do, that would mean more to us than anything else right now."

Ruben nodded. "I'll see to it that the body is released as soon as possible."

Now there were tears in the father's eyes. "Get the bastard who did this to my little girl," he whispered.

Ruben drove back to Graham Hall with his mind more on his interview with the Breckenridges than on the road he was following.

It was a sad commentary on the world in which he lived, he decided, that his investigation obliged him to establish Kyle Breckenridge's whereabouts at the time of the murder. The man was obviously grief-stricken, and as a father Ruben couldn't help but put himself in Breckenridge's place. The very idea that anyone might think he could harm a hair on Stacey's head made the police chief's blood run cold with anger, and he knew how he would have responded to such a suggestion.

All things considered, Tara Breckenridge's father had remained a gentleman.

"The police are proceeding on the assumption that Tara Breckenridge was accosted by an assailant or assailants while walking near her home sometime after ten o'clock Saturday night," the *Seward Sentinel* began its lead story the following day.

"According to Mayor Albert Hoch, the popular Island teen might have been on her way to visit a friend, or just out to get some fresh air.

"Said Hoch: 'We have reason to believe that Tara was somewhere in the vicinity of Southwynd when she was abducted by this person or persons, and then taken to Madrona Point, where she met her tragic end.'"

"If there is anything good that can be said of such a terrible tragedy," a member of Seward Episcopal Church where the Breckenridge family worshiped wrote to the editor, "it's that the grief we feel over dear Tara's death has made us cherish every single moment with our own precious children that much more."

"Whether we like it or not, violent crime has come to our island," wrote a crusty fisherman whose son was serving a two-year sentence in a California prison for possession of cocaine. "Perhaps, the only way to keep our young people out of trouble is to keep them off the streets."

8

Malcolm Purdy lived on the west side of Seward Island, on a thirty-acre parcel of land that had been left to him by a great-uncle he never knew. The first thing the crusty ex-Marine did upon acquiring title to the property was to erect a high stone wall around it, secured by an iron gate. The second thing he did was to electrify it.

He had come from nowhere one day about ten years ago, driving off the ferry in a new Jeep Cherokee with a one-eyed dog seated beside him. No one on the Island had ever been able to figure out what he did for a living. He had no apparent job, no visible assets, and aside from his military pension and his modest inheritance, no income anyone could readily identify. He lived alone in the cottage his great-uncle had built, and except for one month each year when he was absent from the Island, he rarely left it.

Those few, mostly delivery people, who got past the gate reported that he was doing nothing with the land. His neighbors said he spent much of his time at target practice, the sound of his rifles carrying easily over the wall. The woman who worked for him three days a week, who did his cleaning, his laundry, and his shopping, and stayed on the property for the entire month he was gone, was as taciturn as her employer. Some said she was also his mistress, but if that were so, it didn't seem to bother her husband very much, a grizzled fisherman who lived aboard his boat for months at a time.

For the first couple of years, Malcolm Purdy was the hot topic of conversation on Seward Island, fueled on by the insatiable curiosity of small-town people to know everything there was to know about everyone. They were told when his fancy computer arrived from a mail-order catalogue company. They knew, almost to the penny, how much he spent on ammunition down at Gus Landry's gun shop. They took note of the NRA literature that regularly filled his mailbox. They assumed he had a small arsenal on his land, but since none of them was ever invited inside to see, they could never prove it. Most of all, they speculated about what he did during the month each year that he left the Island. They would have given almost anything to know where he went, but there was no one to tell them.

Eventually, interest died down, and for a while anyway, the recluse was left to live in relative obscurity. Then strange men began to show up on the Island and find their way to his electrified gate, to stay for a month or two and then be gone.

Shortly after the arrival of the first few visitors, a significant quantity of lumber and other materials was delivered to the property, and the neighbors related that the sounds of target practice had been replaced by the sounds of saws and hammers. Sure enough, a mainland man who installed septic tanks reported that Purdy was building a bunkhouse behind his cottage. A local plumber later confirmed the report.

The Seward gossips began their speculations with renewed fervor. What was going on out there? they wondered. Was he training terrorists? Was he plotting insurrection? Was he harboring wanted criminals?

If Purdy knew how preoccupied the Islanders were with his life, he never let on. It was as if they walked and talked on another planet. He was an orphan from Alabama, who had been handed around from one distant relative to another until he was eighteen years old. The Marine Corps had for many years been everything to him. It gave him an identity he had never had, comrades he would never have found, the discipline he had always lacked, the focus he would otherwise not have gained. And it taught him how to kill: swiftly, cleanly, and without remorse. As much as he was able to love anything, Malcolm Purdy loved the Marines.

He had a wife once, and what he thought was a life with her. One day he came home unexpectedly and found her in bed with another man. He killed them both; coldly, calmly, each with one deliberate shot to the head.

His attorney, a sharp major, managed to exonerate him of any wrongdoing, claiming he had acted out of acute pain and uncontrollable rage in the commission of a justifiable crime of passion, even intimating that the woman and her lover had somehow deserved to die for what they had done.

But the Corps had its image to protect. After twenty-three years of dedicated service, Purdy was quietly and speedily discharged, with all accrued benefits. He didn't blame the Corps; he understood.

He was left with two young daughters, one who was five years old, the other almost three. He took them to a second cousin and her husband in Mobile who were in their thirties and childless.

"I want you to legally adopt the girls," he told them. He gave them a duly executed document in which he renounced all present and future parental claim. "They need a regular home and a good woman to raise them. They don't need to know their mother was a whore and their father was a murderer."

"Where will you go?" his cousin asked. "What will you do?"

"I don't know," he said. "Don't let it concern you."

A month later, a lawyer representing the estate of his great-uncle contacted him.

In the ten years since then, Malcolm Purdy had made no effort to communicate with his cousin, or to find out what had become of his children. He sent no birthday cards and no Christmas presents. But the day after Tara Breckenridge's death was reported in the paper, he picked up the telephone and called Mobile.

"I just wanted to know they were all right," he said.

"They're perfect," his cousin told him. "Bright and beautiful and normal and happy."

"Do they—do they remember . . . anything?" he asked.

"I think they remember only good times," she replied. "Would you like to talk to them?"

"No," he said abruptly. "I just wanted to know they were all right."

9

"All efforts to identify the assailant or assailants whom police believe abducted Tara Breckenridge near her home, and then brutally murdered her, have so far been fruitless," the *Sentinel* told its readers.

"Police are asking anyone who might have seen or heard anything unusual in the vicinity of the Southwynd estate or Madrona Point Park, either late Saturday night or early Sunday morning, to please contact the police as soon as possible.

" 'We believe we are looking for a transient,' Mayor Hoch told this reporter. 'Someone who does not live on Seward Island, but was just visiting on the day of the murder when he committed this random act of violence. If anyone saw, spoke to, or knows anything about such a person, we need to hear from you.'

" 'Sometimes, just the smallest piece of information,' Detective Ginger Earley said, 'no matter how insignificant or unrelated it may seem, can bring about the resolution of a case.' "

"It is our failure to provide our children with good Christian morals that is causing them to go astray," one of the Island's most righteous religious residents wrote to the editor. "They are falling prey to the hedonism that permeates our society, and we must do everything in our power to bring them back to God."

"Tara Breckenridge's death was a sad and horrifying thing," wrote a housewife and mother of four, "but lack of morals didn't kill her—some deranged lunatic did, and we should not lose sight of that. Our kids are basically good kids."

"If Tara Breckenridge had been at home where decent girls should be instead of out walking somewhere in the middle of the night," wondered a divorced carpenter who rarely saw his own daughter, "would she be dead today?"

Magnus Coop sat at one end of a rectangular metal table in the small, windowless room at Graham Hall that the police used for interviews or meetings of more than three people. The morning paper lay open in front of him. "Sometimes, I don't know which is worse," he declared peering at the newsprint through the steel-rimmed spectacles perched on his nose, "the facts or the speculation."

"Lack of the former often leads to a proliferation of the latter," the police chief, seated opposite him, observed. He looked at the folder in front of the medical examiner. "I assume that's the autopsy we've been waiting for."

"It is."

"So what have we got?"

"I should warn you, Magnus," Ginger said, seated along the length of the table, between the two men, "despite what you may read in our esteemed local newspaper, Ruben doesn't think our perp is a transient."

"You don't?" Coop inquired, fastening his beady eyes on the chief of police. "Why not?"

Ruben shrugged. "I'd like to. In many ways, it would make this case a whole lot easier. But it doesn't add up. Besides, I tend to go with the statistics. Well over eighty percent of all homicide victims in this country are killed by someone they know."

"This is true," the medical examiner agreed. "But that does leave a few percent, doesn't it?"

"Okay, just for the sake of argument," Ruben was willing to consider, "let's say our perp *is* a transient, and he just happens to be visiting the Island, and he just happens to be driving by Southwynd in the middle of the night when Tara comes along, and she just happens to let him pick her up and take her out to Madrona Point Park, where he kills her. My first problem with that is—why would Tara go anywhere with a perfect stranger? From all accounts, we're not talking about some wild teenager here, out looking for kicks. She was sweet and shy and well brought up. She didn't do drugs, she hadn't even started to date yet. Would a girl like that really have gotten into a car with someone she didn't know in the middle of the night?"

Charlie Pricker was slouched across from Ginger. "He could have forced her."

"With a gun, yes, but with a knife? From inside a car? In that neighborhood? She would have screamed. She would have run."

"Maybe he got out of the car," Charlie suggested.

"And maybe there were two of them," Ginger added.

"Well, I don't know about that," Charlie said. "We have no indication there was more than one perp."

"Okay," Ruben continued, "let's say, one way or another, the person we're talking about finds a way to force Tara into his car and get her to Madrona Point where he kills her. My question is—why? Don't forget, we saw the body; that poor girl died a brutal death. This was no whim. It was clearly a crime of uncontrollable anger. Now remember, we're dealing with a stranger here. What was his motive?"

"Maybe nothing more complicated than that he was mad at the world," Charlie suggested.

"Then let's say he's mad at the world. So he takes a ferry to a remote island—one that rolls up its sidewalks at nine o'clock at night—to find a victim? And long after most of us are tucked up in our beds, he's still out roaming around, and when he happens on Tara walking along in the most exclusive part of town, he knows exactly where to take her?"

"Isn't something like that possible?" Ginger asked. "Maybe he's been here before; maybe he's a regular."

"Okay, let's suppose that for a moment," Ruben conceded. "He's a repeat visitor, and he picked Tara up, took her out to Madrona Point, and for whatever reason, he killed her. How did he get off the Island? Even assuming the earliest possible time of death, the last ferry was already long gone. And he had to have had blood all over him—we know he tried to wash himself up in the park bathroom. What did he do for the rest of the night? Check into the Island Inn? Sleep on the street? Even if he stayed where he was, where did he go in the morning?"

"That's right," Ginger said with a frown. "He couldn't have been at Madrona Point past six-thirty, or Tom Hildress and his boy would have seen him."

"And the first ferry doesn't leave until eight o'clock on Sunday," Ruben added, "so he could hardly have been at the dock without being noticed. Keep in mind, we had the park, the ferry, the whole island covered by seven-forty-five that morning. How many killers, even mad-at-the-world ones, would set up a mark on an isolated island, and then get themselves trapped with no way to get off?"

"I see what you mean," Ginger murmured. "But maybe he didn't mean to kill her. Maybe he just meant to take her someplace and rape her, and it went down wrong."

"No," Coop said.

Ruben looked at him quickly. "Why no?"

The medical examiner sighed. "Because there were no indications that she had been raped or sexually molested in any way.

There were abrasions on her arms consistent with someone trying to restrain her, and a laceration on her face consistent with someone slapping her, and there were also some contusions on her scalp which I'll get to later, but there was no sign of semen and no anal or vaginal bleeding or bruising."

"What else?"

"The cause of death is what I told you it was," Coop said with a heavy heart. "There were thirteen sharp-force injuries—nine in the abdomen and four in the chest. It was one of the last four—a direct penetration of the left ventricle—that finally killed her."

Ginger shuddered. "What a nightmare it must have been for her."

The medical examiner nodded grimly. "This was not a merciful death," he said. "But surprisingly enough, while I found blood on her hands, there were no defensive wounds, and nothing under her fingernails. Brutal as the assault was, she apparently didn't make any effort to protect herself."

Ginger had little experience with this kind of homicide. "Is that unusual?" she asked.

"When you're attacked, especially with a knife," Coop told her, "the typical reaction is to defend yourself. In a situation like this, Tara should have had cuts and abrasions all over her hands and forearms."

"What else, Doc?" Charlie inquired.

"The majority of the wounds were very deep," the medical examiner continued, "in most cases, right up to the hilt, indicating that whoever killed her was reasonably strong. It's my opinion that all the injuries are consistent with having been made by one person, using one instrument—in all likelihood, a single-edged knife with a curved blade, about six inches long and approximately one and one eighth inches at its widest part. In other words, a hunting knife; the kind of hunting knife that can be bought in no fewer than a hundred places within a fifty-mile radius of here, and is probably already present in at least thirty percent of the homes on this island. Hell, I know for a fact that Jim Petrie's got a whole case of them over at the hardware store."

"That really narrows it down," Ginger muttered.

"Well, maybe it does in a way," Coop said. "Because it's also my opinion, based on the angle and position of the wounds, that our killer was left-handed."

"Left-handed?" Charlie echoed, perking up.

"The way I reconstruct it," the doctor said, "he was holding her by her hair. There were several contusions on her scalp resembling knuckle imprints that conform to a right-handed grasp, and confirm my opinion that he held her with his right hand and stabbed her with his left. It's what I state in my report."

"Okay," declared Ginger, "so now we know our killer is strong—at least strong enough to inflict the injuries and then hoist her into that Dumpster—and he's probably left-handed." She turned to Ruben. "Now what?"

But the police chief had been only half listening, his attention caught on one of the doctor's earlier statements.

"Did you say nine out of the thirteen stab wounds were in the abdomen?" he asked.

Coop's eyes blinked behind his steel-rimmed spectacles. "That's what I said—nine in the abdomen."

Charlie Pricker hunched forward in his seat.

Ginger glanced from one to the other. "Did I miss something?"

"Not yet," Ruben said, and fastened his glance on the medical examiner. "What is it you don't want to tell us, Doc?" he asked softly.

Magnus Coop sighed with unutterable sadness. Barely fifteen years ago, he had brought this child into the world, so clean and innocent and perfect, and now he was about to destroy her, as surely as had some madman with a knife. From now on, whatever else people remembered about her, they would first remember this.

"Tara Breckenridge was pregnant."

10

When Ginger thought about her childhood, one of the first things that always came to mind were the hundreds of jigsaw puzzles she had done with her father. The long rainy winter evenings when the two of them would huddle in front of the living room fire over little interlocking bits of landscapes that increased in difficulty as she increased in years. It never ceased to fascinate her, how all those oddly shaped pieces eventually fit together to form one complete picture.

At the time, she had no way of knowing that an evening's entertainment was also an important learning experience. But as she would later say, doing jigsaw puzzles taught her how to concentrate on the forest, one tree at a time. It also taught her patience. And that combination went a long way toward explaining why she took so readily to police work. She saw each case as a similar sort of puzzle; finding the next clue to put in the proper place or context to reach, ultimately, the one incontrovertible truth.

"You were right all along, and I should have seen it," she told Ruben the moment the medical examiner had departed and Charlie had gone off to review the autopsy report in detail. "We aren't dealing with a transient, and this wasn't a random act. Our perp was someone she knew."

"So it would seem," Ruben concurred.

"That's why she got into the car with him. He wasn't a stranger; she had no reason not to. And that's our motive—he got her pregnant, and then he decided maybe that wasn't such a good idea."

"A pretty drastic form of abortion," the police chief said with a sigh.

"Maybe she didn't give him any alternative," Ginger responded.

"Maybe."

"And of course that's what she was doing that night, too," the detective continued. "She wasn't out for some fresh air, or going to visit a friend—she was meeting *him*. They had a date she didn't want her parents to know about. She probably told him about the baby. Maybe she refused to have an abortion, they got into an argument, and he panicked. All those wounds in the abdomen—he wanted to kill the baby."

"Conjecture is fine," Ruben allowed, "so long as you don't let it cloud up the real picture. Yes, he obviously wanted to end her pregnancy, but does what we know so far tell us that this crime was just about dealing with unwanted fatherhood?"

Ginger considered for a moment. "No, it doesn't," she decided. "He could have talked his way around paternity, he didn't have to slash her to pieces. What it tells us is that this is someone who had a lot more to lose than just becoming a daddy."

"Give me a profile," Ruben prompted.

"All right," Ginger began thoughtfully. "He's someone who's strong, very likely athletic, probably left-handed, and known by his victim. Which means he could be a high school student who has big plans for college or career. He could be a relative or a friend of the family with a high profile. He could be a teacher or a minister or a doctor, or anybody else in a position of respect or authority in the community. He may be married. He either is, or believes himself to be, highly vulnerable. He's almost certainly somebody Tara trusted."

"Who have we excluded?"

"So far, Tom and Billy Hildress and Egon Doyle."

"Who can we include?"

"Everyone else—that is, everyone else who happens to be left-handed." She paused for a moment. "Can we rule out Kyle Breckenridge? He's partly left-handed."

"Partly?"

Ginger shrugged. "I happen to know he's ambidextrous. I've seen him write with his left hand, but he plays golf right-handed."

"He's also got a confirmed alibi for the time of the murder," Ruben told her. "And the sympathy of the entire island. Without any direct evidence that leads us right inside his front door, I think we'd best take him off the list for now."

Albert Hoch had been adamant about that. The mayor was on the telephone barely an hour after Ruben's interview at Southwynd had concluded.

"That man's done more for Seward Island than anyone in the last hundred years," Hoch screamed in Ruben's ear. "I happen to know he's devastated by the death of his daughter. So unless you can wrap the actual murder weapon around his neck and no one else's, don't you dare go dragging his good name through the mud."

"Getting back to our profile," Ruben continued. "If we assume everything you've said so far to be so—what was our perp's greatest fear?"

As before, Ginger took a moment to think. "Exposure," she declared. "And not just to the wrath of the Breckenridge family, although that would have been considerable. But Tara was only fifteen—which means, even if she consented, he was still looking at a rape charge. A felony conviction. A prison sentence. Total ruin."

"So what else can we add to the profile?"

"He's at least eighteen years old."

"And you got nothing on a boyfriend?"

Ginger shook her head. "I talked to the kids Tara hung with. They were positive she wasn't seeing anyone."

"So were her parents," Ruben said.

"Do you think they knew she was pregnant?"

"I'd say there's a good chance the mother didn't know, but the father's a hard read. He might have suspected, but I think he wanted to protect his daughter, and he figured, if it didn't come out in the autopsy, it was none of our business."

"None of our business?" Ginger cried. "It just defines the whole case. It just establishes that we're looking for someone right here on Seward. Look out, folks, he could be living in the house next door."

"Or in the bedroom upstairs," Ruben murmured.

The detective sighed. "Nobody's going to like this, you know. But in a way, it could be a good thing. Most of the locals are decent people. They're just used to taking potshots from a comfortable distance instead of getting involved up close and messy. Now they're going to know that we aren't dealing with a transient, that the killer is one of their own, still here, and to all intents and purposes, ready and able to kill again. No mother on this island is ever going to turn in her son, and most wives would have a pretty tough time turning in their husbands, but knowing he's here may motivate someone else to give him up."

Ruben smiled. Whatever her personal opinions might be on an issue, he could always count on her for a clear and accurate analysis of the place and the people she had known for the better part of her life.

"I sure did a smart thing when I hired you, didn't I?" he thought aloud.

Unaccountably, Ginger blushed, even as her hazel eyes twinkled. "For such a hotshot cop, it took you long enough to figure that out," she retorted.

It rained the day of Tara's funeral. A downpour that Father Paul, the aged priest of Seward Episcopal Church, was quick to attribute to the tears of God at having to take one so young into His fold.

There were hundreds of people in attendance, all of them wanting the opportunity to say a final good-bye. The high school had canceled classes for the afternoon so that those students who wished to do so could be present at the service. Local businesses had shut down for two hours so that workers could pay their last respects. Housewives did their shopping early that morning. Commuters flocked home on the midday ferry.

There were also sizable contingents from both Seattle and Olympia in attendance; mainlanders who felt motivated to make an appearance. The Sewards had pioneered this part of the country, and the family's interests spread across Puget Sound.

The grand stone church that crowned the north end of the Village Green was by far the largest and most prestigious on the Island. The original building dated back to the days of Nathaniel Seward and his tribe. On this day, its ancient carved mahogany pews overflowed, the crowd spilling out of the antechamber, an armada of umbrellas bobbing over a soggy sea of grass.

The ceremony was sad and beautiful. The choir sang the hymns that Mary Breckenridge identified as Tara's favorites. At least two dozen people spoke, each recalling funny, happy, touching little stories about the girl who had been part of their lives for such a brief moment in time.

"She may have been beautiful, and she may have been rich, and she may have had all the advantages that the rest of us just dreamed of having," Melissa Senn said. "But she was just too nice for anyone to hate. So we loved her instead."

"She was not just my goddaughter," sobbed an emotional Albert Hoch, "she was one of His favorites here on earth. And there's no doubt in my mind that she'll go right on being His favorite now that she's with Him in heaven."

"I gave Tara her first smack on the bottom and her first vaccination," Magnus Coop recounted. "Every time she came to my office, she earned a lollipop for good behavior. I sat with her when she had the measles and the mumps. I put her arm in a cast when she broke it, and taped up her ankle when she sprained it. I watched her grow from a beautiful child into a lovely teenager. I have the marks on my office wall where we measured her height each year; just like a lot of you, she got to put her name below it. As long as I live, that wall will never be repainted."

Out of respect for Tara, the chairwoman of the Harvest Festival announced that the festivities would be canceled for this year. Nobody objected.

Ruben and Ginger stood at the back of the church.

"Remember the old detective stories," Ginger whispered, "where the inspector goes to the funeral to see who's there who doesn't quite fit?"

The police chief nodded. "You mean the one who can't quite help looking guilty?" he whispered back.

"Yeah," Ginger said. "That's the one."

Ruben smiled. "Do you really think he showed up?"

Ginger studied the crowd: the family, the friends, the entire bank staff, various civic leaders, representatives from Mary's numerous charitable organizations, Kyle's golf buddies, members of the Rotary, the Elks, and the Hunt Club, and the crowd of students and teachers.

"Oh, he's here, all right," she murmured. "He couldn't risk not showing up."

✦   ✦   ✦

Jerry Frankel left the church in the company of half a dozen other teachers from the high school, quite moved by the out-pouring of sympathy for the dead girl.

"It's rather extraordinary that one so young could have touched so many lives," he murmured.

"I know you're relatively new here, but don't be naive," someone replied cynically. "That show wasn't about Tara. It was about being seen."

"Are the Breckenridges really that important?" Jerry asked.

"Let's put it this way," another teacher responded. "I wouldn't want to get on the wrong side of them. Old man Sew-ard, Tara's grandfather, had a teacher summarily dismissed some years back for referring to the Commodore as a pirate."

Jerry laughed. "He *was* a pirate," he said. "One of the best of them, too."

The other teachers looked around hastily.

"You'd be wise to keep your voice down and your opinions to yourself," one of them said. "Kyle Breckenridge isn't exactly a person to mess around with, either."

Mary Breckenridge walked slowly down Southwynd's grand second-floor hallway, hugging the wall as though to diminish her-self. She had been taught to walk that way by nuns. Her mother, being Catholic, had insisted on sending her daughter to a con-vent school in Seattle. Mary was always so quiet and obedient that perhaps the woman hoped the girl would take to religious life.

She didn't. Quiet, she may have been, and obedient, most definitely, but Mary had her own ideas about the kind of life she wanted for herself, and it had nothing to do with a solitary exis-tence shut off from such things as marriage and children.

"She's a good girl," reported the nuns, "but not suited to the sisterhood."

Like a flower, Mary had the kind of looks that were fresh

and delicate as a girl and faded into womanhood. She met Kyle Breckenridge when she was twenty years old and a sophomore in college. He had come to work at her father's bank and was ten years her senior.

"That young man has a damn good head on his shoulders," her father said after a month. "If he sticks with the banking business, he could be a real asset to us, I think."

"And he has such fine manners," her mother added. "He obviously comes from a good family that took the time to raise him properly."

In fact, Kyle Breckenridge was the ninth of twelve children born to a Minnesota strip miner and his common-law wife. The state had been mostly responsible for raising him until the age of eighteen, whereupon he turned an athletic scholarship into an honors degree from the University of Minnesota, followed by a graduate degree in finance from the University of Chicago, and never looked back.

He taught himself how to speak and how to behave by watching Cary Grant movies over and over again, invented a tragic background to explain the absence of family, and proposed to the bank president's daughter a year to the day after they met.

Mary was delirious. She had hoped and dreamed and fantasized, of course, but despite her wealth and position, she had never really expected that anyone as charming, as attractive, or as exciting as Kyle Breckenridge would fall in love with her. As a result, she promptly fell madly, deeply, completely, and irrevocably in love with him.

She abandoned college, they married, she gave him two daughters, he took over the bank after her parents drowned in a tragic boating accident, and they lived in the gracious home that had first been built by her great-great-great-great-grandfather. And slowly, so slowly that Mary didn't even realize it was happening, Kyle's needs became her needs, his dreams became her dreams, and his life became her life, until she almost ceased to exist.

Everyone they knew applauded them for their dedicated community involvement, appreciated them for their charitable support, admired them for their obvious family commitment, and envied them their affluent lifestyle. But Mary knew it was only an extension of their own desires. Like a house with shuttered windows, no one ever really saw what went on inside. They never glimpsed the heartache that Mary lived with every day, once she was forced to accept the fact that Kyle had married her not so much for love as for a bank and an estate and everything that went along with that.

And it was never more obvious than right now, when she needed him the most, when her whole carefully constructed world was about to explode into a million irretrievable pieces, and he was somewhere else.

Almost at the end of the hall, she reached the door to Tara's room—a pink and yellow cocoon that had once nurtured such promise, so briefly occupied by the beautiful little girl who had always made her mother so proud. It was all ruined now. Her daughter had gone to a place where Mary was unable to reach her, to hold her, or to wipe away her tears. And as if that were not bad enough, her precious memory would soon be forever tarnished. Once tomorrow's issue of the *Sentinel* reached the breakfast tables, everyone who had applauded, admired, appreciated, and envied them, everyone who had sobbed as the casket was lowered into the cold, wet ground, would know that the image of sweet innocence that had always defined Tara was nothing more than a facade.

A facade, Mary thought bitterly, much like a marriage could be. Sinking down on the pink and yellow canopy bed and wrapping her arms tightly around her body as though to keep herself from falling apart, she wept.

❖   ❖   ❖

Despite the combined protests of both Albert Hoch and Kyle Breckenridge, news of Tara's pregnancy did indeed find Its way onto the front page of the newspaper the morning after the funeral.

"Revealing this information to the general public could seriously hamper the investigation," the mayor told the editor.

"That's a load of crap and you know it," Gail Brown shot back with an indignant toss of her ponytail. "The fact is, it might just help find the bastard."

"Don't go up against me, Ms. Brown," the bank president warned, "or I'll damn well put you and your newspaper right out of business. I'll call in your loan, and if that doesn't do it, I'll lean on your advertisers until they turn and run."

"Go ahead," Gail retorted fearlessly. "I'll print what you just said, in the presence of a witness, and let not just Seward Island but the whole of Puget County decide the issue of the people's right to know."

"But running this story will make you so unpopular," the mayor pleaded. "All it will do is ruin the good name of an innocent girl."

"I'm not in the popularity business, I'm in the newspaper business," the editor declared. "And I don't make the news—I just report it. Besides, whatever you know about today, Albert, the whole world will know about tomorrow anyway, so what difference does it make if I print it?"

"I hope you'll at least have the sensitivity to wait until after the funeral," Kyle said.

"As a result of startling new evidence that has been confirmed by the county coroner's office," the *Sentinel*'s lead story began as promised, "local authorities now believe that Tara Breckenridge's killer was not a transient, as had been previously assumed, but a resident of Seward Island who almost certainly knew his victim."

* * *

"Well, at least she waited until the poor girl was buried," Charlie Pricker observed, tossing the paper into the trash can.

"A lot of comfort that'll be to the family," Ginger said with a sigh.

The story eclipsed the funeral, even the murder itself, as the main topic of conversation down at the Gull Harbor Drug Store, the Commodore Street Bakery, the Seward Island Library, and the Waterside Cafe, where little knots of people spoke in hushed whispers that broke off in mid-sentence if either Kyle or Mary or young Tori Breckenridge happened by.

"It's twice the tragedy," an assistant librarian felt compelled to tell the editor. "Now the Breckenridges have been devastated by two murders instead of one."

" 'The wages of sin is death,' " quoted the wife of the Baptist minister, with her husband's permission. "Tara Breckenridge sinned and has been punished for her sin. May God have mercy on her soul."

"If parents can't properly educate their kids about sex, and if churches won't even admit that teenage sex is here to stay," wrote an angry biologist, "maybe it's time we let the schools dispense condoms."

Everyone, it seemed, had an opinion, whether it was about the murder or about teenage pregnancy or about the recklessness of unbridled youth. But as the days began to slip into weeks, no one stepped forward with any information that would assist the police in their investigation.

"More than ever, local authorities need your help in identifying Tara Breckenridge's killer," the *Sentinel* reiterated. "If you saw Tara on the evening of her death, or were near Madrona Point Park between midnight and two o'clock on that Sunday morning, Mayor Albert Hoch urges you to come forward.

"'If we are to make Seward Island safe for our children again,' he said, 'we need your support. We cannot let this murderer escape justice.'"

The Breckenridge case was almost three weeks old and going nowhere, and the people were growing restless.

"Why is Tara Breckenridge's killer still at large?" the frightened father of two young girls asked the editor. "Surely, on an island as small as this, the police should already have a suspect in mind, have gathered enough evidence, be close to making an arrest. We pay taxes to have a police force that will keep our community safe. Why aren't they doing their job?"

"Is it possible that he lives just down the street?" inquired an eighty-year-old grandmother. "Is it possible that I've known him since he was a boy, watched him grow up, and never saw the evil that was taking possession of him? Is it possible he played with my grandson or dated my daughter? I've lived here all my life. Do I really want to know?"

"I'm afraid to go out of my house now," a seventh-grader wrote. "I'm afraid the killer might get me."

"I've never seen anything like it," Hoch admitted to Ruben, brandishing the latest issue of the newspaper as evidence. "People are running scared. Parents are locking up their kids at night. They're staying home themselves. Restaurants reported a sixty percent drop in dinner revenues last week; the movie theater says attendance was off by almost half. Nobody ever thought about locking their doors on this island before. Now Jim Petrie down at the hardware store says he can't keep enough dead bolts in stock. Nobody knows who to trust anymore. Folks are suddenly suspicious of neighbors they've known all their lives. Everyone's walking on eggshells."

"That's perfectly understandable," the police chief told him. "Cold-blooded murder is a whole new thing to this community, and people don't know how they're supposed to react to it."

"And, of course, everyone's trying to figure out who the next victim will be."

"Next victim?" Ruben echoed. "Why are they assuming there'll be another murder?"

"Because the maniac lives right here, where he can strike at any time," Hoch declared. "Maniacs don't stop at one killing, do they?"

"Based on the nature of the crime, we believe the killer was enraged," the police chief replied. "But not necessarily that he was deranged. Whether he kills a second time depends on why he killed the first time."

The mayor's eyes popped in his bald head. "Don't you think he'll kill again?"

Ruben leaned against his chair, stretching his back, and contemplated the wall for a long moment while he weighed the pros and cons of telling Albert Hoch what he really thought.

"Mind you, this is nothing more than my own personal opinion, based on past experience," he said at last, knowing that within the hour his words would be reported the length and breadth of the Island as official fact, "but I tend to see this crime as having been a deliberate assault on a single person for a specific reason. There's nothing we've uncovered so far that would lead me to assume that our killer will kill again. Of course, I could be wrong, but all the circumstances of this case seem to indicate that it was an isolated incident."

11

It was just her eyes he saw. In the moonlight, they seemed to burn with a life of their own, as though they had no relation to the rest of her, as though there were no rest of her. Twist and turn though he might, he couldn't get away from them, or from the hideous indictment in them.

He covered his face with his hands so he wouldn't have to see. But even with his face covered, there were the eyes. Always the eyes. He tried to hide himself, whimpering and cowering because he knew what was coming next. He covered his ears, hoping to shut it out. But even with his ears covered, the wretched scream split the night in half as it denounced him to the world.

And then he woke, in a panting, sweat-soaked panic. There was no moon, no scream; the room was dark and silent. He had not been exposed. It was only a nightmare.

For a moment, his throat was so tight he couldn't seem to breathe, the pain in his chest so sharp he wondered if he might be having some kind of heart attack. What an inexcusable blunder it would be, he thought, were he to die right here, right now, over a bad dream, when he had so much of life yet to live.

He forced himself to take several deep breaths, filling his lungs to the bursting point before he let the air out as slowly as he could, knowing this would relax his throat and ease the pain in his chest.

When he was reasonably calm, he pushed his pillows against the headboard, leaned back into them, and began to reconstruct the entire scenario, from start to finish, assuring himself each step of the way that he had taken the only option available to him. What she had demanded would have destroyed him, ruined his entire life. He would probably even have gone to prison. But she never once made an effort to see that from his perspective. As many times as he tried to tell her, she refused to listen. He couldn't believe how stubborn she had been. In the end, she left him no choice.

The stupidity of it was that something could have been worked out. All she had to do was go along. He had more than made that clear enough. So, in reality, she had brought it on herself, out of her own sense of shame or guilt; forced his hand, out of some misjudged sense of power. She had gambled with her very life, and lost. Which meant the consequences were hers.

With a satisfied sigh, he closed his eyes and waited for sleep to return, having persuaded himself that, in the end, at least, she understood what she had done—what she had compelled him to do. It was the reason she hadn't struggled.

12

"For the next several weeks, we're going to be taking a look at World War II, up close and personal, as they say," Jerry Frankel told his sophomore history class on the Monday after Halloween, when Tara Breckenridge had been dead for three weeks.

"As some of you may already know, this was a war that, aside from the loss of life and the defeat of Fascism, had an enormous socioeconomic impact on this country, and we'll examine that impact very closely. But just to get our feet wet a bit, do any of you have family members who were involved?"

Three hands went up.

"My grandfather fought in the war," Lucy Neiland said. "He lost an arm on D-Day."

Many members of the class nodded. They knew Lars Neiland. He owned the sail shop down at South Cove, and could tie a knot faster with his steel claw than anyone with two hands.

"I had a great-uncle who was in the Navy," Jack Tannauer reported. "But I never met him. The Japs sank his boat in the Pacific way before I was even born."

Jerry looked at the teenager for a moment. "You mean the Japanese, don't you?" he suggested.

Jack shrugged. "Yeah, sure, whatever," he said.

"My grandmother's whole family died in the war," Daniel Cohen said. "Her parents, her brothers, and her sisters, all her aunts and uncles and cousins, too. They were gassed at Auschwitz. She was the only one who survived."

There was a loud snicker at the back of the room.

"Hank, did you have a comment?" Jerry asked.

"That stuff about gassing—that's all such garbage," Hank Kriedler said.

"What do you mean by 'garbage'?" the teacher inquired. "Are you saying Daniel just made up that story about his grandmother's family?"

"Well, he might think it's true," Hank said with a careless shrug, "because that's what they told him. That's what they told everybody."

"They? What 'they' are you talking about?"

"The Jews, of course," Hank Kriedler replied. "It's all propaganda that the Jews spread around to give Hitler a bad name because they didn't like the way he was getting Germany back on her feet."

Jerry considered the sixteen-year-old for a long moment before he spoke. "My father has a tattoo on his arm that reads: M4362," he said finally. "He covers it up with long sleeves so no one will see it because he's ashamed. He got it on the day he arrived at Majdanek—which we'll learn was one of Hitler's most notorious death camps—the same day he saw his parents herded into a communal bathhouse and never saw them come out again. He's ashamed because he couldn't do anything to save them. He was twelve years old. Is that what you mean by propaganda, Hank? You think my father made it all up?"

"The Jews were destroying Germany," the teenager maintained. "They controlled all the money. They were strangling the economy. Everybody knows they engineered the Great Depression so they could get even richer and have more power. And they got France and England to start the war with Germany. Hitler was right to get rid of them while he was defending his country. But there were no death camps like everyone thinks—they were just detention camps, like we had for the Japs—uh, Japanese—here. That whole mass murder stuff is crap."

"Then what do you think happened to the six million Jews, and the millions of political dissidents, and others designated as undesirable by the Third Reich, who disappeared during the war?"

"Like I said—propaganda," Hank repeated. "Most of them probably never existed in the first place."

"You seem to be quite well versed in this particular subject," the teacher observed. "May I ask where you got your information?"

Hank shrugged again. "From books," he said. "My dad has real history books that me and my brother have read, books that tell the true story, not the lies they always try to feed us in school."

Jerry Frankel looked around the class of twenty-three, a perfectly ordinary group on the face of it. "Are there any more of you who feel the way Hank does?" he asked. "Who feel that the textbooks we have are feeding you lies?"

Hank glared at his classmates, especially those who were part of his immediate social circle. Jack Tannauer shrugged and raised his hand. After a moment, Kristen Andersen did, too. Several others looked as though they might, but then apparently thought better of it.

"At least three of you," Jerry murmured, feeling the hair at the back of his neck begin to rise. He made a quick decision. "Hank, I'll tell you what," he said. "You bring in those books of your father's. We'll read them together, right here in class, where we can compare them to the texts that have, for almost fifty years now, been accepted by pretty much every educational institution in the country. Then we'll separate the facts from the fiction of the matter, and see if we can come up with the real truth."

The whole room began to buzz. Everyone turned to look at Hank Kriedler. He was big for his age, good-looking, and one of the few sophomores to drive his own car. He was generally acknowledged to be one of the class leaders, and he had been challenged.

"I'll have to ask my dad," the teenager mumbled, his face coloring to the roots of his platinum hair. "They're his books. I don't know if he's gonna let me bring them to school."

"Why not?" Jerry Frankel inquired mildly. "This is a neutral place. Our primary objective here is to learn. You've presented us with a fairly contrary view of history today—one you obviously believe we should all embrace. I'm simply offering you the opportunity to achieve your goal; to back up your beliefs with documentation that can stand the scrutiny of your peers."

In a basement room, lit by a single candle, seven men talked late into the night. It was not a regularly scheduled meeting of any official organization, nor even a social get-together, for few of these men moved in the same circles. Rather, it was a hastily called gathering of certain like-minded citizens who, when the occasion arose, came together for the purpose of discussing a specific issue.

Their voices were too low to overhear, their faces too shadowed to identify. The only thing that was clearly distinguishable in the flickering light was a red banner mounted on the back wall with a distorted Greek cross in its center.

13

Ginger's least favorite part of any investigation was having to go back to people she had already interviewed and press them even harder—perfectly innocent people, who wanted nothing more than to be left alone to live their lives—in an effort to persuade one of them to give up his or her brother, best friend, neighbor.

In the weeks following the funeral, she went back to the group of students who had been closest to Tara Breckenridge. Had anyone seen Tara displaying any kind of special interest in another student, a teacher, an adult man in the community—anyone at all, at any time—that might give the police a lead to follow? The answer was no.

Had anyone seen a student, a teacher, an adult man in the community—anyone at all, at any time—displaying any special interest in Tara? Again, the answer was no.

"Tara was my best friend," Melissa Senn said, "and I happen to know she was very sheltered. She wasn't even allowed to date. I guess her parents felt she was too young and naive about some things. I think they were afraid she might end up getting pregnant or something." The black-haired teenager stopped short, coloring deeply, when she realized what she had said. "I guess they were right, weren't they?"

"There was this sort of 'hands-off' thing about Tara," Bill Graham observed. "I don't think she knew it. I think it was just the way everyone related to her. You know, look but don't touch. She was part of our crowd sometimes, we kidded around, but that's as far as it went."

"And that was okay with you?"

Bill shrugged. "My dad is a mortician, Detective Earley. He dresses dead bodies and digs graves. I'm gonna be lucky if I get to go to college. Hank Kriedler's dad sells cars. Jack Tannauer's dad collects tickets and cleans toilets at the movie theater. We're not exactly the kind of people who'd be welcomed at Southwynd, if you know what I mean. When it came to Tara, I think the Breckenridges had their sights set a little higher than someone from Seward Island."

Ginger moved on to the boys in the senior class. How many of them had known Tara? Had they ever been out with her? Had they ever seen her in any situation that seemed unusual, out of the ordinary? She was met with another blank wall.

Then she interviewed each of them separately. What were you doing on the night Tara died? Is there anyone who can corroborate your alibi? Would you be willing, if asked, to come down to Graham Hall and take a polygraph test?

Next, the detective went to the office and asked to see the victim's academic record. Coming into high school, Tara's grades had been solid As and Bs. By the end of her freshman year, however, they had quietly slipped down to Cs. She had taken three remedial classes in summer school and received Bs in two of them. In the third class, history, she had gotten an A.

Finally, Ginger went back to the teachers. Having had time to consider, did any of them remember anything that might help the investigation? Was there anything about Tara that had changed during the last weeks of her life?

"Her grades certainly weren't what they should have been," her science teacher acknowledged. "I think she was a good deal brighter than the quality of her work indicated."

"Algebra wasn't her best subject," reported her math teacher. "But I do know she was trying. I checked—she got an A on her last exam."

"She was good in grammar and composition, but she really didn't have her mind on school," her English teacher conceded sadly. "I wish I'd been more alert. Certainly, if I'd had any idea what was going on, I would have tried to do something. But I assumed it was just about getting into a new school year, and like a lot of other kids, she would eventually settle down."

"Tara earned that A in summer school," Jerry Frankel, the history teacher, asserted. "It was no gift. She worked hard for it. But she wasn't the same after the fall term started. Her homework assignments were frequently late or missing altogether, and I noticed she had trouble concentrating in class."

Ginger went over to the intermediate school, which was actually an adjunct of the high school, and asked to see Tori Breckenridge. They went to the library and sat at a table at the far end of the room.

"I don't know anything," the twelve-year-old said. "My mother always says that Tara and I were, you know, close, but we weren't. Not really. We got along okay, I mean; she wasn't bad to me or anything. But she never, like, confided in me about stuff going on in her life, or talked to me about her problems or anything."

"Do you know anyone she might have talked to?" Ginger prompted.

Tori shrugged. "Maybe Father Paul. Tara used to be real involved in church stuff."

The massive doors to the Seward Episcopal Church stood open to the autumn wind. Ginger found the aged priest on his knees at the altar, shivering beneath his vestment.

"It's cold, Father Paul," she said gently. "Could we have some tea?"

The priest struggled to his feet and led the way to his office. The man was over eighty and had been in his church for almost fifty years. His assistant, a gaunt man of around forty, brought tea.

"Tara was a true believer," Father Paul said, his tea sitting untouched beside him. "She helped teach the young ones in Sunday School, you know. She never missed a service, never missed communion. It seemed to lift her spirits so, and renew her soul."

"Right up until her death?" Ginger asked.

"No," the priest admitted. "Sometime, I think it was in early September, she didn't come to church for two weeks in a row. I assumed she must have been sick. She came back after that, but she stopped receiving communion, and she wouldn't teach the children anymore."

"Did you ask her why?"

The priest sighed. "I meant to," he said.

"Didn't you wonder?"

"Of course I wondered."

"She didn't come to you?"

"No."

"Was there anyone else here, one of your assistants, perhaps, that she might have confided in?"

"Father Timothy is my only assistant at present," he said. "Unfortunately, Tara didn't come to him, either. She came to no one here. And that's the failure I will take to my grave." Tears filled the old man's eyes. "She was a beautiful child," he said. "As pure and as clean as the angels of heaven, and given to us by God as a gift of love. Whatever befell her here on earth was surely the work of the devil."

❖   ❖   ❖

Ginger's last appointment of the day was with Magnus Coop at the medical center.

"You were her doctor," she pressed the crusty physician. "You really didn't know she was pregnant?"

"No," he sighed, wagging his white head. "I wish to God I had. I gave her a routine school physical at the beginning of August. I noticed nothing amiss, and she didn't complain of anything. Of course, I wasn't looking for a pregnancy. She didn't come to me after that."

"Did she go to anyone else?"

"Not at this clinic," he declared. "Of course, she may have gone to someone in Seattle."

"On her own?" the detective wondered.

"Probably not," Coop conceded.

"But she had to know she was pregnant," Ginger pressed. "Otherwise, none of this would fit. Do you think she might have gotten herself one of those do-it-yourself-at-home tests?"

"That would certainly make sense," Coop agreed.

"She didn't talk to her parents or her sister, she didn't talk to her friends, she didn't talk to her priest, and she didn't talk to you," Ginger reflected sadly. "How horribly alone she must have felt."

Ruben sat at his desk in Graham Hall, eating the lunch Stacey insisted on preparing for him every morning. This was Tuesday, which meant a meatloaf sandwich smothered in salsa, just the way he liked it. But he ate mechanically and hardly tasted a thing.

It was three weeks since the death of Tara Breckenridge, and Ruben was still trying to find something in the few fragments of evidence that Charlie Pricker had retrieved from Madrona Point Park that would put him on the trail of a killer.

The entire department had been working on the case, and all they had to show for it was a piece of bloodstained carpet, a

number of hairs and fibers that did not belong to the victim and may or may not have belonged to the person they sought, the partial fingerprint on the cross around Tara Breckenridge's neck that apparently did not match anyone among her close friends and family, a hundred or so other fingerprints that could take months to identify—if indeed they could be identified at all—and the certain and infuriating knowledge that he was out there, somewhere, watching their every move, laughing at them.

Ginger had reported talking to at least two hundred people. In addition to the victim's friends, classmates, and teachers, she had reinterviewed family members, neighbors, and townspeople, asking all of them the same questions: Were they absolutely positive they hadn't seen Tara that evening? Hadn't talked to her? Hadn't known of her dating anyone? Hadn't seen her with anyone? Hadn't heard her speak of anyone?

All of them were positive. They hadn't seen her, they hadn't talked to her, there was no one, there was nothing. Besides, deep down, none of them could really believe that one of their own had committed such a heinous crime. A few of them had voluntarily come down to police headquarters and taken polygraph tests. All of them had been excluded as potential suspects.

And yet there had to be somebody out there, Ruben was convinced, somebody who knew something, even if he or she didn't realize it. There was always something. He sighed and picked up the forensic reports for the twentieth time. Fingerprints, fibers, hair, blood. It was all right here. All they needed was a place to start.

"Knock, knock," said Helen Ballinger. The plump, affable, middle-aged police department clerk stood at Ruben's open office door, wagging her head as she saw the folders in one hand and the sandwich in the other. "You're going to get indigestion doing that," she warned.

"Probably," he agreed.

"Well, take a break. There's a young man out here wants to talk to you."

Ruben dropped the reports onto the desk, set aside his sandwich, and leaned back in his chair. "Okay," he said, "send him on in."

The boy looked to be about seventeen years old, with auburn hair, blue eyes, and acne.

"My name's Owen Petrie," he said, standing awkwardly by the door, his voice cracking slightly.

"No need to be nervous, son," Ruben told him with a reassuring smile. "We're pretty informal around here." He indicated the spare chair. "Why don't you have a seat, get comfortable, and then you can tell me what's on your mind."

The teenager hesitated for a few seconds, as if debating the wisdom of this suggestion, and then slid onto the chair and swallowed hard. "Well, the thing is, I guess I might know something, you know, about the murder," he said, staring down at his Air Jordans.

Ruben's posture didn't change, nor did his expression, but his eyes suddenly began to study the youngster with great care. "If you mean Tara Breckenridge's murder," he said in the same casual tone, "it sure would be helpful if you did."

"Yeah, well, I didn't think it was anything, but then, see, I told my dad about it, and he said, just in case it *was* something, I ought to come and tell you about it."

"Is your dad Jim Petrie, from the hardware store?"

The boy looked up. "Yeah, he is. D'ya know him?"

"Sure do," Ruben said. "He's on the city council, which makes him one of my bosses."

Owen twisted in his seat. "Oh yeah. Well, you see, I was there that night—at Madrona Point Park. The night Tara was killed, I mean. It's a pretty secluded place at night, and sometimes some of the guys go up there to, like, hang out, you know, with girls. Well, you see, I'm not really supposed to go there, which was why I didn't say anything before this, but then I got to thinking, you know, about like what if what I saw was important, and I was the only one who saw it, and so, well, I decided maybe I'd better risk being grounded for a month and tell my dad."

"What did you see, Owen?" Ruben asked carefully.

"Well, I didn't see Tara or anything like that, or I'd have spoke up right away, you understand," the teenager said. "But I did see a car come into the park. It was around eleven o'clock, which was way before, you know, the murder was supposed to have happened, so that's why I didn't really think anything about it. But I'm pretty sure that the car was still there when we left, and that was about eleven-thirty. So, I don't know, maybe it could mean something."

"Did you see anyone inside the car?" Ruben queried.

Owen shook his head. "Not really. Well, I mean, it didn't pull up near us or anything—it went all the way around to the other side of the parking lot from where we were, over near the Dumpster, and there aren't exactly a lot of bright lights around the place." The boy blushed. "That's kinda the reason we go up there, you know, because it's, like, dark and quiet and all."

Ruben nodded. Although his own youth was long past, he could still remember a quiet hill overlooking Los Angeles where he had taken a girl or two. "Could you tell how many people were in the car?"

The youngster shrugged. "Well, there had to be at least one, of course," he said. "There could've been two, I guess. I don't know. To tell you the truth, I wasn't really paying that much attention."

The police chief tried not to smile. "Do you think the young lady who was with you might have seen something?" he asked hopefully.

"No, she didn't see anything," Owen replied, blushing even harder. "She wasn't exactly looking out the window at the time, if you know what I mean."

"Yes, I think I do," Ruben murmured. "Did you know Tara Brockenridge, Owen?"

"Not really," the senior replied, looking straight at the police chief. "I mean, sure, I knew her. Our families know each other; we go to the same church, and to some of the same parties, and we belong to the same country club. But she was just a kid. Jail bait, as my dad says. I never made a move on her, if that's what you're asking, and nobody I hang out with would have, either. Jeez, her father would've killed anyone that tried."

"Getting back to the car," Ruben said, "I don't suppose you got a license number, did you?"

"No, I didn't. How was I supposed to know it would be important? I thought it was just another guy with a girl."

It was too much to hope for. "Well then," Ruben inquired, "could you at least describe the car for me?"

"Oh, sure," the teenager said. "I wouldn't have come talk to you unless I could do that. It was a Ford Taurus wagon, or I guess it could have been a Mercury Sable—they're pretty much the same, you know. My mom drives a Taurus. That's how I recognized it for certain. Except hers is white and this one was dark. Not black, I don't think, but dark green, maybe, or maroon, or brown."

"Three weeks, and finally our first solid lead," Ginger said when she heard.

"First *possible* lead," Ruben cautioned. "It could turn out to be perfectly innocent—just another junior Don Juan out for a hot time."

The detective shrugged. "Well, there can't be that many Taurus or Sable wagons on the Island, so we should be able to find it."

"Start with Kriedler," the police chief suggested, referring to the Ford dealership on Center Island Road. "He ought to be able to give you a list of customers. Then put every uniform we can spare out on the street."

While he might caution Ginger not to get too excited, a lead was still a lead. After weeks of blowing up dust, at least this was something concrete they could investigate. Ruben felt a familiar surge of adrenaline. Old habits, he thought to himself.

14

By the time nine months had passed, Matthew Frankel had decided that living on Seward Island wasn't so bad after all. He had made a best friend, Billy Hildress, who lived several streets over, and that had gone a long way toward making up for the pain of having to leave Scarsdale, his grandparents, his childhood chums, and the only home he'd ever really known.

The boys were in the same fourth-grade class at Madrona Elementary School, and inseparable. Their teacher called them her two peas in a pod. They sat next to each other, teamed up for class projects, and helped each other study. They ate lunch together, spent recess together, walked home together, and played with each other after school. So it was only natural that Matthew would invite Billy to share his ninth birthday celebration.

It was bright and sunny and unusually warm for the second Saturday in November, perfect for a ride on the top deck of the ferry to Seattle. The first stop for the Frankels and their guest was the Museum of Flight down at Boeing Field, where the boys sat in a space capsule, checked out the enormous Blackbird, and climbed aboard a vintage B-52 where they pretended to be pilots and bombardiers. Then there was lunch and games at Chuck E.

Cheese. And now they were back at Matthew's house, playing in the yard with his new golden retriever puppy.

"I named him Chase, because he chases after me all the time," Matthew told his friend.

"Puppies are neat," Billy said. "Our dog is too old to play with me anymore." He flopped down on the grass and the retriever began to lick his face. "Where does he sleep?"

"He'll sleep in my room as soon as he's housebroken," Matthew replied. "And I get to feed him and walk him and take him to obedience school when it's time, too."

"Maybe I'll get a new puppy for my next birthday," Billy said hopefully, "and then the two of them can play together."

From the corner of his eye, Matthew saw a curtain flutter out a second-floor window in the house next door. Justin Keller stood at the window, watching. A serious, solitary boy, Justin was eleven years old and in the sixth grade, and in nine months had not spoken more than a dozen words to his new neighbor.

"It's my birthday," Matthew called up to him. "I got a new puppy. You can come over and play with him if you want."

Almost instantly, Justin disappeared, his round eyeglasses catching a quick glint of late afternoon sunlight as he went. Then a hand reached out to retrieve the errant curtain and shut the window with a wordless response.

"How weird," Billy said.

Matthew shrugged. "I guess so."

"Even weirder," Billy added. "There's a police car coming up your driveway."

Matthew looked. Sure enough, a black Blazer with the Seward Island police seal on its door came to a stop at the top of the drive, and a man and a woman got out.

"That's Chief Martinez," Billy whispered. "And that's Detective Earley with him. She's the one me and my dad talked to the day we found that body in the Dumpster. I wonder what they're doing here."

"I don't know," Matthew said, his dark eyes, which were so like his father's, following the officers up the path to the front door of the house.

The police had identified three Ford Taurus wagons and one Mercury Sable registered on the Island that fit Owen Petrie's description, and Ginger and Ruben were spending Matthew Frankel's birthday interviewing the owners.

The first Taurus on the list, they quickly learned, had been in the repair shop the weekend of the murder.

"That damn car spends more time in Kriedler's garage than it does in mine," the owner grumbled. "I don't know why I let my wife talk me into buying it."

He gave Ruben the receipt for the repairs and the name of the mechanic.

The second Taurus had been in Yakima the weekend of the murder.

"It was my mother-in-law's seventy-fifth birthday," the owner explained. "We left early Friday afternoon and caught the late ferry back on Sunday night. My wife's whole family was there, even the noisy cousins from Albuquerque showed up. Fifty-two people."

He gave Ginger a list of the attendees and his mother-in-law's telephone number.

The Mercury Sable belonged to Dr. Frederick Winthur, a forty-two-year-old divorced father who, it turned out, was the Breckenridge family dentist.

"Where was I the night of Tara's murder?" he asked. "I was right here at home with my two boys. According to my custody agreement, I get them every other weekend."

"How old are your sons, Doctor?" Ruben inquired.

"Eight and ten."

"Do you remember what you did that night?"

"Let's see, we probably went out for pizza—that's what we usually do on Saturday nights. And then I suppose we came home and watched movies on the science fiction channel. That's also what we usually do."

"And, if you recall, approximately what time did your boys go to bed?"

"Probably around eleven," Winthur said. "Although I'd appreciate your not making a big issue of that. My ex-wife has a real fit when I let them stay up past nine."

"And you?"

"Well, I don't really remember, but I guess I'd say I went to bed maybe half an hour after that. I generally hang around for the late news."

"Is there anyone else who would have had access to the Sable that night?" Ginger wanted to know. "Did anyone ask to borrow it? Could a relative or a friend or a neighbor have used it?"

"No," the dentist replied. "I'm not in the habit of lending my car to anyone, and I can't recall anyone ever asking to borrow it."

"Would you mind if Detective Earley and I took a look at your car?" Ruben inquired.

"What for? Do you think I'm lying to you?"

"Not at all," the police chief said smoothly. "It's simply that we have information that a car fitting the description of your car was seen at Madrona Point shortly before we believe the murder took place. We'd like the opportunity to exclude even the possibility that it was your car."

The dentist shrugged. "As long as I can be there to make sure there's no funny business going on, you can look all you want to," he said.

"Thank you," Ruben murmured.

"By the way," Ginger asked, as the dentist led the way to the garage, "when was the last time you saw Tara?"

"Let me see," Winthur said, frowning in thought. "I believe her last checkup was sometime in July. Of course, it could have been June. I think I saw both girls at the same time, but I'd have to review my records to be certain."

It took Ginger less than ten minutes to determine that, on the surface, at least, the car was clean. There were no obvious bloodstains, no suspicious strands of blond hair, no clearly visible "smoking gun."

"One last thing, Doctor," Ruben asked as he and Ginger were about to leave. "Are you right-handed or left-handed?"

"I'm right-handed," came the reply. He pulled back the cuff of his sweater to reveal a contorted left hand. "Good thing, too, because I've had limited use of this one since I was twelve."

"I'm sorry," Ginger murmured.

The dentist shrugged. "I was playing macho man and got careless with a handgun. The damn thing discharged—almost blew away my arm. My boys are never going to come within ten feet of a gun. It's the only thing my ex and I ever agreed on."

The last Taurus on Ginger's list was registered to a Deborah Frankel, the vice president of a major investment firm in Seattle.

As they pulled into the driveway, Ginger saw two boys playing with a puppy in the backyard. As she walked up the path beside Ruben, she could feel three pairs of eyes on her back.

"Good afternoon," Ruben said to the dark-haired woman who answered the door. "I'm Chief Martinez and this is Detective Earley, from the Seward Island police. I wonder if we could talk to you for a moment. It's in connection with the Breckenridge case."

"I beg your pardon?" Deborah Frankel said in surprise. Police officers didn't generally show up at her home on a peaceful Saturday afternoon, wanting to talk about murder.

"The girl who was found in the Dumpster last month," Ginger clarified.

"Yes, I know what case it is," Deborah assured them. "I just don't know anything about it."

"This has to do with a maroon Taurus wagon," Ruben told her. "You do drive one, don't you?"

"No, I don't," Deborah corrected him. "My husband drives it, but you've already talked to him." Ruben glanced at Ginger. "At school," Deborah added. "He was one of the dead girl's teachers."

"Yes, of course," Ginger said. "I talked to a number of Tara's teachers about her grades and general attitude. This is about something else."

The double garage door was open, and Ruben could see the maroon Taurus parked inside. "Perhaps we could talk to your husband, if he's here."

"Yes, of course," Deborah murmured. "Come in."

She led the two police officers to the library where Jerry sat at the rolltop desk, grading a pile of essays.

"Kids," he said with a chuckle. "They think Dunkerque is a city in Iowa, and Churchill used to be President of the United States." He smiled at the intruders. "Hello again, Detective Earley. What has you out working on a weekend?"

"We're following up on a lead we received in connection with the Breckenridge case," Ginger explained. "About a Taurus wagon being seen driving into Madrona Point Park around eleven o'clock on the night of the murder. We're asking everyone on the Island who has such a vehicle whether they were there, and if so, whether they saw anything that might help us, anything at all."

Jerry shrugged. "Well, I do drive a Taurus wagon, but I wasn't out in it that night."

"Is there anyone else who would have had access to the car?" Ginger asked.

"Only me," Deborah replied, "but I didn't drive it that night either."

Ruben looked from one to the other. "Could anybody have borrowed the car? A teenage son or daughter perhaps?"

Both the teacher and his wife shook their heads. "We have only one child," Deborah said. "He's nine—nine today, in fact."

"We're sorry to interrupt such a happy occasion," Ruben said sincerely. "Unfortunately, criminal investigations have a way of intruding at the least appropriate times. To wrap this up then, you're pretty sure that your car was in the garage all evening?"

Jerry's eyes slid past the police chief's shoulder. "As I recall, I was in the shop, working on a kite for my son that evening. My shop area is right in the garage, and I think I would have noticed if the car were missing. I must have been in there from somewhere around ten o'clock until about midnight."

"I was in bed by eleven," Deborah said, although Ruben hadn't asked.

"We were there that afternoon, though," Jerry offered. "At Madrona Point Park, I mean. We took our bicycles and went for a ride around the trails. But we were back home by four o'clock at the latest."

Deborah nodded in confirmation.

"Well, it was a long shot," Ruben said, as he and Ginger prepared to leave.

Jerry gave them a boyish smile. "I thought teaching was tough," he said. "But your job is even tougher. I don't envy you."

"I wonder," Ruben said as though the thought had just occurred to him. "You wouldn't mind letting us take a look at your car, would you?"

"A look?"

"Well, yes. You say you didn't take the car to the park that night, and no one borrowed it, so we'd like to be able to exclude it from our investigation. Occasionally, that's how we have to solve a crime—by excluding everything until we're left with only one possibility."

Jerry looked directly at the police chief. "I thought you came here to find a witness, Chief Martinez—or was it a suspect?"

Ruben shrugged apologetically. "That's just it," he conceded. "Sometimes, we never know."

"Then, by all means, look at the car," the teacher said. "My wife can show you where it is. I have to finish grading these essays."

As with Fred Winthur's Sable, a casual inspection of Frankel's Taurus revealed nothing that either placed the vehicle at the scene or implicated it in the crime.

"Well, what do you think?" Ruben asked as he and Ginger climbed back into the Blazer. "Could he be a reluctant witness?"

"I don't know," Ginger replied cautiously. "From everything I hear, he's one of the good guys. He's got a first-rate reputation at school, and his students say he was all broken up about the murder. I think, if he'd been anywhere near the park that night, he would have told us."

"Unless he had a reason not to get involved," Ruben suggested.

"You mean, he might be stepping out on his wife and had nowhere else to go but Madrona Point, where he witnesses a murder and decides, for the preservation of this illicit relationship, and/or his marriage, to keep quiet about it?" Ginger played out the scenario with a hint of skepticism in her voice.

"Is it possible?"

Ginger shrugged. "I guess anything's possible, but I'd have a hard time swallowing it. To begin with, you saw the wife; she's a knockout. Why would he be looking elsewhere? But let's just say he was. Madrona Point is about teenagers, not adults. Even if he didn't know that, the minute he drove in and saw another car parked there, he would have split."

"He might not have noticed the other car."

"In a town as small as this," Ginger said, "a guy who's doing something he doesn't want anyone to know about would look—very carefully."

"You might be right," Ruben conceded, starting up the Blazer's engine. "Okay, so if he's not a witness—could he be a suspect? He does drive a maroon Taurus—and he *is* left-handed."

"I know," Ginger allowed. She, too, had noticed him grading the essays. "Of course, it could be a coincidence."

"Maybe," the police chief hedged. "But I don't like coincidences. So just to be on the safe side, let's see what we can find out about him."

"Okay," Ginger said. "Drop me off at Graham Hall and I'll get started on it right away."

Ruben looked at his watch. It was after five o'clock. "On Saturday evening?" he protested. "Come on. Don't tell me you don't have something better to do than investigate a murder?"

"Not really," Ginger admitted. "This is just another night in the week as far as I'm concerned." She shrugged. "If you must know, my social life isn't exactly what you'd call active right now. But I don't mind. I love my work."

"If you really don't have any plans," Ruben said without thinking, "maybe we could have dinner together. My daughter is out for the evening, and I guess you could say my social life isn't all that active either."

"You mean a working dinner?" Ginger asked. "To talk about the case?"

Ruben hesitated. What was he doing? Was he crazy? "No," he heard himself say. "I mean a regular dinner, at a nice restaurant, with tablecloths and wine. And we can talk about anything we want to talk about."

15

On the second Saturday in November, Ginger Earley and Ruben Martinez had known each other for exactly twenty-one months and five days, and there had never been anything between them but the job.

As soon as the invitation was out of his mouth, Ruben couldn't believe he had issued it. He couldn't believe he had actually suggested that they go out on what clearly amounted to a date. He had never dated a policewoman before, much less one who worked for him. Come to that, he had hardly dated at all in the past thirteen years. But even as his words took him by surprise, he realized that the idea must have been in his mind for some time.

Ginger had such freshness, and an eagerness about her work that had not yet grown jaded. She reminded him of himself, before the bullet. He liked being around her. And he had to admit she wasn't bad to look at, either. With that red hair and those freckles, it was easy to see the winsome woman she really was peeking through the tomboy facade she had cultivated. He couldn't believe there weren't hordes of suitors tripping all over themselves to get to her, and he felt a strange stab of pleasure in hearing that there weren't.

Of course, he knew he couldn't let himself get carried away with any of this. She was, after all, much too young for the used-up man he knew himself to be. The eighteen years that lay between them was far more than a mere span of months and minutes; it was a lifetime of disappointment and disillusion. But he couldn't help it; he wanted to know what it would be like to sit across a table from her for one evening, away from the turmoil of the office and the pressures of the job. Just once, he told himself—once would be enough. He held his breath and waited for her response.

Ginger was caught completely off guard. In twenty-one months and five days, Ruben had never indicated anything other than a professional interest in her. More than that, he had always been careful not to treat her any differently than he treated the men on the force, or even acknowledge that there *was* a difference. Regardless of the fact that she was the only female officer in the department, she had always felt like one of the guys.

Yet here he was, after all this time, asking her out for dinner on a Saturday night as though it were the most natural thing in the world. What had Ginger so flustered was that she had spent a significant portion of those twenty-one months and five days fantasizing about him doing exactly that.

In the long, quiet evenings alone in the cozy apartment she had leased shortly after returning to Seward Island, as she read a book or listened to music or watched a television program, she would find her mind drifting toward him, find herself wondering what he was doing at that moment, trying to imagine what kind of life he led away from the office, what kind of woman he preferred . . . what he would be like in bed.

Next to her father, she certainly admired him more than any man she knew. His knowledge, his intuitiveness, his patience all spoke of a man who was sensitive, caring, genuinely concerned about people, and dedicated to his work. From the mayor and city council to the members of his staff to the pettiest of vandals, Ruben always treated everyone with respect.

The difference in their ages never entered her mind. There was as yet no gray in his thick black hair, no wrinkles around his intelligent brown eyes, no sag to his square jaw, no telltale thickening in the midsection. Everything about him spoke of vitality and endurance.

He was not overly tall, barely taller than she, in fact. But he kept himself in excellent condition, despite the back brace she knew he wore beneath his shirt, and his body was still lean and hard. Ginger knew about the bullet, of course; everyone in the department knew. The story had become part of office lore, and as far as she was concerned, only added to his appeal.

"Dinner sounds fine," she heard herself say.

Ginger lived on the ground floor of a three-story building on Green Street, two blocks off Seward Way, that had been designed to look more like a mansion than an apartment house. It had a comfortable bedroom and bath, a modest kitchen, a living room with a well-used fireplace and a glass wall that opened into a small backyard, and an alcove that was just big enough for her round oak dining table and four chairs.

She had chosen it in part for the location, being a stone's throw from work, but mostly for the exquisite little garden of rhododendron, rock daphne, andromeda, and ceanothus, surrounded by a high hedge of photinia, that the previous tenants had lovingly planted and left in her care. Ginger wasn't particularly good with plants, but she loved having them, and she made a sincere effort to keep them all well and happy. She did a lot better with animals, and her current cat, an enormous marmalade named Twink, stood guard over the slugs and sow bugs and other parasites that threatened her blooms with bodily harm.

Ruben found the place easily, and then sat in his car for ten minutes until his watch read exactly seven o'clock. Thirty seconds later, he was ringing her doorbell, feeling every bit as nervous and as awkward as a sixteen-year-old on his first date.

One of her mother's homilies that had actually stuck with Ginger down through the years was on the virtue of promptness, and she was ready and waiting in a simple black dress with a scooped neck and a short skirt. Ruben could not remember ever seeing her in a skirt before—she always wore pants to work—and it didn't take him long to notice that she had extremely nice legs. Her fiery hair, normally bound in a neat French braid down her back, had been turned loose to curl softly about her shoulders.

"You look just great," he murmured, wondering what she had done with the tomboy he had invited to dinner.

"You don't look so bad yourself," she replied with a grin. His dark blue suit may have been a little shiny in spots, and his white shirt may have been a bit frayed around the collar, but he was freshly scrubbed and eager, and Ginger couldn't remember him ever looking better.

Because of the murder, quite a number of Island families were still choosing to stay at home these days. Ruben had no trouble getting a last-minute reservation at Gull House, the renowned restaurant crowning the northern arm of the harbor that offered its patrons the finest seafood to be found in the Northwest, and an unparalleled panorama of Puget Sound through a series of leaded glass window walls. The place had much more the atmosphere of an exclusive private club than a public eating establishment. The lighting was soft, the carpets were thick, and the service was as impeccable as the fare.

Ruben had been to Gull House only once before, at a pre-employment luncheon interview with the mayor and members of the city council. The last time for Ginger had been a dinner party to celebrate her twenty-first birthday.

The maître d' showed them directly to a window table in the smallest but most elegant of the three dining rooms.

"My goodness, the best table in the house," Ginger whispered. "I didn't realize I was dining with such a celebrity."

"Neither did I," Ruben whispered back.

They were not unaware of the stunned looks and startled murmurs their entrance garnered from the small contingent of locals who had ventured out, and they let themselves be amused by the sidelong glances that followed their progress across the restaurant.

"What do you think they're thinking?" Ginger asked with a mischievous glint in her eye.

"Why, they're thinking how lucky I am to be out with such an attractive young lady, of course," Ruben replied with a grin.

"I'm delighted you chose this restaurant," she told him carelessly. "Maybe it'll give them something to gossip about besides how little headway we're making on the Breckenridge case."

They ordered Caesar salads, grilled swordfish for him, Dungeness crab for her, and a decent bottle of chardonnay. Over the food, they talked about being on a small island, from his perspective of having more or less recently arrived, and from her perspective of having lived there most of her life.

"How long does it take before you stop feeling like an outsider?" he asked.

"I don't know yet," she replied. "Probably three or four generations."

They talked about what they did when they were away from the office, on weekends and holidays.

"I love to hike," she said. "I've been roaming the Olympics since I was ten."

"I've only gotten as far as Hurricane Ridge," he admitted. "But someday, I'd like to get up to the glacier."

They talked about lifestyles.

"I love the water," Ginger told him. "I'd live on a houseboat if I could figure out how to swing it."

Ruben nodded. "I used to fantasize about living on some

deserted beach one day," he said, "in a little cabin with a dog to keep me company. After I retired, and after Stacey was grown and gone, of course."

They talked about hobbies and favorite activities, and surprised each other when they both put bird-watching near the top of their lists.

"It's not so much the birds," she began.

"As the quiet," he finished.

He applauded her efforts against animal cruelty. She was delighted to learn that he abhorred hunting of any kind. "I know I probably shouldn't say this," he said, "but I think I'd sooner kill another person than a defenseless animal."

They spoke about music and movies and books. It was as easy for them to talk to one another as if they had known each other all their lives, and it didn't take long for them to discover they had a lot in common.

Too soon, much too soon, dinner was over, the last bite of shared satin cheesecake swallowed, the last drop of coffee drunk, and he had driven her back to her apartment house and walked her to her door.

"Thank you," she said, feeling awkward standing there on her front step. "This was really fun."

"Yes, it was," he assured her.

She didn't want the evening to end. She wanted to invite him in, for another cup of coffee, an after-dinner drink, more conversation, anything, because she felt light and carefree and happy, happier than she had in years, and she wanted it to last just a little while longer, like maybe for the rest of her life.

"I guess I'll see you Monday," she said.

"First thing," he promised.

There was just the slightest of pauses, and then he was turning and leaving. The moment was lost. She couldn't go running after him; he'd think her such a fool. She stood on the threshold, watching, until he was out of sight. Then she went inside and shut the door with a resolute click.

He was her boss, after all, and she knew it would be foolish to start anything personal with him. It would only confuse things, or worse, mess up their working relationship, and perhaps even end up costing her a job she loved. Maybe it was the wine that had her feeling so good, she decided, not him. Maybe it was the dinner and the restaurant that made her so giddy, and the fact that this was her first date in over a year.

She kicked off her shoes and padded down the hall into the bedroom to undress. They had chatted on like old friends because, to some extent, they *were* old friends. They had worked within arm's reach of each other for almost two years and that kind of togetherness almost had to create a bond. It wasn't all that surprising; she considered at least half the men on the force to be friends.

As for the things they had in common, well, they weren't such unusual things, really. Hiking and boating—almost everyone in the Pacific Northwest liked them. And as far as birdwatching, classical music, David Lean films, and Tony Hillerman novels were concerned, she supposed she could have those things in common with any number of people.

Ginger scrubbed her face and brushed her teeth and climbed into bed, resolving to make an extra effort to get out more and meet new men. The cat jumped up and stretched out beside her.

"I don't know what I'd do without you, Twink," she said, scratching his ears. "But I'm afraid, when it comes to sharing a bed, you just don't cut it, you know what I mean?"

The cat snuggled against her and began to purr.

Ginger sighed. She loved her job, but the truth of it was, there was a hole in her life that her work just couldn't fill. Surely, there had to be someone out there meant for her—someone who would understand her commitment to her career, who would applaud her work and not flinch from her profession. There had to be someplace where she could meet such a person.

She thought about her girlfriends from high school, most of them married and mothers. She thought about the boys with whom she had grown up. They were either married or gone. The Island was predominantly a family community, not a haven for singles. The chances of meeting Mr. Right here were slim to none, and she dreaded the idea of going into Seattle to hang out at bars.

Maybe she should consider taking an adult education class, or an extension course at the university, or join the Sierra Club. Yes, that was the thing to do—expand her horizons, look somewhere else, somewhere less complicated.

Ruben was a very special person, there was no doubt about that. But what would be the point in getting herself involved in something that had the deck stacked against it right from the start?

Ruben reached home before Stacey. He mixed himself a weak Scotch and water, and sat down in the living room, wondering why he had cut the evening off short of eleven o'clock.

The tables near them at the restaurant had emptied while he and Ginger dallied over each dish, talking and laughing, in no particular hurry to get to the next course. Still, they had run out of food long before they had run out of conversation. Ruben smiled into his Scotch. He had the feeling that, given all the time in the world, they would never run out of conversation.

There had been a fleeting moment, at her door, when he thought she would invite him in, and he wondered how he should respond. But the moment passed, she didn't give him the choice, and he was both disappointed and relieved.

It was easy enough to keep things on a friendly level at the restaurant, with other people around them, but it might not have been so easy once they found themselves alone in her apartment.

He knew it was wiser not to let this go beyond casual, not to get involved. He also knew that neither of them needed complications at work that might hinder their effectiveness or set idle tongues to unnecessary wagging.

It was no big revelation that personal and professional relationships rarely succeeded, and usually ended up hurting one or both of the parties concerned. He had wanted one evening with her and now he'd had it. Dinner was over.

Ruben downed the last of his Scotch with a resolute sigh and pulled himself to his feet. Whatever else, he always tried to be honest with himself. And he knew, despite what he might have believed earlier, that just one evening with her was not going to be enough.

16

The dream woke her—a disturbing dream, not quite a nightmare. Deborah Frankel opened her eyes with a start, expecting to see the girl. But there was only the moonlight slipping through the window, and the shadowy shapes of her solid rosewood bedroom furniture. Who was the girl? Deborah wondered. Where had she come from? And what was she doing in the middle of a dream about Jerry falling off a cliff?

Deborah didn't have a very clear image of her, and even that was fading now with wakefulness, but she had definitely been there, a peculiar spectator who calmly stood and watched and waited—for what?—as Deborah tried frantically to save her husband.

"Help me!" Deborah remembered crying. "Help me!"

But the girl hadn't replied, hadn't moved, hadn't even blinked.

Deborah glanced at the clock on the nightstand. The digital numbers read three-eighteen in ghostly green. She looked over to the other side of the bed. Jerry was fast asleep, safe and sound, all curled up around his pillow like a little boy hugging a teddy bear.

Deborah sighed. It was a major trait of his that she had somehow failed to notice in the beginning: the innocence, the beguiling playfulness . . . the dependency. But that was twelve years ago, and she saw so many things differently now than she had then.

Twelve years ago, she was a junior at Bryn Mawr, trying to decide on a future, and he already had his master's in hand, and was teaching history in an inner-city Philadelphia high school. They met, of all places, at a synagogue on Rosh Hashanah. He was there with his father; she was there with her roommate. Being Jewish wasn't a very big thing in Deborah's life, but it was part of her heritage, and she knew it pleased her parents back home in Scarsdale, New York, when she at least made an effort to observe the holidays.

They spotted each other immediately, across the aisle in the Reform temple, and stole cautious glances whenever they thought the other wasn't looking. After the service, they found a way to meet.

"I haven't seen you here before," he said.

"I haven't been here before," she replied.

He was a taller and much more attractive version of his father, but with the same sensitive, expressive eyes. In retrospect, she decided, it was the eyes she had first fallen in love with. The eyes that had looked so deep into hers that she felt engulfed by them on the night he asked her to marry him. The eyes that danced at the birth of their son, the eyes that cried when their daughter died . . . the eyes that seemed to slide past Ruben Martinez's shoulder when Jerry said he was working in the shop on the night that Tara Breckenridge was killed.

Deborah knew that look. She was sure he meant it to convey concentration, but sometimes she wondered if it hid evasion. She remembered the morning after the murder; the bandaged thumb, the bloody sweatshirt. She hadn't thought anything about it then. For some reason, she found herself thinking about it now, and a cold chill slid down the length of her body as she wondered whether her husband had been telling the truth.

Even after twelve years, she was not quite sure. There had been good communication between them once, or so she thought, when she was young and still impressionable. But as time went on, she came to realize that he had put a barrier between them, like a protective suit of armor which allowed her to know only that part of him that he wanted her to know. In their early years together, she had tried every way she could to penetrate that barrier, but after a while the effort began to seem greater than the reward, and she abandoned it.

Life, she couldn't help reflect, was sometimes like a big black hole—a dark and scary unknown that you plunged into with no clear idea of what awaited you—much like the murky pond behind her childhood home that her mother used to caution her about. You made decisions that seemed to be reasonable and informed at the time, only to learn later that they may have been imprudent. You thought you knew what you wanted, only to discover that perhaps you did not. You saw yourself as wise and worldly and mature enough to make the right choices, only to realize you were not. And then, without quite understanding how you got there, you found yourself in a place you didn't really want to be, with no viable way out.

She remembered how often her elders had waxed eloquently about the particular joys of marriage and motherhood— and wondered why nobody had ever thought to warn her about the mistakes one could make. Not that she was ready to admit that her marriage was a mistake, but there were things she wished she had known beforehand, things she would perhaps have been better prepared for, things she might have been able to handle a little differently.

With a small yawn, Deborah plumped her pillows and snuggled down under the covers. She could go back to sleep now. The analytical side of her brain had taken over—what she always referred to as her working mind. It was already beginning the process of evaluating situations, assessing results, and considering options.

The dream was gone. So was the girl.

17

"Tara Breckenridge has been dead for almost a month now," Gail Brown editorialized in the *Sentinel*, "and yet the police are no closer to apprehending the person responsible than they were on the day it happened. How can this be? With all the modern technology law enforcement has at its fingertips, why does this case remain open?

"Chief Ruben Martinez came to Seward Island three years ago with impeccable credentials, and he has built a first-rate staff. I know most of these people; they are dedicated professionals, and yet they have so far been unequal to the task of solving the single most heinous crime this community has ever known. What's wrong with this picture?

"If we who live here are to blame, if there is someone among us who knows something that will help lead authorities to Tara's killer, and has not come forward, then shame on us, for even the finest police force cannot be expected to work in a vacuum.

"Our idyllic island has been severely rocked and is now being sorely tested. Living here will never be the same. I see fear and distrust everywhere I go. Friends and neighbors who deliberately chose this place to distance themselves and their families from the dangers of big-city life are locking their doors and looking over their shoulders. Tara's death, the way in which she died, touched us all. It's an open wound that will not—and cannot—heal until the person responsible has been brought to justice.

"Whether we knew her well or not at all, we want Tara to rest in peace. We want the Breckenridge family to have some closure. *We* want to be able to get on with our lives. She deserves, they deserve, we deserve to have this matter resolved. If this resolution is being thwarted by someone out there who has pertinent information and has purposely chosen not to share it with the proper authorities, then shame, shame, shame on us all."

"She took aim at the whole island this time," Charlie Pricker remarked, dropping the paper on Ruben's desk.

"It was a mistake," declared Ginger.

"Why?" Ruben asked. The three had once again squeezed themselves into the police chief's tiny office.

"Because she's a native," replied Ginger. "She should know better. All this is going to do is alienate everyone, and make our job even harder."

"I can't see as it matters much," Charlie said, sighing.

Ginger shook her head. "Islanders are basically good people, but they're the kind of people who go to church every Sunday, listen to the sermon, pray piously—and then go home thinking they're square with God. If you rub their noses in it, they'll turn on you. But if you just let them alone, sooner or later, they'll get around to doing the right thing."

"Yeah, but how much later?" Charlie drawled.

Their investigation of the mystery Taurus wagon that had been seen in the Madrona Point parking lot on the night of the murder had come to nothing, and Ginger's look into the life of the history teacher had turned up no indication that her initial assessment of him was in any way inaccurate.

"He's clean," she said. "I haven't found anything to suggest otherwise."

Charlie shrugged. "Back to square one."

"It's infuriating," Ruben said. "The guy we're looking for is out there, right under our noses, and we're just missing him. Here we sit, on an isolated island, with a population of twelve thousand people. That gives us a potential suspect pool of maybe thirty-five hundred males between the ages of eighteen and let's say seventy, only a small fraction of which are going to turn out to be left-handed. Tara obviously had a relationship with one of them, and it didn't happen in a vacuum. So why are we having so much trouble finding him?"

"Maybe because we're coming at it the wrong way," Ginger said slowly.

"What do you mean?"

"Well, instead of investigating Tara, maybe it's the men we should be investigating."

Ruben looked at her. "You want to investigate thirty-five hundred men?"

Ginger shrugged. "Either we can sit around waiting for something to happen, or we can try to make something happen for ourselves."

The police chief frowned. "How exactly would you go about doing this?"

Ginger thought for a moment. "It's the blood that's going to solve this case," she said finally. "So I'd be right up front about it. And I'd start with an easily identifiable group—let's say, high school seniors. That's only around seventy or so. I'd tell them exactly what we're doing. Then I'd ask each of them to voluntarily give us a sample of his blood to be used for a paternity test. If the kid is innocent, it's the best way to clear himself. If he refuses, well, at least we've narrowed the field. Then, of those who refuse, we can strike the ones that are right-handed, and con-centrate on the rest. If that doesn't give us what we want, we ex-pand the selection and repeat the process until we get him."

"Those tests cost a fortune," Charlie reminded her, "and they take months to process."

"We can probably eliminate a lot on basic blood typing alone," Ginger replied. "And remember, we're concentrating on left-handers, which will narrow the field dramatically. So we send off only those samples provided by left-handed donors that have a possible chance of matching."

"How do we determine who's left-handed and who isn't?" Charlie inquired.

"Let Magnus do that," Ginger said, "as a casual part of tak-ing the blood sample. You know, you take the blood out of the arm the donor either uses most of the time or doesn't use as much, or something like that. And the technician can mark down which it is."

"Has it occurred to you," Charlie suggested, "that we could be looking for someone who might not be strictly left-handed, but ambidextrous?"

"It's possible," Ginger conceded. "But I think it's safe to as-sume that the number of ambidextrous men on this island is small enough to ignore at this point. I'd go with the obvious. If we have to increase the sample at a later date, so be it. And if we don't let on that we're only looking for lefties, we won't give any-thing away."

It was the one piece of information that they had been able to keep from Albert Hoch, and therefore from the Island as a whole.

"Are we clear with the Constitution on this?" Ruben asked. "I don't want to go stepping on anyone's personal freedoms."

"I think we are," Ginger asserted, "as long as we make it strictly voluntary."

Charlie shrugged. "You know, it's so obvious, it might just work."

Ruben had to agree. He looked at the redhead he had known for almost two years, and was just beginning to know. If the department ever got around to solving this case, he felt certain it would be because of her. She combined an instinct for police work that could not be taught, with a thorough understanding of the community in which she performed that work. It was how he had operated in the barrios, blending into the background. It was not like here, where he was so out of place. Here, *she* was the one who blended, and he had come to rely heavily on that.

There had been their dinner together on Saturday night. This was Wednesday afternoon. Hardly a moment had passed between then and now that he wasn't thinking about her, recounting the evening in his mind from beginning to end—every word, every gesture, every smile. It was like returning from a long exile in an Arctic waste to find the world was a warm and wonderful place, and to know, after so many years, that it was okay to be alive.

He was thrown clear of the auto accident that killed his wife—a pickup truck skidding on a slick patch of road, spinning out of control, smashing into the passenger side of the old Chevy. It all happened too fast. There was no time to react, to swerve, to avoid the collision. Everyone said so. But that didn't stop the guilt from engulfing Ruben, or the pain, or the loneliness. He had loved his wife as much as he could. Afterward, he began to wonder whether he had loved her enough. That made it worse.

It was Stacey who saved his life. She was only two years old at the time of the accident, suddenly motherless, and she needed him. He couldn't deny her. He taught himself to shut off all the parts of himself that didn't directly relate to his daughter or his work, and he had been quite successful at it.

Until Saturday night.

Now there were a dozen different doors opening inside of

him, exposing him to the expectations, the uncertainties, the joys, and the fears of connecting with another human being. Because, of course, they *had* connected. As much as he wanted to tell himself—tried to tell himself—they hadn't, he knew better.

It was all wrong, everything about it was wrong—the difference in their ages, their positions, their backgrounds. He was well aware of that. But it didn't matter, because it was clear to him that nothing had ever been or would ever be more right.

He talked it over with Stacey at breakfast on Sunday; they had few secrets between them.

"It sounds like you two really hit it off," she said. She had encountered the no-nonsense redhead at police headquarters on any number of occasions, and pretty much liked what she saw. "So, do you want to see her again?"

"There's really no point in it," her father replied with perhaps more candor than he intended. "This is such a small island. Our working relationship could be jeopardized. Then there's the potential gossip that could cause problems. Not to mention the difference in our ages. She's closer to your age than mine. No, there's no point; it can't go anywhere."

"That's not what I asked you," Stacey observed.

Sometimes, he thought, she was too wise for her years. The obvious answer was yes, but he couldn't seem to say it. He was afraid that he had caught Ginger off guard, giving her no choice but to accept his invitation once she had told him that she was free for the evening. He didn't want her to go out with him just because he was her boss and she didn't know how to refuse, and he wasn't sure he would be able to tell the difference. Ruben had already had enough rejection in his life; he was not particularly anxious to open himself up to more.

"What if I do want to see her again?" he countered. "She may not want to see me. And I certainly don't want her to feel she has to be polite."

Stacey tossed her silky blond hair that was so like her

mother's. "Invite her home to dinner," she suggested. "If she accepts that kind of offer, I think you can assume she's not just being polite. Then I'll get a good up-close, out-of-the-office look at her, and we'll know what's what."

"You really think I should?"

His daughter looked at him quizzically. "What's the worst thing that can happen?" she asked shrewdly. "That she says no—or that she says yes?"

Ever since that conversation, the fearless police chief had been trying to summon the courage.

The Sunday after the dinner at Gull House was brisk and blustery; a steely overcast threatened rain.

Ginger spent the better part of the day holed up inside her apartment, listening to an all-Beethoven concert being rebroadcast from New York's Lincoln Center and cleaning out her closets. Anything to keep herself busy, to keep her mind and her body occupied, to keep from thinking about Ruben.

In the clear light of day, she decided it wasn't fair. To be twenty-eight years old and finally find what could be the right man—only to have him be her highly visible boss in a small town where the gossip alone could destroy them. There were so many things wrong with the two of them being together—and everything right. They thought alike, they shared so many interests, their senses of humor seemed to harmonize. She had no doubt that their bodies would fit together perfectly as well.

Despite her resolution of the night before to get out and meet other men, she began to think about the possibility of finding a job in another police department, in another county, which might then make it permissible for them to see each other. Even though she would hate leaving the Island, if it meant she could have a relationship with Ruben, it might be worth it.

At three-thirty in the afternoon, the Beethoven concert having concluded, Ginger abandoned her closets, changed her clothes, and set off for the rambling farmhouse on the western side of the Island where she had been raised, and where her parents still lived. It was a weekly ritual that she rarely missed because it brought her three brothers and their families back to Seward.

Sunday dinner at the Earley homestead was normally a boisterous affair with her nieces and nephews out of control, and she and her father and her youngest brother squaring off against the rest in a game of touch football. But it was a somber group that greeted Ginger this particular day. The children were strangely silent, her brothers perplexed, her father distracted, and her mother agitated.

"Eleanor Jewel just couldn't wait to tell me," the buxom woman with unnaturally blond hair declared the moment her daughter was past the front door. "Why, she fairly pounced like a cat the moment we walked into church."

"Tell you what?" Ginger asked.

"All about you going to Gull House, of all places, with that Chief Martinez person, of course," Verna Earley replied.

"So what?"

"So how do you think it looks?" her mother complained. "You being seen having dinner with—with your boss?"

"We worked late on a case, and on the spur of the moment, we decided to have dinner," Ginger said. "If I'd thought there was anything wrong with that, I wouldn't have done it."

Verna looked to her husband for support.

"I think your mother is concerned more with how it was perceived than by how it really was," Jack Earley suggested with an unhappy sigh at being put in the middle.

"That's not true," Verna argued. "I'm just as concerned with how it was. It's bad enough you have to work for him, but to be seen with him when you're on your own time, to flaunt your association in the faces of our friends, our neighbors, all the people you grew up with—well, it's not the done thing."

Ginger looked from her mother to her father and back to her mother again. "Did I miss something here?"

"It was a good many years before we became part of this community, young lady," her mother said. "Although you were too young to remember, it didn't just happen. Your father and I had to make it happen. We had to attend a particular church. We had to join the right clubs. We had to cultivate the proper friends. As you well know, Seward Island can be a very cliquish place, and coming from the other side of the state, as we did, your father and I had to work especially hard to be accepted here. It took a long time, but this is our home now, the people are important to us, and their opinion of us matters."

"I guess I must be dense," Ginger said, "because I still don't get it."

Her mother sighed in exasperation. "You were seen giggling and laughing and sharing your food with him, like you were out on a date, for God's sake," Verna said. "Out on a date at the most expensive restaurant in town, in a low-cut dress with—well, I shouldn't even have to mention it, and I'm sorry, but I guess there's only one way to say it—with a Mexican."

The word was aimed like a dart at Ginger, and it landed with the precision of an expert marksman, almost knocking the wind out of her. For a moment, she was so stunned she was unable to speak.

"I never realized there was anything wrong in being friends with a Mexican," she said finally. "You never told me there was anything wrong with that."

"There were never any of them around here," her mother retorted. "So we didn't think there was any reason to tell you."

"And you're saying the whole island feels this way?"

"Well of course I can't speak for the whole island," Verna said, backing off slightly, "but I'm sure I speak for those in our social circle. There are people who belong and there are people who don't, and it doesn't do to mix the two."

"I'm sorry," Ginger said slowly. "I didn't know."

There had always been remarks, passing comments of one sort or another, but never anything as blatant as this, and Ginger had always been able to dismiss them as thoughtless chatter. She looked at her mother as though unsure whether she had ever really seen her before.

"Well then," Verna said, "what's done is done, and now that you understand, we'll say no more about it."

A collective sigh ran through the entire family. Her mother trotted off to the kitchen to tend to her roast. The children began to chase each other around the backyard. The touch football game took over the front lawn. A thorny matter had been dealt with, and now life could return to normal. Nobody seemed to notice that Ginger played with an unusual lack of enthusiasm, or that she hardly said a word to any of them all evening, or that she merely pushed the food around her plate at dinner.

Only when she was back in the safety of her apartment did the anger inside her erupt, and the violence of it made her hurl her handbag at the bookcase crammed into the corner of the entry foyer, knocking several volumes askew and smashing a small porcelain angel that had been a sixteenth-birthday gift from her late grandmother.

For the first time, she realized how apart she had grown from the close-knit family she cherished. More than just the life experiences that had taken her out of the cloistered atmosphere of Seward Island and into the harsh reality of police work, she simply didn't see things the way her parents did. Their values were not her values, their world no longer her world.

She tried to picture herself at ten or twelve, perched on a stool in the big, friendly kitchen as her mother baked cookies, or sitting shoulder to shoulder with her father as they worried over a jigsaw puzzle. Had they really told her that some people were less acceptable than others, and she had missed it? Or had she, like most children, simply allowed them to think and act for her until she was grown up enough to shed their influence and think and act for herself?

Unbidden, a memory pushed its way into Ginger's mind of a Japanese-American girl she had liked in grade school, and how her mother had, for no specific reason, discouraged the friendship. And she recalled a Jewish boy in high school who had been one of the few ever interested enough to ask her out. Verna had clearly not wanted her to date him. So it *was* there, that undercurrent. Never very overt, never too hostile, just there. Never anything specific that you could put your finger on, just something you were apparently expected to understand.

Ginger understood, all right. She knelt down on the floor to retrieve the shattered pieces of the porcelain angel. Gone were all her doubts and fears about an office relationship. Gone was the idea of seeking employment in another district. She was going to stay right here where she belonged, on Seward Island, and live her own life. Because that's exactly what it was—her own life; whatever the pitfalls, whatever the consequences.

There, on her knees, she prayed as hard as she had ever prayed before that Ruben Martinez would ask her out again.

He did. Four days later.

"I guess I should have said something a whole lot earlier," he began cautiously on Thursday morning, when they found themselves alone in his office for a rare moment, "but I really wanted to thank you for having dinner with me the other night. You're a lot of fun to be with, and I had a terrific time."

"So did I," she said. "In fact, I can't recall when I had a better time."

"Really?" he asked, brightening. "Because I thought maybe I didn't exactly give you a choice."

"Of course you did," she told him. "I didn't have to say yes."

"Well then," he said, his courage soaring. "I was—uh—well, wondering if maybe—uh—we might do it again sometime?"

Ginger felt her heart skip a beat. "I'd like that," she replied.

A big grin spread across Ruben's face. "That's great," he said. "That's just great." He turned to the work in front of him and then turned back to her. "I don't suppose you'd be free on Sunday, would you?"

"As it happens, I am," she said without the slightest hesitation.

"Stacey said I should invite you home for dinner so she can look you over, but we can go out someplace, if you'd prefer."

Ginger laughed. "Gosh, I can't remember the last time anyone wanted to look me over," she told him. "I'd be delighted to have dinner at your place."

Ruben shoved his hands into his trouser pockets because he was afraid he might do something stupid, like clap.

"Is six o'clock okay?" he asked.

"Six is just fine, and I think I know the way to your place."

"Oh, no," he said. Despite the desperate life of the barrio, he had been taught his manners. "I'll pick you up at six."

"Okay," Ginger agreed. "I'll be looking forward to it."

Ruben grinned. "So will I."

Ginger grinned, too. Her parents were just going to have to manage without her on Sunday. She began to plan in her mind exactly how she would tell them.

"They're at another dead end," Albert Hoch reported to Kyle Breckenridge. "The car-in-the-park angle didn't pan out. They're back to square one."

The bank president wagged his silver-blond head. "A month and still nothing. This isn't good, Albert. It sends a very dangerous message that our police force is weak at best and incompetent at worst. People are starting to ask how it can be so difficult to catch one murdering bastard on an island with only twelve thousand people."

"I know, Kyle, I know," Hoch said. "But they've got a new plan. They want to use DNA to find him. They want to start with the high school seniors, get them to give a blood sample, and try to match it with Tara's unborn child. If they come up dry, they'll expand the circle to others who knew her. They think they can catch him that way."

"This is terrible," Breckenridge declared. "To have the people in this community subjected to such a thing. What are we coming to—that we must interrogate our lifelong friends and neighbors, invade their privacy, strip them of their dignity?"

"They've got nothing else to go on," Hoch protested. "You want them to find Tara's killer, don't you? Well, they can't just pluck a viable suspect out of thin air, can they?"

"No," Kyle Breckenridge conceded with an unhappy sigh. "They can't just pluck a suspect out of thin air."

Ginger began her telephone calls on Thursday afternoon. By Friday, she had contacted all seventy-two male members of the Seward High School senior class. Of that number, forty-six agreed to be tested, eleven said they would get back to her, and fifteen flat out refused.

"A lot of the parents aren't happy about the idea," she reported to Ruben. "But most of them got the point. If they refuse to let their sons be tested, it could make them look guilty."

She arranged with Magnus Coop to take the blood samples at the clinic on Saturday. Both Coop and Charlie Pricker would be on hand, as well as all three of the clinic's laboratory technicians, who would be instructed to determine whether each subject was right- or left-handed. Once the samples were properly identified and typed, Charlie would hand-deliver those to be tested to the state crime laboratory in Seattle. With a little luck, they could expect to have the results back in two months.

18

Ruben was up, showered, and dressed by seven-forty-five on Sunday morning, but Stacey was way ahead of him. The fifteen-year-old not only was dressed herself, but had his breakfast ready.

"I thought you'd want to go to mass this morning," she said, as she set a plate of scrambled eggs with sausage in front of him, poured his coffee, and then sat down quietly with her hands folded in her lap.

Going to church was something Ruben did as infrequently as possible and mainly on holidays. Even then, it was more for Stacey than himself. Yet there were some things that could not be ignored, that had to be honored.

"Yes," he said, thinking that nobody made coffee like his daughter, thick and black and delicious.

When he invited Ginger to dinner, with Stacey's full approval, he hadn't stopped to think about the date. But this was the thirteenth anniversary of the accident that had taken his wife, and every year since, he and his daughter had observed the occasion by going to mass together.

"We'll have plenty of time to clean up the house when we get back," Stacey assured him. "And do dinner, too."

Ruben nodded sadly, thinking how easy it was for her to slip from past to present, knowing that the ritual they celebrated was his, because she could have no real memory of her mother.

Saint Aloysius Catholic Church was a pristine structure located two blocks west of the Village Green. Built of white clapboard and shingles, with a series of fabulous stained glass windows, it had been destroyed by fire three times in its history and restored, each time just a little bit sturdier, a little bit grander than before. The three percent of the Island population that supported the church did so generously.

A majority of the pews were already filled by the time Ruben and Stacey arrived. As was their custom, they quietly took up seats at the rear. Immediately, Stacey moved forward onto her knees, and began to pray. Ruben stayed where he was. Since the death of his wife, he had been unable to recover his faith. Over the years, he and God had developed a more or less laissez-faire relationship with each other that seemed to work well enough. At least, as far as he was concerned.

The mass was traditional, the sermon a rather bland version of doctrine. The priest was an agreeable enough man, but not much of an orator. Ruben watched with detachment while Stacey took communion, glad if it could bring her a measure of comfort that it no longer brought him. Then he went with her to light a candle for his wife.

It was after the service was over, when the congregation was slowly filing out of the church, that he and Stacey happened to overhear part of a conversation going on ahead of them.

". . . chief favored us with an appearance today," John O'Connor was saying.

"The Breckenridge case must be keeping him busy," Kevin Mahar responded.

"More likely a case of a redheaded detective," O'Connor suggested and laughed.

"Can you believe that?" Lucy Mahar exclaimed. "I don't know what she could be thinking of."

"That she's twenty-eight years old and still unmarried, my dear," Doris O'Connor replied with a shrug.

"For all he's accomplished on the Breckenridge case, we might just as well have hired ourselves a chihuahua," John O'Connor said.

At that, Stacey tucked her arm through her father's. "Come on, Dad," she said in a bright, clear voice. "If we hurry, I can get your kibble on the table before you can say woof."

The O'Connors slunk away without a word. Kevin Mahar had the grace to look embarrassed.

"I'm sorry, Ruben," he mumbled. "We didn't realize you were behind us."

"That shouldn't change your opinion any," Ruben replied with quiet dignity. "One of the great things about this country is the freedom we have to speak our minds without fear of the consequences."

"White American trash," Stacey remarked as they climbed into the Blazer.

"No," Ruben said with a sigh. "They're just ordinary people who aren't used to being afraid of the dark."

The apple pie was cooling, the rib roast was cooking, the little house was scrubbed and sparkling, and the table was set for three by the time Ruben left to pick up Ginger. Stacey selected a red sweater for him to wear over a white shirt, and then liberally dosed his hands with Vaseline Intensive Care lotion.

"Just in case you happen to take her elbow or something, you understand," she said with an impish twinkle in her dark brown eyes. "After all, you don't want her thinking you do housework, do you?"

Ginger was ready when he rang the bell. She was wearing a pair of slacks and a soft sweater in bright blue that looked wonderful with her red hair, which was swept off her face and caught in back with a big blue bow.

"Red, white, and blue," she said in greeting. "We're certainly a patriotic pair."

Ruben Martinez was a straightforward man who believed in tackling a problem head-on. It was simply not in his nature to deceive.

"Look," he said. "Before we go, I think I should tell you that, well—some people are talking. About us, I mean. Normally, I don't pay much attention to that sort of thing, but some remarks were made at my church today, and I just wanted you to know that, well, I'd understand if you thought it best to call dinner off."

"Remarks?" Ginger echoed. "What sort of remarks?"

"Well, I'm afraid they were about you—being seen with me."

"I stopped going to church years ago," Ginger told him with a toss of her head. "Now I know why."

"This is a small town," he said.

"Yes, and some of the people have small minds," she said.

"Still, it's the place where you've lived most of your life," he reminded her. "I don't want to cause you any embarrassment. So the decision is up to you."

"In that case," Ginger declared, "I hope you're a good cook, because I'm starved."

Like an old bathrobe, there was something warm and cozy and familiar about the Martinez home that wrapped itself around Ginger the moment she stepped through the door. Although the place was undeniably small and the furnishings a bit shabby, comfort and caring oozed out of every corner. Had she had the slightest hesitation about going to Ruben's house on just their second date, the feeling vanished the moment Stacey stepped forward with a smile and a hug.

"I hope you like roast beef," the teenager said. "It was the only thing Dad and I could agree on."

The roast was delicious, done just the way Ginger liked it—still red in the middle; the carrots crunched with just a hint of cinnamon; the salad was simple but substantial, and the salsa rice and beans was an unexpected, but perfect, accompaniment.

"Dad wanted to go totally ethnic," Stacey confided, passing a plate of hot buttered tortillas, "but I convinced him that too much too soon might scare you away."

Ginger laughed. "I guess I don't scare that easy," she said with a glance at Ruben.

Dinner lasted well past nine o'clock. No one seemed to be in any hurry. The wine was inexpensive but mellow, the coffee superb. They talked more than they ate, and they ate everything. Several times they laughed so hard they almost cried. Ginger couldn't remember when she had felt so relaxed, so welcome—and so totally content. It was after eleven when Ruben drove her back to her apartment. Five hours had passed in hardly a blink.

"I had a terrific time," she said at her front door, wishing the evening were just beginning and she had five more hours to spend with him.

"So did I," he agreed, hoping this time she would invite him in for a nightcap or another cup of coffee, or even a glass of water, come to that, because he didn't want to leave her just yet.

"I don't know where the time went," she added, wanting to open her door to him but afraid he might refuse. And if he didn't refuse, afraid of the expectations—hers as much as his—and it was much too soon to deal with that. "It's really amazing how we never seem to run out of things to talk about."

"I'm glad you could come," he said. "I guess I'll see you to-morrow."

"Bright and early," she assured him.

They stood there for a moment, neither quite sure what to do next. Then he leaned over and kissed her lightly on the cheek.

"Sleep well," he murmured and was gone, gliding quickly down the pathway, through the shadows, into the dark.

Ginger went inside, alone again, and yet not quite. His kiss was still on her cheek. She touched her fingers to the spot. It felt soft and warm, and the warmth spread down through her body as though he were a part of her.

She wrapped her arms around herself to hold on to him as long as she could. When the feeling began to fade, she went into the bedroom and took off her clothes. Then she ran a hot bath, which was something she rarely did, and soaked in it, trying to recapture the sense of him.

For close to two years, she had talked to him, listened to him, worked beside him, and learned from him, never really believing that he would ever be anything more to her than the chief of police. And now, in just one short week, all that had changed.

The spare cinder block building at the end of Commodore Street was suddenly the most beautiful place in the world to her. Just the thought of going to work made her smile; just the idea of seeing him each day sent her spirits soaring. She no longer thought about how this might end. After all, it was just beginning. And in the beginning, it was always so easy to believe it would last forever.

She tried to recall the young man from Pomeroy, the one in the farm equipment business. But his face had grown fuzzy with time, and it was hard to gauge feelings that no longer existed. How absurd that broken heart seemed to her now; now that her heart was full again, and on the verge of what could well be true happiness.

It was long past midnight by the time she slipped into bed and snapped off the light. She had to be at the office early in the morning, but she didn't bother to set her alarm. There was too much to think about, to dream about while she was still awake enough to steer the outcome. The last thing she wanted to do was sleep.

19

Ginger spent most of Monday going over a list of those high school seniors who had failed to present themselves at the clinic to give a blood sample. There was a total of eighteen names.

"Do you really think he's in there?" Charlie Pricker asked, peering over her shoulder.

"Who knows," Ginger replied with a shrug and a sigh. "But it's a start."

Since Charlie's promotion a year ago, the detectives had shared an office that was barely large enough for two desks pushed against opposite walls, two gray metal file cabinets, and one extra chair. They worked out of each other's back pockets, as they often described it, and had grown accustomed to purloining each other's coffee mug, taking each other's telephone messages, signing for each other's mail, and discussing everything.

"You've been in the department four years longer than she has," Charlie's wife, Jane, complained. "Why don't *you* have seniority?"

"She's been a detective longer than I have," he explained patiently.

"But you've been a policeman for thirteen years," Jane persisted, "and you're six years older than she is. That ought to count for something."

Her husband smiled his easy smile. "It does," he teased, because he loved his wife almost as much as he loved his job. "Sometimes, *she* gets the coffee."

Jane sniffed. "And now that she's playing cozy with the chief, I suppose you'll never get the chance to show how good you are."

"I show how good I am every day of the week," he told her, his smile fading slightly. "By doing my job the best I know how. And I don't particularly appreciate my own wife repeating rumors about the people I work with. It only makes my job harder."

If Charlie harbored any resentment toward Ginger for having seniority, it wasn't apparent. They handled separate parts of an investigation, conferred officially on matters that related to both of them, joked around with each other the rest of the time, and got along well. He thought of her as the kid sister he never had. She looked on him as another brother.

"I like Ruben," he said out of the blue, as he folded his lanky frame into his chair, dropped his glasses over his eyes, and began to peruse a report. "I've known him a while longer than you. He's a good person, but I think he's pretty vulnerable here. I like you, too. You're solid, but I think you're not so vulnerable. That means it's up to you to be careful."

Ginger swung around to face his back. "Is this your own opinion I'm hearing, or is the whole damn island talking?"

"I don't listen to gossip," Charlie replied mildly. "I just call it like I see it."

"We've been out with each other exactly twice," she protested. "Why do people need to make such a federal case out of it?"

"Twice?" he echoed. "Damn, I thought it was only once. Some detective I am."

She couldn't be angry with him. "Thanks," she said with a chuckle. "I know you mean well."

"So then, why don't you give me a copy of those names," he said. "One of the English teachers up at the high school is a pal of mine. Maybe I can get some input on how many of your hold-outs are left-handed."

"It's an outrage," Grant Kriedler wrote to the editor of the *Sentinel*. "We are now being asked to give up one of our most basic constitutional liberties in a blatant attempt to implicate our sons in the Breckenridge case. If the police have just cause to suspect that one of them has committed murder, let them present their evidence and secure a duly executed warrant. If not, let them stay out of our homes and our lives. My eighteen-year-old son has refused to take part in this charade, and I support him."

"It seems to me that we're damned if we do, and damned if we don't," wrote a senior who had kept his appointment at the clinic. "But if giving some of my blood is going to help find Tara's killer, then I say what harm does it do?"

"Three of the kids on your no-show list are left-handed," Charlie told Ginger on Wednesday.

"Thanks," she said, looking at the sheet of paper he laid on her desk and the little red asterisks he had placed beside the three names. "This gives us a starting place."

Stacey Martinez passed a bowl of corn chowder to her father.

"Everyone's talking about it," she said. "It's become the Great Debate. I mean, it's not every day that almost the entire male population of the senior class is asked to give blood to prove themselves innocent of a crime."

"I wish there'd been another way," Ruben replied, taking a generous helping of the soup.

"Do you really think the person you're looking for is sitting in school every day as though nothing had happened?"

"I don't know. Do you?"

"I just don't see it," Stacey declared, buttering a tortilla. "I know you say the killer acted out of anger and circumstance, but I can't believe that any of those kids could have killed Tara that way, and then been able to go on about his life, pretending he didn't know a thing about it. I mean, I see them every day. They're not complicated, they're not alienated, they're not cold and calculating. For the most part, they're normal kids, doing whatever it is normal kids do. This thing about the blood—it's getting to everyone."

"How do you mean?" Ruben asked.

"Well, they're starting to take sides. You're either for or you're against. Everyone's lining up, and they're not just being vocal, either, they're being physical about it, too. The principal had to break up two fistfights today."

Ruben looked at his daughter thoughtfully. "Have you noticed anyone who isn't taking sides?" he asked. "Anyone who isn't being vocal or physical? Anyone who's sort of just standing on the sidelines?"

Stacey started to shake her head, but stopped. A face flashed before her eyes. She frowned because the face was not connected to the question her father had asked; it had just popped into her head.

"Danny Leo," she said, attaching a name to the face.

"Danny Leo?" Ruben repeated. "Is he someone who seems to be playing neutral?"

"No, it's not about that," Stacey said. "Remember, right after the murder, you asked me if I'd ever seen Tara with anyone? Well, there was something I couldn't remember back then, but I remember it now. One day after school, I saw Tara with Danny Leo."

"Come on down to dinner, Danny," Rose Leo called from the bottom of the stairs. "Hurry up now. Your father's waiting."

A good-looking eighteen-year-old clambered down the steps and took his seat at the table. He had curly brown hair that he kept neatly trimmed, and clear green eyes that were known to set a girl's heart to fluttering when they chanced to glance her way.

"You've been locked up in your room for days now, son," Peter Leo said. "What's going on? Is something bothering you?"

"No, Dad," Danny replied. "I'm trying to make a model of the *Bounty*. It's a special project, and Mr. Frankel said he might enter it for the state history award if I got it accurate enough. I'm only locking my door because I don't want the girls to get in there and mess it all up."

The two siblings, seated across the table from their brother, sniffed.

"I just wanted my Fiery Nights nail polish back," the thirteen-year-old said.

"And I want my blue hair ribbon," chimed in the ten-year-old.

"I needed them for my project," Danny told them both. "I told you I'd get you some more."

"See that you do, son," Peter said. "And I don't think you'll have to lock your door anymore. I'm sure, now that the girls understand what it's about, they'll leave your project alone."

The girls looked at each other and then at their father and nodded reluctantly. When Peter Leo spoke, the family listened, and obeyed. The only problem was that he almost always took Danny's side. Not that Danny didn't deserve it much of the time, the girls grudgingly had to admit. The high school senior excelled on both the track and ice hockey teams, served as the sports editor of the school newspaper, was president of the student body, maintained a straight-A average, was in line for a scholarship to Harvard University, and always kept his room spotless. It was just that it would be nice if, once in a while, someone would see things from their perspective; to be more specific—how difficult it was to grow up beside Superboy.

"There's something else," Stacey told her father. "I know I'm not supposed to know about this, but I overheard you say something to Ginger the other night—Danny Leo is left-handed."

"Are you sure?"

She nodded. "I work with him on the school paper. I've seen him writing lots of times."

"It's funny how things happen," Ginger said the next morning. "You start with a forest, and before you know it, there are the trees."

Danny Leo's name was on the short list of left-handed seniors who had not provided a blood sample for the paternity test.

"We can certainly justify having a talk with the boy," Ruben acknowledged. "But I doubt we've got enough for a court order. We can ask him to come in, but we can't force him. How do you want to handle it?"

"I know the family," Ginger said. "Let me go talk to them at home first, informally. Then we'll see."

"I don't know what to do," Rose Leo said, flapping her hands in frustration. "Peter isn't home from work yet."

Ginger stood just inside the front door of the Leo home. It was five-forty-five in the evening. She had waited in her car for almost an hour until she saw Danny jump off the late school bus, trot along Lindstrom Avenue, turn the corner at Dover, and then cut across the lawn that fronted a modest gray-shingled house with brown trim.

Between this morning, when she had first spoken to Ruben, and the time she had gotten into her car to drive to Dover Road, the detective had gathered as much information about the teenager as she could. His school health form indicated that he was five feet ten inches tall and weighed approximately one hundred seventy pounds. Generally speaking, she did not consider that to be an overpowering stature, but as she watched him disappear inside the front door, it was clear that most of his weight was in solid muscle.

Ginger also knew about his grades and his scholarship, that his mother worked part-time as a nurse's aide, and that his father worked the day shift at Boeing's production plant in Everett.

"What time does Peter normally get home, Rose?" she asked.

"He gets off work at four-thirty," came the reply. "If he catches the five o'clock ferry, he's usually here by six."

"I don't mind waiting," the detective said smoothly. "This is rather important."

"Important? Why? Danny didn't have anything to do with that girl who was murdered. He's a good boy. If this is about that blood thing on Saturday, you can't blame Danny for that. It was his father who wouldn't let him go."

"Please, Rose," Ginger said. "I wouldn't be here if I didn't have a good reason. But I'm sure it's nothing for you to get upset about. I just have a few things to discuss with Danny."

"Hey, look," the teenager said from the stairway. "I'll talk to you, Detective Earley. You don't have to wait for my dad to get home. Ask me whatever you like. I have nothing to hide."

"No, Danny," Rose interjected anxiously. "You wait for your father."

"It's okay, Mom," the teenager said. "Really. There's no problem."

"I don't want to go against your mother's wishes, Danny," Ginger said clearly. "I'd prefer to wait for your father."

"Why don't you come on in the living room," the boy suggested. "We can talk there. If you ask me any stuff I don't think I should answer, then we can wait for my dad."

Rose Leo looked from one to the other. "I'll go see to dinner," she said lamely.

The living room was done in Early American style, and didn't look as though it were used very much. Ginger and Danny sat down on two cushioned sofas that faced each other across a maple coffee table.

"I don't know what I can tell you," the boy began. "I'm sorry about not taking the blood test. I would've done it, but my dad said it was a matter of principle."

"Why don't we put that aside for the moment," Ginger said. "Right now, I'm more interested in hearing about your relationship with Tara Breckenridge."

Danny blinked. "I never had a relationship with Tara," he said. "I knew her. We weren't exactly what you'd call friends, but we were—friendly."

"How did you get to be friendly?"

"I knew her from the country club. The last two summers I worked there as a busboy in the restaurant, and she used to come around sometimes."

"And?" Ginger prodded.

"If she sat at one of my tables, she would say hello," he said. "And if she was alone, we would talk about stuff."

"You were several years older than Tara," the detective observed. "What kind of stuff did you talk about?"

"I don't know," the senior replied with an uneasy shrug. "Nothing important."

"Danny, why didn't you say anything about knowing Tara when I first talked to you?"

"Just about everyone knew Tara," he said. "I didn't think *how* I knew her was important."

"Well, it could be very important," Ginger told him. "So why don't you tell me about it now."

The boy hesitated. "I made a promise," he said. "I promised not to tell."

"You promised Tara you wouldn't tell anyone about the two of you being friendly?"

He nodded.

"Well, Tara's dead," the detective said. "I really don't think it would matter if you broke the promise now, do you?"

Danny sighed. "It was her folks, you see. They were real strict with her. They didn't let her date or anything or hang out much. She couldn't even go to parties if her father knew that boys were going to be there. It would've been bad for her if her parents even knew we talked in the restaurant. But we did anyway. It seemed like she really needed to talk to someone. Like I said, we were friendly, but that's all. Maybe we met a couple of times, in private, you know, where we didn't think anyone would see us. She said her folks would've raised hell with her if they knew, so I promised I wouldn't tell. But all we ever did was talk. She was a sweet kid. Real shy, but sweet."

"Are you sure that was all you did, Danny?" Ginger asked softly. "Just talk? Or did you do more than that? Did you meet Tara in places so private that you could do whatever you wanted to do? Is that why you didn't say anything? Is that why you weren't willing to give us a blood sample? Because you knew what the results would be?"

"No," Danny exclaimed. "I swear, we didn't do anything but talk. Okay, if you must know, what was really going on was—I was tutoring her."

"Tutoring her?" the detective asked with a blank look.

"Yeah. She was having trouble in school. The second half of her freshman year, her grades started to slip for some reason.

Her folks didn't like that. They even made her go to summer school. She was real upset about that. So she asked me if I'd help her. I think she was embarrassed. She said she didn't want to have to go back next year. I remember her saying something about wanting her dad to be proud of her, not ashamed of her."

"The times when you and Tara met," Ginger prodded. "Tell me about them."

Danny shrugged. "We met after school," he said. "To keep it secret, we would leave separately and then we would meet up again."

"Where would you meet?"

"There's a place, down by the harbor, that's pretty secluded. We went there a couple of times."

"Anywhere else?"

"Once we went down to the beach."

Ginger looked at the boy intently. "Did you ever meet Tara at Madrona Point?"

"No," he declared. "I never met her there. Most times, we just went right back to school, and hung out behind the bleachers."

"What about at night?" the detective asked suddenly. "Did you ever meet Tara at night?"

The teenager twisted uncomfortably in his seat. "Yeah, once," he replied reluctantly. "That's the time I told you we went to the beach. It was on a Saturday night and she had an algebra test the next Monday. She told me her sister went to bed at nine, and her folks were at some big-deal charity dinner in Seattle and wouldn't be home before midnight. So I picked her up outside her house around ten o'clock. We drove down to the beach and sat at one of the picnic tables and studied the stuff by flashlight." The boy grinned. "She aced the test," he said, and then, apparently remembering himself, sobered. "That was a week before, you know, before she died."

"Was this a business arrangement, Danny?" Ginger asked. "Was Tara paying you for these sessions?"

"No," he said. "She didn't pay me. It wasn't like that. I was just helping her out. You know, like a friend."

"Out of the goodness of your heart?"

The teenager shrugged a bit self-consciously. "Well, maybe I did have what you might call an ulterior motive," he conceded. "I was thinking about asking her father for a recommendation for college. He's a pretty important person around here, you know, and I figured having him in my corner couldn't hurt. I thought that tutoring Tara would be a pretty good trade-off. She said, after her grades got better, she'd be willing to tell him that I was the one who helped her."

"What kind of a car do you drive?" Ginger asked, veering abruptly in another direction.

"I don't have a car of my own," he replied, without hesitation. "I drive my mom's car when she's not using it. But it's not a Taurus, Detective Earley, if that's what you're getting at. It's a Honda."

Ginger gazed at him for a long moment. "Look, Danny, I think you may be telling me the truth," she said finally. "But I've got a real problem here. I've got a corpse who was pregnant, and most likely killed by the person who *got* her that way. Now, you've admitted being friendly with Tara. You've even admitted that you saw her secretly on a number of occasions, including at least one evening. It's only your word that you were just tutoring her."

"But I was," the boy blurted.

"Well then, the best way to prove that would be for you to give us a sample of your blood," Ginger declared. "At this moment, I can't compel you to do that, but considering what you've just told me, I'm pretty sure I could get a court order that would. The thing is, I don't really want to have to do that. What I want is for you to give us what we need voluntarily. Trust me, if you're not involved in Tara's death, there's no blood test that's going to say you are."

"I already told you, it wasn't my idea not to—"

"Danny, don't you say another word." Peter Leo stood in the living room doorway. "Get out of here, Ginger. Get out of here right now."

"No, Dad, it's all right," Danny protested. "Really, I want to—"

"I said be quiet," Leo barked at the boy. Then he turned on the detective. "You have no right to be in my house," he charged. "You have no right to come in here and interrogate my son behind my back, without my permission. Eighteen or not, he still lives under my roof, and I say this is a clear violation of his civil rights. Now get out."

Ginger stood up. "I'm sorry you see it that way, Peter," she said. She looked at the boy and sighed. "I'm sorry, Danny, but an innocent person was brutally murdered, and I'm going to find out who did it."

20

"I guess we've got enough for a court order," Ginger told Ruben on Friday. "Danny Leo knew Tara. From September on, they were meeting as often as three times a week. He even admitted he saw her once on a Saturday night. And his father's acting a lot more like he needs to protect his son than defend a principle."

"You didn't believe the boy?"

"It's not that," she said. "I think he was honest about what he told me, but on the other hand, he may have been telling me only what he wanted me to know."

Ruben stretched his back, taking the moment to think. "The autopsy indicated Tara was ten weeks' pregnant. That puts us in early August, a month before the fall term started. Danny claims he didn't start tutoring her until September, but he admits he knew her through his job at the country club. The question is— is that enough to establish a prior relationship?"

"I don't know," Ginger said. "When she went looking for a tutor, I don't think she would have just picked him out of a crowd because he got top grades. And it wasn't a business arrangement—he said she wasn't paying him, with money anyway, for his services. Besides, if what they were doing was so innocent, why did they go out of their way to keep it secret? Just because her parents didn't allow her to date? I should think Kyle Brecken-ridge would have been delighted to have his daughter tutored by one of the Island's best students. I think he would have wel-comed Danny into his home."

Ruben scratched an ear. "It's possible."

"And there's something else that makes me wonder," Gin-ger concluded. "Danny is looking at a scholarship to Harvard. While it hasn't been officially confirmed yet, the principal said he looks like a shoo-in. Not exactly the kind of thing a kid like him could afford to forfeit because of a summer pecca-dillo."

"Okay," Ruben said. "Take it to Judge Jacobs. Let's see if he thinks it's enough."

"What the hell are you doing, Ruben?" Albert Hoch roared the first thing Monday morning. "Going after a court order to test Danny Leo's blood? I thought this whole DNA deal was sup-posed to be voluntary?"

"His father won't let him come in voluntarily," the police chief replied. "We think we've got probable cause."

"What cause? So he knew the girl from the country club. So he tutored her a few times. So he helped her study for a math test one night. What kind of probable cause is that? That's just crap. Danny Leo is one of our finest young men; an exemplary student, a star athlete, a school leader. Anything else is just crap."

"If that's so, Judge Jacobs will refuse our petition."

"Ruben, I have to tell you, I never really liked that hare-brained scheme of yours to test everyone's blood in the first place. But I would have flat out forbid you to do it if I knew it was going to lead you to someone like Danny."

"What did you think?" Ruben countered. "That we were just playing games here?"

"Frankly, you were getting nowhere, so I thought you were trying to make it look like you were actively working on the case," Hoch replied. "You know, so that people would feel better."

Ruben stared at the city official. "You think that's what this investigation is all about?" he charged. "Making people feel better? We've had a murder here, for God's sake. Your own goddaughter's murder. I want to find the person who did it—no matter who he is. Don't you?"

"Well, of course I do," Hoch said irritably. "But you don't really think it's Danny Leo, do you?"

"To tell you the truth, I don't know," Ruben conceded with a heavy sigh. "But at the moment, I'm not about to rule him out."

"This is terrible," Hoch muttered. "This is absolutely terrible. This whole business is tearing the Island apart. I just don't know what to do."

"My son gave his blood in the interests of truth," a mother wrote to the *Sentinel*. "He had nothing to do with Tara Breckenridge's death; he barely even knew her. But he wants her killer caught, and he was willing to do the right thing—help authorities solve a crime that has haunted this community for over a month now. If Danny Leo didn't kill her, what's his father afraid of?"

"Where will it end?" asked a freelance writer. "Should our appointed officials, under the guise of protecting the citizenry, have the right to invade our homes, terrorize our children, and threaten us with prosecution if we object to giving up a single one of our personal freedoms? Has our government finally, and fatally, turned its back on the Constitution?"

"If the chief of police really thinks that a decent young man like Danny Leo could have had anything to do with Tara Breckenridge's murder," suggested the mother of a girl he occasionally dated, "maybe it's time we hired somebody else for the job."

❅ ❅ ❅

"What's everyone being so solicitous of Danny Leo for?" inquired the father of a senior math scholar heading for Stanford. "Why couldn't he have killed that girl? My son didn't kill her, he didn't even know her, but that didn't stop authorities from taking his blood. Why should Danny Leo be exempt?"

"This witch hunt has gone too far," one of the high school teachers wrote to the editor. "Our classrooms have become battlegrounds, teen against teen. I know how important it is to catch Tara Breckenridge's killer, but must we destroy our island in the process?"

Malcolm Purdy stood well over six feet tall, weighed in at two hundred thirty-eight pounds, wore his head shaved in military fashion, and dressed almost exclusively in camouflage fatigues that he ordered from a surplus store in Seattle. When he drove his Jeep Cherokee down Johansen Street on the Friday after Thanksgiving and pulled into a parking space in front of Curtis House, he stopped foot traffic dead in its tracks. It was more than two years since he had been seen in town.

He swung out of the Jeep, strode into the building, and planted himself at the front counter.

"I want to put a notice in the newspaper," he announced to a wide-eyed Iris Tanaka.

"Certainly, sir," she replied, scrambling for a form.

"I'm offering a hundred thousand dollars to anyone who comes forward with information that leads to the arrest and conviction of the butcher who murdered the Breckenridge girl."

Iris stared at the man. "I beg your pardon?" she sputtered.

"You heard me," he said. "I'm sick of all this shit. Put the notice in the paper, inside a big black box on an important page, so everyone can't help but see it, and keep on running it until I say you can stop. I'll pay you for a month in advance."

"Don't you think you should—uh—maybe go to the police with this first, sir?"

"I have no use for cops," he said shortly. "Just tell me how much I owe you."

Iris figured out the amount and watched as he pulled the bills from his wallet.

"Did you know Tara well?" she ventured.

Purdy shook his head. "Nope. Didn't know her at all."

The editorial assistant was clearly at a loss. "Then—why would you want to do this?"

"I've got my reasons," he told her. "They don't concern you."

Iris hurried into the editor's office the moment Purdy had pocketed his receipt and departed the building. "Can we do this?" she asked.

"The man paid his money," Gail Brown replied with a shrug. "He wants to place an advertisement in our newspaper just like anybody else. We may not like his message, but it's still a free press." She looked out her window after the retreating Cherokee. "My, my, my," she reflected. "This ought to cause a nice little stir."

It caused an uproar.

"Who the hell does this guy think he is?" bellowed Mayor Hoch, secretly annoyed that he hadn't thought of the idea himself—on a somewhat smaller scale, of course.

"I won't have the tragic circumstances surrounding the death of my daughter turned into a three-ring circus," warned Kyle Breckenridge.

"What I want to know is where did he all of a sudden get that kind of money?" asked Jim Petrie of the city council. "And how do we know for certain he's really got it, and that this isn't just some kind of scam he's running?"

"There's funny business going on here, for sure," said someone from the chamber of commerce. "And I think it's high time we found out what it is."

The gossip mill reopened. Locals began to fabricate all sorts of excuses to drive by the Purdy place, some even having enough nerve to get out of their vehicles and walk right up to the gate, being careful not to touch it, of course. But the gate was only twelve feet wide, and the property extended for thirty acres up a narrow dirt road and over a rise; there wasn't much for anyone to see.

"We want an immediate investigation," a contingent of respectable Islanders demanded of the police chief. "We want to know exactly what this fella's been up to all these years. We always thought there was something peculiar going on out there. Now we're sure of it. He's too secretive to be legitimate."

"Do you have any evidence that the man has done anything wrong?" Ruben asked them. "Any *concrete* evidence?"

"Well, no," they admitted.

"When you do, please come back," they were told, politely but firmly. "I assure you we'll look into it."

"Every crackpot in the county is going to come crawling out of the woodwork on this one," predicted Charlie Pricker. "Taking up time we don't have. Using up manpower we can't afford to waste."

"Assign Dirksen to screen the calls," Ruben instructed Ginger with a helpless sigh. "But make sure you apologize to him first."

Officer Glen Dirksen, twenty-two years old and a nine-month veteran of the Seward Island police force, had been the first to reach Madrona Point Park on that second Sunday in October. From the moment he climbed up to peer over the edge of the Dumpster, he had been unable to erase the picture of Tara Breckenridge's mutilated body from his mind. He had two teenage sisters back home in Blaine, and he begged to be involved in the case, gladly accepting the assignment that nobody else wanted.

❊   ❊   ❊

"As if the police department's job wasn't tough enough," an environmental engineer wrote to the editor in disgust. "How will it ever sort through the mountain of garbage that's now bound to come pouring in from every lunatic with a money problem?"

"If someone on Seward has any legitimate information about the murder of Tara Breckenridge that he or she has not already divulged to the proper authorities, it is unlikely that this offer of money will persuade him or her to do so," an Island psychologist felt compelled to say. "Therefore, I predict a mad scramble to see who can invent the most plausible fiction."

"Maybe this offer is exactly what Ruben Martinez needs to jump-start his investigation again," the self-ordained minister of a fundamentalist organization told his flock. "And we badly need funds to pave our parking lot. Perhaps God is showing us the way. If any of you has any information that could help solve this crime, now is the time to come forward."

"I'm getting sick to my stomach," Glen Dirksen reported the following Wednesday. "Over sixty calls have come in already, from under just about every rock on the Island, with theories ranging from the South American Mafia to aliens from the 51 Pegasus system. You know, I'm beginning to think some of these people would turn in their own mothers to get their hands on that money."

"Nobody promised you a picnic," Ginger told him.

"I had one guy on the phone from some church group who told me he had seen his next-door neighbor wielding a knife and dripping with blood the night of the murder. When I asked him why it had taken him so long to contact us, he told me that, until the reward was offered, he had no reason to destroy his neighbor's life."

"It's stuff like this that builds character," Ruben told the young officer. "But go ahead and check out the neighbor anyway."

"More to the point," Charlie wondered, "have we checked out Malcolm Purdy?"

"Yes," Ginger said. She had gone out to the Purdy place herself, pressing the intercom that had been installed beside the electrified gate, waiting for what seemed hours until the man answered.

"What do you want?" the ex-Marine demanded.

"Mr. Purdy, I'd like to talk to you about this reward you're offering," Ginger replied after introducing herself.

"What about it? As far as I can tell, it speaks for itself."

"Well, there are a few questions—"

"Questions?" his voice crackled over the wires. "Last time I looked, this was still a free country. You're not here to tell me the government passed a law saying it isn't anymore, are you?"

"Must we have this conversation over the intercom, sir?" the detective asked.

There was a considerable pause, and then the heavy gate slowly began to swing open.

The service people who had gained admittance to the property during the last decade were right, Ginger decided as she drove up the narrow dirt road; he had done nothing with the place. His great-uncle had been a farmer, but now the fields that once produced much of the Island's corn had gone to weed.

Purdy stood on the front steps, a clear indication that he did not intend to invite her inside. That was all right; the cabin looked like it was about ready to fall down anyway. Ginger could see the bunkhouse he had built out back. It looked solid. The one-eyed dog lay on the porch, too old and complacent to care about visitors.

"So what is it you seem to think you have a right to know?" he inquired.

Ginger sized him up quickly. "For openers," she said, "was your intention to help our investigation or hinder it?"

He chuckled. "To help, of course," he said. "It's obvious that somebody on this rock knows something about that poor girl's murder. So far, appealing to his better nature hasn't gotten you very far, has it? So what's wrong with offering him a little incentive to do the right thing?"

"And what happens if your scheme works?"

"You catch yourselves a murderer, and I guess I'm out a hundred thousand bucks," he said.

"You've lived on this island for ten years, Mr. Purdy," Ginger said bluntly, "and you've never seen fit to involve yourself in local affairs before. Why now?"

He stared at her for a moment, with eyes that were a brilliant blue. "Well, I guess if now it's me and my life you're going to investigate, Detective," he said, in an about-face, "we might as well be comfortable about it." He held the cabin door open for her to enter.

As dilapidated as the little house may have looked from the outside, it was immaculate on the inside, with brightly colored pillows and scatter rugs, highly polished hardwood floors, paintings hung all over the walls, and a pristine open kitchen. It was a little, she thought, like going from Kansas into Oz. There was a coffeepot sitting on one side of the stove, and a kettle of something that smelled wonderful simmering on the other. A warm fire crackled pleasantly in a stone hearth. An easel stood in one corner of the main room, with a cloth draped over it.

"You paint, Mr. Purdy?" Ginger asked, not quite able to keep the surprise out of her voice.

"Sometimes," he answered.

She looked again at the artwork on the walls, and knew that it was all his; at least a dozen renderings of sea and land, from a variety of perspectives around the Island, done in clean, sure strokes, and one haunting portrait of two young girls.

"This is quite lovely," she said.

"I did it from memory," he replied gruffly. "They're a lot older now."

"Your daughters?"

He peered at her. "I don't see as my personal affairs are any of your business," he said. "Your only concern is whether I offered this reward to steer any possible suspicion away from myself."

Ginger couldn't help smiling. "Did you?"

"Nope. Didn't have anything to do with the killing, and no one could ever prove that I did."

"Then why?"

"I have my reasons," he told her. "They don't matter to anyone but me. All you need to know is that I'm good for the money."

"Malcolm Purdy doesn't hunt," Ginger reported back. "He's a vegetarian. He owns guns, not knives, which he claims to use only for target practice, and he was at home on the night of the murder."

"Confirmed?" Charlie asked.

Ginger shrugged. "By the woman who works for him."

"Any clue why he's doing this?" Ruben wondered.

"More from what he didn't say than what he did say," Ginger told him. "I think it may have something to do with a couple of daughters."

"Well then, I guess until we learn different we take him at his word," the police chief said.

"We take the money at his word, too," Ginger said. "He says he has it, but he won't tell me where, and I can't find any record of a bank account in his name in the state. He has one Visa card, which he clears every month with a money order, and he pays all the rest of his bills either with money orders or in cash."

Ruben eyed the detective thoughtfully. "All right, for the

sake of argument, let's assume that he's on the up-and-up," he said. "How do you read the local reaction?"

Ginger shrugged. "Typical," she replied. "When it comes right down to it, people are people. The people on Seward are no different than anyone else. A lot of them believe in live and let live; it's one reason why they moved to a place like this. They won't get involved unless someone gives them a good reason. Malcolm Purdy has just given them a hundred thousand good reasons. For some folks, there's nothing quite like greed to kick the conscience into high gear."

"You mean, there could really be something in some of these calls?" Dirksen asked.

"That's the thing about these people," Ginger told him. "You never know."

The basement meeting ended early. There was only one topic of discussion and it brought little argument. It was barely ten o'clock when the shadow men filed silently back out into the night.

21

Stacey Martinez usually walked the five blocks to her home alone after school. Her close friends took buses to other parts of the Island, and those few classmates who lived in her direction liked to stop off at Pizzazz, the local arcade and pizza parlor, to play a few games, share a snack and a Coke, and generally let off some steam. On Thursday, however, Kristen Andersen caught up with her before she was barely a block away.

"Mind if I walk along with you?" she asked.

"Of course not," Stacey replied, hiding her surprise. Kristen was a nice enough girl. They sat next to each other in history class, they had worked together on a biology project, and occasionally the green-eyed blonde would pass out free cosmetic samples from the pharmacy where her father worked. But she traveled with Hank Kriedler's crowd, and had never gone out of her way to be particularly friendly.

"I—uh—I've been wanting to talk to you," she said hesitantly. "There's something that's like really sort of been bothering me, you see, and I'm not sure what to do about it. I mean, it could be nothing at all, you know, just my imagination, but it's been on my mind, and like well, I thought, you being the police chief's daughter and all, maybe you could tell me what to do."

"I'll be glad to help, if I can," Stacey assured her.

"Well, you see, it's about something I saw a while ago. You know, something to do with Tara."

Stacey looked at her classmate sharply. "If you have information about Tara, you should be talking to my father, not me."

"But that's just the point," Kristen replied. "I don't know if this has anything to do with—you know, her murder or anything. That's why I wanted to talk it over with you first. I can always go to your dad afterward, if you say I should."

The police chief's daughter nodded slowly. "Okay," she said.

"Look, I don't want to get anyone in trouble," Kristen insisted. "What I saw—well, it involves somebody else. Besides Tara, I mean. For all I know, he's already told your dad about it. I mean, he probably has, and the whole thing was all probably totally innocent anyway, so I shouldn't really be worried, right?"

"If you're asking me if there's someone in particular who's come forward to talk to my father about Tara, I don't have any idea," Stacey told her. "But if you know something that might help solve the case, then I don't think I'd worry about getting anyone in trouble."

Kristen let out her breath. "Okay," she said, her words coming in a rush. "Well, as you probably already know, Tara and I were in gymnastics together. And one afternoon, I think it was the Wednesday before—before she died, I stayed on at the end of class because it was my turn to put up the mats and stuff. Well, I thought everyone else would be long gone, but when I came out of the gym, I guess it was like maybe half an hour later, I saw that Tara was still there. She was in the back hall, and she was crying. I was going to go over, you know, to see what was wrong, but then I saw she wasn't alone. There was someone with her. I saw him put his arms around her, and he was holding her, you know, like really close and all, and I didn't want to interrupt, but

I couldn't help it—I had to walk right past them to get out of the building. He let go of her as soon as he saw me. I was pretty embarrassed, and I just dashed out of there as fast as I could."

Stacey thought Kristen was looking pretty embarrassed right now. Her face was all flushed, she was almost tripping over her words in her haste to get them out, and her eyes were fastened on her feet.

"You're saying you saw Tara with someone?" the police chief's daughter prompted.

"Yes, well, Detective Earley asked us about that—if we'd ever seen Tara with anyone, but I didn't really think of it that way then. I thought she meant, you know, like boyfriends. But then, I got to thinking about seeing the two of them there like that." Kristen paused uncertainly for a moment. "I don't know," she added, "maybe there was nothing to it. Do you think I should tell?"

"I don't know if somebody hugging Tara in a hallway at school means anything or not," Stacey said. "It'd probably depend on the circumstances, and on who it was."

Kristen pried her eyes from her feet and looked around as though worried that someone might be listening.

"That's the whole point," she whispered. "That's why I wasn't sure what to do. You see, the police seem to think the killer is one of the seniors, but the person I saw Tara with— well, it might have been at school, but it wasn't a student. It was a teacher. It was Mr. Frankel."

PART TWO

The Suspect

"Nothing is more dangerous than an idea, when it's the only one we have."

—*Emile-Auguste Chartier*

1

Jerry Frankel was the only child of parents who began their marriage knowing very little about each other, and ended it knowing even less. He grew up in a house that never laughed. His mother, Emma, was born in the concentration camp at Buchenwald to a thirteen-year-old Jewish girl who did not survive the birth and a German officer who was later executed by the Allies. She wound up in Philadelphia after the war, adopted by the Kaufman family, who, having barely gotten out of Germany ahead of Hitler, did their best to forget she had been fathered by a Nazi.

But Emma never forgot. She felt the shame of it every day of her life. She was a beautiful girl who had inherited her mother's dark hair and her father's pale eyes in a dramatic blend that, from her earliest days, caused people to stop and stare in admiration. Deep down, however, she felt herself ugly.

She was not much of a student. After graduation from high school at the age of seventeen, she married the first man to show any serious interest in her, because he owned his own business and made a good living, and because he didn't know her father was a Nazi. The Kaufmans did not object. They were decent people, but they were relieved to see her go.

Aaron Frankel was thirteen years older than Emma. He thought she was the most exquisite creature he had ever seen. Further, like himself, she was a survivor of the Holocaust—an event that, in the aftermath of World War II, most Americans seemed to want to forget. He felt that Emma, unlike a girl who had not known the war, would understand his nightmares. He could not believe his good fortune when she promptly agreed to marry him.

After the war, Aaron came from Majdanek to his only surviving relative, a distant cousin who lived in York, Pennsylvania. The cousin was a good man, but he had a wife and five children, and could ill afford to take care of another. So he set the boy up with his wife's uncle, a crusty bachelor who owned a small company near Philadelphia that manufactured surgical instruments.

Aaron had little formal education, but he had a good mind. The uncle, already in his sixties, was delighted with the chance to teach the boy everything he knew before he died. To his surprise, Aaron took to the business. He worked hard and lived cheaply, saving every penny he could toward the day when the uncle would let him buy in. By the time he met Emma, the company was not only his, but one of the fastest growing and most reputable producers of precision surgical instruments in the country. At the age of thirty, having achieved his goal of financial security, Aaron decided it was time he took a wife.

But Emma knew nothing about being a wife, and cared even less. She had never learned to cook, had no interest in making a home, and suffered his attentions in bed with silent distaste.

Aaron forgave her. She was so young and so beautiful, it filled him with joy just to look at her. He determined that he could be patient until she learned. That she flatly refused to discuss anything having to do with the Holocaust was but a momentary disappointment. After all, he reasoned, she had been just a baby, she could hardly be expected to remember. That she showed no interest in his work, and even yawned on those occasions when he tried to explain it to her, was a more lasting disappointment, for it would have thrilled him to have someone with whom he could share his excitement. But then, he decided, her beauty more than made up for any lack of attention she displayed. Over the next ten years, he forgave her everything.

As for Emma, once she realized her marriage was not the fairy tale that the movies and magazines had led her to expect, the discontent returned. Her antidote was to spend money, lots of money, much more than Aaron could afford. It was like a narcotic—the more she spent, the happier she felt. And as soon as the euphoria of one spree wore off, she would set out on another. She bought everything: several sets of fine china and crystal, far more furniture than even their gracious home in Cheltenham could hold, expensive jewelry that she wore once before tossing into a drawer, and clothing that enhanced her lovely figure and overflowed her closets, store tags still attached to them.

When she discovered she was pregnant with Jerry, Emma cried for a week.

"I don't want a baby," she wailed. "It'll make me fat! What would I do with a baby?"

"You'll see," Aaron assured her, elated by the news. "Having a baby will make all the difference. We'll be a real family at last, and you'll love being a mother. Every woman does."

Emma hated being a mother. She was useless at caring for the baby, sometimes forgetting to feed him, frequently forgetting to change him, often leaving him unattended for hours at a time as she resumed her shopping excursions.

Aaron finally hired a nanny to look after the boy. He returned much of the clothing and household items and most of the jewelry to pay for it. He made arrangements with the shops Emma frequented to notify him of her purchases. He hoped that perhaps the buying was enough, and the having was inconsequential. He was right. Emma never missed the items that found their way back onto the racks and into the display cases.

Eventually, though, the antidote began to lose its effectiveness, and then Emma turned to vodka. The clear, almost tasteless liquor made its way into her morning orange juice, her afternoon tea, her dinner coffee, and any time in between.

"This is Mommy's water," she would snap at her son when he reached for her glass. "Go get your own."

When she complained of not sleeping, Aaron found a doctor who would prescribe pills. After that, she slept a great deal, often not awakening until past noon and retiring before eight. Aaron didn't know what to do for her, so he did nothing. Whatever the problem was, he convinced himself it was temporary and would soon go away.

It didn't. Emma sank deeper and deeper into depression. She stopped shopping. She stopped taking care of herself. She ate next to nothing. She began to wander listlessly around the house, vodka in hand, sometimes not even bothering to dress.

The war in Vietnam fascinated her. She would spend hours sitting in front of the television set, waiting for news reports of the carnage.

"It's amazing how a war can come right into your living room and yet not touch you," she would marvel. "You can see everything that's going on without getting hurt."

She was furious with the protesters.

"What do they want?" she would rant. "Do they want to stop the war? Then what would I do all day?"

It was not that Aaron turned a blind eye, exactly. It was more that he couldn't get past his original image of her to see what she had become.

She paid no attention to her son, never noticing how handsome he was, how bright, how sweet-tempered. The only part of him she ever really looked at were his eyes, and she sighed with relief when she saw that he had inherited Aaron's eyes, not pale and cold, but wide and innocent and the color of warm molasses.

Then, on May 4, 1970, the same day that four students protesting the war were shot to death by National Guardsmen at Kent State University, Emma Kaufman Frankel, aged twenty-seven, swallowed half a bottle of sleeping pills with a whole glass of vodka and died.

Jerry found her when he came home from school. She was lying in bed as though asleep, with an expression on her face that the boy had never seen before. She looked happy.

Aaron was shattered. He refused to believe she had done it on purpose. He blamed it on the vodka, claiming she could not have known what she was doing.

It didn't really matter to Jerry. His mother was dead, that was all. He tried to think what that would mean to him. He thought of his friends, and the way their mothers hugged them and fussed over them, and were always there to provide after-noon snacks and chauffeur them to and from Little League games. But his mother had never done any of that. In fact, he could not recall that she had ever done very much of anything for him. He decided her death did not have to make a significant dif-ference in his life.

His nanny, the latest in a long line of women his father had hired to look after him, dressed him in dark clothes and told him he should cry for Emma.

"Why?" asked the pensive eight-year-old. "She's not sad any-more."

Aaron Frankel turned to his son to fill the void. They grew as close as a bewildered man and an abandoned boy could grow. Aaron had tried so hard to re-create a semblance of the family he had lost at Majdanek, and could not understand why he had failed so miserably.

He had no particular interest in other women. To his way of thinking, he had already had the best and would not settle for less. There were many who tried to change his mind—after all, he was a well-to-do widower and considered a fine catch. He was wined and dined by parents from all over the Philadelphia area. He ate their food and drank their liquor, but he did not pursue any of their daughters.

Meanwhile, Jerry grew tall and strong. He excelled at soccer, the debate club, and academics, and discovered that he genuinely liked school, liked learning, liked the *process* of learning. He admired a great many of his teachers, and he thrived on the give-and-take of the classroom. The public library, with its air of quiet authority, its distinct mustiness, and faint smell of sweat, became as familiar and comfortable to him as the teddy bear blanket he had clung to through childhood. Often, he would spend hours after school, wandering through the stacks, pulling out a book here, a volume there, not looking for anything in particular, just to wrap himself inside the walls of the institution. There were many evenings when he would reach home barely minutes before his father.

Outwardly, he was the cheerful, dutiful son he knew Aaron wanted him to be. But it was like looking in a mirror and seeing someone else's reflection, because he knew his real self to be so very different. He preferred shadow to sun, calm to commotion, solitude to society.

As a child, when he was invited to parties, he loved to play hide and seek, but never wanted to be "it." Instead, he wanted to be one of the ones who got to hide. Then he would hunt out a place so secure he could stay hidden for hours. Sometimes, even when there was no party and there was no game, he would hide himself away where he could not be found. He would hear his nanny calling for him and would keep silent. Only when it was his father's voice reaching into the corner of the attic where he crouched under the eaves would he reluctantly crawl out and clatter down the ladder steps.

Jerry was always careful to mask the scary dark moods that

took hold of him for no reason, because he didn't understand what they meant, and he didn't want his father to find out and worry that he would end up like his mother. Or maybe it was he, himself, who was afraid he might end up like Emma.

He had a large circle of acquaintances, but few real friends, unwilling to let anyone get too close. He dated his share of girls, managing to advance past the stage of heavy breathing and feeble protests on more than one occasion, but sooner or later, they all sought a commitment that he found himself unable to make.

The times he treasured most were those when he and his father sat together in the library, reading, listening to music, and talking. It was with Jerry that Aaron finally got to speak about Majdanek. With the boy a willing audience, he would talk for hours at a time, recounting everything he could remember about that piece of the past that had shamed the entire world.

"Those of us who survived," he would say in his still lightly accented English, "survived for a reason. And I think it was not just to bear witness to what happened at that time and in that place, but to make certain it is never allowed to happen again, at any other time or in any other place. Because it is only by studying our past and learning from it that we can prevent ourselves from repeating it."

"How?" the boy would ask.

Aaron would think for a moment. "Each generation must be taught that genocide is not just about Germany thirty years ago," he would say. "It has happened before, and it can happen again, anytime, anyplace—in Europe, in Asia, in Africa. It happened right here, to the American Indians, did it not?"

The boy would nod.

"Well then, it could happen again," his father would predict. "To the Jews, the blacks, the Hispanics, or any other identifiable group that an apathetic public is willing to let be abused. All it takes is the coming together of even a small number of people who require a scapegoat to explain away their own insecurities, lack of abilities, or low self-esteem, and you have the environment for creating another Hitler."

"Do you really think something like that can happen now, Dad?" Jerry would ask. "When the world is so much smaller and people are so much smarter?"

Aaron would wag his head. "It wasn't the intelligentsia who did the bidding of Hitler and his cronies," he would tell the boy. "They were annihilated right along with the Jews and all the others that Hitler determined were political adversaries or of 'inferior breeding.' It was the scum who followed their grand führer; the bigots, the have-nots, the greedy who saw a way to profit by taking what they could never have created on their own. Mark my words, if you let the quality of public education deteriorate far enough, let the economy go sour enough, let unemployment rise high enough, and give people reason enough to lose confidence in their government—it could happen anywhere."

It was those words from his father that cemented Jerry's future. What better way to ensure that the nation's children learned about the perils of the past, he decided, than by being the one to teach them?

He graduated from Cheltenham High School at the top of his class, politely refused an academic scholarship to Princeton because his father could well afford to send him to college, and went on to complete both his undergraduate and graduate work at the University of Pennsylvania.

Jerry loved teaching. Not only was he able to linger in the classrooms and libraries of his youth, where he had always felt safe and protected, but he was fascinated by his subject. The more he learned about history, the more he came to see it as a giant and never-ending tapestry of threads woven together in intricate patterns that kept repeating themselves.

For example, there were so many similar socioeconomic and political threads in the fall of most of the great empires in the world, from Greece to Rome to Russia. And it was a similar set of conditions that had opened the door to Hitler in post–World War I Germany. It began with social unrest, engendered in part by Germany's humiliation over the Versailles treaty, was compounded by severe economic decline resulting from the Great Depression, and ended in a level of moral decay that led directly to the disintegration of respect for the law and the total abdication of personal responsibility. Or, as his father always put it, "thugism."

In many instances, Jerry discovered, life could be as predictable as mathematics; although times and circumstances changed, people basically did not. And he tried to portray this idea of the cycle of history to his classes.

He loved the light of learning he saw go on inside the heads of his students when they finally understood something he had taken great care and patience to explain. It gave him a real rush to stand in front of a class with twenty-odd pairs of eyes trained on him, and know that twenty-odd minds hung on his next revelation. They were like blank computer screens on which he could imprint his lasting images. It was heady stuff, the sense of power that teaching gave him, this daily measure of his own value.

He had just begun his second year of teaching at a public high school in Philadelphia when he met Deborah Stein. She was still at Bryn Mawr, and looked up to him very much the way his students did. Being with her gave him the same kind of rush he experienced in his classroom. She also had dark hair and light eyes like Emma.

"Everyone says you look too much like my mother," he told her, only half joking, when he knew that, this time, he would not be able to get out of the relationship. "If I marry you, they'll say I have an Oedipus complex."

"Perhaps," she returned with a toss of her hair and a mischievous twinkle in her eye. "But if you don't marry me, they'll say you're crazy."

They were married two months later.

*   *   *

Deborah Frankel graduated from Bryn Mawr, and went on to earn a business degree at the University of Pennsylvania's Wharton School. Each evening over dinner in their cozy little apartment, the young couple would tell one another everything about their day apart, letting even the most inconsequential moments assume major proportions. Then, washing the dishes, they would dream about the wonderful future they would share, the home they would have one day, the family they would raise together, the exciting journeys they would take, the exotic places they would explore, walking in the steps of Jerry's beloved heroes of history. Finally, when the last dish was done, they would whisk the cloth off the table and spread out their homework.

Jerry took enormous pride in Deborah, in her mind, her ambition, her accomplishments. Although, in all honesty, he could not claim much of the credit, he felt like Pygmalion to her Galatea, and it pleased him enormously when she came to him for help with her assignments.

"I don't know why I can't figure this out," she would say.

"Let's see if we can find a way to make it clearer," he would reply.

She asked for his help almost every evening until the middle of her first year at Wharton when she finally passed his level of expertise in her specialty. Two or three nights a week after that, she would come home an hour or so later than usual, having stopped by a friend's place to study.

Then they would throw a quick meal together, provide each other with abbreviated accounts of their respective days as they ate, and hurry to their separate assignments.

"Need any help?" he would ask, poised over his own stack of papers.

"Thanks, but I think I can handle it," she would reply.

Eventually, he stopped asking. He was happy for her achievement, but it was also a loss, and he felt it as a parent

would who watched a child grow up and take off on his own—
with both pride and pain.

It was during Deborah's second year at Wharton that
Matthew was born. She was out of school until after the Christmas break, adjusting to motherhood even as she kept up with the
work she was missing. After that, she strapped the baby into a
backpack and wore him to class.

Jerry had not believed it possible that he could love another
human being as much as he loved his son. The depth of his emotion stunned him. He adored his wife, but there was a distinct
difference between what he felt for her and what he felt for
Matthew. Here was a brand-new person that was part of him,
someone who was totally dependent on him, someone he could
nurture and mold and teach from the very beginning.

Standing in the hospital corridor with his nose pressed to
the glass wall of the nursery, Jerry could hardly wait to introduce
the boy to his grandfather. It meant a great deal to him that he
could give Aaron back the family he had lost at Majdanek; this
time, a family that would not abandon him.

"I want to go back to New York," Deborah announced when
Matthew was seven months old and she had her master's degree
in hand. "My parents are there. My whole family is there. I've
been recruited by a really good Wall Street firm, and I'd like to
take the job. I know you've lived your whole life in Pennsylvania,
and you're close to Aaron and all, but I'm close to my family, too,
and I've been away from them for six years now, and I want to go
home."

The last thing Jerry wanted to do was move to New York,
but he couldn't find an objection that she didn't dismiss as selfish. So, reluctantly, he prepared a résumé, and within a month
found a teaching position at a private high school in Scarsdale,
the town in Westchester County where Deborah's parents lived.

Aaron gave them a down payment for a small house about
fifteen minutes from the school. Deborah commuted by train to

New York City. Her mother volunteered to look after Matthew until Jerry could take over, and then Deborah would rush home in the evening to prepare the baby's dinner, give him his bath, and put him to bed.

The following year, after a miserable pregnancy, the Frankels' second child, a daughter, was born with a malformed brain. They named her Emily. She lived twenty-six hours and died. The young couple was devastated, clinging numbly to each other through the ordeal of the funeral and the long week of condolences. Then, surprising everyone, Jerry most of all, Deborah took two weeks of her planned maternity leave and went off to the Caribbean. She returned, tanned and rested, to throw herself back into her work with almost a manic determination, no longer hurrying home at night to her son and husband, and sometimes, if she worked very late, not even bothering to come home at all.

Jerry thought he understood; after all, she had endured an emotionally shattering experience, and as he saw it, her job provided a temporary diversion that could go a long way toward helping her come to terms with that experience.

Eight months later, on the same day her company offered her a major promotion, she told Jerry that she did not want to have any more children.

"The doctors can't guarantee the same thing won't happen again," she said, "and I'm afraid to risk it. I couldn't go through losing another baby like that. But we have Matthew, and he's such a wonderful little boy, I can't help thinking that we're really very lucky. Anyway, I've just been promoted, and I'd like to concentrate on my career for a while."

Concentrating on her career, Jerry soon learned, meant she would now be working late into most evenings and even on weekends. He hid his disappointment. While he was willing to concede that she was bright and talented and had a right to make her mark in the business world, he missed her. He missed the young woman who used to look up to him, who had once be-lieved he had all the answers. Jerry had little in common with the new Deborah. On the increasingly rare occasions when she made it home in time for dinner, she would rattle on about things he barely understood, and then hardly bother to listen when it was his turn to share a few snippets of his daily life.

As more of her energy went into her work, she had less to spend on her husband. They spoke mostly about money now, and about Matthew. Somewhere along the way, they stopped talking about the exciting future they had planned to have, and focused instead on the present.

Jerry never questioned his commitment to his wife. She and Matthew were the center around which his life revolved. Yet, more and more, it seemed to him that he was no longer the cen-ter of *her* life; that he had become a satellite to her needs and de-sires. He tried to talk to her about it, because he wanted desperately to fix what was broken. Only he either couldn't seem to find the right words to use, or she really wasn't listening. After a while, he stopped trying.

They continued on that way, drifting along in different di-rections, until it became familiar. And with familiarity came a pe-culiar sense of comfort, and with comfort came no further need for understanding.

Still, there was something that tugged at him, something he was unable to articulate—or probably even acknowledge, given how deeply it was rooted in his past—something he could only sense. Jerry Frankel was lonely.

2

"May I have a word with you, Mr. Frankel?" Ginger asked.

It was Friday, and although well past the last school bell, she found the teacher still in his classroom.

"Sure, come on in," Jerry replied. "I'm just finishing up some paperwork."

He was wearing a navy blazer with a striped shirt and gray slacks, and looked more like a preppy college student than a high school teacher.

Ginger glanced around the room. Some twenty-odd metal desk units were lined up in front of a raised platform on which sat a large wooden desk that clearly showed the scars of time and place. Behind it were suspended two thick rolls of maps. Even without looking, she knew which maps were coiled inside which roll. She knew that blackboards ran the length of three of the room's walls, and that windows lined the fourth.

The detective calculated quickly. If she took one of the student seats, she would in effect be putting herself in a subordinate position. If she remained standing while he sat, she would tend to put him in a defensive position. If she leaned against his desk, her attitude might appear too familiar. If she stayed by the door, it could indicate that she felt somehow intimidated. She chose the first seat in the middle row, directly in front of Frankel.

"This was my seat when I was in school here," she said. "It still feels familiar."

Jerry smiled. "I spend most of my life in classrooms," he told her. "But a couple of years ago, I went to my fifteenth high school reunion, and walked around a building I once knew better than my own home. I couldn't believe how totally lost I got, and how out of place I felt."

In her mind, Ginger flipped through the dossier she had compiled on the history teacher, starting on the Monday morning after she and Ruben went calling about the Taurus wagon, and ending yesterday afternoon after Stacey had brought Kristen Andersen to see her. She knew he was thirty-five years old, and that his fifteenth reunion had been held two years ago. She knew his high school was in Cheltenham, a wealthy suburb of Philadelphia, and that he had graduated first in his class. She also knew he held a *summa cum laude* in liberal arts from the University of Pennsylvania, as well as a master's with honors in education. But of course there was no reason to tell him that she knew all this.

As far as she could determine, his teaching credentials were impeccable. He had taught at a public high school in Philadelphia for five years before taking a position at the Holman Academy, a classy private high school in Scarsdale, New York. The principal at the Philadelphia school had been very sorry to see him go. The headmaster at the Scarsdale school said his resignation had been accepted with great regret.

Frankel had arrived on Seward Island at the end of last January, after his wife's investment firm transferred her to its Seattle office. It was interesting that both of his job moves had apparently been made in deference to his wife's career, but not particularly significant.

In the opinion of Seward High School principal Jordan Huxley, which was based on one spring semester, a summer session and the fall quarter, Frankel was an exemplary teacher, popular with colleagues and students alike, and the Island was lucky to have him. A casual survey of a number of those colleagues and students confirmed Huxley's assessment.

Ginger could find no police record for the teacher, no arrest, no conviction, no trouble of any kind with the law. Not even so much as a parking ticket had shown up in either of the two states where Jerry Frankel had lived and worked. In fact, there was not a shred of information whatsoever that he was anything other than what he appeared to be—a dedicated teacher, a devoted husband, and a proud father.

Still, when Kristen Andersen presented herself at Graham Hall, and repeated the story she had told to Stacey, Ginger could not ignore it.

"It's possible I could be wrong about him," she told Ruben.

"You could," he agreed.

"Of course, at this point, all we've got is a secondhand account of an incident that might have a perfectly reasonable explanation."

"And a bunch of odd little coincidences."

"That's true," she conceded. "So how about if I go talk to him again? One-on-one, you know, friendly like, on his own turf, and see what happens."

The police chief smiled because it was exactly what he would have said under the circumstances, exactly what he would have done.

"As I'm sure you know, we're still investigating the Breckenridge murder," Ginger told Jerry Frankel as he sat behind his desk on the platform, looking down at her.

"I certainly assumed as much," the teacher replied.

"And whenever we receive any information that might be relevant to that investigation, we're of course obligated to look into it."

"I assumed that as well."

"In a case like this, we get all sorts of tips, you know," the detective said, trying to study the teacher without appearing to do so, even as she had the distinct impression that *he* was studying *her*. "People always think they know something they're sure will solve the case for us. Most of what we get doesn't amount to anything, but following up on all of it at least makes us feel like we're doing our job."

Jerry nodded. "And what tip did you get that's led you to my door?" he asked pleasantly enough.

"One of the students here at the high school mentioned having seen you and Tara alone together just three days before her death."

The teacher frowned slightly. "I'm not sure I know what you're talking about, so I can neither confirm nor deny what you've been told," he said. "Perhaps if you gave me some more information, or told me who saw what and where, it might refresh my memory."

"One of your students," Ginger repeated, intentionally omitting Kristen Andersen's name, "claims to have seen you with Tara in the hallway behind the gym at around five-thirty on the Wednesday afternoon before her death."

"It's possible," Jerry said. "I don't seem to remember the specific occasion, but I can't say for sure I didn't see Tara in that particular hall on that particular day."

"I understand she was crying," Ginger prompted. "And that you had your arms around her."

The teacher's eyes widened slightly. "*That* day," he murmured. He stood up from his desk and came down off the platform to take the seat beside the detective. "I do remember now. I was using the inside route past the gym to get to the office, and I did see her there. And she *was* crying. I guess I might have put my arms around her to comfort her."

"Did she tell you why she was crying?"

"No, she didn't," he said, his glance sliding past the police officer's shoulder as though trying to recall. "She just said something about her life being a total mess. I confess I didn't really think that much about it. Kids that age, especially girls, tend to be emotional and often think their lives are a mess."

"After she was murdered," Ginger inquired, "why didn't you tell us about that? Knowing she had been upset to the point of crying shortly before her death might have been important."

"I'm sorry," he said. "I guess it never occurred to me. To be perfectly honest with you, I'd forgotten all about it until just now."

"You'll pardon me for asking this, Mr. Frankel, but was that day in the hall the only time you can recall when you and Tara were alone together?"

"No, it wasn't, Detective Earley," Jerry said, and now he looked her straight in the eye. "On a number of occasions, Tara came to see me after school for extra help. As I think I mentioned before, her grades weren't as good as they should have been. I told her she was welcome anytime."

"Was Tara the only student who needed help?"

Jerry started to smile and then stopped himself. "No, she wasn't. I currently have about a dozen students who come in on a fairly regular basis."

"I wonder if you would be kind enough to give me their names?"

"Of course." He got up and returned to his desk where he scribbled the names on a pad, then ripped off the sheet and held it out to her.

"Thank you," the detective said, rising to retrieve it. "I hope you understand that we're looking for a killer here, and we can't let even the most insignificant of incidents involving the victim go unexplained."

"I understand," the teacher assured her. "It was my fault for not remembering to tell you about it in the first place."

"In police work, you learn to question everything," she added on a sudden impulse. "First, we have someone who claims to have seen a dark-colored Taurus wagon in the park near the time of the murder—and we find that you drive just such a car. And now we have you being observed in a potentially compromising situation with the murdered girl shortly before her death." She was careful to omit any reference to the additional coincidence of his being left-handed.

"And that quite naturally led you to the conclusion that I was a child-molesting monster?" This time he did smile a little.

"Sometimes, it's a lousy world," Ginger said. "But for the record, other than being a concerned teacher, you didn't have any special relationship with Tara Breckenridge, did you?"

It seemed to her that he hesitated an instant before he answered, but she couldn't be sure that it wasn't just her imagination.

"No, I didn't," Jerry Frankel replied.

"And if I were to ask you, on a purely voluntary basis, you understand, to come in for a polygraph test, and maybe to give us a sample of your blood for a DNA analysis, you wouldn't have any objection, would you?"

This time, there was no mistaking the hesitation.

"Probably not," he said. "But I'd want the chance to think about it first."

"Of course," Ginger said.

"I don't know," she declared an hour later, dropping into the spare chair in Ruben's tiny office. "Either this guy doesn't have a thing to do with this case, or he's the smoothest liar I've ever come up against."

"And you can't decide which?" the police chief asked.

"I really leaned on him," Ginger admitted. " 'Forget about the witness thing,' I as good as told him. 'Now we're looking at you for the murder itself.' If he'd been there, if he'd seen anything, knew anything—one way or another, I think he'd have given it up. But I watched him like a hawk. He didn't even blink. Everything he said was exactly what he should have said, every gesture was absolutely correct, every expression had just the right note of sincerity."

"And that's why you think he could be lying?"

"Sounds silly, doesn't it?"

Ruben shrugged. "Do I conclude from this conversation that you're not ready to cut him loose?"

Ginger thought about that for a moment. "Not yet," she said finally.

"Do you consider him a material witness?"

"Probably not," she said.

"Do you consider him a suspect?"

"I'm not sure."

"Do your instincts tell you he could be a killer?" Ruben asked.

"Given the right motivation," Ginger said with a toss of her red hair, "I think anyone could be a killer."

"Does he fit your profile?"

"Sure he does," the detective acknowledged, remembering the characteristics of the killer they had defined. "Right down the line—he's physically strong enough, he has no alibi, he drives the right car, he's left-handed, and he knew the victim. But, except for the car, Danny Leo fits the profile, too. And probably a couple of hundred other people we don't even know about."

"Then what have we got?" Ruben asked.

"An itch I can't scratch," she said. "I've just got this funny feeling he knows something he isn't telling us."

"Okay, supposing you're right, how do you want to handle it?"

"Well, for the moment, the ball is in his court. I invited him in for a polygraph."

"I assume he declined your invitation?"

"He didn't outright decline it," Ginger replied. "He just deferred it."

"Smart."

"What do you think he'll do?"

Ruben shrugged. "I think he'll call a lawyer."

"That's what I figured," Ginger said.

"So suppose he talks to his lawyer and then declines your invitation?"

"I'll take it one step at a time," she replied, leaning back and locking her hands together on top of her head. "I don't really want to harass the guy. But if he's holding something back that has anything to do with this case, I'm going to find out what it is."

She had on navy pants and a blue shirt, and her red hair was bound in a braid down her back. She wore little makeup and her freckles stood out plainly. If it weren't for the gun holster clipped to her belt, she would have looked a good deal more like a troubled teenager than an embattled police officer. Ruben smiled to himself.

It was almost three weeks since she had come to dinner at his place. The longest three weeks he could remember. She was clearly being cautious and he didn't want to move too fast, risk scaring her off by asking her out too often, or give the local gossips any more grist for the mill than was necessary. But he missed her; he missed being able to look at her and talk to her and laugh with her.

They had little time alone together at work, although police headquarters was definitely not the place in which to carry on personal business. There were always people in and out. It was more than a week since they had even had the opportunity to talk in private. He knew he was free to telephone her, in the evening, after hours, but Ruben preferred the direct face-to-face approach, where he could see, not just hear, her reaction and then judge whether she was really interested in going out with him again, or just being polite.

"What about the Leo boy?" he asked.

"I don't know whether that's going to come to anything, but he's still at the top of my list," she told him. The top of a very, very short list, she thought.

Ruben nodded slowly. "People are already yelling witch hunt," he said. "First, we did the blood thing, then we went after one of the Island's top high school seniors, and now we're breathing down the neck of one of the most popular teachers. Whatever you do, make sure you do it by the book, and then make sure you back yourself up, every step of the way."

"I promise."

Ginger smiled to herself, wondering why she had never realized before how cautious he was. It was almost three weeks since she had been to his house for dinner, and the evening had been such fun that she couldn't understand why he hadn't asked her out again. She could read nothing in his behavior at work, but that was to be expected. Without either of them ever saying a word, it was clear that their personal lives had to be kept out of the office. But it was pure hell, waiting for him to speak, and wondering if she had done something to displease him.

Their conversation seemed to be at an end, so Ginger got up and started for the door.

"By the way," she said, turning back, unable to keep the words from coming out of her mouth, "I've acquired two New York steaks, and one of them has your name on it, if you're free tomorrow night."

Ruben's face lit up. "I am," he said. "As a matter of fact, I, uh, was just getting ready to mention something along those lines myself."

"Fine then. How's seven o'clock?"

"Seven is great," he replied. "I'll be there."

As a child, she had often climbed recklessly out onto an untested tree limb. She could remember how fearful she had been to discover that it was much thinner than she expected, and then how exhilarated she was when she realized that it wasn't going to break beneath her. She felt that way now.

Steak, salad, baked potatoes, something for dessert, and a good bottle of wine, she thought quickly. She would stop at the market on her way home tonight. That would give her all day tomorrow to clean her apartment.

"See you then," she said.

"You bet," he said.

Neither of them mentioned that it would be just the two of them, alone together, for the first time.

3

Danny Leo caught the late bus home from school on Friday. It seemed the closer he got to graduation, the more activities he found himself involved in. This particular day, it was a meeting of the holiday dance committee that kept him way past the last bell.

Whenever his mother complained about his hours, or his father chided him for being tardy in doing his chores, Danny would remind them that his school record was not just about good grades, that Harvard University was looking for well-rounded students who displayed a real sense of community commitment. It was enough to get them to back off for a while. Peter Leo had been born and raised in the shadow of Harvard, and had promised himself that, if he ever had a son, the boy would be educated where he himself had been neither bright enough nor rich enough to gain admittance.

"Detective Earley was up at school this afternoon," Danny told his father.

Peter bristled. "Is she harassing you again?"

"No," Danny assured him. "She didn't come to see me. She came to talk to one of Tara's teachers."

"What's so unusual about that?"

"Nothing really," Danny replied, "except that she already talked to all the teachers weeks ago, right after the murder. And today, she made a special trip, after school was out, just to see one of them. I saw her going into his classroom."

"Well, well, well," Peter murmured as a slow smile spread across his face. "Now that's another matter entirely, isn't it? Let's hope it's something that will take the heat off you."

"But I told you, Dad," Danny insisted. "I'm perfectly willing to give blood. I can clear myself if you'd only let me do it."

"You don't understand, son," Peter said, as the boy knew he would. "In this country, you don't have to clear yourself of anything. You are completely innocent until someone can prove otherwise."

"I, uh, won't be home tomorrow night," Ruben told Stacey as they sat down to supper. "I'm going to have dinner with Ginger."

The teenager grinned. "Again, so soon?" she murmured.

"What do you mean so soon?" he protested. "It's been three weeks."

Stacey burst into laughter. "Gosh, Dad, you sound more like a kid than a parent."

"Give me a break," her father retorted. "I'm not used to this father-talking-to-daughter-about-him-dating thing."

"Neither am I," she reminded him.

Ruben frowned suddenly, because the thought had not occurred to him until this moment. "Hey, are you okay with this?" he asked. "I mean, is it a problem, my going out with Ginger?"

Actually, Stacey had not been all that sure how she would feel about her father seriously dating someone. She knew he had seen other women over the years, but rarely more than once or twice, and he had never brought any of them home. She used to wish he would remarry, back when she was little and really needed a mother. But as she grew older, she realized that marriage was not about taking care of children or making a warm, cozy home; it was about a very special relationship between two people that happened when it was supposed to happen and not necessarily when you wanted it to.

"It's no problem," she assured him. "I like Ginger. I like you and Ginger."

He peered at her. "That sounded awfully grown-up," he observed. "When did you get so grown-up?"

Stacey grinned. "Oh, about a minute ago," she said. "So, tell me, are you going to splurge and go into Seattle tomorrow night?"

Much as she might not wish to do anything that would discourage her father's relationship with Ginger, she was all too aware of the gossip that had begun a few weeks ago with the snide remarks at church, and progressed to a fairly steady bombardment of wisecracks from several of her classmates.

Ruben tried to look casual. "As a matter of fact, we're staying on the Island," he said. "Ginger's, uh, invited me over to her place."

The fifteen-year-old digested that bit of information for a moment. "In that case," she said, "be sure and take a condom with you."

Had Ruben's skin been a shade or two lighter, the hot flush that suddenly flooded his face and spread down his neck would have been a lot more visible. His discomfort was in part because this was not exactly the kind of conversation he thought appropriate to be having with his teenage daughter, but mostly because the same thought had already occurred to him.

"Give me a break," he managed to repeat.

"I heard the strangest thing down at the market," Libby Hildress declared over dinner. The wife of the man who had discovered Tara Breckenridge's body was the opposite of her husband in more ways than one. Physically, she was short and plump, with soft blond hair that framed a pretty face, and clear blue eyes.

"What's that?" Tom asked, a spoonful of tomato soup halfway to his mouth.

"Somebody said that the police are investigating Jerry Frankel."

Tom blinked. "For what?"

"I guess maybe they think he might be involved in the Breckenridge case."

"You've got to be kidding," her husband said.

Libby shrugged. "That's what I heard."

"Why would anyone be dumb enough to think that?" Billy scoffed. "I know Mr. Frankel. He's Matthew's dad, a regular person. He can't be the killer."

"Why can't he?" challenged Billy's brother, Bud. "Just because you've been in his house doesn't mean you know anything about him or what he'd do. Besides, the cops have to pin the murder on someone, and it might as well be a teacher." Bud was thirteen years old, in the eighth grade, and not particularly fond of school.

"Dad, the police wouldn't do that, would they?" Billy asked in alarm. "Matthew's my best friend."

"I don't think the police would pin anything on anyone without good cause," Tom assured him.

"We don't even know if it's true," Libby said. "It's just what I heard. Naturally, I called Deborah at her office as soon as I got home." The Frankels and the Hildresses did not really socialize, but because of the friendship between Matthew and Billy, they had exchanged telephone numbers for emergency situations. "She said something about the police wanting to tie up a loose end."

"There, you see?" Tom declared, buttering a biscuit. "Last week, if you remember, the big flap was over Danny Leo. Now it's Jerry's turn. Next week, it'll probably be somebody else."

*   *   *

"I don't understand," Deborah Frankel declared. "The police already talked to you several times about that murder. Why would they need to talk to you again?"

Jerry shrugged. "Your guess is as good as mine," he replied.

"Oh, come on, they must have had some reason," she persisted. She was furious. She couldn't believe he hadn't called and told her himself about Ginger's visit, that she had to hear about it from the mother of one of her son's friends. "A woman I hardly know interrupts me at work, in the middle of a very important meeting," she stormed. "She wants to know why the police are investigating my husband in connection with the Breckenridge case. I didn't know what to tell her."

"I didn't think it was that important," he said.

"Well, I guess it must be, if the whole town is talking about it."

Jerry could see that she would not be put off, that she was determined to make a big thing out of it.

"One afternoon after school, I guess it was shortly before her death, I came across Tara in tears over something," he said with a sigh. "I don't know, I must have put my arm around her to comfort her. To tell you the truth, I don't really remember doing that, but apparently I did, and somebody saw me, and totally misinterpreted the situation, and reported it to the police."

Deborah felt a cold shiver dart down her back. "You had your arms around the murdered girl?" she asked.

He glared at her. "There was nothing to it," he said coldly.

Scott Cohen was considered by his peers to be among the best criminal defense attorneys in the State of Washington, if not the entire country. He was not bombastic in the manner of an F. Lee Bailey, perhaps, or folksy in the style of a Gerry Spence. But in his own quiet, unassuming way, he could demolish a prosecutor's case with the skill of a precision bomber.

A man of less than medium height and more than medium

weight, Scott had a froth of light brown hair that, by the time he turned forty, had receded almost to the crown of his head, giving him an odd halo effect, and explaining why it amused his colleagues to refer to him as the Cherub. But it was his eyes that drew the attention of most people; they were large, hooded eyes, sea green in color, and filled with a combination of intelligence and compassion that could hearten even the most desperate of defendants.

Scott, his wife, Rachel, and their son, Daniel, had lived on Seward Island for five years, ever since Scott was invited to join the law partnership of Morgan, Kaperstein and Cole, and they had purchased their 1909 farmhouse. Rachel picked the place for the lovely little pond and well-tended orchard that went with it. Scott took to it for all the renovation work he could do in his spare time.

"Are you sure you won't mind having to commute?" Rachel asked, as they packed up the house on Queen Anne Hill that was barely ten minutes from his office.

"Actually, I think I'll like it," he told her. "It'll give me separation time."

Commuters on the seven o'clock ferry from Seward to Seattle got used to seeing the Cherub every morning, sitting in the lounge, looking oddly impish in his three-piece suit, sipping a cup of coffee, and watching the scenery. He never looked at a file nor wrote a note. Only after he reached his office, and settled himself behind his desk with his third cup of coffee, was he prepared to begin his workday.

It was a hard-and-fast rule of Scott's to work Sundays through Fridays, but never on Saturdays; he had been raised to respect the Sabbath. There was no synagogue on Seward Island when the Cohens arrived, barely even a Jewish presence at all. But after two years of trudging back to Seattle for services, Scott became instrumental in urging several local families to form a small congregation. He convinced the rabbi at his old temple to let his assistant take on a part-time flock, and made a deal with the Unitarians for the use of their church on Friday nights, Saturday mornings, and the high holy days in exchange for a reasonable sum. There were fewer than thirty Jewish families on the Island at the time, not nearly enough to support a facility of their own, so Daniel had celebrated his bar mitzvah in the sanctuary of the Cedar Valley Unitarian Church.

"God lives in many houses," the rabbi had asserted. "He rejoices with us no matter which one we are in."

Scott was not an obsessive man, but everyone who knew him knew he took the traditions of his religion seriously. Therefore, when Jerry Frankel came knocking at the Cohens' front door in the middle of a quiet Saturday afternoon, the attorney assumed his friend was making a social call.

"How's it going?" he inquired amiably.

The Cohens and the Frankels had met the previous March, about two months after Jerry and Deborah moved to the Island and chose to attend the Passover service at the church. They discovered that they lived only three blocks from each other, and it was not long before the two couples had become friends.

"Can I talk to you for a minute?" the teacher asked.

"Sure," Scott said. "Come on in."

Jerry shook his head. "Can we take a walk around?" he suggested instead.

The attorney blinked. "If this is business," he said, "can it keep until tomorrow?"

"I'm sorry, I forgot," Jerry said, flustered. "Sure, it's not important, it can keep."

He turned away, but Scott had already seen something in the teacher's eyes that he had seen on far too many other occasions to misread: panic.

"Why don't we take a stroll down by the pond," he offered. "Rachel has been talking about building a little bridge over one end of it, and I've been wanting to ask your opinion."

The two men headed down the slope of lawn behind the farmhouse, Jerry walking with his shoulders bent and his hands shoved into the pockets of his khakis. Scott sighed inwardly.

"I may be getting into something over my head," the teacher said as soon as they were out of earshot of the house. "And I don't know what to do."

"Well, I'm sure it isn't anything that can't be worked out," Scott replied.

Jerry looked at his friend. "I think the police think I'm involved in the Breckenridge case."

"*Are* you?" the attorney asked, caught completely off guard.

Jerry eyes fastened on his friend's halo. "No, of course not."

The Cherub shrugged. "Then I wouldn't worry about it."

"But they want me to take a lie detector test and give them a sample of my blood. If it gets out that they even asked me, pass or fail, I lose all my credibility as a teacher in this community."

Scott took what he liked to call a judicious moment to assess the situation. "You can always refuse," he said finally.

"Won't that look even worse?"

"As I understand it, they've been asking a lot of people to give blood and take polygraphs. How many of them have we heard about?"

"This is different," Jerry muttered. "Most of them were students or regular townspeople. I'm a teacher. I work with kids. My success depends on their trust and respect. Even a hint of scandal will ruin me."

Scott Cohen always prided himself on his instincts about people, and on his ability to evaluate a situation quickly and accurately. "I've been speaking to you so far as a friend," he said now. "Do you want me to represent you as an attorney?"

The teacher sighed. "I guess so," he replied.

"All right then, this is how it works. They can't compel you to take the polygraph. That's strictly voluntary. If you refuse to give them a blood sample, the only way they can force you is to get a court order. For that, they need probable cause. If they *had* probable cause, they wouldn't be asking. So I think we can assume they're on what we call a fishing expedition. Now if, as you say, you're not involved and have nothing to hide, they won't catch any fish, and they'll move on to another part of the pond."

"And it won't look bad that I refused? It won't make me look guilty of anything?"

Scott shrugged. "You have a clear right to refuse; it's called the Fifth Amendment. But you're a history teacher—I shouldn't have to tell you that."

Jerry seemed to perk up at that. "Of course, you're right. I guess I forgot."

The attorney smiled. "In that case, I think your crisis is past."

But the teacher didn't smile back. "If I hear from them again," he said instead, "if they try to pressure me, can I call you?"

"You're my client now," Scott told him. "You can call me anytime, Sundays through Fridays."

4

By five o'clock Saturday afternoon, Ginger's apartment looked like a set for a television commercial to promote cleaning products. The windows were Windexed, the hardwood floors were Johnson Waxed, the carpeting was Hoovered, and the dining room table was Pledged.

Everything that didn't have a proper place had been swept into the back of the bedroom closet. By the time she had Ajaxed the kitchen, it looked as though no one had ever cooked in it. She then Lysoled the bathroom, removed her underwear from the shower bar, and put out a clean guest towel and a fresh cake of soap. At the last moment, she changed the sheets on her queen-sized bed.

With two hours left in which to get dinner, and herself, ready, she headed for the kitchen. She had a salad whipped up in no time. Then she mixed up some sour cream and chives for the potatoes. Finally, she trimmed up a bunch of asparagus to pop into the microwave. She would put the potatoes in the oven at six; they were big and the cookbook said they would take an hour and a half to bake. Since Ruben liked his meat as rare as she did, the steaks would go on the Jenn-Air grill at the last minute.

Dessert was already prepared—chocolate mousse out of a package. Granted, it might not be considered a gourmet meal, but then she was a working woman, not a full-time cook, and she thought Ruben would understand that.

At five-thirty, she jumped in the shower, washed and blow-dried her hair, came out to get the potatoes going, and returned to the bathroom to apply her usual modicum of makeup. At six-fifteen, she headed for her closet. By ten minutes to seven, she had considered and discarded almost its entire contents and was ready to scream.

"We're looking for something simple here," she said to her reflection in the cheval mirror that sat in the corner of the bedroom. "Something attractive, but not too suggestive. Something that says I'm comfortable, but not necessarily available. Something soft; very soft."

From his perch on the bed, Twink, the marmalade cat, let out a low meow.

"Of course," Ginger exclaimed. She raced to her dresser and rummaged around the bottom drawer until she came out with an oversized gray angora turtleneck, a birthday gift from her parents some years back. "Perfect," she said with a wicked smile. "Let's see you try to keep your hands off this, Mr. Chief of Police."

She had just finished buttoning a pair of black wool slacks, slipping her feet into black leather flats, and fastening silver hoops in her ears when the doorbell rang. It was thirty seconds after seven.

"I hope I'm not late," Ruben said.

"Your timing is perfect," she replied.

He, too, was wearing a turtleneck sweater, beige and made of something thick and cuddly, like lambswool, and he wore it with neat brown slacks. He looked so put together, she wondered if he'd had as much trouble choosing his outfit as she had.

He was carrying a bouquet of winter flowers, which he shyly

presented to her. "I'm afraid I'm out of practice," he admitted. "I wasn't sure what to bring."

"You didn't have to bring anything," she told him. "But these are beautiful, so I'm glad you did."

Ginger turned into her little kitchen and busied herself finding a vase. She had been looking forward to this evening all day, but now that he was here, she was suddenly nervous.

"How about a drink?" she asked to cover her jitters.

"Sure," he said.

"Is Scotch okay?" Ginger didn't drink hard liquor. She bought the Scotch because it was what he had been drinking at his house.

"Scotch is fine," he told her.

She fixed the drink the way she remembered he had fixed it, with ice and a little water.

"How did you know?" he asked.

Her hazel eyes twinkled. "I'm a detective, remember?"

She poured a little Scotch over ice for herself, filling the rest of the glass with water, and then they went into the living room. A fire smoldered in the fireplace, threatening to go out.

"May I?" he asked.

"Please do."

He inspected the pile of wood she had stacked next to the hearth, and she watched as he selected a combination of logs and kindling that would best suit his purpose. The beige sweater rippled across his back, and she wondered if he were wearing his brace. He began to rekindle the blaze, alternately rising up to reach for pieces of wood and then squatting to arrange them, while his brown slacks tightened and loosened against his body. Ginger downed her Scotch in two long gulps and went back to the kitchen for more. This time, she doubled the amount of the alcohol and cut the water in half.

At first, tonight had simply been about her wanting to see him again. She would have felt uncomfortable inviting him out to a restaurant, even in the 1990s, and since he had already had her to *his* home, it seemed perfectly appropriate that she ask him to hers. It was only after he accepted the invitation that she began to consider where it might lead. Not that anything was inevitable, of course; not even that it was likely. It was just something to contemplate, maybe even fantasize about while she cleaned the apartment. But now that he was here, she wasn't sure what she wanted.

Ruben reset the fire, taking far more time than the task actually required because it gave him something to do. He had really looked forward to spending the evening alone with Ginger, but now that he was here, he wondered whether he should have suggested they go out to dinner instead.

"There, I think that should do it," he declared as flames began to lick around the fresh wood. He stood up and retrieved his drink from the mantel. Ginger was curled at one end of a dusty blue sofa. He sat down in a green and blue striped chair across from her.

"I'm afraid I'm not very good with fires," Ginger said. "I can start them, but I can't seem to keep them going."

"Well, there's no big trick to it," he told her. "You just have to leave plenty of space around the logs so the air can circulate. It's air that keeps the wood burning."

"I'll have to remember that."

"Of course, you have to use the right combination of wood, too," he said, sipping his Scotch.

"I'll certainly keep that in mind."

"And of course, different kinds of fireplaces react differently," he added. "There are some that don't draw as well as others, and I suppose there are some that might draw too much, but yours seems to work just fine."

"That's good to know," she murmured.

There was silence then, because Ruben had exhausted his

knowledge of fire tending, and didn't quite know where to go next. He took a long drink of Scotch.

"Today certainly was a beautiful day," he said finally, just to say something.

"Yes," she agreed. "Unusually warm for December."

"I walked around my yard in my shirtsleeves."

"I went out without a coat."

"The climate here still surprises me," he said. "You'd think it would get so much colder than it does, being so far north."

"It's one of our best-kept secrets," she told him.

Twink sat by the sliding glass doors, his tail slapping the carpet as though bored with the conversation and impatient for the topic to change.

"I still haven't seen as much of the state as I'd like to," Ruben said, beginning to feel desperate. "I know there are a lot of places we should visit, like the San Juan Islands and Skagit Valley and Leavenworth. Stacey and I keep talking about taking a picnic up to Mount Rainier, and I think a trip to Mount St. Helens would be fascinating. But so far, we haven't been able to make the time."

"Yes, there are some wonderful places around here," Ginger replied.

Sight-seeing? The weather? She couldn't believe they were sitting here, talking like two people who had never met each other before. They hadn't discussed the weather on their first date, or even their second. They had been so comfortable with each other before; he had been so easy to talk to. It made their present conversation seem almost comical. Only Ginger didn't feel like laughing—she felt like crying. The evening wasn't going at all the way she had planned. She downed the rest of her drink.

"I like the way you've done this room," Ruben said, grasping at anything to keep himself from doing something stupid—like fleeing. "The colors you picked work really well together."

"I'm kind of limited," she admitted. "There aren't too many

colors I can live with. Red hair does tend to put a damper on one's options."

"Reds and yellows are my heritage," he told her, "but I like blues and greens. They're softer, and they suit you."

She could feel the warmth of the Scotch wriggling around inside her body.

"I always wanted to wear bright red," she confessed with a sudden giggle. "And swing my hips down Commodore Street. My mother used to tell me that only wicked women wore bright red, but I think I only believed her a little bit."

Ruben was delighted. "So that's where the tomboy came from," he charged. "To cover up your wild side."

A big grin split her freckled face. "Of course. And I did it so well that I talked myself into it."

"Well, be sure and let me know if your true self ever gets the urge to emerge," he told her with a chuckle. "I almost think I'd give up my pension to watch the Honorable Albert Hoch have a coronary right at the corner of Commodore and Seward."

Ginger hooted.

The ice was broken. They sensed it immediately. Both of them sank back into their seats, each with a silent sigh of relief. Even Twink noticed. He came over and stretched out in front of the fire.

"I've never drunk two Scotches before," Ginger said with a giggle.

"I can't tell you how glad I am you did," Ruben said.

While she grilled the steaks, he tossed the salad. While she zapped the asparagus, he rescued the potatoes. While she set the table, he lit the candles. While she turned on the stereo, he poured the wine. Finally, they were seated across from each other, the food between them.

"I was beginning to think I'd made a terrible mistake by asking you over here," she said as she forked up a piece of sour-creamed potato.

"I don't know why, but I can't remember the last time I was so nervous," he admitted, slicing into his steak.

"You'd think we were a couple of teenagers," she said.

"On a blind date," he added.

"Instead of friends . . ." she began.

". . . enjoying an evening together," he finished.

They smiled at each other through the candlelight.

Ruben picked up his wine. "To good food and better company," he said.

Ginger raised her glass to his. "To perseverance," she murmured.

After dinner, Ruben insisted on helping her wash up the dishes.

"You don't have to do that," she protested.

"Of course I do," he replied. "I wouldn't want you to think my Stacey didn't raise me up right."

Ginger chuckled. "She's lucky to have you for a dad."

But Ruben shook his head. "No," he told her with a soft smile. "I'm the lucky one."

When the kitchen was back in order, Ginger took a bottle of Kahlúa from a cabinet and poured two glasses. Then they went back into the living room. A Tchaikovsky symphony had begun to play on the stereo. They sat down on the sofa.

"The *Pathétique*," he murmured. "One of my favorites."

"Mine, too," she said with a nod.

They sat there, sipping the Kahlúa and listening to the music. After a while, he reached over and picked up her hand, entwining his fingers with hers. She didn't pull away. Instead, she let the symphony and the liqueur and the fire and the quiet strength that flowed from his hand to hers lull her into a world of warmth and wonder. A flood of sensations washed over her, from excitement to anxiety to desire to fear.

The last time Ginger had been to bed with a man was almost five years ago, a brief affair with a Seattle reporter assigned to cover one of her small-town cases that left her feeling very used. She concluded that sex, just for the sake of sex, was not a sufficient reason to take off her clothes.

But this time, she hoped it would be different, *wanted* it to be different. In the last few weeks, since she had begun to see Ruben in a new light, she had felt drawn to him in a way that hadn't happened since the young man in the farm equipment business. While she wasn't quite ready to pin a label on what she was feeling, she thought she was at least ready to consider taking the next step.

Of course, she had no idea what was going on in Ruben's head. This was, after all, just their third date, and on both previous occasions he had appeared somewhat reticent. Which meant it was entirely possible that she was no more to him than a momentary diversion, someone to enjoy for a while until the novelty wore off, someone to help push away the loneliness for a time; not someone with whom he would allow himself to get seriously involved. In which case, she would be wise to wait for him to make the next move.

By the same token, it could also mean that he was shy, and awkward at dealing with the unique language of the single set, despite the length of time he had been a widower. In which case, it might very well be up to her to make the next move. For all her intuitive ability on the job, when it came to personal relationships, Ginger had never been much good at reading men's minds.

Ruben, however, had no such problem. He could read his mind quite well. And he knew that, in Ginger, he had found someone quite extraordinary. Not only someone warm and compassionate and singularly compatible, but someone with whom he was beginning to let himself believe he could share the rest of his life. The thought both thrilled and panicked him. In many ways, he had spent a very long and very lonely thirteen years. It was only now that he was beginning to realize what had been missing since the death of his wife; what he had denied himself over grief and guilt. He thought that finding Ginger might be a sign that his penance was over.

All of which was good to know, he acknowledged, but did little to solve his present problem; namely—what to do now? He stole a look at his watch. It read ten minutes past ten. The *Pathétique* was about to conclude. Was he going to thank her for a lovely dinner and depart? Or was he going to seize the moment and let it carry them both as high as they chose to go? Ruben heard the last notes of the symphony. It was time to decide.

He turned to her at the very second that she turned to him, and their words collided in midair.

"Dinner was terrific."

"I'm glad you could come tonight."

There was a sudden pause, during which they both stood up.

She must not be interested, he thought.

He doesn't want to get involved, she thought.

Still, they found themselves searching for something else to say, anything that would keep this evening from ending, until, for the second time, their words, spoken in the same instant, tumbled over each other.

"It's still pretty early."

"Would you like another Kahlúa?"

"Yes," he said.

"Yes," she said.

And then suddenly, without any thought, he was holding her, and her body seemed to melt into his. Ruben couldn't believe how sweet she smelled, how good she felt, how vibrant, how alive. Memories of the handful of women he had clung to out of need over the years vanished in a rush of desire he had not known since his wife.

He had felt guilty on those other occasions, because they meant nothing to him. But he felt no guilt now as he turned Ginger's face to his and began to kiss her, on the forehead, at the corner of her eye, along the line of her cheek, moving down until he reached her mouth. Kissing her softly, because he was still unsure—of her, of himself.

It was only when he realized she was kissing him back that he grew bolder, more insistent, parting her lips with his, drinking from her, deeper and deeper, until he was dizzy and trembling. Then he pulled her close against him and just held her, while the world around him spun wildly.

"I'm a little rusty," he murmured into her hair. "So, if this isn't what you want, tell me now, and I'll go."

"Stay," she breathed.

She was wrapped in his arms and she had never felt so complete, so totally within herself. Not even with Farm Equipment. It was almost as though, at twenty-eight, she was just discovering what being a woman was really about. Every nerve ending in her body tingled, every sense was heightened. She had never been so sure of who she was, and what she wanted. She took him by the hand and led him to the bedroom.

Behind them, Twink curled up on the dusty blue sofa, in the warm spot they had abandoned, and began to lick his huge paws.

The moment they entered the bedroom, they began to reach for each other with their hands, their arms, their lips, their legs. Between kisses, he pulled her sweater over her head, she pulled his sweater over his. With their mouths locked together, he undid the buttons on her slacks, she unfastened his belt. With their tongues exploring each other's depths, he kicked off his loafers, she kicked off her flats. Then they stood there, in their underwear and stockings, and started to giggle.

"This was supposed to be an incredibly romantic moment," he scolded, smiling.

"Well, I guess we'll just have to settle for fun," she replied.

They fell into each other's arms, laughing, losing their balance and tumbling onto the bed.

"That's all right," he murmured. "It's where we were headed anyway."

He pulled off his undershirt.

"You're not wearing your brace," she observed.

Ruben looked embarrassed. "It's not very attractive, and I thought it might, you know, be something of a turnoff," he confessed. "I guess that was pretty presumptuous of me, wasn't it?"

"That's okay," she told him. "I changed the sheets."

He reached for her with a grateful groan. In less than a minute, they had rid themselves of the remainder of their clothing, and then there was no more need for words as their bodies began to communicate with one another.

She smelled of spring flowers, and her skin felt as soft as rose petals. Beneath the tomboy facade, Ruben found a woman's body, expertly molded, eager and welcoming. Ginger was long and lean and nothing like his wife, who had been quite petite, but he felt the same wave of emotion, rising in him like the surf, building toward the moment when it would crest and break and engulf them both.

His body felt strange against hers. The compact shape, the rough skin sliding over taut muscles, the strong hands, the soft warm lips, the dense hair that covered his chest—they were all so unfamiliar. And perhaps because of that, the room, the very bed she had slept in every night for almost two years felt different, as though it were a place she had never been before. But when they finally came together, one and inseparable, she forgot about the strangeness, the self-consciousness. She forgot about everything except the extraordinary sweetness of being with him, the exhilaration of it, and the absolute rightness of it.

Like a hymn from her childhood, she felt as though she were being borne on the wings of an eagle, soaring higher and higher and higher. Sex was not new to Ginger, but this was not just sex. She knew beyond any doubt that what she was feeling was unlike anything she had ever experienced before.

When it was over and they lay apart, their hands clasped together, their energy spent, neither of them could find adequate words to express what had taken place, or what it had meant.

"How awful to think," she said after a while, "that I could have gone to my grave without ever once knowing what it should be like."

"I'd like to think we'll know it more than once," he remarked.

She squeezed his fingers. "Count on it," she told him.

Somewhere along the way, they had remembered the condom, but neither of them could recall exactly when. It had just been handled, at the appropriate time, in the right context, without interruption.

"It's a pity we aren't married," he murmured, thinking of that now. "A night like this should have created life."

5

On Sunday, Ginger drove over to the Earley house shortly after noon, knowing that her brothers would not yet have arrived. Indeed, her parents had barely returned from church.

"What's the matter?" her mother wanted to know, hurrying to answer the doorbell.

"Nothing," Ginger assured her. "I just want to talk to you and Dad before the others get here."

"Talk to us? About what?"

"Do you really want me to tell you right now, on the front porch, in front of God and the neighbors?" Ginger inquired. "Or would you like to let me come in first?"

"Oh, don't be silly," Verna retorted. "Of course, come in."

The three of them sat in the living room, tentatively, her father trying to light his pipe, her mother twisting her hands in her lap.

"I wanted to tell you this myself," Ginger began in a matter-of-fact tone, "before you heard it from Eleanor Jewel, and didn't know how to respond. Ruben Martinez and I are seeing each other . . . socially, I mean. We've had several dates so far, and we've decided that we want to pursue a relationship."

"You mean, you're going to get *married?*" Verna blurted, horrified.

"No," her daughter replied. "I mean we're going to date each other on a regular basis; go to dinner, to the movies, out dancing, anything we like, and see where it leads us."

"You mean, you're *thinking* about getting married?"

"We're not thinking about anything right now," Ginger said, "except spending time with each other."

"But that's exactly where this sort of thing leads, you know."

"If it does, then that's when we'll deal with it."

"You mean, when it's too late to talk any sense into you. Do you have any idea what you're asking for? People like that have no morals. People like that would just as soon get you in trouble and then leave you high and dry."

"People like what, Mother?" Ginger inquired, with a definite edge to her voice. "Decent, hardworking people who earn their paychecks every week, just like Dad? People who dedicate their lives to cleaning up other people's messes? People who stick around to raise children all on their own after their wives die? Are those the people you're talking about?"

Verna looked to her husband for support. "You tell her, Jack. Obviously, she won't listen to me."

Jack Earley sighed. "What do you want me to tell her?" he asked his wife. "I think Sheriff Martinez is a good man, and that's more than I can say for a lot of men I know, wherever they may have come from. If Ginger wants to date him, I don't see as we have any right to tell her she can't."

"Any right?" Verna cried from the very depths of her soul. "After all the years I've spent making a place for us on this island—you think she has the right to ruin it?"

Jack puffed on his pipe. "Seems to me," he said after a moment, looking down the last quarter century of life with his wife, "if her dating a Mexican fellow is going to ruin your reputation, maybe it's because you spent all those years circulating in the wrong circles."

"Late Friday afternoon," the weekend edition of the *Sentinel* summarized, "Detective Ginger Earley was back at Seward High School to talk with one of Tara Breckenridge's teachers. This was apparently in relation to the recent report that a classmate of the murdered girl had seen Tara and the teacher alone together several days before her death.

"While details of the conversation between the teacher and Detective Earley were not released, this could mean that the Breckenridge investigation is now headed in a totally new direction."

"Well, they may not have come right out and named him, but you know as well as I do who they're talking about," Libby Hildress told her husband when she read the article. "So I guess I was right about what I heard."

Tom sighed. "That doesn't mean he's involved in the case," he suggested. "It just means they talked to him."

"Of course," Libby agreed. "But where there's smoke, there's usually fire."

They were lingering over coffee, and as was their habit after church and Sunday dinner, they were reading the weekend *Sentinel* to catch up on the Island news. The boys, having been released from the table, were out playing.

"Just the same," Tom said, "do me a favor and don't go making a big thing of it. Matthew is Billy's friend, and I think we owe him and his parents our support."

"I have no intention of saying anything to anyone," Libby promised. "But mark my words, this isn't going to go away next week."

"Every single day, all we ever get is the Breckenridge case, smeared over practically every page of the newspaper," Deborah

Frankel grumbled. "And when they run out of things to report, do they just move on to another issue? No, they invent something, and then spin their wheels speculating about it. You'd think there was nothing more important going on in the world."

"The thing you have to keep in mind is that there's nothing more important going on *here,*" Rachel Cohen reminded her gently. The attorney's wife was almost a head shorter than Deborah, with auburn hair, soft brown eyes, and a heart-shaped face.

"That's the difference between us," Deborah said with a heavy sigh. "You like living in the middle of nowhere—I don't."

It was Sunday afternoon, the laundry was done, and the two women were in the kitchen, sharing a cup of coffee while Jerry, Scott, and the two boys were off on a bicycle ride. The newspaper lay on the table between them.

"I hated being here for the first few months," Rachel admitted. "I felt so cut off from everything I thought was important. Now, you couldn't get me to go back to living in the city."

"But don't you get bored out of your skull sometimes?" Deborah cried in exasperation.

The attorney's wife shrugged. "I can get on a ferry and spend a day in Seattle anytime I want to," she said.

While the Frankels had acquired a rather sizable circle of acquaintances on Seward Island since their arrival, Rachel was the only real friend Deborah had made. It wasn't that she was unsociable or snobbish or even shy. It was more that she was a very private person, and did not care to become a topic of small-town gossip.

"I don't think I could stand it if I didn't have my job to go to every day," she confessed. "I don't know how you do it—spend so much of your time here, I mean. It's so claustrophobic."

"You get used to it," Rachel said. "After a while, you start to appreciate things like the peace and quiet, and the clean air, and not having to lock your doors. You find you really enjoy doing things like gardening and baking bread. And pretty soon, you discover the benefits of not having to put on two inches of makeup every day."

"But some of the people here are so small-minded and mean-spirited," Deborah argued. "They smile to your face readily enough, but then they turn around and stab you in the back."

"I don't think the people in our neighborhood are like that," Rachel said.

"Well, no," Deborah conceded. "I guess some of them are okay. But there are others."

In many ways, Rachel was every bit as perceptive as her husband. "You know, I think people are people, wherever they happen to be," she said, casually picking up the *Sentinel* and dropping it on the floor beside her chair. "With all the same dreams, and all the same fears. I don't think it makes much difference whether they live in big cities or small towns."

But Deborah was staring at the spot on the table where the newspaper had been. "Jerry didn't have anything to do with that girl's murder," she blurted suddenly, desperately. "I don't care what they're saying—he just couldn't have."

"Ginger doesn't tell us very much about the case," Verna Earley said over the telephone to Eleanor Jewel, relieved that the topic of the Sunday evening call was going to be murder, not marriage. "After all, the work she does has to be kept confidential."

"But she must have said something," Eleanor insisted. "Now that she and the police chief have become so, shall we say, intimately involved in the case, she surely must know everything that's going on."

On the heels of the conversation with her daughter, Verna bristled. "What my daughter does and what she knows are no concern of yours," she retorted.

"On the contrary, I have two grandchildren up at the high school," Eleanor argued. "If one of the teachers is involved in Tara Breckenridge's death, shouldn't everyone know about it?"

"Well, I wouldn't jump to any conclusions just yet, if I were you," Verna relented, smiling into the receiver because, after looking down her nose at the Earleys for so many years, the gossip queen had finally come begging. "When the time is right, I'm sure you'll be told whatever you need to know."

"You *do* know something," Eleanor pounced.

"I didn't say that," Verna protested.

"You didn't have to say it. I can hear it in your voice, plain as day. That teacher they talked to *is* the one, isn't he? He killed poor Tara, didn't he?"

Ginger had never said a word to her parents about the Breckenridge case, nor did Verna know anything more than the newspaper had reported. But she wasn't about to tell that to Eleanor Jewel.

"I'm sorry," she said sweetly, "but I really can't say any more."

6

"I've spoken to my attorney, Detective Earley," Jerry Frankel said over the telephone on Monday. "He advises me that I am under no obligation to submit to a polygraph test or to give you a sample of my blood."

"Your attorney is absolutely correct," Ginger replied.

"Well then, unless you have some real evidence that I'm involved in this case, I must decline to put myself in a position that would very likely compromise my career."

"If you have nothing to hide, Mr. Frankel," Ginger said smoothly, "your career wouldn't be compromised."

"I'm not that naive, Detective," Jerry responded. "Don't you read the local newspapers? I do. Even the hint that you're seriously investigating me could be enough to get me suspended from my job. And although I'm sure your tests would establish my noninvolvement beyond any doubt, the suspicion would always be there and my credibility at school would be destroyed."

His argument was reasonable; Ginger couldn't fault it. She was, in fact, furious about the article describing her visit to the school, and she resented having to defend any part of it.

"The *Sentinel* didn't refer to you by name," she said.

"It didn't have to," he replied. "This is a very small community. There were still students and teachers and staff at school last Friday when you showed up. How long do you think it will take people to figure it out? I have no information about the murder of Tara Breckenridge. If I did, I would have given it to you a long time ago. Now, please, leave me alone."

There was a definitive click at the other end of the line. Ginger sat there with the dead receiver in her hand. She had assured Ruben that she had no wish to harass the teacher, and she didn't. More than that, he was acting exactly as an innocent man would act in such circumstances, controlling his anger, making his point.

Despite the pressure they were under to come up with a suspect, despite the little itch at the back of her neck that told her he very well might know something that would help the investigation, she wondered if it weren't time to move on.

"First, one of our outstanding seniors was suspected of being involved in Tara Breckenridge's murder, and now it's one of our teachers," the assistant principal of Seward High School complained to the editor of the *Sentinel*. "And not just any teacher, mind you, but one of the finest we've ever been lucky enough to have here on the Island. And for some reason, your newspaper just can't seem to resist reporting every trivial piece of information as though it meant the impending resolution of the case. Perhaps you should display more integrity, and exercise more care before a decent man's career is ruined by innuendo rather than fact."

"I know which teacher it is that the police are now supposedly investigating," wrote the mother of a high school junior. "This is too small a community for anyone not to know. And I can't believe they're serious. My daughter is in one of his classes. She's learned more from him in the short time he's been here than from any other teacher in school, and she has the marks to prove it. A man like that inspires, he doesn't destroy."

"Has anyone noticed what's happening at the high school?" asked one of the English teachers. "It's now a place where learning has become secondary to speculation, and knowledge less important than rumor. If the police really want to find a killer, let them look where killers live, not where young minds are encouraged to grow."

"I don't know who's crazier, the *Sentinel* or its readers," the mother of twin sophomores told the editor. "Does the fact that Detective Earley 'talked' to one of the teachers automatically qualify him for hanging?"

"Where do we draw the line between what is legitimate investigation and what is harassment?" wondered a member of Scott Cohen's modest congregation. "And where do we draw the line between harassment and persecution? The police have now spoken four times to the teacher referred to in your recent article. If there were anything that connected him to the Breckenridge case, wouldn't they be doing a lot more than just talking to him by now?"

"Shouldn't we have a trial first, and see some hard evidence, before we rush out to crucify one of the best teachers we've ever had?" asked a local secretary.

"I have it on very good authority," Eleanor Jewel told a close acquaintance over a double tall latte at The Pelican, a popular coffee shop next to the ferry dock, "the teacher did it. The police know it for a fact, but they just don't have enough evidence yet to arrest him."

"What teacher?" the acquaintance asked.

"Why, my dear," Eleanor cooed, "I thought everybody knew."

"I can't believe the police really think Mr. Frankel could have murdered Tara," Melissa Senn declared during lunch break, between bites of an egg salad sandwich.

As Jerry himself had predicted, Ginger's conversation with the teacher had become common knowledge.

"Well, that's what I heard," Hank Kriedler said.

"How do you hear all these things?" Jeannie Gemmetta demanded.

Hank shrugged. "People talk," he said. "You know how it is."

"More like Kristen Andersen talked," Jeannie scoffed. "She was blabbing that silly story to everyone who would listen to her. All about seeing the two of them together with their arms wrapped around each other."

"What do you think—that she made it up?" Bill Graham asked.

"Maybe not," Jeannie conceded. "But she could have made a lot more out of it than it really was. You know Kristen—she always exaggerates."

"And don't you remember the Monday after Tara died?" Melissa insisted. "I do. Mr. Frankel didn't know a thing about it. We had to tell him what happened. He looked positively sick."

"So maybe the guy's a good actor," Jack Tannauer said.

"If he was that good," Jeannie retorted, "he'd be making movies in Hollywood instead of teaching history on Seward Island."

"I don't believe for a minute there was anything going on between the two of them," Melissa scoffed. "First of all, he's married. Second, Tara might have been pretty, but she wasn't nearly smart enough for someone like him. Third, we see him every day in class, looking perfectly normal, and you know that murderers can't help but give themselves away. And besides, Tara wasn't into going out with guys yet. I was her best friend; she'd have told me if she was."

"Still waters run deep," Hank said.

"What does that mean?" asked Jeannie.

"I don't know about the rest of you," Jim Petrie said, "but I'm getting pretty damned concerned over the lack of progress in the Breckenridge case."

The city council was having lunch, an informal monthly get-together that cleverly preempted the need for public participation, and allowed for what Albert Hoch liked to call "straight talk." As was their habit, they occupied the small dining room at Gull House, with full confidence that the restaurant management would honor their privacy.

"I don't feel any better about it than you do, Jim," Maxine Coopersmith responded. "But as far as I can tell, the police are doing everything humanly possible, and I don't know what more we can expect of them."

"Wasn't that the reason we hired Martinez?" Dale Egaard asked. "Because he was such a hotshot with all that big-city experience?"

"If that was the reason," Petrie countered, "it looks like we made a mistake."

"What are you saying?" Ed Hingham inquired. "You saying you want to fire the guy because he couldn't solve the murder in sixty minutes?"

"How about sixty days?" Petrie shot back.

"Do you think you can do better, Jim?" drawled Henry Lewiston. "Do you want the job?"

"Certainly not," snapped Petrie. "I just want the case solved and the killer caught so we can all get back to living normal lives. But Martinez is going off in all directions, wasting valuable time and resources running down ridiculous leads, and as far as I can tell, getting nowhere."

"Well, I agree the Purdy thing was untimely," Maxine conceded. "Stirring everyone up like it has. And it can't have helped any, to bring out all the crackpots. But no one had any control over that, and we can hardly blame Ruben."

"I'm not blaming anyone," Petrie said. "All I'm saying is that I want results. And if we can't get them from our current chief of police, well then, maybe we should think about bringing in someone else."

"They're looking at some teacher now, aren't they?" Ed Hingham asked. "Maybe something will come of that."

"At this point, I don't think we need to talk about firing anyone." Albert Hoch spoke for the first time. "Let's let the Purdy thing play itself out for a bit, and keep an eye on the teacher situation, and see what happens. The issue is on the table. We know it's there. We can always come back to it later on, if we need to."

"Hey, I've got one for you," Glen Dirksen said, catching Ginger on her way back from lunch. "This twelve-year-old kid says his seventy-year-old grandmother admitted to whacking Tara Breckenridge with an ax. The old lady claimed she needed sweet young bones for her winter soup."

Ginger rolled her eyes. "And I bet you came out of the academy thinking police work was going to be all cops and robbers."

Ruben called to her as she passed his door, heading to her office.

"Fill me in," he requested. "Where are we?"

"It all depends on your point of view," she replied. "We're either in the middle of an intensive investigation, or we're grasping at some pretty skinny straws. Dirksen's got a hot lead on a granny angle."

Ruben shook his head in disbelief. "Anything new on the teacher?"

"No," Ginger told him. "And I'm not so sure there ever will be. But Peter Leo lost his battle in court. Judge Jacobs refused to quash the order on Danny. He's got a week to report to the clinic."

"If his DNA comes up negative, and we cut the teacher loose," he reminded her, "that means we're back at nowhere."

But Ginger didn't need reminding.

"You were right to stand up to them, Albert," declared Kyle Breckenridge. "I'm glad we have one level head at City Hall. Anyone with any brains at all knows you don't change horses in the middle of the river."

"That's exactly what I told them," the mayor agreed, preening a bit from the compliment. "Ruben still has leads to follow. The teacher, for one, although I gather nothing's come of that. And much as it pains me to say it, there's still Danny Leo. Not to mention all the stuff that's been pouring in since the Purdy reward was put up. I told them to wait and see."

Breckenridge nodded. "Something's bound to break," he said. "I don't think it'll be much longer."

Jordan Huxley had been the principal of Seward High School for almost sixteen years. In that time, he had seen a lot of teachers come and go, good ones and bad ones, and he considered himself lucky to have Jerry Frankel on his staff.

The timing had been perfect. First there was Jim Duffy dropping dead of a heart attack the way he had, at the premature age of fifty-two, leaving a rather sizable hole in the history department in the middle of January. And then there was Frankel's wife suddenly being transferred to Seattle, and a letter of inquiry arriving on his desk on the very heels of poor Duffy's funeral. He had just lost a history teacher, and here was a history teacher for the grabbing. After a brief but thorough examination of Frankel's credentials, the principal grabbed. His reward was that Frankel had been able to slip right into Duffy's place, almost without missing a beat.

Huxley was fifty-eight years old, of considerable size, with small brown eyes that tended to get lost in folds of fat when he smiled, and bushy hair that was now more gray than brown. He came from Enumclaw, just east of Tacoma, had gotten his education at Washington State University, and had spent his entire professional life on Seward Island, first as a math teacher for twelve years, and then as assistant principal for seven years before being appointed principal. In all that time, he had never come across a teacher of Jerry Frankel's caliber.

From the start of last year's second semester, through the summer session and right into the fall quarter, the new teacher's performance had been an unqualified success. Somehow, he had managed to arouse a level of enthusiasm for history that the small community had never before enjoyed—an enthusiasm that was now beginning to spill over into other subjects.

"How do you do it?" the principal asked.

The teacher shrugged. "There's no real secret," he replied. "I just try to show the kids that education isn't just some bad-tasting medicine that adults make you swallow in order to matriculate. And that history isn't something old and dry and dead—but something that's living right here with us, influencing everything we do. Once they understand that they're creating history themselves every single day, they begin to realize how important it is to learn from other people's successes and failures."

Truancy in the history teacher's classes dropped to an all-time low. Test scores were on the rise. Frankel had set up an after-school chat room, so to speak, where his students could drop in for help with homework, to participate in informal study groups, or to discuss any of a number of far-reaching topics within the teacher's purview. He was having so much success with this approach that other members of the staff had begun to think about following suit. Despite his brief tenure, Frankel was already being acknowledged by his colleagues as an excellent addition to the school, and an innovator. And Jordan Huxley was getting the credit.

A natural-born leader, the principal thought to himself, dismissing out of hand all those ridiculous rumors about the Breckenridge murder; a leader that might be able to help him with a very sticky problem.

It was no secret that Frankel was Jewish. It didn't matter to Huxley. All he cared about was the quality of a man's work, not the salvation of his soul. But now there was a serious effort afoot to cancel the annual Christmas pageant at the last moment—a pageant that had been held at Seward High School for as long as the principal could remember. In front of him, laid out on a massive polished mahogany desk—his one extravagance after thirty-five years—was a formal petition that contained several hundred names, including the majority of the Island's Jewish residents. To be honest, Huxley hadn't realized there were that many of them.

There had been some grumbling about the pageant, off and on for the last five years or so, but this was the first time any official protest had been lodged. Huxley had two options: he could kick the petition up to the school board and step out of the loop, or he could try to diffuse the situation himself. Not a man to pass the buck, he chose the second option. And he intended to start with the man who was just coming into the front office.

Jerry Frankel knew it was only a matter of time before his effectiveness as a teacher at Seward High School would be compromised. There had been whispers flying around the corridors for the past two days, curious glances, sudden gasps. In class, the students seemed to be studying *him* more than his subject. During the breaks, his colleagues went out of their way to offer support, without really saying what it was they were being supportive about. It was humiliating.

And now this abrupt summons from Huxley: *May I see you after school*, the note delivered during the last period said, and it was not a question.

After everything else, Jerry concluded such a summons could mean only one thing: that his presence at the school had become too disruptive.

"Don't just stand there, my boy, come, come," Huxley beckoned genially, waving Jerry into the private office, and then taking the time to close the door firmly behind him.

At that, Jerry's stomach sank to his feet.

"Sit down," the principal invited, moving back behind his buttress of a desk.

The history teacher sat on the edge of his chair and waited, wondering what form the suspension would take.

"I'm going to come right out and say it," Huxley began. "I need your help."

So his tactic was going to be to ask for a voluntary resignation, Jerry thought. Never mind a suspension and what could be a lengthy and messy investigation—just cut the cancer out, neat and clean. He clenched his teeth.

"You see," Huxley continued, "I've got this petition here, signed by a whole lot of people, and I don't exactly know what to make of it."

Jerry frowned around his clenched teeth, and wondered how a petition about him could possibly have been produced so quickly. Granted this was a small island, and the local newspaper had been eager to jump on his case, but it was hardly more than a weekend since his conversation with Ginger Earley, and only yesterday that he had officially declined to submit to her tests.

"And seeing as it's got your signature on it," Huxley went on. "I was hoping to get your thoughts on the matter."

Jerry looked at the man blankly. What was he talking about? He certainly hadn't had anything to do with signing something that demanded his own dismissal.

"The petition," the principal prompted. "The one I have sitting right here on my desk from all you people who want us to cancel the annual Christmas pageant."

Jerry fell back against his chair in relief. "I thought you were . . . I thought this was . . . well, you know, I thought this meeting was because of the rumors," he stammered.

Now it was Huxley's turn to look blank. "Rumors?" he asked. "What rumors? I'm not talking about rumors, I'm talking about a school tradition here."

Jerry shook his head as though to clear it. "Excuse me," he said. "It's been a rough day. Now, what about the pageant?"

"Well, that's what I was asking you," the principal replied. "You want us to cancel something we've been doing for decades. I want to know why."

"I guess maybe it's because there are enough people now living on the Island who feel that the way it's structured is no longer appropriate," Jerry said.

"But it's just a pageant," Huxley argued. "A nativity reenactment, some recitations, a little dancing, a few songs. Something to get the kids involved. They've been working on it for over a month. What's the harm in it?"

"All the kids, or just some of the kids?" Jerry asked. "Does it include reenactments from all the major religions—or just one?"

"Well, it certainly represents the overwhelming majority of the people on this island, and we do still live in a democracy, don't we?"

"Mr. Huxley, I'm a history teacher," Jerry said slowly, thoughtfully. "A Jewish history teacher. Perhaps that gives me a somewhat different perspective on things, but I don't happen to believe that majority rule should be thought of as synonymous with exclusionary rule."

The little brown eyes blinked between their folds of fat. "So you think the minority should win?"

"If you put it that way, the minority has already won," Jerry replied with a shrug. "It's in the Constitution. But in this case, why can't everyone win?"

"What do you mean?"

"This is a school, isn't it? A place to learn? So why not use the pageant to educate as well as entertain? You can keep your nativity reenactment, but add a skit about Hanukkah and maybe sing a Jewish song or perform a Jewish folk dance. And do the same thing for Ramadan."

"Ramadan, eh?" Huxley mumbled. He hadn't the faintest idea what that was, couldn't remember ever even hearing the word before, but he wasn't about to tell Frankel that.

"Also, I understand we've had a significant Buddhist population here for generations, so why not celebrate some of their traditions?" Jerry added. "And any other religion practiced on the Island. It certainly can't hurt any of our children to learn about the culture and customs of people who are different from themselves. On the contrary, knowledge is always the first line of defense against intolerance."

Jordan Huxley smiled broadly. "Damn if you haven't got a first-rate idea there," he declared. "Don't know why I didn't think of it myself. The pageant's not for a couple of weeks yet. There's still time to make a few little changes. I'll run it past the committee first thing tomorrow, and we'll see how it flies." The principal stood up and came around the desk with an out-stretched hand. "I'm pleased you took the time to come in and see me, real pleased. I knew you were the right fellow to talk to."

Jerry took the hand and felt his shoulder almost come out of its socket. "I was happy to help," he murmured as he was ushered out the door.

Martin Keller answered the door himself. "Yes, may I help you?" he asked.

He was a short man, dressed in a dark brown business suit

that befitted his job as senior bookkeeper for a Seattle hospital. It was impeccably shaped to his compact figure, and he wore it with a starched white shirt and a paisley bow tie. A matching handkerchief peeked out of his breast pocket. His brown shoes were polished to a mirror shine. He looked to be somewhere in his early fifties. He had a small mustache and thin hair of a non-descript color, and his eyes, behind gold-rimmed spectacles, were a faded blue.

Ginger pulled out her identification. "I'm Detective Virginia Earley from the Seward Island Police Department," she said, looking down at him from a two-inch advantage. "If I'm not interrupting your dinner, I'd like to ask you a few questions."

"A few questions?" he repeated in a voice that was somewhat high-pitched. "About what?"

Ginger looked around. "About the neighborhood," she replied.

"I don't discuss my neighbors," the man said. He started to close the door.

"It's very important, sir, or I wouldn't be here. It's about the Breckenridge murder."

Martin Keller peered at her through his spectacles. "All right," he said after a moment, and stepped aside to let her enter. He led her across the foyer, a large, high-ceilinged space defeated by dark, gloomy wallpaper, and into the living room.

Like photographs snapping, Ginger absorbed it all in a series of glances. The room was uninspired, decorated in musty browns and rusts and drab earth tones. The furniture was old and ungainly, the scattered rugs well worn and almost colorless. Even the draperies were dull and heavy. Practical was the word that popped into Ginger's head. Little dirt would show in this room; little light would shine in it, as well. The one aesthetic note was a corner curio cabinet that housed an extensive collection of Meissen.

"My wife's," Keller said as if reading her mind. "Left to her by her grandmother."

"Lovely," she murmured.

"Sit down, Detective," he invited, gesturing to two wing chairs drawn up before a neat fire. A well-used book with no jacket lay open on the chair he took for himself. Keller picked it up and closed it as he sat down, and then casually dropped it onto the floor behind him. "I don't believe I know anything about the Breckenridge case," he said. "But I'm curious to know why you think I do."

Ginger sat down opposite him and wondered what it was about him that made her so uncomfortable. He seemed such a harmless little man, and he was being perfectly polite, even gracious. But something about him made her spine twitch. As a matter of course, she was used to taking charge of such conversations, yet she had the distinct impression that he was the one in control; that he was taking her measure even more carefully than she was taking his, analyzing her with those washed-out eyes as intently as a scientist would study a specimen under a microscope.

"We generally get a great many tips from people during an investigation such as this," she began. "And no matter how far-fetched they might sound, we're obliged to check them all out."

"That seems prudent," he said.

"We've been given some information that concerns one of your neighbors, and we're trying to determine whether it has any merit."

"Which neighbor?" Martin Keller asked.

"Jerry Frankel," Ginger replied.

The washed-out eyes fixed on her for a full ten seconds before he spoke. "The Frankels live right next door, as I'm sure you already know," he said. "They purchased the house about a year ago. They keep their lawn mowed, they do not have loud parties, and as far as I can determine, they are law-abiding."

At that moment, a boy of eleven or twelve came skidding into the room, perhaps for the purpose of having a word with his father.

"Justin, we do not slide on your mother's floors, and we do not enter a room without permission," Keller said sternly.

The boy, seemingly taken by surprise to see a stranger seated by the fire, blinked several times behind his round eyeglasses, and then darted out without a sound.

"Children," Keller murmured with a sigh. "I apologize for my son's lapse in manners."

"Do you know them well?" Ginger asked, returning to the purpose of her visit.

"Who?"

"The Frankels."

"I don't know them at all," Keller corrected her. "My wife and son and I are very private people, Detective Earley. We don't intrude on others, and by example we expect others not to intrude on us."

"But is it possible," Ginger persisted, "that, without intruding, you may have seen or heard something that might now help us either to include or to exclude Mr. Frankel from our investigation? In particular, on the night of Tara Breckenridge's death?"

Again, there was a contemplative silence.

"I'm sorry to disappoint you," Martin Keller said at last. "But I saw nothing and I heard nothing."

A moment later, Ginger stood in the Keller driveway and looked across at the Frankel house. Lights burned brightly from the windows, spilling out into the chill evening. A boy called out; a dog barked. The family was obviously at home, going about the business of living. It looked just like any of the houses on Seward Island—friendly and inviting.

This had been her last shot. She had interviewed all seven of the teacher's nearest neighbors and learned nothing. The night of the murder, none of them could recall seeing or hearing anything out of the ordinary. As far as anybody knew, Jerry Frankel was a great guy, a fantastic teacher, and a genuine asset to the community.

Ginger sighed. It was almost eight o'clock, she was tired and hungry, and she couldn't think of anything else to do. She got behind the wheel of her car and drove away.

From the slimmest of cracks between the heavy living room draperies, Martin Keller watched her go.

"You don't really think Mr. Frankel murdered Tara, do you?" Stacey asked her father.

"What makes you ask?" Ruben countered.

"Because of what Kristen said," she told him. "It's all over school, you know, that Kristen talked to me, and then I took her to talk to Ginger, and then right away Ginger went back to talk to him. And now, a lot of the kids are going around saying he's the killer."

"Small towns," he said, shaking his head. "To answer your question—I don't know."

"I like Mr. Frankel, Dad," Stacey said earnestly. "He's not just a good teacher. He really cares about the stuff he teaches us, and I think he cares about us, too. He's really into his head a lot, and he knows so much about what makes people tick, from a thousand years ago right up to yesterday. I don't see him as a hot-head. I see him as the kind of person like you want *me* to be— one who would think his way out of a problem before he'd act his way out of it. Maybe he was fond of Tara, but I don't believe he could have killed her."

"What do you mean, he was fond of her?"

"Well, I've been thinking about it," the teenager said. "And it's possible that he might have treated her a little differently than he treated the rest of us."

✿   ✿   ✿

This time there was an angry debate during the basement meeting, snatches of conversation rising well above the usual muted pitch.

". . . never have a better opportunity," declared one.

". . . as subtle as a sledgehammer," scoffed another.

". . . a real chance of exposure here," cautioned a third.

". . . can't risk being identified," warned a fourth.

"Cowards," sneered the first.

"Enough," the acknowledged leader said in a soft but firm voice. "This kind of bickering is getting us nowhere. Let's keep focused."

The men looked at one another. There was a purpose to this meeting, they knew; options to be discussed, a decision to be reached, a plan of action to be devised. All of them had the same objective, personalities notwithstanding. Each took a deep breath and then they began again.

An hour and a half later, the leader rose. "All right, are we agreed?" he asked.

One by one, the men nodded.

7

Gail Brown sat curled on a wicker couch in the living room of her beachfront cottage, which sat at the very edge of North Point, absently tugging at her ponytail. A forgotten cup of tea was balanced on the cushion beside her.

Beyond her window, Mount Baker loomed like a ghost in a clear blue sky. The winter rains were now two months late, and meteorologists, who for weeks had been predicting fronts that never materialized, were beginning to tiptoe around the possibility of a drought.

There was nothing quite like the beauty of the Pacific Northwest on a fine day, but the editor's brown eyes behind the thick glasses stared out at nothing.

Although she was perfectly all right, Gail had called in sick this morning, in the middle of a workweek, a thing she had never done before in her entire professional life. But she had a decision to make, and she needed some distance from the office and her staff in order to make it.

At the heart of it, Gail was a person divided, and being tugged in both directions. The side of her that loved Seward Island and everything it represented was centered in her very marrow and could never be denied. This was not just the place where her family had lived for almost eighty years, or where she had been born and raised. This was her safe haven in an increasingly turbulent world, the one place she knew where she felt unconditionally accepted. There had never been any doubt in her mind, despite electing to go east for her education and experience, that she would come back. It was why she had gone away—to gain the skills she would need to return and succeed.

The little house in which she now lived had been left to her by her grandmother. The old woman had called it her "hut of humble thoughts"; the refuge where she had come whenever she needed to be alone to sort out a problem; the sanctuary where she had insisted on spending her final few months.

Gail felt much as her grandmother had about the rustic cottage perched on Seward's northeasternmost tip, providing as it did a spectacular panorama of Puget Sound from the vantage point of being able to see but not be seen. It was both her window on the world and her preserve of private counsel.

The pull of the Island had cost Gail her marriage. She could not understand why anyone would not want to live on an isolated rock in the middle of nowhere with only a water connection to the rest of civilization; he could not understand why anyone would. He wanted the kind of excitement that only a big-city newspaper could provide, and Seattle apparently wasn't big enough. They left Boston together: he heading for Chicago, she heading for home. She loved him, but she loved the Island more.

That was one side of Gail Brown—the side that would protect this place and these people with her last drop of blood, her final spurt of energy, her one remaining breath.

The other side was the part of her that was smart and determined and totally devoted to her profession. She believed in the Bill of Rights every bit as much as she believed in the Ten Commandments. She was convinced of the people's right to know, and committed to the First Amendment as the only true safeguard of the nation. And for her dedication to that principle, she craved the recognition and respect of her peers.

It never occurred to Gail that the day might come when one side of her would be in serious conflict with the other. But it was two months since the murder of Tara Breckenridge, and notwithstanding the editor's exhaustive efforts to be the conscience of the community, or to put it less charitably, her resolve to milk every ounce of revenue from the story, very little headway had been made in the case. Of course, this was both a plus and a minus. While public confidence was way down, the newspaper's sales were way up—an irony that did not escape her.

The question she now had to answer was—how much further was she willing to go? How thin was she willing to stretch the rules? How narrow was the line she was about to walk?

Although the *Sentinel* had been careful not to identify him by name, Gail knew it was Jerry Frankel who had been the most recent focus of Ginger Earley's attention, and it was likely that, by now, a significant part of Seward knew it, too. The editor could just imagine the conversations taking place in the aisles at the Island Market and under the dryers at Wanda's Hairworks.

She picked up the letter for the hundredth time, and with some measure of cynicism, wondered what people would be saying if they knew about this.

It was typewritten, on plain white paper, and had come with no signature and no return address. Bearing a Seattle postmark, it had been sent, not to the office, but to her home. Under ordinary circumstances, Gail would have dismissed such a letter out of hand. But these were not ordinary circumstances, and she gave in to the little pump of adrenaline that told her this might not be the time to get hung up on ethics.

As a matter of journalistic policy, anonymous letters were never printed in the *Sentinel*. In fact, Gail made a point of personally contacting the author of each letter before it was published to confirm the opinions expressed. Yet there was something about this particular one that could not be dismissed.

Had anyone else received it, he or she would probably have turned it directly over to the police, and let them deal with it. Only Gail Brown was not anyone else. Her hometown ties notwithstanding, she was the ambitious editor of a small daily newspaper that had yet to make its mark, a critical factor that played a part in every decision she made.

On the one hand, she held herself and the *Sentinel* to the highest standards of journalistic integrity. On the other hand, a letter like this, with what it imported, could be the key to breaking the Island's first homicide case wide open, and she was enough of a professional—all right, egoist—to want a piece of the action for herself.

For whatever reason, she had been made part of the equation. In the wake of Malcom Purdy's bizarre offer, the letter had come to her. That gave her an absolute right to use it to her best advantage. The question was—how?

She had never met Jerry Frankel. She had, however, spoken at some length to Jordan Huxley, as well as a couple of dozen assorted teachers, students, and parents. Frankel got top marks from all of them.

"He's a remarkable teacher," said a colleague who taught science.

"He has definitely raised the standards at Seward High School," said another who also taught history.

"He has a true gift," said one of the English teachers.

"He makes learning fun," said a student.

"I like going to his class every day," said another. "All those boring dates of battles and stuff we used to have to memorize—they make sense to me now."

"My son used to be a D student in history," said a parent. "Now he earns As, and he's talking abut majoring in history when he goes to college."

Clearly, Jerry Frankel was a significant asset to the Island. Whatever the subject, Gail knew that a teacher who could inspire his pupils as this one obviously had was a rare commodity in this age of undereducation.

Still, there was the letter. The editor leaned back against the sofa pillows and took a sip of cold tea. With the instincts of a barracuda, she understood its potential value for an obscure newspaper. In fact, she was already envisioning a whole series of articles that would cast the *Sentinel* in the role of mentor to the police. A series that would not only serve to further the investigation, but might aid authorities in the actual capturing of the killer. A series that would give her little newspaper the national recognition she craved. Perhaps, she let herself dream, the kind of recognition that would lead to a Pulitzer.

It was the ultimate dream of every journalist. Just thinking the word sent chills down Gail's back. Despite what she knew her actions might do to the tranquil community she so cherished, it was an opportunity she was not sure she could pass up. The rationalization was easy. What was more important? she debated with herself. To protect a teacher, highly regarded though he may be, educational benefactor though he may be— or to rid Seward Island of a dangerous killer? Besides, there was always the chance that the whole thing was a fool's errand, and would come to nothing.

Put that way, her decision was clear. She picked up the telephone and dialed the number of her travel agent. As it began to ring, she glanced at the letter one more time.

"To the editor:" it read. "Better late than never for the police to get around to a certain history teacher at the high school. If anyone is really interested in solving the Breckenridge case, they should be talking to the people at the Holman Academy in Scarsdale, New York."

8

"I've had over a hundred calls so far," Glen Dirksen reported on Wednesday afternoon. "And more are coming in every day. I've followed up on about two dozen. There's just nothing there."

"Well, we knew it was a slim chance at best," Ruben told him. "But don't give up."

The young officer shook his head. "There was a call from one guy who said he wasn't interested in the money, only in justice. Wouldn't even give his name. All he said was: 'Where there's dirt, there's dirty doings,' and hung up."

"Sounds like one of our Island whackos," Charlie Pricker told him.

"Or an environmentalist," Ginger quipped.

"Hey, Stacey, wait up," Danny Leo called, catching her as she was leaving the high school campus.

The police chief's daughter stopped. "Hi, Danny," she said. "I know I'm a little late with the girls' basketball story. I'll have it in by tomorrow."

"That's okay," he said. "It's not about that." There was an awkward pause. "Look, could I, uh, talk to you about something?"

"Sure."

Danny had gold-flecked brown hair and thickly lashed green eyes that most of the girls at school openly drooled over. Right now, they were fastened on something around the tip of his Reeboks. In the year and a half that Stacey had worked with him on the school paper, she had seen him angry, excited, confused, and even embarrassed, but she had never seen him at a loss for words.

"I guess you know all about me," he said finally. "I mean, your father must have told you about me and Tara."

"Actually, Danny, I was the one who told him," Stacey replied. "I saw the two of you together one time. I'm sorry."

"Yeah, well, that's okay," he said. "I should've been up front about it myself. Anyway, I'm in this kind of jam, and I wondered if maybe you could help me out."

"What kind of jam?"

"Well, you see, Detective Earley got this court order to take a sample of my blood. My dad tried to fight it, but he lost so I have to go to the clinic. But the results of the test won't come back for at least two months, and meanwhile it's screwing up my scholarship to Harvard. Going to Harvard is real important to me, and I swear I didn't have anything to do with Tara's death, and I thought, if I could take the polygraph test, the results of that would be in, like right away, and then everyone would know, and I'd be off the hook."

"Well, if you want to do that, I'm sure all you have to do is go in and see Ginger Earley."

"If my dad found out, he would kill me," Danny said. "He's so hung up on his principles, he doesn't understand it's my life he's messing around with. And I'm afraid he could get himself in a lot of trouble over this. I want to take the polygraph, but I don't want him to know about it until it's done. Do you think you could talk to your dad and see if something could be arranged?"

"I'll talk to him," Stacey promised.

❀   ❀   ❀

"I was happy three years ago when the city council hired Ruben Martinez," a local businessman wrote to the editor. "I knew it was only a matter of time before the rest of the world began to slip across the water, and change our idyllic island for the worse. I read about Ruben's twenty-five years of law enforcement experience, and I felt he was the right man to meet those changes head-on, and deal with them. Now it's been two months since Tara Breckenridge was murdered, and I'm not so sure anymore."

"What do our police do all day?" asked a housewife. "All I see them doing is issuing parking tickets, lying in wait for traffic violators, and assisting elderly people across the street. These are all noble endeavors, to be sure, but Chief Martinez says everyone in his department is working on the Breckenridge case. Do they really think the killer is parking too close to a fire hydrant, or speeding down Center Island Road, or eighty years old and feeble?"

"Ruben, we have a problem," Albert Hoch declared, his voice carrying easily from the police chief's office, despite the closed door. "It's been two months, and you're no closer to solving this murder than you were on the day it happened."

It was Wednesday evening. The police chief, after having a conversation with his daughter, had just arranged for Danny Leo to take a polygraph test. He was getting ready to head for home when the mayor appeared.

"Some things take time," he told Hoch calmly.

"Time? How much time? The more time goes by, the colder the trail gets. You've got Danny Leo giving blood. What about the teacher?"

"We've come up with no evidence that he has any involvement in the case."

"Is there anyone else?"

"Not at the moment."

Hoch sighed heavily. "Three years ago, I went out on a limb for you. A lot of people around here didn't exactly think you were the right man for the job, but I told them you were, that you had the experience we needed. And now look what happens: the first major crime to come along, and you're spinning your wheels like an amateur."

From her office down the hall, Ginger grit her teeth. It wasn't fair. If the mayor wanted to blame someone for the lack of results, he should have come to see her. After all, she was the one running the investigation. If nothing was happening, it was her fault.

"Some cases don't solve easy," she heard Ruben say. "I was hoping this one would, but it hasn't. And unless we're willing to suspend all civil rights, and haul every man on Seward Island down here for mandatory blood and polygraph tests, we're just going to have to rely on something breaking for us."

"How much longer do you think we can wait?"

"As long as we have to, I guess."

"Dammit, Ruben, that's not good enough."

"If you think another man can do a better job," came the response, "that's certainly your decision to make."

Ginger gasped. She couldn't believe that Albert Hoch could really be talking about firing Ruben. Not now. Not when they had finally found each other.

"People are pounding on my door," the mayor said. "They want action. They want to know why our esteemed police force can't seem to solve a simple crime. What am I supposed to tell them?"

"Tell them that Seward Island has a department filled with dedicated professionals whose top priority is the well-being of this community," Ruben replied

Albert Hoch was a glad-hander, not a backhander. He

sighed. "The city council isn't happy," he said. "Frankly, I don't know how much longer I can hold them off."

"My name is Heidi Tannauer," the voice on the telephone said.

"Yes, ma'am," Officer Dirksen replied, stifling a yawn. "How can I help you?"

"I'm a freshman at Northwestern University," she said. "I didn't know anything about the Breckenridge case until I came home for Thanksgiving. But now my parents tell me you think a teacher may be involved?"

Dirksen suddenly sat up in his seat. "I'm sorry, ma'am, but that's not something I'm at liberty to discuss at this time," he said.

"Well, I don't know if this has anything to do with that," Heidi continued, "but I had to take a makeup class in summer school last year, and I distinctly remember seeing Tara several times after school hours with one of the teachers."

"Do you happen to recall which teacher?" the officer asked casually.

"I don't remember his name," Heidi replied, "but I'm pretty sure he was the new history teacher."

9

The telephone was ringing. Jerry Frankel shifted the bag of groceries he was carrying from his left arm to his right and inserted the key into the lock on the back door of his house. He dropped the groceries on the kitchen counter and reached for the receiver.

"Mr. Frankel, this is Detective Earley," the voice at the other end said. "I wonder if you'd be kind enough to come in and see me tomorrow after school."

Jerry sighed. The curious stares and whispers were still following him. And it wasn't confined to the school anymore, but everywhere he went. He had thought, or perhaps hoped, that all the curiosity and speculation would have died down by this time, but it hadn't. Rather, it seemed to be the opposite. Just a few moments ago, two women in line at the Island Market abruptly stopped talking the moment he approached the checkout counter.

"What is it now, Detective?" he asked.

"Well, I really don't want to go into it over the telephone," Ginger replied. "There's something we need to discuss, and it would be better if you'd come in." There was the slightest of pauses. "You're certainly free to bring your attorney, if you like," she added.

"Do you really think that's necessary?"

"It's entirely up to you," she said. "Whatever would make you most comfortable. Shall we say four o'clock?"

"Four o'clock," he repeated dully.

Jerry hung up the receiver and turned automatically to put away the groceries, slipping the jar of peanut butter into the refrigerator and setting the carton of milk on the pantry shelf before he realized what he was doing.

He reached Scott Cohen at his office.

"Are they going to charge you with anything?" the lawyer asked.

"I don't know what they're going to do," Jerry replied. "She said she wanted to talk. She said I could bring you with me."

Scott paused. "Well, it doesn't sound like you're in imminent danger of arrest," he said finally, "but she's putting you on notice that this is more than just a friendly chat. So hold on a minute while I check my schedule."

Jerry waited while the lawyer went off to scan his appointment book and speak to his secretary. His head ached and his brain felt like mush; he couldn't think straight. He wanted Scott to think for him.

"I can meet you there at four o'clock," Scott said, coming back on the line.

"Do you think it will look bad," Jerry asked, "that I'm bringing my lawyer with me?"

"At this point," Scott said bluntly, "that's the last thing you should be worried about."

They gathered in the windowless interview room, the detective on one side of the rectangular metal table, the teacher and his attorney on the other. It was apparently going to be just a conversation; there was no stenographer present, no tape recorder in sight.

"The reason I've asked you to come in, Mr. Frankel," Ginger began, "is because I find myself with so many coincidences here that I feel perhaps you haven't been totally candid with me."

"What sort of coincidences, Detective Earley?" Scott inquired.

"Let's begin with the ones Mr. Frankel and I have already discussed," Ginger said to the attorney. "The fact that a dark-colored Taurus station wagon was seen in Madrona Point Park on the night of the murder, and your client drives such a car; the fact that your client lacks a corroborating alibi for the time of the murder; the fact that your client was one of the victim's teachers, and thereby known by him; and the fact that he was seen with her shortly before her death in what could clearly be construed as compromising circumstances. Now add to that a new report that he was seen alone with Tara several times after school during the summer session. And finally, a piece of information that we have not yet released to the public—the fact that we believe our killer is left-handed, and so is your client. Granted that all this is purely circumstantial, but it does seem to suggest that your client may be more involved in this case than he's told us."

"But I'm not," Jerry interjected.

Scott laid a hand on his client's arm. "Detective Earley, my client has already told you that he was home on the night of the murder. You checked his car and found nothing. I sincerely doubt that he is the only left-handed man who knew Tara Breckenridge. And I could probably find any number of people who were seen alone with the victim prior to her death; such as Danny Leo, such as our esteemed Mayor Albert Hoch, such as Magnus Coop—all of whom, by the way, happen to be left-handed. So since you have nothing that even remotely connects my client to the commission of any crime, I don't see what the purpose of this conversation is, other than harassment."

"Mr. Cohen, I'm not naive," Ginger said. "I'm in no position to charge Mr. Frankel with anything. If I were, I would be standing on his doorstep with a warrant. But I have a brutal murder case to solve, and an intuition that tells me your client is either connected in some way or knows something that could help us. It's not my intention to embarrass him or harass him. I'm just trying to do my job."

"What exactly do you think he knows?"

Ginger looked directly at Jerry. "I think you had something more than just a teacher-student relationship with Tara Breckenridge," she said. "I think, even if you didn't kill her yourself, you know something—whether you realize it or not—that could lead us to the person who did."

Jerry looked at his attorney.

"Would you excuse us for a few moments, Detective?" Scott requested. "I'd like to talk with my client."

"Certainly." Ginger stood up without hesitation and left the room, closing the door behind her.

"How is it going?" Ruben asked.

Ginger shrugged. "They're having a powwow," she said.

Ten minutes later, Scott opened the door. "Would you please come in, Detective Earley. My client would like to make a statement."

"You mean, on the record?" Ginger asked.

Scott glanced at Frankel. "I don't see why not," he replied.

A tape recorder was brought in and set up in a matter of minutes.

"I'd like to have Chief Martinez present, if that's all right with you," Ginger said.

Scott nodded. Ruben entered the room and took a seat beside Ginger. The detective pushed the red button on the recorder and spoke into the microphone.

"This is a voluntary statement being made by Mr. Jeremy Frankel in the presence of his attorney, Mr. Scott Cohen, Chief of Police Ruben Martinez, and Detective Virginia Earley."

She pushed the microphone across the table. The teacher sat up in his chair and cleared his throat.

"Let me say, right from the start, that I had nothing to do with the death of Tara Breckenridge," he said. "I did know her, and we developed a relationship that may have extended, but never ever exceeded, the boundaries of a normal teacher-student relationship." He paused for a moment. "There was something about her that I noticed from the first days of summer school— a kind of melancholy is the best way I can describe it—that clearly went a lot deeper than just the boredom or the embarrassment of having to make up classes. On top of that, she seemed to be far brighter than her grades indicated, which got me curious. I wanted to find out what the problem was and help her work through it, if I could. I might have paid more attention to her than I did some of the other students, because I was trying to get a dialogue going with her, trying to build a rapport. As usually happens when a teacher takes an interest in a student, she responded. Her grades started to improve. I thought that was a good sign, and I acknowledged it. She began to come out of her shell and talk to me—that rapport I mentioned. I've always found that kids who are relaxed absorb more, and sure enough, her grades got better. I saw no harm in that. If she sought me out after school, I didn't turn her off. If I saw her between classes, I was friendly. If she came in for extra help, I gave it to her. I'm in the business of educating, Detective Earley—of opening minds—and different students need different approaches. I was nice to her, I encouraged her, and my efforts paid off. She worked hard and earned an excellent grade, and that was all there was to it."

He stopped. Ginger waited until she was sure he was not going to continue before she leaned toward the microphone.

"You say you and Tara had a rapport, Mr. Frankel," she said. "You say she came out of her shell. What did she talk about?"

Jerry took a moment to think. "Mostly about growing up,"

he said. "She talked about her family. She said she wished she had been a boy instead of a girl."

"Did she say why?"

"I think it had something to do with her father—that she didn't feel she could live up to his expectations. He apparently wanted her to go to a top university and have an important career, but she really wasn't interested in that. She thought he would have been happier with a son."

"Did she say what she wanted out of life?"

"She talked once about becoming a nun," he said.

"I beg your pardon?"

"She said she wanted to be a nun," he repeated. "But she was afraid God wouldn't want her."

Although the Breckenridge family worshiped at Seward Episcopal, Ginger knew that Mary Breckenridge had been raised a Catholic. "Did Tara say why she thought God wouldn't want her?"

"She said it was because she wasn't good enough. That God chose only the best people to serve Him."

"The daughter of the Island's most prestigious family, and she didn't think she was good enough to be a nun?"

Jerry shrugged. "Sometimes, Detective Earley, self-esteem has little to do with wealth or position or even beauty," he said softly. "During the time that I knew her, Tara was a very troubled girl."

"Did she ever talk to you about being involved with someone—a boy, a man?"

The teacher's eyes narrowed as if in thought. "I don't recall that she did," he said.

"Are you sure?" Ginger pressed. "Obviously, you can appreciate how important this is."

"I'm sorry. She never said. Even that day in the back hall that you asked me about. All I can recall is what I told you—she said something very general about how awful her whole life was.

I think her actual words were 'a total disaster.' But kids are always saying things like that and I didn't take it very seriously. I'm sorry now that I didn't. But she never mentioned anyone by name."

"And your own relationship with Tara—are you stating here for the record that it was strictly professional and never sexual?"

Jerry glared at the detective. "What's the matter with you?" he demanded. "She was a child, for God's sake. Just a child."

"Can I borrow the car Saturday night?" Danny Leo asked.

"What for, son?" Peter inquired.

"I'm taking a girl to the movies."

"How nice, dear," Rose said. "Of course you can have the car."

While he was one of the most popular teenagers on Seward Island, Danny dated only occasionally, preferring, in the current local fashion, to socialize with friends in groups.

"What girl?" Peter asked.

Danny took a breath. "Stacey Martinez," he replied.

Peter looked surprised. "The police chief's daughter? Why would you want to date the police chief's daughter?"

"I know her from the school paper, and I like her."

"You know a lot of people. Why this one?"

Danny shrugged. "I'd like to get to know her better."

"Isn't she a little young for you?"

"She's pretty mature for a sophomore."

Peter contemplated the boy. "She's also the police chief's daughter," he said. "I'd be very careful, if I were you."

"It's just a movie, Dad."

"I don't care what you say," Libby Hildress told her husband as they were getting ready for bed. "Something's not right."

"About what?" Tom asked, knowing full well what it would be about.

"I was talking to Judy Parker at choir practice tonight. She told me that Mildred MacDonald told her she saw Jerry Frankel and Scott Cohen going into the police station this afternoon. Now why would he need a lawyer?"

"Scott's also his friend," Tom reminded her.

"Do people normally take their friends with them when they go talk to the police?"

10

If Gail Brown had thought to prioritize all the things she wanted to do in the middle of December, going to Scarsdale, New York, would not even have been on her list. Yet here she was, driving her rental car from Kennedy Airport up the Hutchinson River Parkway, in the dark, through a dense freezing rain.

She had called the Holman Academy before confirming her plane reservations, and was told that, while the school was officially closed on weekends, one or two members of the staff were usually around. Which suited Gail just fine. The fewer people who knew why she had come flying all the way across the country, the better.

From her earliest days as a reporter, Gail had always preferred to slip into a situation, rather than jump into it. That way, she found she offended fewer people and embarrassed herself less often. Such an approach was especially prudent here, where she really wasn't sure what she was looking for.

The anonymous letter may have set off alarm bells and propelled her into this cross-country odyssey, but there were no specifics contained in it, just the cryptic charge. For all she knew, she could be on a wild goose chase.

Gail found the inn her travel agent had booked for her, a quaint little gabled structure adjacent to a friendly-looking restaurant. She checked in, unpacked a few things, and headed for food. The restaurant was doing a brisk business, always a good sign.

"What'll you have," the waitress asked, when she finally made it to Gail's table. The woman looked to be about fifty, with thin brown hair and tired eyes. Her name tag identified her as Sally.

"What's good?" Gail asked.

Sally shrugged. "The stew's always good," she said. "Some of the regulars prefer the chicken. The pasta's fresh. The fish chowder's first-rate."

Gail looked at her. "What do *you* eat?"

The waitress smiled at that, and Gail realized she was a lot younger than she looked, and with a little makeup would have been quite pretty.

"I like the chowder," Sally said.

"The chowder it is, then," Gail ordered.

During all the years that the editor had spent on the East Coast, going to college and graduate school, working on various newspapers, she had never been to Scarsdale. But she knew that it was a fashionable town, with a reputation for having big money. She also knew that most of the people who lived in a town such as this would not be forthcoming with information, preferring instead to protect one another, and by so doing, protect themselves. In a wealthy community, Gail understood, there were always many more closets to hold skeletons.

"Are you here on business or pleasure?" Sally asked conversationally as she set the bowl of chowder, a plate of salad, and a basket of bread down in front of Gail.

"Business," the editor told her.

"Oh? What kind of business are you in?"

"I work for a newspaper," Gail replied.

"Really?" Sally said, because the skinny woman with the bushy ponytail and thick eyeglasses didn't fit the image. "One of those big-city reporters who are always looking to dig up dirt on other people?"

"Not exactly," came the response. "I'm an editor, not a reporter. And I work for a very small newspaper on the other side of the country."

"Oh," Sally murmured, apparently no longer interested.

"You sound disappointed," Gail said with a smile. "Why? Is there a lot of dirt to dig up in Scarsdale?"

The waitress shrugged. "We've got our share, I guess, just like any other town." She walked away before Gail could ask her anything more.

The chowder was as good as advertised, although Gail ate hardly any of it. She left a generous tip.

"For the recommendation as well as the service," she said as she paid her bill.

"Thanks," the woman said, tucking the bills into the pocket of her pink uniform.

Gail went back to her room at the inn and snapped on the television. There was nothing she could do tonight. In the morning, she would locate the Holman Academy.

"What's going on with your dad?" Billy Hildress asked Matthew. The two boys were playing a video game in Matthew's bedroom. Chase, the retriever pup, who was now fully housebroken and allowed the run of the house, sat watching their every move.

"What do you mean?" Matthew asked.

"Well, I don't know," Billy said, "but my mom says that people are saying your dad's got something to do with that body me and my dad found in the Dumpster."

Matthew stared at his friend. "*My* dad?" he replied. "Why would anyone think that?"

Billy shrugged. "I don't know, but it's what my mom heard. Did your dad know the dead girl?"

"Yeah. I think she was in one of his classes," Matthew conceded. "But that doesn't mean anything—he knows lots of kids."

"I gotta tell you," Billy admitted, "it's kinda creepy, having your best friend's dad being talked about like that."

Matthew frowned. Now that he thought of it, his mother had seemed out of sorts the past few days. He wondered if there were some connection.

"Say, Dad, why do people think you're involved in the murder?" he asked at dinner.

"Matthew!" his mother declared. "That's no question to ask your father. He's not responsible for what other people think."

"But Billy said something about it, and I didn't know what to tell him," the nine-year-old replied, not noticing that she hadn't taken exception to his question, only to his asking it.

"Tell Billy that the police have to investigate everyone who could possibly be connected to a crime," his father said. "It's their job. And one of the ways they solve crimes is to eliminate everyone that isn't involved in order to find the one who is. It just happens to be my turn to be eliminated."

That seemed to make sense. "I get it," Matthew said. "They make a list with everybody's name on it, and they keep crossing the names off until they're left with the last one—and that has to be the killer."

"Something like that," his father said.

The Holman Academy was located at the southern edge of Scarsdale, a three-story red-brick building in an upper-class neighborhood that had once been home to a banking magnate. The manager of the inn gave Gail directions, and she found the place easily. A high brick wall surrounded the grounds, just as he said it would. The iron gates stood open. The gravel parking lot that flanked the service wing was empty except for an old Ford pickup and a blue Oldsmobile sedan. It was exactly ten minutes past ten on Saturday morning when Gail pulled her rental up beside them.

It must have been a magnificent estate, she thought as she climbed out of the car and started around toward the front door. The freezing rain of last night had given way to a watery sunlight that set the whole landscape to shimmering. There were acres of lawns, massive elms, graceful maples, and enormous rhododendrons that looked impressive even out of season. Little paths meandered through vast flower beds. And down a little slope, off to one side, she caught a glimpse of a duck pond.

The front door was unlocked and Gail walked right in. The entry corridor was laid in big diamonds of black and white marble; the walls were paneled in rich mahogany. A small brass plaque mounted on the wall made it clear that this was indeed the Holman Academy, an institution of higher education for young women, established in 1943.

The clack of a typewriter came from an open door halfway down the corridor, and Gail followed the sound to a room that might once have been a small parlor but was clearly now an office.

A gray-haired woman was seated behind a vintage Smith-Corona; a plaque on the desk in front of her identified her as Mrs. Quinlan. "May I help you?" she asked, looking up with a bright smile.

"My name is Gail Brown," the editor replied, "and I'm hoping to get some information about a teacher who used to work here."

"Every teacher employed at the Holman Academy has been outstanding," Mrs. Quinlan said, as if by rote. "We're most particular, we have very stringent standards, and we can afford to pay for the highest quality. If you're looking for a reference, I'm sure we'll have no trouble providing you with one." She turned to a file cabinet. "Now which teacher was that?"

"Jeremy Frankel."

Did she imagine it, Gail wondered, or did the woman seem to hesitate for an instant? There was no overt change in her expression or her manner, but Gail was not a journalist for nothing.

Mrs. Quinlan opened the bottom drawer of a metal file cabinet and flipped through a row of folders, finally pulling one out. "Mr. Frankel was on staff here at the academy until January of last year," she said, reading from it. "He taught history. He was with us for six and a half years, and he was a very fine teacher." She replaced the folder and shut the drawer with a sharp click.

"This seems such an ideal place to work," Gail observed. "Can you tell me why he left?"

"Teachers come and teachers go," the woman said. "Now, if that's all, I'm really quite busy."

"I don't mean to bother you, Mrs. Quinlan, but I've come a long way," Gail said. "All the way across the country, as a matter of fact. It's extremely important that I find out why Mr. Frankel left the Holman Academy."

"I don't know what to say that would help you," the woman replied. "All I know is that he resigned in the middle of the school year. I couldn't say why. Why don't you ask *him* why he left?"

"Please understand that, if I could, I would." Gail carefully weighed what to say next. "You see, he currently teaches at the high school in the town where I live, and it's possible that he might be involved in a situation there that could be detrimental to the community. I was told that I could find out what I wanted to know here."

"I'm sorry," Mrs. Quinlan said, and now it seemed that her voice held a note of compassion. "I hope your situation resolves itself appropriately, but there really isn't anything more I can say. Our records are supposed to be confidential, and I've already told you more than I should have."

"Is there anyone else here who might be able to help me?" Gail asked.

Mrs. Quinlan shook her head. "The only other person here at the moment is one of our janitorial staff. He would hardly be in a position to tell you anything."

"Well, thank you for your time," Gail said.

She turned to leave the office and collided with a man wearing blue coveralls with the name "Ezekiel" stitched on the front pocket.

" 'Scuse me, ma'am," he exclaimed, looking embarrassed. "I sure didn't mean to get in your way like that."

"No, please, it was my fault," Gail said quickly. "I'm afraid I have a habit of not always looking where I'm going."

She turned down the corridor in the direction of the front door, but once there, with her hand on the knob, she looked back. Ezekiel was staring after her.

"I think I'll try the pasta tonight," Gail said to the waitress in the restaurant.

"Sure thing," Sally replied.

It was early, not yet six o'clock on a Saturday night, but the place was already more than half full. It was a testament, Gail decided, to modern America's continuing love of home cooking and dislike of cooking at home.

From the Holman Academy, she had gone directly to the local newspaper office, which was housed in the public library building on Olmstead Road, identified herself, and asked for help.

"We have a situation in my community that might involve a teacher who used to be out at the Holman Academy," she said. "I'm trying to determine if there's any connection. Can you give me a hand?"

"What exactly are you looking for?" a pretty redheaded clerk asked.

"Does the name Jerry Frankel ring a bell?"

There was a pause, a blank stare, and then a polite shake of her head. "Aside from graduation and honors stuff, we don't report much on the academy," Gail was told.

"Why not?"

"I guess because it's a private institution, and they go to great lengths to keep it that way."

"Why? What are they hiding?" The question was meant mostly in jest.

"Oh, I don't think they're trying to hide anything," the clerk was quick to reply. "I think it's more that they feel an obligation to protect their students. It's a pretty exclusive school. They've got a lot of rich kids up there, with prominent parents who probably wouldn't appreciate a lot of town gossip. I've been here six months, and we haven't reported a single thing about the academy in all that time."

"Do you think your editor would have any information?" Gail inquired, thinking she might get more from a peer.

The redhead shrugged. "He might, but he's not here. A death in the family. He won't be back until the end of next week."

Gail thanked the clerk, and being right there, stopped in at the library where she spent the afternoon poring over old issues of all of the area newspapers. She went back to the time when she knew Jerry Frankel had first come to the Holman Academy, and worked forward, searching for anything that might give her a clue, suggest someplace else to look, or even, for that matter, give her a hint about what it was she was looking for. There was nothing.

Finally she went to the police station.

"I'm looking into some allegations that were made about a teacher named Jeremy Frankel," she told the officer in charge, a short man with thinning dark hair and a shaggy mustache. "Do you know anything that might help me?"

"No, ma'am," Detective Derek McNally replied without the slightest hesitation. "I can't say as I do."

"Look," Gail said wearily. "I'm not after dirt, and I wouldn't be here if it weren't important. To be honest with you, I'm hoping I'm wrong, that there's absolutely nothing to the allegations. But I have to find out."

"I don't know what I can tell you," he said.

"Did you know Frankel?" she asked.

He shook his head. "No, I didn't. But that's not so unusual. A lot of the teachers around here don't live in Scarsdale, so I'd have no reason to know them."

"My understanding is that Frankel *did* live here."

McNally shrugged. "I still didn't know him."

"Do you know if there was anything that he might have been involved in anytime during his last year? Anything criminal?"

"I believe I spoke to someone in your police department about this guy just a few weeks ago," McNally told her. "A Detective Earley, I think her name was."

"Ginger Earley is a good cop," Gail said. "She's very smart and very thorough. But she doesn't know what I know. And before I tell her what I know, I want to find out if I really know anything at all."

Detective McNally considered the skinny woman with the frustrated expression behind her eyeglasses.

"There have never been any charges brought against your Mr. Frankel," he said. "Not even for jaywalking."

"All right, so there were no charges brought," Gail conceded shrewdly. "But were there any allegations made? Was there any investigation?"

"We have no record of any investigation."

Gail nodded. It had been a long day, and she had spent it running into a series of dead ends. "Well, thanks for talking to me," she told McNally. "I just needed to know, one way or the other. I'm really glad it's turned out this way, because he's an excellent teacher."

"Extraordinary," the detective conceded.

She made her way out of the building and climbed into her rental car. Ginger and Ruben were going to have to solve the Breckenridge case without her help, she decided as she started up the engine. She certainly wasn't going to waste any more time trying to find something that wasn't there. The letter had obviously been a prank. She pulled out into the traffic of Fenimore Road and headed back toward the inn. She had skipped lunch; she would have an early dinner. Then she would see if she could get a seat on tomorrow morning's plane back to Seattle.

Detective Derek McNally stood just inside the doorway of the police station, and watched until she was gone.

Sally brought her salad.

"Did you take care of your business?" she asked.

"I guess so," Gail replied.

"That Holman Academy sure is a pretty place, isn't it?"

"Yes, it is." Gail looked up. "How did you know I was there?"

"I don't know," Sally said with a shrug. "Guess you said something about it at breakfast."

Gail took a bite of her salad and tried to recall the conversation.

"I don't remember mentioning where I was going this morning," she said as Sally returned with her pasta.

The waitress shrugged. "Then maybe I heard it from my husband," she said as she walked away. "He runs the inn."

The pasta was tasty. When she could eat no more, Gail paid the bill and left the restaurant. An icy rain had begun to fall and the walk was slick as she hurried toward the inn. She hoped the weather would clear by tomorrow; she didn't much fancy driving all the way back to Kennedy Airport in the same miserable weather she had driven through to get here.

She did not regret having come. She meant what she had said to Derek McNally; either way, her mission was going to be a success, and truth to tell, she was a lot happier to learn that the anonymous letter was a prank than she would have been to discover that the history teacher was a two-headed monster.

Returning to her room, she called the airline and made a reservation for tomorrow's flight back to Seattle. Then she tuned the television to CNN, and relaxed against the bed pillows to watch the news. Jerry Frankel drifted out of her mind. In ten minutes, she was sound asleep.

It was a little past nine o'clock on the other side of the country. A fire crackled contentedly in the small stone hearth in Ruben's living room. Ruben and Ginger had pulled the cushions off the sofa and now lay propped against them, sipping Kahlúa, as a winter wind whirled and whined around the little house.

"It's all arranged," Ruben said on Thursday. "Danny Leo is going to take Stacey to a movie on Saturday night."

"Where will you do it?" Ginger asked.

"My place," he replied. "We can have everything set up by seven o'clock. He'll be through in about an hour and a half, and that'll still give them plenty of time to catch the nine o'clock show."

"I hope it goes all right," she said. "I'd hate to see Stacey caught in the middle."

Ruben nodded. "So would I," he said uneasily.

Stacey had come to him immediately after she talked to Danny.

"His father doesn't have to know, does he?" she asked. "I mean, before the fact?"

Ruben had to think about that. "The boy is eighteen. If he

comes in voluntarily, it's not our responsibility to determine whether he should have had his father's consent."

"Good," she said, "because I don't think he had anything to do with killing Tara."

"You may be right," Ruben told her, "but I have to warn you: if the test doesn't go his way, we *will* have to notify his parents. And you won't be going to any movie with him."

"But if it does go his way? If he does pass the test?"

Ruben shrugged. "Then it's up to him whether he tells his father or not. And you can tell me all about the movie on Sunday morning."

The polygraph had taken exactly an hour and seventeen minutes. Danny answered every question that was put to him about the death of Tara Breckenridge without a blink.

"Were you having an affair with Tara Breckenridge?"

"No."

"Were you the father of her unborn child?"

"No."

"Did you kill Tara Breckenridge?"

"No."

"What's the verdict?" Ruben asked when it was over.

"There are always ways to beat the test," the examiner qualified his answer. "It's never an absolute. But as far as I can determine, the boy answered truthfully."

Now the teenagers and the machine and the technician were gone, and Ruben and Ginger were alone.

"I guess that knocks Danny off the list," she said.

From the beginning, Ruben had been troubled by the whole idea, especially because the Leo boy had involved Stacey in his plan. As a result, he watched the senior like a hawk, looking for the slightest indication that something was amiss. But the teenager had appeared comfortable throughout the entire procedure, following instructions, taking his time and answering clearly.

"So it would seem," Ruben said cautiously. "But let's run his blood sample anyway."

"Okay," Ginger agreed with a smile. Her boss was a real stickler for detail. They settled down in front of the fire, the unasked question still hanging between them—now what?

"I'd keep after the teacher if I thought there was any more to get," she said. "But I've listened to his statement backward and forward, and I can't find a flaw. I've gone over the notes of my other conversations with him at least a dozen times, and I can't find a single inconsistency. I think he's given us everything he's got, and without a new lead, I'd just be stabbing in the dark." Then she realized what she had said. "Forgive my abominably poor choice of words," she added hastily.

"I think you're right about Frankel," Ruben told her. "We all want to close this case. Me, especially, since it now seems to have put my job on the line. But railroading someone just to stay employed doesn't sit too well with me. The guy looks as clean as snow. So, unless something else surfaces to implicate him, he's off the list, too."

Gail awoke with a sense of urgency, stiff from being cramped in a half-upright position. The lamp beside the bed was still lit; the television was still on. She glanced at her watch. It was after midnight, which meant she had been asleep for more than five hours.

She twisted her neck around to ease the tension, and tried to remember what it was that had jolted her into wakefulness. Was it just a dream, or had something been trying to push its way to the surface? Her mind was blank. She closed her eyes and tried to reconstruct the dream. A montage of the day's events floated into her mind, all out of context: a policeman, a school secretary, a waitress, a newspaper clerk, a custodian in coveralls.

Gail sat up, now positive: there was something about today she had missed. But what was it? She went back over everything—a secretary who was reluctant to talk about a former teacher; an overcourteous policeman who claimed he knew nothing about Jerry Frankel; a chatty waitress who knew she had gone to the Holman Academy; a redheaded clerk who said the newspaper didn't report on the academy; a custodian in coveralls who had stared at her.

Gail jumped off the bed and started to pace around the small room. What was it McNally had said? Not that there had been no investigation of Jerry Frankel—only that there was no *record* of an investigation. And Mrs. Quinlan had said that Frankel resigned, but even when pressed, wouldn't say why, when the record should have listed his wife's transfer as the reason.

The blood began to pound in her temples. It had been right in front of her, and she had missed it. Was she ever rusty! Gail Brown the reporter would have seen it instantly. The newspaper clerk's words echoed in her head: "It's a private institution, and they go to great lengths . . . to protect their students."

She couldn't understand how she could have been so blind. The anonymous letter was no prank. It had sent her in the right direction. The runaround she had gotten was nothing less than the first layer of a major cover-up. And the reason she had missed it was obvious—it wasn't Jerry Frankel these people were shielding.

Her brain was reengaged now, the wheels clicking. It wasn't the teacher and it wasn't the school. Oh, the school would protect itself in any way it could, but she sensed the town as a whole would feel no great obligation to assist in such an effort. Not unless someone was involved whom the town *would* choose to shield, someone prominent or, perhaps, she thought with a shiver, the *daughter* of someone prominent.

Gail called the airline again, this time to cancel her return flight. Then she sat down and began to make a plan.

11

The icy night rain became a fine drizzle by morning. Gail returned to the Holman Academy shortly after eleven o'clock. As before, the iron gates stood open, allowing her to drive right through. And as she had hoped, the Oldsmobile was gone; only the pickup was parked in the gravel lot. Gail pulled up beside it. There was no telling where she would find him; he could be anywhere on the estate.

She climbed out of her car and made her way to the service door that faced the parking lot, relieved to find it unlocked. Pushing it open, she went inside.

It took her twenty minutes to find him, or to be more precise, for him to find her. She was wandering aimlessly down corridors, peering into every room, when a voice behind her said, "You ain't supposed to be here. There ain't no school today."

She whirled around and there he was, in the same blue coveralls, with his name above his pocket.

"Ezekiel, isn't it?" she asked with a smile. "My name is Gail. I was here yesterday, talking with Mrs. Quinlan. Do you remember me?"

Ezekiel squinted at her for a moment and then nodded. "I remember. You talked about the teacher."

Gail's heart bounced. "Yes, I did," she said. "Do you remember the teacher?"

"Sure do," Ezekiel said with a smile. It was a sweet, child-like smile, trusting and toothless. "He was a right fine teacher. Sometimes, he let me come in his classroom after school was done, and he tell me about all sorts of things that happen long before I was even born. I sure did like listenin' to him talk."

"Do you know why he left the school, Ezekiel?"

The man's expression darkened. "It was her fault," he replied. "She said awful things, and the police came."

"The Scarsdale police?" Gail asked.

"Uh-huh. They had nice uniforms."

"What happened then?"

"The headmaster sent them away and told me I shouldn't think about it. But the teacher was all upset and he forgot about lettin' me come in his classroom, so how was I supposed to do what the headmaster told me and not think about it?"

"I don't know, Ezekiel," Gail replied. "But tell me: after the girl said the awful things, and the headmaster sent the police away, what happened next?"

"The teacher went away."

"Right afterward?" Gail pressed. "Did the teacher leave the school right after that?"

"Pretty soon right after," Ezekiel told her. "I know it was after the holidays, 'cause that's when the headmaster told me the teacher was gone and wasn't never comin' back."

Gail held her breath. "Do you know who the girl was?" she asked.

"I miss him," the janitor said wistfully. "Nobody talks to me like the teacher did."

"Ezekiel," Gail repeated, "do you know who the girl was?"

He nodded. "She was a nice girl," he said.

"What happened to her? Do you know what happened to her?"

The janitor shrugged. "Nothin' happen to her, I guess."

Gail stared at him. "What do you mean, nothing? Is she all right? Is she still here?"

"Uh-huh," he said. "I see her all the time. She's a nice girl. All the girls here are nice. Some of them like to tease me." He started to fidget. "But I'm not supposed to talk about her. The headmaster said so."

"That's all right, Ezekiel, you don't have to talk about her," Gail assured him. "You've told me enough. Now just tell me how to get out of this place."

He walked her to the front door and opened it for her. "You don't come from here," he said.

"No, I don't," Gail told him. "I come from all the way across the country."

"Then how do you know about Alice?"

Gail looked at him. "Is that her name?" she asked, holding her breath. "Is that the girl's name—Alice?"

"Alice is a nice name," Ezekiel said as he closed the door.

Gail went back to Fenimore Road and the police station.

"I think you lied to me, Detective McNally," she said. "To begin with, you said you'd never met Jerry Frankel, and didn't know him—yet you referred to him as an extraordinary teacher."

"I thought you were asking me for personal knowledge," the police officer replied smoothly. "I'd heard of his reputation."

"Really? One teacher in a school supposedly filled with outstanding teachers? How did you hear of his reputation? He taught at a school that makes a particular point of staying out of the public eye. How would anything about him have come to your attention?"

"It happens."

"You also led me to believe there was no investigation involving him. That wasn't true, either, was it?"

McNally sighed. "Look, Ms. Brown, I didn't really have to talk to you at all. I was only trying to be polite."

"Then all you had to do was tell me you were not at liberty to discuss the case," Gail retorted.

"And that would have made you go away?"

"Look, McNally, I'm not the enemy. And I didn't come here to take the cure. I came here because two months ago, we had a homicide in my hometown—the first ever. It was the brutal murder of a fifteen-year-old girl, and so far our police department, which is very good indeed, hasn't been able to come up with the killer. Then I get an anonymous tip about a new teacher in the community that directs me right to the Holman Academy. Now, if you were me, what would you have done?"

McNally sighed. "All right, there was an allegation made. We did go up to the school to look into it. The teacher denied it, the headmaster told us it was a private matter, and we went away. No investigation. End of story."

"Can you tell me what the alleged incident involved?"

"It involved a male teacher and a female student."

"Was the teacher Jerry Frankel?"

The detective nodded reluctantly.

"All right, McNally," Gail said carefully. "Jerry Frankel is long gone, which leaves you with no reason to cover for him. So who is it that you've gone to such lengths to protect? By any chance, would her name be Alice?"

The detective looked her straight in the eye. "You got what you came for, Ms. Brown. This conversation is over. It was real nice meeting you, and I hope you have a safe journey home."

An hour later, Gail sat in the restaurant, over an uneaten ham sandwich and a cooling cup of coffee, and put the pieces together.

Obviously, the allegation made against Jerry Frankel by one of his students had been serious enough to cause the police to go out to the academy. And just as obviously, the entire town, while probably willing to give Frankel up without a great deal of concern, was prepared to go to the wall for the student. Which told Gail that she had to be the daughter of someone who had a lot of clout.

The eerie similarity between this Alice and Tara Breckenridge sent a chill through her. Yet Ezekiel had told her that Alice was still a student at the Holman Academy, which meant that whatever had happened between the two in Scarsdale had not resulted in the extreme level of criminal behavior that had occurred on Seward Island.

Gail pondered her options. She now knew that Jerry Frankel had been involved with a female student, but she didn't yet know the nature of that involvement. Had she fulfilled her mission anyway? Could she leave Scarsdale without discovering what that allegation was, and whether there was any merit to it?

While the media in general did not enjoy a reputation for being particularly fair-minded, Gail tried to be. She had always done her best to report both sides of a story, and to give both sides equal weight, distasteful though that often was. Could she now go home and make an accusation without corroboration?

"Coffee need freshening?" Sally asked. "The ham not to your liking?"

Gail looked up. "Thanks," she said. "I guess I could use some hot coffee. But the ham's fine. I just got a little lost in my thoughts."

"Stirring up quite a hornet's nest around here, aren't you?" the waitress observed, exchanging the cold coffee for a freshly brewed cup.

"Am I?" Gail said, her eyes narrowing slightly behind her thick glasses. "I didn't realize."

"The teacher's gone. The rest is best left alone."

"I didn't tell you I was going to the Holman Academy, did I?"

"Does it matter?" Sally replied with a careless shrug.

Gail took a gamble. "I guess Alice is a pretty special girl," she said.

"Which Alice is that?" Sally inquired blandly.

"The one who was involved with the teacher."

The waitress shrugged again. "Well, I wouldn't know about that," she replied.

"Sure," Gail said. "I just assumed. You know, all the trouble they went to, to hush the whole thing up."

Sally let out a short laugh. "You mean, *tried* to hush it up," she said without thinking.

Gail allowed herself a canny grin. "That's what I figured. I was born and raised in a small town myself."

"Yeah, well, then I guess you understand."

"Yes, of course. Someone as special as Alice must be protected at all costs."

"I suppose," Sally said.

"You weren't in favor of the cover-up?" Gail inquired.

The waitress snorted. "I wasn't exactly asked for my opinion," she replied. "But seeing as you managed to find out about it all on your own, let me tell you, those girls up at that academy aren't anything more than a bunch of spoiled rich bitches. None of them will ever have to work a day in their lives—can you imagine that? But does that make them any more special than anyone else? Not in my book. Far as I'm concerned, they deserve whatever trouble they get into."

"Even Alice?"

"Why not? Her daddy's got more money than God, and goes around thinking he's so much better than the rest of us just because he's some hotshot doctor who supports worthwhile causes. I see her, she comes in here sometimes with her friends, acting as if working folk like me are nothing more than dirt on the floor. You can take my word for it, she's no better than any of them."

The gamble had paid off. Gail took a sip of her fresh coffee and a big bite of her ham sandwich, and smiled benignly at Sally. Once again, her stay in Scarsdale was going to be extended.

"I'm not a suspect in the Breckenridge murder anymore," Danny Leo told his parents after church on Sunday.

"What do you mean?" Peter asked. "Have they found the killer? I didn't hear anything about it." He looked at his wife.

Rose shook her head. "I didn't hear anything about it, either."

"I don't know who they've found or not found," Danny said. "I just know they're not interested in me anymore."

"How do you know that?"

"Detective Earley told me so."

Peter frowned. "She made a point of seeking you out to tell you this?"

"Yes sir."

"How come?"

Danny shrugged. "I guess I must have convinced them."

"How did you do that, son?"

"Well, if you must know," Danny said, "I took their poly-graph test."

Peter glared at the boy. "I'll sue the uniforms off those bas-tards," he roared, furious. "They had no right to come after you behind my back!"

"They didn't come after me," Danny corrected him. "I went to them. I wanted to take the test. I wanted to put an end to all this."

"But I told you this was a matter of principle."

"You were making too big a deal out of it. Fighting the court order! Even my friends were starting to look at me funny, like maybe my own father believed I might be guilty or something."

"Your friends must not be worth very much if they can't understand the importance of standing up for a principle."

"The hell with your principles, Dad. Mr. Huxley's the only principal I care about right now, and he told me, flat out, because of what you were doing, I was about to lose my scholarship to Harvard. Is that what you wanted?"

For a moment, Peter looked as though he might strike the boy. Then, in the next moment, he shrugged his shoulders and chuckled.

"Passed the polygraph, huh?"

Danny grinned. "I didn't just pass it," he said. "I aced it."

It took four hours at the library and an hour and a half with the local telephone directory for Gail to come up with Dr. Stuart Easton, his wife, Denise, and their seventeen-year-old daughter, Alice.

The Eastons lived in a six-bedroom Tudor-style home that was rumored to have belonged to a notorious gangster in the 1930s. Dr. Easton was the chief of surgery at a prominent local hospital—an entire wing of which bore his name—and every mention of him included a long list of his medical accomplishments, and a tribute to his many years of community philanthropy.

Gail turned her rental in to the circular drive at ten minutes past eight on Monday morning. A maid answered the door and ushered her down a thickly carpeted corridor to a small parlor where Stuart Easton was waiting. He was about fifty, of little more than average height, slender and dark, with a presence about him that reminded Gail of a stalking panther.

"I have to tell you that I resent your being here, Ms. Brown," he said as soon as the introductions were out of the way. "We're a very private family, and we do not intend to air our dirty linen in public. I've agreed to talk to you as a favor to Derek McNally, but only on the understanding that our entire conversation will be strictly off the record. I warn you—take one step over the line, and this meeting will be over."

"Dr. Easton, I appreciate your seeing me on such short notice, and please understand that I am not here with any intention of embarrassing you or any member of your family," Gail assured him. "As I believe Detective McNally explained, because of a situation in my hometown, I just need to clarify a few things for background only."

He sat down in a leather chair and gestured her to a nearby sofa. "What is it you want to know?" he asked.

She told him about the murder of Tara Breckenridge, and the string of small coincidences that appeared to connect Jerry Frankel to that crime, and then she told him, in general terms, about the contents of the letter.

"Now I don't normally give much credence to anonymous tips," she said. "But under the circumstances, I felt I had to follow up on this one. All I need to know is what the allegation against the teacher was about, and whether there was any real merit to it."

"My daughter was in his junior history class," Easton said. "She was having difficulty with some of the work, and he invited her to come in after school for extra help. He took the opportunity of those private sessions to sexually molest her."

"How did you find out about it?"

"Alice told us. But apparently not until it had been going on for several months."

"What did you do after she told you?"

"What do you mean—what did I do?" he snapped. "I notified the police, of course."

"Did you have Alice examined by a doctor?"

"Ms. Brown," he said irritably, "*I'm* a doctor."

"Please don't misunderstand me, Dr. Easton," Gail said hastily. "I'm simply looking for corroboration."

"Are we still off the record?" he asked warily.

"Of course."

"All right, yes, I had her examined by a doctor."

"And?"

"She was pregnant, of course."

"Were DNA tests done? Was it determined that Jerry Frankel was the father?"

"The teacher was unwilling to submit to any such tests."

"You could have compelled him."

"That would have meant a court battle, and a lot of hurtful publicity," he said with a sigh. "At the very least, my daughter's reputation would have been destroyed. And for what, really? Alice is a very fragile, very vulnerable girl, Ms. Brown. I felt she had been through enough. My first priority was to make sure there would be no baby. After that, I wasn't interested in dragging her name through the mud."

"Detective McNally told me that Frankel denied having had a sexual relationship with your daughter."

"Does that surprise you?"

"No. But without the tests, or a thorough police investigation, it does raise a rather significant he said/she said issue. Frankel has the reputation of being a very dedicated, very caring teacher. Is it possible that Alice could have been, let's say, less than candid with you about her situation?"

"I'm not in the habit of doubting my daughter's word," Easton stated flatly. "If she said he did it, then he did it."

"You mean, she told you Jerry Frankel was responsible, and that was all?"

"In essence, yes."

"Did Alice say she was a willing participant in this alleged affair between the two of them?"

"It doesn't matter whether she was willing or not," he said. "She was sixteen years old at the time—his student. He was in a position of authority—her teacher. She looked up to him. He took advantage of her."

"Can you tell me, Doctor, had your daughter been, well, sexually active prior to the alleged involvement with Jerry Frankel?"

Easton was clearly uncomfortable. "Look, I'm a very busy man. Maybe I'm not at home as much as I should be. Maybe I'm not as close to my daughter as I could be. But I do the best I can. If she was sexually active, I didn't know about it."

"I appreciate how difficult this is for you," Gail said, although, in reality, she found herself feeling very little compassion for the man. "I know, if she were my daughter, I would be every bit as outraged as you are. I hate putting you through this, and believe me, I wouldn't, if it weren't so important."

"I understand," he conceded.

"I only have a few more questions."

"Go ahead."

"What exactly did Alice tell the police?"

The surgeon blinked. "She didn't tell them anything," he replied. "I wouldn't permit it. She told her mother and me what happened, and *we* told the police."

"And based on that, on just what your daughter told you had taken place, Frankel was—what? Forced to resign his position at the Holman Academy?"

"Certainly," Easton declared. "You don't think I would have permitted Alice to stay at the school if he were still teaching there, do you?"

"I see."

"And let me assure you, dedicated teacher or not, a lot of other parents were behind us on this."

"You've told me that there were no DNA tests performed, and Detective McNally told me the police investigation was cut short by the headmaster at Holman. So there was never an objective determination of the facts—just Alice's charge?"

"I'm not sure I appreciate your implication, Ms. Brown."

"Dr. Easton, a man's life is at stake here. If Jerry Frankel molested your daughter and murdered the girl on Seward Island, I want him to pay for it. If he didn't, I don't want to implicate him with innuendo. All we seem to have here is an uncorroborated allegation told to you by your daughter and subsequently related through you to the police." Gail paused. "I don't suppose you'd be willing to let me talk to Alice, would you?"

"Absolutely not."

Gail nodded. You win some, you lose some, she thought as she gathered herself together and stood up. In many ways, she was leaving with more questions than answers.

"Thank you for seeing me."

A moment later, she was back in her car, starting the engine and preparing to swing out of the driveway. She wasn't sure what made her glance toward the house at the last moment; perhaps a sudden movement had caught her eye, perhaps it was just a feeling. A girl with blond hair stood in an upstairs window. It might have been a trick of light, or simply her imagination, but it looked to Gail as though the girl were crying.

He awoke in a panic, his eyes flying open, sockets dry. He was gasping for breath, his heart pounding, sweat pouring from his body. It was the nightmare again, now coming with relentless regularity. Only this time, there was something new—his skull felt as though it were being crushed in a vise. He had never had a headache before, never understood the agony. He wondered if he would have them from now on.

It was the third time this week that his sleep had been interrupted, that he had been jolted out of oblivion. The same faceless eyes stared up at him, indicting him; the same wretched scream split the darkness, denouncing him. Like a snippet of movie newsreel that willfully replayed a piece of history the way it actually happened, rather than the way one might wish to remember it, his nightmare was a moment frozen in eternity that would neither soften, nor blur, nor twist itself around to fit his fancy.

When he was conscious, it was easy to convince himself that *she* was the villain, not he. That, at the very worst, he had acted in self-defense, protecting himself from ruination or worse. It was exasperating that the dream continued to rob him of his rest.

He staggered out of bed and into the bathroom, where he fumbled for the bottle of headache medicine he knew was there, downing three of the tablets with a glass of water. Then he put his head under the faucet and let the cold water run over his hot neck.

When he started to shiver, he dried himself off and crept back between the sheets. The clock on the nightstand told him it was twelve-thirty-five, little more than an hour since he had gone to bed. It was early for the nightmare to have come. He settled down under the covers and began to massage his temples with his fingers. After a while, the pain in his head began to ease, and he went back to sleep.

12

Gail fought a battle with herself all the way back to Seattle. But in the end, she went to Ginger with what she had learned.

"There's not really anything I can ethically use," she conceded, "just a bunch of possibles. But there may be enough for you to move on."

"You couldn't get to the girl?" Ginger asked.

Gail shook her head. "I tried. Her father refused to let me see her. He even admitted that the police had never talked to her. I went back to the school, but the headmaster wouldn't see me. He sent his secretary out to say that under no circumstances would they discuss Alice Easton with me, and that whatever measures they had taken to resolve a specific matter had been taken in the best interests of the school."

"I can't help but say that I wish you'd come to me first," Ginger told her. "I very likely would have gone with you."

Gail shrugged. "Once a journalist, always a journalist, I guess."

"The son of a bitch!" Ginger cried the moment Gail was gone. "He really played me like a violin."

"He's obviously smoother than we gave him credit for," Ruben said.

"Sure, but where were all my finely honed instincts—my professional intuition?"

"Don't be so hard on yourself. He's apparently fooled a lot of people, hasn't he?"

"But I'm a trained police officer," she argued. "I'm supposed to see through all that. He seemed so open, so sincere. Now, of course, I realize he was just prepared. He'd been down the road before."

"Well, not exactly," Ruben suggested. "Alice Easton is still alive."

"A dress rehearsal," Ginger said. She didn't know which was worse—that Frankel was in fact a child-molesting murderer, or that he had manipulated her so easily. She felt so stupid, so betrayed.

"Well, at least now we know," Ruben said.

"Yes." Ginger nodded. "And now that we do, I think it's time to tighten the screws on our dear teacher. I'm going to squeeze him until there's not a lying breath left in his body."

A born cop, Ruben thought.

"Some additional information has come to our attention, Mr. Frankel," Ginger said over the telephone. "I wonder if you'd be kind enough to come in and discuss it with us—perhaps tomorrow afternoon, after school?"

"What is it now, Detective Earley?" he asked with an unmistakable edge to his voice.

"We'd like to talk to you about the Holman Academy."

There was an audible intake of breath at the other end of the line. "How did you find out about that?" he demanded.

"Does it matter?" she responded smoothly.

There was a momentary silence and then a clearly audible sigh. "I'll get back to you," he said and hung up.

❄   ❄   ❄

At four-twenty-five the following afternoon, the history teacher walked into Graham Hall, unaccompanied.

"I think you should have your attorney with you," Ginger cautioned.

"He'll be here at five," Jerry told her. "But I came early so I could talk to you first."

She escorted him to the interview room, where he took the same seat that he had occupied on his previous visit. The tape recorder was already in place on top of the table, along with a folder containing a transcript of the teacher's prior statement, and a tray with a pitcher of water and several glasses.

"You are currently being represented by counsel," Ginger said, sitting down across from him. "Which means that you can't waive your rights except in his presence. So we'll wait until he gets here. It's for your own protection." She was not about to play any more games with this man; she wanted every word he said to be admissible in court.

Jerry looked at her with a half smile. "Do I need protecting, Detective Earley?"

"I don't know, Mr. Frankel," she said. "But that's the way it works."

"I didn't kill that poor girl," he said.

"Please don't say anything more."

"I didn't kill her," he insisted. "And you've got it all wrong about the Holman Academy."

"Mr. Frankel," she responded calmly, "as an officer of the court, I can't allow you to continue."

"But I'm trying to tell you," he said. "I didn't—"

"Mr. Frankel, please," she interrupted him. "Unless you agree to say nothing more until you are in the presence of your attorney, I'll have to leave the room."

He shook his head. "This had nothing to do with the Breck-enridge case," he said. "It's a totally different matter, and I don't understand why I can't talk about it without my attorney."

Ginger stood up. "I'll wait outside," she told him.

"No, that's all right," he said wearily. "You don't have to go. I won't say anything more. I promise. Please stay."

She retook her seat, and the two of them waited in silence, the teacher fidgeting in obvious discomfort, the detective calmly observing every move he made.

"Can we at least talk about the weather?" he asked after a moment. "I understand it's very mild for December."

"It really would be better if we didn't talk at all," she said.

He sighed heavily and began to look around; blank gray walls stared back at him. After a few moments, he reached for a glass from the tray on the table, poured water into it from the pitcher and drank. When the glass was empty, he returned it to the tray. Ginger sat and watched.

At three minutes past five, Scott Cohen entered the room and sat down next to his client. "All right," he said. "Where are we, and what are we doing here?"

"We are here to discuss some new information regarding an incident at your client's previous place of employment," Ginger said. "Mr. Frankel arrived here half an hour ago, wanting to talk about the matter, but I advised him that he could not do so until he was in your presence."

"As I understand it, you're referring to an alleged incident that is not connected to the Breckenridge case, is that correct?" Scott inquired.

"That's correct."

"Then I see no relevance here."

"Wait a minute," Jerry put in. "I want to talk about it. I want to get this whole thing cleared up once and for all."

"I'd like a moment with my client," Scott said.

Ginger stood up immediately and left the room.

"Jerry," Scott urged. "I don't think this is the time for—"

"I don't care," the teacher said. "This investigation of theirs has turned my whole life upside down, and I want it to stop. Now, I'm going to tell them whatever it is they want to know."

"I'm advising against this."

"They just have the wrong idea about something," Jerry told him. "It has nothing to do with the Breckenridge case."

"Listen to me, and listen very carefully," the lawyer instructed. "Anything you say to them, anything at all, has to do with the Breckenridge case. They're after a killer, and they'll do whatever they have to do to find one. They're looking for a motive, for a pattern of behavior, for whatever they need to make an arrest. The situation at your previous school, as you've described it to me, may just give them all three."

Jerry blinked. "But they already know the other side of the story," he said. "I just want to tell them my side so they have it straight."

Scott sighed. "All right," he said. "But I won't allow you to go on record."

He got up and went to the door. When Ginger returned, Ruben was with her.

"This will be a conversation only," Scott said. "No tape recording, no stenographer. Nothing said here will be on record. Is that understood?"

The two police officers exchanged glances and then Ginger pushed the recorder aside and leaned back in her chair. "Tell us what happened at the Holman Academy."

"As I'm sure you already know, her name was Alice Easton and she was a student there," Jerry Frankel began. "She was the only child of some important doctor and his socialite wife, neither of whom apparently had much time for her. She was a very unhappy girl. She used to tell me she couldn't understand why they'd ever bothered to have a child because she was raised mostly by housekeepers. By the time I met her, she was fourteen years old and so starved for affection, she didn't particularly care where she found it. And I was—there. Alice wasn't the first student to have a crush on me; it goes with the territory. But she was the first who carried her fantasy too far."

"Fantasy?"

"Yes," he said. "That's all it was—a fantasy. She had problems with history right from the beginning of her freshman year, but it wasn't until her junior year that she took to stopping by after school for help. I've always encouraged my students to do that. We don't all learn at the same pace, you know, and sometimes, when we teach at one level, we can lose kids who are at different levels. Alice Easton was an average student, not particularly motivated. She started showing up for help immediately after the fall term began, coming in maybe once or twice a week. By the end of October, she was coming in every day."

"Didn't that strike you as unusual?"

"Of course it did. She had never shown much interest in history before. But I didn't turn her off. I thought of it as at least a safe place for her to hang out, because it was clear very early on that she had nowhere else to go."

"Was she the only student you tutored?"

"No. But if other kids were there ahead of her, she wouldn't join in; she'd sit in the back of the room and wait until they were done. If kids came in after her, she would step aside and insist that I help them first." He sighed. "In the beginning, we talked strictly about history, and her grades even started to improve a little. But after a while, she started to tell me about herself, about her life, and sometimes she would ask me questions about my life and my family—which, by the way, I answered only in the most general of terms. I felt sorry for her. She didn't seem to have many friends, and she apparently wasn't very popular with the boys. She seemed to me to be quite lonely, and I thought it was very sad. She had money and position and advantages that many people would envy, and yet she was depressed and unhappy. So I let her talk. It didn't seem like such a big thing. You know, it's not uncommon for teachers to counsel a student about something peripheral to schoolwork. I thought I was in control of it. A lonely student—a caring teacher, I thought that's all it was."

"But it wasn't?" Ginger prompted.

"One day at the end of November, she came into my classroom quite late," he said. "I was just about to leave. She said she had waited outside on purpose, to make sure no one else would be coming, because we were going to need total privacy. I asked her what she was talking about, and she said she was talking about making love, of course. That she had decided she was ready."

"She came on to you?"

"Came on to me?" Jerry echoed. "She stood there in the middle of my classroom, Detective Earley, and took off all her clothes. Right there, at school, when anybody could have walked in. They prepare you for a lot of things when you're learning to be a teacher, but let me tell you, they don't prepare you to deal with that. I was scared. I tried to be kind, but I guess I wasn't as—diplomatic as I might have been. I'm not proud of myself, but I ended up walking right out of the room and leaving her there, naked. The next thing I knew, I was being accused of child molestation, indecent behavior, statutory rape, consorting with a minor—you name it, her father cried it."

"And none of what she claimed was true?" Ginger asked.

"None of it," Jerry said firmly. "Did I cross the teacher-student line with her? I don't know. Sometimes that line gets a little fuzzy for me when I have an especially needy kid in my class. Did I hug her, did I praise her, did I try to instill in her some measure of self-worth? Yes, I admit to that. But I never did any of the other things they said I did."

"So, you're saying that your attempts to help Alice Easton in your capacity as her history teacher were totally misinterpreted by her?"

"Yes," Jerry declared.

"And it was pure fantasy on her part that the two of you were romantically involved?"

"Yes."

"And that, when you rebuffed her that day in your classroom, she retaliated by accusing you of being the father of her unborn child?"

"Yes," Jerry affirmed. "Now, my attorney tells me I was wrong to tell you all this. He tells me you'll try to use it to build a case against me in the Breckenridge matter. So I want to say that it was my intention to stay at the Holman Academy and fight the accusations, because I know I would have won. But when it became clear that my effectiveness as an educator had been compromised, there was no point. Kids, it turns out, are the harshest judges of all."

Ginger looked him in the eye. "You were not the father of Alice Easton's unborn child?"

Jerry looked right back at her. "No, I was not."

"Did you decline to submit to DNA testing?"

"No. The police never really asked. The officer who interviewed me at school mentioned it in passing as an option if I wanted to exonerate myself. I told him there was absolutely no foundation to the charge, and unless one could be established, I didn't feel I was under any obligation at that point to jeopardize my career."

"Pretty much the same thing you told us, isn't it?"

"And for just about the same reason."

"An interesting coincidence, though, wouldn't you say?"

"They do occur," the teacher replied. "However, the Scarsdale police chose not to pursue an investigation, so DNA testing became a nonissue."

Ruben leaned forward and rested his arms on the table. "I've been a policeman for more than twenty-five years, Mr. Frankel," he said. "Maybe my work has made a cynic out of me, but I don't happen to believe in coincidence. I sit here and I see a man who fits our profile of Tara Breckenridge's killer to a T, who admits to what many would consider an unorthodox pattern of behavior with his students, and who was associated with two pregnant teenage girls—one of whom implicated you in her pregnancy and one of whom ended up dead. Now, that adds up to a whole passel of coincidences. From where I'm sitting, it's starting to look like Alice Easton was responsible for you losing your last job—and maybe you weren't about to let Tara Breckenridge lose you this one."

"Are you prepared to charge my client with anything at this time?" Scott asked abruptly.

"No," Ruben conceded.

"Then this interview is over."

The attorney stood up, took his client by the elbow, and steered him out of the room.

"A pretty cool customer," Ruben observed.

"Which one?" Ginger asked. "The teacher or the lawyer?"

Ruben chuckled. "Take your choice."

"The bastard did it," she said. "It's so obvious to me now, I can't believe I didn't see it before."

"It's happening all over again," Jerry cried as he stumbled toward the parking lot where he had left his car. He had put on a brave show in the interview room, but now he was shaking like jelly.

"It's still a fishing expedition," Scott told him. "They've got nothing more than they had before. So just keep your cool."

"It's all over school, you know. I see it in the way the kids look at me in class. Without their trust and respect, I'm useless to them. Hell, it's not just in school, it's all over the whole damn island. Even Matthew's friends have started asking him about it. Why am I standing on principle? Maybe I should take their damn polygraph and let them test my blood. I don't see how things could be much worse."

Scott shrugged. "That's always an option."

"One you recommend?"

"Right now, I think you're still coming from a position of strength," the lawyer said, weighing his words. "You've denied any involvement in the murder, and while they may have suspicions, they haven't a shred of evidence to the contrary. The Alice Easton matter is most unfortunate, a very awkward parallel indeed, but the argument could be made that it has no real bearing on this case. My advice would be: don't give anything away unless you have to. The winter break starts on Friday. Get some rest. Maybe things will look better after the New Year."

Ginger waited until she was sure the teacher and his attorney were gone and then, very carefully, retrieved the drinking glass that Jerry Frankel had used.

"From what I hear, Scott Cohen is a top-notch lawyer," Ruben said, nodding at the glass. "I'm surprised he let you get away with that."

"He wasn't here," Ginger told him. "I'll get Charlie to take it over to the lab. The teacher thinks we have no proof; he thinks he's going to get away with it. Well, we'll just see about that. If the prints on this glass match the partial on Tara Breckenridge's cross, we've got him!"

"That's twice now that Jerry's been down at the police station," Libby Hildress told her husband that night, her blue eyes troubled. "I saw him myself, this time, around six o'clock. He and Scott were just coming out of Graham Hall, and both of them looked pretty upset."

"Maybe we should call the Frankels, and see if there's anything we can do to help," Tom suggested.

"I don't know," Libby said. "I'm beginning to get bad feelings about this. With everything that's going on, maybe it isn't such a good idea for Billy to be playing over there so much."

✿   ✿   ✿

"What did they want *this* time?" Deborah inquired.

"They wanted to know about Alice Easton," Jerry replied.

She gasped. "They found out about that?"

"Apparently."

"I thought the school wasn't supposed to say anything; it was part of the agreement."

"I thought so, too."

She shrugged. "Well, I don't know why either one of us should be surprised. Someone was bound to find out sooner or later."

"I guess so."

"What did you tell them?" she asked.

"I told them the allegation was false, of course," he said with a look of disgust.

"Did they believe you?"

"I don't know, Deborah," he snapped at her. "Why don't you go ask them?"

"Is it the teacher?" Albert Hoch questioned his police chief the following morning, his voice, as usual, resonating throughout the building. "That's twice you've had him down here. Are you on to something? Are you close to an arrest?"

"We're only at the talking stage," Ruben replied. "We have reason to believe he may be involved in the case, but we can't be sure."

"Then why are you pussyfooting around?" the Bald Eagle demanded. "Why don't you go after him, turn his place upside down, find something?"

Ruben sighed. "He's got a very sharp lawyer, and we don't have probable cause for a search warrant," he replied, wishing the mayor would let him alone to do his job. "We have to keep working the situation."

"I gotta tell you, you're running out of time, Ruben," Hoch warned. "The city council is getting pressured. I'm getting pressured. We've got to have a break in the case, something I can take to people and say: 'Here, this is what we're doing; this is what we've accomplished.' You're running out of time."

"I appreciate your efforts in my behalf," the police chief said evenly. "I know you understand that real police work doesn't always happen in an instant; that more often than not it takes great patience and careful strategy to solve a case as complex as this one."

"Do you at least have a strategy for this teacher guy?" Hoch asked.

"At the moment, we're considering several different ones," Ruben told him. "We still have some evaluating to do before we decide which one will be most productive."

"When are we likely to see some results?"

"It's hard to say just now."

Hoch wagged his bald head. "I don't know if that's going to satisfy the city council."

"I'm sorry," said Ruben. "I don't know what else to tell you."

The mayor was clearly frustrated. "What I'm hearing is that you think he probably did it, but you can't nail him for it, is that right?"

Ruben shrugged. "Unfortunately, what we suspect isn't always the same as what we can prove."

Down the hall, Ginger wrapped her legs around her chair to keep from jumping up and running to Ruben's defense. Why couldn't everyone see he was doing his best? With almost no physical evidence, no murder weapon, and no eyewitnesses, what did the damn city council expect?

They had the teacher in their sights, and they weren't about to blink. If they could just get that fingerprint match, they would have their first piece of solid evidence; more than enough to secure a search warrant. And Ginger was positive that a thorough examination of Jerry Frankel's home would turn up all they would need to charge him with murder. It was just a matter of time.

In reality, there was no guarantee that the fingerprint on Tara's cross belonged to the murderer; it was just a possibility. But if it turned out to be Jerry Frankel's fingerprint, then the possibility became a probability. Ginger began to pray for just that. All they needed was a little break; just one thing to show the city council that they were on the right track; something that would get them off Ruben's back. She wondered how much time he had left.

"Stacey?" asked the voice at the other end of the telephone.

"Yes," she replied.

"This is Danny." There was a pause. "Danny Leo."

"Oh, hi," she said. "I didn't recognize your voice. I guess I never talked to you on the telephone before."

"I just wanted to say thank you again for last Saturday night. I really appreciate what you did. I told my folks. My dad was pretty steamed at first, but then I think he was happy about it."

"I'm glad."

"I also wanted to tell you what a terrific time I had—afterward, at the movie, I mean. It was a lot of fun."

"I had fun, too," she admitted.

"You know, working on the paper and all, we've known each other for over a year," he said, "but we really don't know each other very well."

"I guess not."

"Well, I was wondering—do you have any plans for New Year's Eve yet?"

Stacey's heart thumped. Was the school hunk about to ask her for a date? "No, I don't," she told him.

"A classmate of mine is having a party, and I thought maybe you might like to go with me?"

Kids on Seward didn't go in for dating very much, Stacey knew. They went out in groups, usually with other kids in the same grade. She knew very well that Danny Leo showing up at a party with a sophomore would be all over the Island by morning.

"Sounds like fun," she said. "I'd like to go."

It was well after midnight, but a wide-awake Matthew Frankel lay in bed with his arms crossed under his head and thought about school. Outside his window, the world was dark and quiet, the best time for thinking. Chase was curled up on the floor beside him, breathing softly.

Matthew was trying to figure out how he could tell his parents that he didn't want to go to school anymore without having to tell them why. He didn't want to tell them why because he knew it would hurt his father, and there was no one in this world that Matthew loved as much as he loved his father.

He thought of asking them if he could go to private school, but he knew the only one on the Island was a Christian school that Billy had told him about, and that would be, as his mother sometimes said, like jumping from the frying pan into the fire.

But maybe he wouldn't have to go to a real school at all, Matthew thought. Maybe he could just stay home and learn from his father in the evenings. There were parents on the Island who home-schooled their kids; he had heard his father say so. That would be great. He could stay right here, where he was safe, and never have to go back to that place or see those kids again.

"Did you know your daddy's a murderer?" a trio of fifth-graders had taunted him on the playground during recess.

"How does it feel to be the son of a murderer?"

"Son of a Jew bastard murderer!"

"Son of a Jew bastard and a Jew bitch!"

They had grabbed his brand-new jacket and thrown it in a mud puddle and stomped all over it. Then they had pushed him down in the puddle and held his face in the mud until he choked and sputtered.

"Hey, look!" they said, laughing as they walked away. "The kike kid's crying!"

Tears oozed out of Matthew's eyes onto his pillow. No one had ever treated him like that before. He knew he was different from a lot of the kids on the Island, because he was Jewish, but he had always tried his best to be nice to everyone. He didn't understand; he didn't even know those fifth-graders.

"I slipped and fell," he told the playground teacher who pulled him out of the puddle.

"I slipped and fell," he told the school nurse who cleaned him up.

"I slipped and fell," he told his parents.

Matthew didn't like to lie, but something had kept him from telling the truth.

Friday was the last day of school before the winter holiday began. That gave him two weeks to think up a plan that would be persuasive enough to convince his parents not to send him back.

13

On the heels of Jerry Frankel's second visit to Graham Hall came a new spate of letters to the editor that were distinctly different from those previously received, and Gail Brown couldn't resist publishing a cross-section of them.

"It wouldn't come as no surprise to me (sic) that it was a teacher who killed that girl," wrote a high school dropout. "I've seen them get off on power trips where they really think they're like God or somebody."

"I don't care how good a teacher everybody thinks he is," objected the manager of the local liquor store. "Just because he can teach doesn't mean he wasn't involved in that poor girl's murder."

"If the police are seriously considering the possibility that one of the teachers at the high school murdered Tara Breckenridge," inquired a worried mother, "shouldn't he be removed from his classroom until the matter is resolved?"

❖   ❖   ❖

"This is no different than those Wenatchee sex crimes, where that preacher got off," an electrician and the father of six wrote. "Only this time, the victim wasn't just molested, she was murdered. Teachers are supposed to be people we can trust, just like preachers, aren't they?"

Jerry Frankel read the letters and sighed. "Somehow, this whole thing has gotten way out of control," he said. "I don't understand how it happened."

"How did they find out about Holman?" Deborah asked.

"I don't know. They didn't say."

"This place is like a sieve," she complained. "There's no such thing as confidentiality around here. Maybe we should think about moving."

"In the middle of a murder investigation?" he demanded. "Now wouldn't that make me look innocent."

"I was thinking more of Matthew," she said. "This is bound to affect him sooner or later."

"Scott says it'll be okay," Jerry told her. "He says they have no evidence, and without it, they can't charge me with anything. He says he can go to court to get them to stop harassing me."

"It's going to be the same damn thing all over again, isn't it?"

"No, it isn't," he said.

Ginger was not looking forward to the session with her parents, but the feisty redhead intended to stand her ground.

"I absolutely refuse to have that man in my house," Verna Earley declared. "Not on Christmas or any other day. The very idea! What would I tell your brothers? Why, my goodness, I would never be able to hold my head up in polite society again."

"Then I'm afraid you won't have me in your house, either," Ginger shot back. "What will you tell my brothers, then?"

"I suppose I'll have to tell them that you preferred the company of others," her mother replied. "I certainly can't be held responsible for that, now can I?"

"Wait a minute," Jack Earley said. He was a fair-minded man who, when it came to his daughter and his wife, too often found himself in the role of mediator. "Aren't the holidays supposed to be a time for people to come together and forget their differences?"

"The holidays are a time for *family* to come together," Verna retorted.

"How Christian of you, Mother," said Ginger.

"Don't you dare say that to me, young lady. I'm as good a Christian as the next person."

Ginger turned to her father. "Dad, you know Ruben. You work with him. Is he diseased? Does he have horns? Has being around him blackened your reputation in any way?"

"A business association is one thing," Verna interjected before Jack could respond. "Your father can't help who he has to work with, just the same as you can't. But a social association is something quite different. That's a choice."

Ginger shook her head in exasperation. "I don't know how I ever grew up in this house and never saw it," she said.

"Never saw what?" Verna demanded.

"How much of a bigot you are."

"You mind your mouth, young lady," her mother snapped. "I'm nothing of the kind."

"Why don't we all back off a bit here," Jack urged. "I think maybe we're starting to say things we'll regret."

"I don't regret anything," Verna retorted. "I tried my best to instill decent values in her, but she always threw it back in my face. Now she'll have to learn the hard way that like goes with like or there'll be no happiness."

Ginger looked at her mother and sighed. "Ruben and I have a relationship—a committed relationship," she said. "He's part of my life, maybe for a very long time. I'd like you to be glad for me, but I'm twenty-eight years old and I don't need your permission. I'm sorry you feel the way you do, about someone you don't even know, but I'm sorrier for you than I am for me. Now you can deal with this situation in one of two ways. You can cut me loose and tell the world I'm no longer your daughter. That might not say much for your family loyalty, but you'll be able to hold your head way up in the rarefied air of racial snobbery. Or you can take the time to get to know two very special people, and possibly even learn something valuable about what really matters in this world. It's up to you."

Verna looked from her daughter to her husband. It was obvious that she had not anticipated the ultimatum, not seen the trap. She turned on her heel and disappeared into the kitchen.

Jack turned to his daughter and shrugged. "You brought up the heavy artillery for what was probably nothing more than a minor skirmish," he said.

"I know," Ginger replied. "But I'm hoping it won't be a very long war."

"I have a double-edged invitation for you," Ginger told Ruben. "Christmas dinner at my parents' house."

"What's so bad about that?" he asked.

She sighed. "Let me tell you about my mother."

"It could be a little rough," Ruben conceded when he told his daughter. "Her mother isn't exactly ethnically open-minded."

"Oh, great," Stacey said.

"We don't have to go, if you don't want to," he assured her. "We can have our Christmas dinner, just like we always do, and I'll be perfectly happy. The decision is yours."

The very last thing Stacey Martinez wanted to do was spend the most important holiday of the year with a bunch of people who were going to have to force themselves to be nice to her. She already knew enough bigots from school to last her well into the next century. But she didn't have the heart to say no.

"Do you want to go?" she asked.

Ruben thought about that for a moment. "Ginger's pretty important to me," he admitted. "More important than any woman since your mother. I'd be lying to you if I said she wasn't. Which means that, sooner or later, I'm probably going to have to deal with her family. This might be as good a time as any. I know Jack Earley. He's a decent man. As for the mother, I'd like to think that the attitude Ginger describes has more to do with fear of the unknown than any deep-rooted philosophy."

"I guess that means you want to go," Stacey said.

"Never mind me—what about you?" he asked.

"It's okay."

"You sure?"

She shrugged. "Why not? As you say, it has to happen sooner or later."

"I promise you, if it's bad, we'll get up and leave," he told her.

"Dad, I said it's okay. In fact," she added with a malicious smile, "it might be fun to slip a little hot pepper into their stuffing."

"I have attended the high school's Christmas pageant ever since I first moved to Seward Island," a woman wrote to the editor of the *Sentinel*. "It was a source of enormous comfort to me, especially in this age of moral decay, to see our young people carrying on the important traditions of Christianity. But now the pageant has been ruined for me by the intrusion of foreign rituals that have no place in our holiday celebration, and that have undermined its purpose and marred its purity. I will not go again."

"First the Jews objected to prayer in school," wrote Mildred MacDonald. "Then they stopped letting us decorate the won-

derful Douglas fir that was planted on the Village Green a hundred years ago for that very purpose. Now they've ruined our
pageant. It's nothing to do with them, why can't just they go away
and leave us alone?"

"The high school's holiday pageant—for it can no longer be
called just a Christmas pageant," wrote a local pediatrician, "was
a superb example of how a community such as ours can join in
celebrating its diverse heritage. If our young people can come together in such an outstanding effort, is it such an impossible
dream to think that, one day, the rest of us might as well?"

"If the high school wanted to change the Christmas
pageant," Doris O'Connor charged the editor, "why couldn't they
have just sung some different carols? This is our holiday, and we
should have the right to celebrate it the way we want to—which
is the way it always was."

"Since it's the Jewish retail businesses that profit most from
the commercial side of Christmas," wrote an elderly widow, "why
are they always complaining about it?"

"Why do we have to print all this drivel?" Iris Tanaka asked.
"The school board finally had the guts to do a good thing for this
community, and some of these people are being downright big-
oted about it."

"That's why we print it," Gail told her. "To let some light
shine on things that are usually allowed to foment in the dark."

"What is all this garbage?" Deborah Frankel wondered.
"Where is it coming from? Are these people for real?"

"A few, I guess," Rachel Cohen conceded. "They keep it
pretty much under wraps most of the time. I think the stress of
the holidays tends to bring it to the surface."

Deborah snorted. "You mean the universally recognized season of Peace on Earth Good Will Toward Men?"

Although he would never admit it to anyone, not even to himself, Christmas was the most difficult time of the year for Malcolm Purdy. The festive decorations, the holiday spirit, the sound of carols, the eagerness of children—it all reminded him of just how alone he was. Even the woman who worked for him and stayed with him whenever he asked had family obligations at Christmas.

Malcolm had no one. The men who came to his compound meant little to him. They connected for a month or two, but they were not family. He taught them what they wanted to know, they paid handsomely for his services, and then they departed. He never heard from any of them again.

Once a year, Malcolm left the Island and went to a place in Montana where he met with others who were like himself, disillusioned, disenfranchised, lost. The few weeks of camaraderie he shared there came as close to the Corps as anything in his life ever would. The philosophies may have differed, Malcolm agreeing with some of them and disagreeing with others, but the intensity was there, the excitement—the awareness that something was happening in the country, and that things, albeit slowly, might finally be starting to change.

When the holidays came, however, he was alone, with his thoughts, his memories, his shattered dreams. On the day before Christmas, he wrote a long letter to his daughters, sheet after sheet of tightly penned lines that told of his life, and begged their forgiveness. When he was finished, well into the evening, he read the letter through, and then, page by page, threw it into the fire.

Ruben brought a pizza over to Ginger's place. They ate it in front of the fire and washed it down with a bottle of Chianti. Twink was now munching on the last bit of crust left in the box.

"I want to give you this now, while we're alone," Ruben said, pulling a small package from his pocket.

"I hope it isn't too extravagant," Ginger said, eyeing the package.

"Terribly," he told her.

Ginger giggled as she tore off the wrapping. Inside the box, nested in blue velvet, was a thin gold necklace, and hanging from it was a small gold heart.

"I love it," she cried. "It's very extravagant and it's just perfect. Here, put it on for me, will you?"

She lifted her heavy hair away and he fastened the clasp around her neck. Then he leaned over and kissed the little hollow where her neck met her shoulder.

"I love that, too," she murmured. "But first things first."

She reached over and selected a package from the pile she had stacked on the floor.

"For me?" he asked with a smile.

"Well, actually, it was for the mailman," she said, poking him playfully in the ribs. "But you put me on the spot."

He undid the wrapping carefully, preserving the ribbon and the paper, while she wriggled impatiently. She had bought him a pale blue cashmere sweater with an elegant cable knit pattern. It had cost her well over half a week's salary, but she didn't care. She didn't know it was the first cashmere he had ever owned.

"I will treasure this," he said, putting on the sweater and then running his fingers over the fine wool.

She fingered her necklace. "I'll never take this off."

"We've known each other for two years," he said. "We had our first date hardly more than six weeks ago. Why does it seem as though we've been together forever?"

She snuggled against him. "There are some that say we keep meeting up with the people we knew in other lives," she told him.

"Do you believe that?" he asked.

She shrugged. "I don't know," she said. "I don't think I believe in much of anything, except what I feel—I believe in that." She ran her finger slowly down his cheek. "And right now, I feel like taking that sweater off you, and everything else that's on you, and then having you do the same to me. Except for my necklace, of course. That stays on."

Not a moment had gone by since the second Sunday in October that Mary Breckenridge didn't think of Tara. There were many mornings when she would awaken expecting to see her, many evenings when she would sit down at the dinner table and wonder why the girl was late. A number of times, she was almost positive that she heard her daughter's voice echoing down the halls of Southwynd.

On one level, she knew Tara was gone. But on another level, she couldn't seem to let her go.

Christmas was Mary's favorite day of the entire year because it had always meant a time that the family would spend together, laughing, playing, enjoying their presents, having fun. But this year there was no joy, no laughter. The house had not been decorated; there wasn't even a tree.

It snowed on Christmas Day; a rare dusting of white that settled over the Island like a gentle blessing. There was not enough accumulation to clog traffic or cause any major accidents, just enough to lift the spirits and mark the occasion as something special.

Mary never noticed. She spent the day in her room with the curtains drawn, pretending to read. She knew she wasn't being fair to Tori; after all, the girl was only twelve. But she couldn't help it. She felt sick inside, and empty, and her tears were never far from the surface.

What made the pain so much worse was that it wouldn't go away; no one would let it. It was like a worrisome wound that couldn't heal because so many took advantage of every opportu-

nity to pick at the scab. Even when Mary didn't want to think
about Tara, the newspaper came to remind her. Every issue carried yet another story, offering a new detail or the rehash of an
old theory. And the letters to the editor! Mary wondered whether
any of these people, most of whom she didn't even know, realized
how hurtful they were being. On top of that, whenever she got
up the courage to venture into town, there were all those solicitous souls who looked at her with such pity, or tried not to look
at her, or lowered their voices to a whisper when she came near.

"You're making it worse," she wanted to scream at them.
But of course she didn't; she hadn't been raised to call attention
to herself.

"Don't blame the *Sentinel*," Kyle told her. "They just want
to help. They think, if they keep the story going, something they
print might lead to the killer. And don't blame the people, either.
They're trying to be kind; they just don't know how."

Mary shook her head slowly. Her daughter was gone. What
did it really matter?

14

At three o'clock on Christmas afternoon, Ruben and Stacey collected Ginger at her apartment and the three of them drove to the Earley home.

From the outside, it looked like a comfortable house; old and brown with white trim, set back off the road to gain some privacy and an ample front lawn. A giant maple tree stood guard on either side of the driveway, rhododendron beds looked well tended, and window boxes hinted at spring flowers to come. The Earleys had draped colorful lights over the bushes, and a life-sized Santa drove his reindeer across the roof. Through a big front window, Ruben and Stacey caught a glimpse of an enormous blue spruce laden with decorations. It was exactly the kind of place where grandparents would live, Ruben thought; the kind of place he had never known, and had never been able to give his daughter.

"Let's hope looks aren't deceiving," Ginger murmured as though reading his mind. They climbed out of the Blazer, retrieved a pile of gaily wrapped packages from the back, and made their way up the path.

Jack Earley opened the front door. "Merry Christmas," he said, giving Ginger a big hug, offering his hand to Ruben, and smiling at Stacey. "Come in out of the cold. Here, let me take your coats. I've got a good fire going in the living room."

The inside of the house was as welcoming as the outside, with comfortable, well-used furniture, polished hardwood floors, scattered rugs, and a seemingly endless array of family photographs that covered almost every surface. The living room was a spacious rectangle with a great stone fireplace taking up almost one whole wall. On closer inspection, the tree was even more spectacular than the initial glimpse had revealed, with hundreds of lights that sparkled on and off and a magnificent display of ornaments that bespoke a lifetime of collecting.

"What a wonderful tree," Stacey cried, her brown eyes dancing.

"That's my wife's pride and joy," Jack told her. "Takes her three weeks to get the thing up every year."

Stacey took a step closer to look at a miniature wooden sleigh, so exquisitively carved that it looked like lace.

"Don't touch that," a voice barked behind her. "My grandfather made that. It's over a hundred years old."

Stacey turned around to see Verna standing in the doorway. "I wouldn't dream of touching it, Mrs. Earley," she said. "I was just admiring it."

"Humph," Verna said.

"I've never seen a Christmas tree so beautiful."

"You don't decorate a tree of your own?" Verna asked. She could afford to be magnanimous; she knew these people could never have anything that would compare.

"Not with this kind of history," Stacey told her. "My mother was an orphan and my dad's parents are long gone, so it's pretty much just the two of us. I have a few things from my grandmother, but nothing like this."

"That's too bad."

Verna had fully intended to despise the interlopers—these two people who were ruining her holiday. But looking at Stacey, she couldn't stop a pang of sympathy for the motherless child who had no family to fall back on. Why, the girl hardly looked Mexican at all, with her silky blond hair and sweet face and simple velvet dress. All that gave her away really was the color of her skin.

She looked at Ruben. Now there was a different story altogether. Even in his best blue suit and his polished shoes, with his arms full of Christmas packages, there was no mistaking where he had come from. She prayed that none of her neighbors had seen him come in, or would notice his vehicle parked in the driveway, and then go spreading the news all over town. She wondered if Ginger had insisted he drive on purpose. She forced her lips into a brittle smile.

"How do you do, Chief Martinez."

"It's a pleasure to meet you, Mrs. Earley," Ruben replied smoothly. "Thank you for having us to your lovely home."

"Yes, well, you're welcome, of course," Verna replied. So he had some manners and he didn't speak with an accent, she thought. What did that mean? Underneath, he was still what he was.

"This teenage terror with the eyes popping out of her head is my daughter, Stacey," Ruben said.

"Hello," the teenager said politely.

"What a pretty name," Verna murmured. She wondered if these people really believed that their children would be more American if they gave them American names.

Ginger laid her packages under the tree. It gave her something to do so that she wouldn't throttle her mother. She knew exactly what Verna was thinking.

"Ruben, bring that stuff over here," she said, as much to get him out from under the glare as to relieve him of his load.

He did as he was told, giving her an amused wink when he was sure no one could see. He, too, knew what Verna was thinking.

"Don't let it get to you," he said under his breath. "It doesn't matter." But even as the words came out of his mouth, he knew that, this time, it did matter.

"Jack says it takes you three weeks to put up the tree, Mrs. Earley," he said politely. "Do you do it all yourself?"

"I don't actually put it up," she said, preening a little. "Jack does that. But I do the trimming."

"Do you have a set place for each ornament, or do you do it differently each year?"

"Oh, differently, of course," she said, warming to her subject in spite of herself. "The moment it comes down, I forget everything about it, so I won't be tempted to repeat anything the next time. That's the whole fun of it: each year, it's brand-new. I never even—"

She brought herself up sharply. What was she doing, standing here, having a conversation with him when she had intended to ignore him?

"Well, enough chitchat," she said. "I have a dinner to prepare."

Across the hall, Stacey had seen the dining room table; the crisp linen cloth, the candles, the setting for sixteen.

"You're not doing all the work yourself, are you?" she asked. "For so many people?"

"Of course, I am," Verna said. "Who else would be doing it?"

"I'd be happy to help," Stacey offered.

Verna looked at her in surprise. "What do you know about cooking?"

"I think you can trust her, Mom," Ginger said with a chuckle. "She's been cooking for Ruben since she was ten."

"Well, I suppose I could use some help," the woman conceded, wondering if the child had any experience preparing American food. There were a number of simple but necessary chores that needed doing. "Ginger certainly never offers."

"I'm great with stuffing," Stacey said, smiling benignly at her father as she followed Verna out of the room.

"How about a drink?" Jack Earley offered. "We can probably squeeze one in before the rest of them show up."

"Scotch," Ginger and Ruben said together. "On the rocks."

Jack went off toward the bar, and Ginger and Ruben turned to each other with a nervous giggle.

"I've been holding my breath so long, I'm dizzy," she whispered. "I keep waiting for the earthquake to hit."

"My back is so stiff, I can't bend," he whispered in reply.

Jack returned with the drinks. "To a Merry Christmas," he said as they touched glasses all around.

"I'll drink to that," Ruben said.

Somewhere between the afternoon and the evening, Verna had to admit to herself that perhaps she had prejudged Ruben Martinez too harshly. He displayed none of the traits she had always believed were associated with Mexicans. His fingernails weren't dirty, his hair wasn't greasy, he spoke English just like an American, his job apparently didn't permit him to be lazy, his language wasn't crude, his manners were as good as anyone else's around her table, and he wasn't stupid. In fact, he led the conversation on a variety of subjects.

Of course, Verna had never really known any Mexicans personally. Growing up, she had been kept away from the migrant workers who seasonally descended on Pomeroy, and had always relied on second- and thirdhand reports of their behavior for her evaluation of them. She had perhaps been somewhat more willing to make allowances for Stacey, since the girl was obviously half white, but her reevaluation of Ruben came as something of a shock to her. Not that she would ever admit it out loud, of course, but she thought she could see a little of what Ginger saw in him. He sat up straight, he looked a person right in the eye, and he had a very engaging smile.

She was as amazed as anyone that her Christmas dinner was not the disaster she had feared. She noted that the boys made at least an effort to be amiable, engaging the police chief in a game of pool at the antique table that occupied one end of the family room. Even their wives took the presence of the intruders in stride. The grandchildren weren't old enough to know the difference and were delighted to have someone new to bedevil with their antics.

Perhaps most responsible for her altered view of Ruben was the gift he had brought for her. When she first saw the box, she anticipated it contained something cheap or garish or totally inappropriate. But when she opened it, she found a fine lace runner nestled inside a cocoon of tissue paper. It was obviously old, obviously costly, and in exquisite taste.

"Why it's beautiful," she cried.

"Ginger told us a little something about you," Stacey explained. "And when Dad saw this in an antique shop, he thought it might suit you."

"He was absolutely right," Verna said, beaming. Indeed, it would be perfect for her dining room table. Eleanor Jewel had one that she said had been in her family for generations, and it was not nearly so nice as this.

"A thank-you might be in order at this time," Ginger prompted.

"I know my manners, young lady," Verna snapped at her daughter. "I even tried to teach them to you!" She turned to Ruben. "Thank you," she said. "It's quite lovely."

Ruben smiled.

As soon as the holidays were over, Verna decided, she would invite Eleanor over for coffee, and casually escort her through the dining room. Of course, she wouldn't tell the gossip where the runner had come from. Maybe, in time, she found herself thinking, she would be able to forget who gave it to her, and just enjoy it for what it was.

Then, at the very moment of her thought, the most extraordinary thing occurred. She happened to catch Ruben's glance, and knew he had read her mind. But rather than reproach, she saw understanding in his expression. I know how you feel, his eyes seemed to say. I'm sorry you feel that way, but I understand. Verna looked away, feeling both vindicated and ashamed in the same instant.

"I'm going to keep it on the dining room table," she heard herself say. "And I'll think of you fondly every time I look at it."

Ginger did a double take, her father blinked, her brothers stared. But Ruben just smiled.

"You bewitched her," Ginger declared as they drove home. "I wouldn't have believed it if I didn't see it with my own eyes and hear it with my own ears. You absolutely bewitched her."

"Did I?" he replied, a twinkle in his eye.

"Don't sit there looking so smug. You know you did. I don't know how, but you got to her."

"There was no magic involved," he said. "I think it was more a matter of her having the chance to see the enemy up close and personal, and realizing there was nothing to fear."

Verna had even allowed Ruben to hug her when he and Stacey and Ginger were leaving. "I'm glad you could come," she had said, and it wasn't entirely untrue.

"Glad you could come?" Ginger repeated now. "Well, if it wasn't magic, it was certainly a miracle."

The telephone rang in the Earley house at just past nine the next morning.

"Tell me it isn't so," Eleanor Jewel trilled over the line. "Tell me you didn't really do it?"

Verna grit her teeth, wondering how, even on this small an island, word had gotten around so fast.

"Do what?" she asked with a leaden heart.

"Why, have that Martinez person in your home, of course."

"As a matter of fact, I did," Verna replied. "It was Ginger's idea, of course. Apparently the man and his daughter have no family and had nowhere to go. Ginger works with him, you know, and I'm sure she took pity on him. I couldn't very well tell her to uninvite him once the damage was done. That would have been too rude."

"But my dear, it must have been horrible for you."

"Of course it was horrible," Verna replied. "But I'm a Christian woman. What else could I do?"

"You're a martyr, that's what you are," Eleanor declared emphatically. "A real martyr."

"It's all true," Eleanor reported to a friend five minutes later. "He was there for dinner. Verna tried to make it sound like it was nothing more than one of those employer-employee things, but of course we know better, don't we?"

"What can she be thinking?" the friend asked. "That we're stupid? Or blind? Her daughter certainly isn't going out of her way to hide the affair."

"On the contrary, my dear," Eleanor said, "she seems to be flaunting it. Mildred MacDonald saw the two of them together coming out of the movies last week—and they were holding hands."

"Poor Verna," the friend said with a sigh. "She has three fine sons, but that daughter of hers has always been a cross she's had to bear."

15

Stacey Martinez stood in her tiny bedroom putting the finishing touches on an outfit of black velvet pants, a cream silk blouse, and a brocade vest. At fifteen and a half years old, she was about to go out on her first real date.

Ginger had helped her select the clothes. After an hour of frustration with everything in her wardrobe, Stacey had gone looking for advice.

"I want to look soft and maybe a little sophisticated," she said. "I don't mind looking my age, but I want everyone to know I have possibilities."

"Silk," Ginger said at once with a knowing smile. "And velvet. You're perfect in velvet."

They put the ensemble together in five minutes. To finish it all off, Stacey tied a black velvet ribbon around her neck, and then added her mother's pearl earrings, a touch of mascara, and a pale coat of lipstick.

"You look absolutely fabulous," Ginger told her when she came into the living room.

Ruben beamed.

"I don't know how she got to be so terrific," he said after

Danny had come to collect her and they had swept out on a wave of excitement and expectation.

"She had a great role model," Ginger said, sitting down on the sofa beside him and resting her chin on his shoulder.

"You know, I always thought it would be the worst day of my life when I stopped being the center of her universe," he confessed. "Now I'm so proud of her, I could cry."

Ginger smiled. The more she learned about this man, the more she liked him. "I have an idea," she proposed. "Let's not wait for midnight to open the champagne. I think we have something much more important to celebrate right now."

"What?" he asked. "Stacey's emancipation?"

"No," she told him. "Yours."

The New Year's Eve party was at the Petrie home, an imposing two-story gray house on the east side of the Island that sat on a gentle rise well back from the road and was fronted by exquisitely manicured lawns.

"Owen's dad owns the hardware store and garden center in town," Danny told her. "He has a full-time gardener working here, and he writes the expense off on his income taxes as advertising and promotion."

The interior of the house was every bit as splendid as the exterior, featuring large rooms that were filled with an assortment of antiques that, genuine or not, must have cost a fortune. There was an extravagant and apparently endless array of food and drink; two maids in gray uniforms scurried about, serving and clearing; a man in a gray suit stood waiting to take their coats.

Stacey had never been inside such a fine home. It had never occurred to her that there were people right here on Seward Island—other than the Breckenridges, of course—who could afford to live like this, and who would think nothing of putting on this kind of party for a bunch of teenagers.

"Hey, Danny," the acne-faced Owen Petrie called, weaving his way across the foyer with a bottle of beer in his hand. "Glad you could make it. Who's this ravishing thing you got with you?"

"This is Stacey," Danny told him. "Stacey, this is Owen."

"Stacey? Stacey who?" Owen asked. It was clearly not his first bottle of beer.

"Stacey Martinez," she replied for herself.

Owen blinked. "The police chief's daughter?"

"The one and only."

"Well, I'll be damned."

With that, Owen reeled away to greet another guest.

"Is he always this rude?" Stacey asked with a chuckle. "Or is it just on New Year's?"

Danny shrugged. "Maybe we shouldn't have come. Would you like to go someplace else?"

"Oh no," she told him. "I think it'll be fun."

"Happy New Year," Ruben said at midnight, as he and Ginger watched the televised fireworks exploding from the Space Needle in downtown Seattle. "I have a feeling it's going to be a great one."

"So do I," she said.

They had finished the champagne before dinner, so now they toasted each other with glasses of Kahlúa.

"I'm glad we didn't go anywhere tonight," he said. "It's so much better to be here alone with you than out with a lot of strangers looking for an excuse to be happy."

Ginger giggled. "Of course, when you think of it—what's to be happy about?" she pondered. "The world and everyone in it getting another year older?"

"No," he said pulling her close. "What's to be happy about is you and me, finding each other."

The Petries' party was in full swing. Midnight had come and gone; food was still being consumed; punch bowls were being refilled. Many of the kids were walking around with glassy eyes and dumb expressions. The beer was flowing. Danny was drinking ginger ale.

"What's the matter, old man?" Bert Kriedler, a taller, heavier version of his younger brother, Hank, teased. "In training?"

"Nope," Danny replied. "Just the designated driver."

"How about you, Stacey? Did you find the tequila?"

"I found the punch," she told him. "Is there tequila in it?"

Bert didn't reply. He just laughed and turned away.

"I hope he didn't hurt your feelings," Danny said. "He's just a jerk."

"His brother is in a couple of my classes," Stacey told him. "It must run in the family."

Sometime later, as she made her way upstairs in search of a bathroom, she saw Bert and a couple of other senior boys through an open bedroom door. It didn't take an expert, or even a policeman's daughter, to know what they were doing with the lines of white powder in front of them.

"Oh shit!" she heard one of them exclaim as she passed. "Now Miss Tijuana is gonna run and tell her daddy on us!"

"I don't think you had a very good time tonight," Danny said on the way home.

"No, I had fun," Stacey assured him. "It was just—different, that's all. Not what I'm used to."

"I don't hang out a lot with those guys," he told her. "And in case your dad wants to know, I don't do drugs, either."

Stacey smiled. "I didn't think so," she said.

"I've got better things to do with my life."

"I'm glad."

They were silent the rest of the way home.

"Well, uh, d'you think maybe you might want to go out again sometime?" he asked as he pulled up in front of her house.

"Sure," she replied.

"We could go to another movie?"

"That sounds great."

"Well, uh, how about Saturday night?"

"Okay."

Even in the dark, she could see the big grin that spread across his face.

"Terrific," he said. "Do you like pizza? Maybe we could get a pizza before the movie."

"I love pizza."

"Six o'clock then?"

"Okay."

Danny jumped out of the car and came around to open the door for her. On the front porch, he leaned down, and for an instant, his lips brushed her cheek.

"Good night," he whispered.

"Good night," she whispered back.

Stacey watched as he drove off. She was a little high from the punch, but far from drunk. Still, she felt as if the whole world were dancing around her.

Despite the display of opulence, it had truly been a terrible party. Almost everyone there had either made an unpleasant remark or simply ignored her, and she had seen several of the girls staring at her with less than gracious expressions that clearly wondered why she, and not one of them, was out with one of the most sought after boys in school. Stacey had no answer for them; she didn't understand it herself. But she didn't dwell on it. The fact that Danny Leo, the high school hunk, wanted to see her again made the whole evening worthwhile. She opened the front door and floated into the house.

16

"We were willing to give Chief Martinez the benefit of the doubt," a television repairman wrote to the editor of the *Seward Sentinel* on the first Monday of the New Year. "Even though a number of us thought that he was an unusual choice to head up the Island's police department, we were told he had the credentials to handle any law enforcement problem that the 1990s might bring our way. Only it's now more than two months since the Breckenridge murder, and it's clear to me, at least, that we were told wrong. Ruben Martinez is obviously not the man for the job. I say, it's time for a change."

"First it was some unidentified maniac who murdered Tara Breckenridge, then it was an exemplary high school student, then it was an outstanding educator, and now who is it, pray tell?" asked a homemaker. "It seems to me that the police are fishing in some murky pond they can't see into, and just pulling up whatever happens to get snagged on their line. My daughters are now thoroughly frightened of strangers, teenage boys, and teachers. Is that what the city council had in mind when it hired an outsider to be our police chief?"

*   *   *

"When a project fails," wrote a high-powered business consultant, "management is almost always to blame. Maybe it's time for Seward Island's police department to have some new management."

"All right," a weary Albert Hoch told Jim Petrie over the telephone. "You want to start interviewing, go ahead."

"You mean Kyle has given you his permission?" Petrie asked with just a hint of derision.

"I haven't even talked to Kyle," Hoch snapped. "I'm just sick of all the bickering. I don't happen to think anyone else is going to come in here and do any better than Ruben, but I'm tired of arguing about it."

In fact, he was tired of the constant criticism, the letters that questioned his leadership, the irate phone calls that insulted his judgment. He was hurt by being snubbed on the street by people he'd known for decades, and embarrassed when he realized that he had become the butt of snide jokes. Some less charitable residents had begun to call for his resignation. Even his wife, Phoebe, was feeling the indignity of being ostracized by some of her social circle.

"You can't say I didn't warn you," Petrie said.

"No, I can't," Hoch replied with a sigh.

Before becoming Seward's mayor, Albert Hoch was a successful insurance salesman. Nothing less than a massive coronary at the age of forty-eight could have persuaded him to give up his agency and take on the benign responsibilities of Island leadership.

Being liked, trusted, and accepted were Hoch's stock-in-trade. They were the traits that had made him a millionaire and gotten him elected to office three times. When push came to shove, his principles would always take second seat to his reputation, and his reputation was far too important for him to risk damaging it in a no-win situation.

After his coronary, his doctors had warned him about avoiding stress, and he did not now want to put himself in the unpopular, and therefore stressful, position of going against the city council. Besides, when it came right down to it, he didn't really owe Ruben a thing.

"It's out of my hands now," he told the police chief less than an hour later, having first stopped by Kyle Breckenridge's office at the bank before walking over to Graham Hall. "The city council has decided to look for someone to replace you."

Ruben shrugged. "It's certainly their prerogative," he said with dignity. Not once in his entire career had he ever been fired.

"No one's cutting you off, you understand," Hoch was quick to add, remembering the two years still left on the police chief's contract. "We'll make it right for you. Time to look for another position, references, whatever."

"I wasn't worried," Ruben replied. "And since it's likely that the interview process will take some time on both sides, I want you to know that I'm willing to stay on the job until you've found a suitable replacement."

The mayor nodded. "I was hoping you would say that," he said. "I certainly do appreciate it, and I'm sure the city council will, too."

With that bit of unpleasant business taken care of, the mayor made a hasty withdrawal.

It was after six o'clock. Ruben had gone home, Charlie had gone off to keep a doctor's appointment, the day shift had been replaced by the swing shift. Although she had officially been off duty for more than an hour, Ginger was still in her office, trying to catch up on paperwork. But the anger kept getting in her way.

As far as she was concerned, Albert Hoch was nothing more than a lily-livered coward, and the city council nothing more than a bunch of mealy-mouthed slugs. To hold Ruben responsible for not catching Tara Breckenridge's killer was a little like holding one of those idiot TV meteorologists responsible for failing to predict an earthquake.

Ginger was as frustrated as anyone about the case, even more so now that she knew who had murdered the fifteen-year-old. To have to stand by and watch Ruben get fired because there wasn't enough evidence to arrest Jerry Frankel was almost more than she could bear.

On the heels of the anger came the guilt. It was her fault this was happening. After all, it was she who was actively conducting the investigation, interviewing the teacher, evaluating the information. If the city council had a problem, it was with her, not Ruben.

Hot tears began to sting her eyes. If Ruben left, what was she going to do? Their relationship was progressing, but it was still fragile; she couldn't just pick up and follow him. And if he ended up in some city clear across the country, what would happen to them then? With conflicting work schedules and the cost of travel, long-distance romances were usually doomed; especially ones that hadn't had time to cement. Just when it seemed that life had finally taken the right turn for her, politics stepped in to block the road. She blinked back the tears.

Dammit it, she thought, the teacher was guilty as sin, and being unable to prove it was not only going to cost Ruben his job, but likely going to cost her a future of real happiness. Ginger could no longer keep the tears in check; they began to run freely down her cheeks.

"Knock, knock," Helen Ballinger said, poking her head in the door. She was wearing her coat and obviously on her way out. "This just came in for Charlie."

She held out an envelope.

"I'll take it," Ginger said over her shoulder.

Helen dropped it on Ginger's desk. "See you tomorrow," she said, and hurried off.

Ginger blinked through her tears; the envelope bore the return address of the state crime lab in Seattle. Her heart suddenly skipped a beat. She knew exactly what it was—the report on Jerry Frankel's fingerprints.

The two detectives often accepted mail for the other, but never opened it. Ginger fingered the envelope. Invasion of privacy or not, overstepping the boundaries or not, she felt sure Charlie would understand. With trembling hands, she ripped it open, almost tearing the report in half in her haste to get to it. She read it once, and then she read it a second time, and a third time. Long after the words were imprinted on her brain, she sat there, staring at the piece of paper.

PART THREE

The Victim

"He that is without sin among you, let him first cast a stone. . . ."

—*John 8:7*

1

Malcolm Purdy survived the holidays the way he usually did. He got drunk on Christmas morning, stayed drunk through New Year's Eve, and remembered next to nothing in between.

The woman who worked for him came in now and again to make sure he was all right. Once, she ended up spending the night, trying to get a little solid food into him, cleaning up after he vomited, holding him when he passed out. He rambled on a lot, about people she didn't know and places she'd never been, and about the sorry state of the country, but most of what he said was unintelligible.

When he ran out of liquor, he sobered up, bathed, shaved, and brushed his teeth. He was expecting two men shortly after the first of January, and it would not have been appropriate for them to see him mewling and puking like a baby.

The men arrived late on Tuesday and were shown to the bunkhouse. The woman unpacked for them and then cooked a hot meal. Afterward, the three men sat around drinking beer, talking, laughing. It was understood that they would relax today, and get down to work tomorrow. Sometime around ten o'clock, they went to bed, the visitors staggering out to the bunkhousebunkhouse, their host collapsing on the sofa in front of the dying fire.

Purdy was a happy man. He knew very little about the two who had come; he would not know much more about them when they left. It didn't matter; he was no longer alone.

"Why, Verna Earley, your table runner is nothing short of magnificent," Eleanor Jewel declared on her way through the dining room. "I don't believe I've seen it before. Was it a Christmas gift?"

"That old thing?" Verna replied. "It belonged to my great-grandmother. I've had it packed away for years."

Eleanor arrived on Wednesday morning in response to the invitation for coffee, bursting with curiosity. It was all she could do to hold her tongue until Verna had propelled her past all her finery and into the breakfast nook, where they sat down with their cups and cake.

"Now tell me just everything," she said at the first possible moment, her triple chins quivering.

"About what?" Verna asked cautiously.

"Well, about the teacher, of course. Are they going to arrest him?" Nothing new had been reported about the Breckenridge case since before Christmas, and the gossip had been itching to get hold of a fresh source.

"Oh, that," Verna said brightly, relieved that the conversation was not going to be about Ruben Martinez. "Well, I expect they'll arrest him when they have enough evidence."

"Then they *are* going to arrest him?" Eleanor gushed. "You mean, he really did it?"

As before, Verna had no more information about the murder investigation than did Eleanor. In fact, when the subject came up at dinner on Christmas Day, both Ruben and Ginger had declined to discuss it. But this was a chance to gain some much-coveted stature, and she wasn't about to let it pass.

"Of course, he did it," she asserted carelessly. "And I'm sure it won't be very long now before Ginger has what she needs to put that horrid man in the hangman's noose."

By the time the holidays were over, Matthew Frankel had reevaluated the incident on the playground, and decided that school probably wasn't such a bad place after all. At least he reasoned that it wasn't fair to judge everyone by the actions of a few.

His grandfather helped him reach that conclusion, during the part of the holiday vacation that the Frankels spent with Aaron in Pennsylvania.

"You're growing into a fine young man," the older version of his father told him. "Tell me, how are you doing in school?"

The two were alone together for an afternoon, and Aaron had taken the boy to the cemetery to visit Emma.

"Okay, I guess, Grandpa," Matthew said. He kicked a stray pebble along the side of the grave.

"Are your grades good?" the old man asked.

"Yes, sir."

"Have you made friends?"

"Sure. Well, one. His name is Billy."

Aaron peered down at the boy and saw an expression that reminded him sharply of Emma.

"What's wrong, son?" he prodded gently.

Matthew squirmed a little. He didn't really know his grandfather very well, but he suspected that Aaron was very much like Jerry.

"Some fifth-graders said some things to me at school one day," he replied hesitantly. "Not very nice things—about me being Jewish." He decided not to mention the other part, the part about his father being a murderer.

Aaron stiffened. He had wondered and even worried when Jerry so abruptly up and relocated his family to the other side of the country. In the past couple of years, he had heard and read some very distressing things about the Northwest; about anti-government militia groups, about small enclaves of neo-Nazis, about skinheads, about the rise in hate crimes.

"Children like that are to be pitied," he told his grandson, a shiver running down his back as he remembered the abusive, goose-stepping youth of the Third Reich. "If you show them you're not afraid, you probably won't have any more trouble with them."

"But why would they do that?" Matthew asked. "I never did anything to them. I don't even know them."

Aaron sighed. "There are people in this world who don't feel very good about themselves," he said. "Some of them aren't very smart, or wealthy, or good-looking; a lot of them have just had bad parenting. Whatever the reason, they're unhappy, and unhappy people somehow get the idea they'll feel better about themselves if they make someone else unhappy. They also have very limited vocabularies."

"*Do* they feel better when they make someone else unhappy?" the boy wanted to know.

"Not for very long," Aaron told him. "You can pretty much hide from the world if you want to, but you can't hide from yourself. Even people who hate others so they won't have to hate themselves sooner or later have to look in the mirror."

"Grandpa," Matthew said, "let's not tell Mom and Dad about this, okay? It's no big deal, and I don't want them to worry."

Aaron nodded. "It'll be just between the two of us," he agreed. "But if it happens again, then you must give me your word that you'll tell your parents. Because they love you and it's their job to protect you."

Matthew considered a moment. "Okay," he promised.

"Again" came four days after school resumed.

The fifth-graders cornered Matthew behind the gymnasium.

"Hey, it's the Jew-boy again!" they exclaimed, closing in.

Matthew stood his ground.

"You're bigger than I am," he said. "And there are three of you. You can push my face in the mud and I probably can't stop you. So if doing it makes you feel better about yourselves, go ahead," he said. "Because after the mud washes off, I'm still gonna like the person I see in the mirror."

The three boys looked at one another for a moment and then back at Matthew.

"The kike kid wants us to push his face in the mud," one said.

"Yeah," said a second. "I heard him ask for it."

"So, what are we waiting for?" asked the last.

The three laughed and started toward him. Matthew didn't fight back. He let them knock him to the ground; he let them push his face into the mud. He shut his eyes and held his breath, and he didn't cry. After a while, they let him up.

"Son of a Jew bitch whore!" they cried.

"Son of a Jew bastard murderer!"

Matthew didn't even let that bother him. He stood as tall as he could. "Did anyone ever tell you that you have a very limited vocabulary?" he told them and then he smiled, his teeth very white in his muddied face.

The three bullies looked at one another, clearly perplexed. None of them stopped Matthew when he turned and walked away.

This time, he told the school nurse who helped clean him up. And he told his parents.

"Are you all right?" Deborah asked in alarm.

"Why didn't you tell us the first time?" Jerry demanded.

Matthew shrugged. "They didn't hurt me the first time; they just scared me. This time, they didn't even scare me, but Grandpa said I had to tell you. They pushed me down in the mud and called me names, that's all. I think doing that makes them feel better about themselves."

Jerry almost smiled because it was exactly the kind of thing Aaron would have said.

"Come on, let's get you into the bathtub, young man," his mother said. She picked him up, hugging him so hard he could barely breathe, and bundled him up the stairs.

Jerry sat down at the kitchen table and clasped his hands until his knuckles turned white. He was a man who was usually slow to anger, but he could feel the burn beginning deep inside him. It was one thing for the police to harass him; it was quite another when a bunch of bullies went after his son. That was hitting way below the belt. Even more, it hinted at something truly malevolent in this serene, pristine community—something that went a good deal deeper than an immature letter to the editor now and then. He had never himself been the target of religious animosity, and despite Aaron's admonitions, he had almost lulled himself into believing he could protect his son from it as well. But now it was here, staring him in the face, and he had to decide what to do about it.

"He's playing naval bombardment as though nothing had happened," Deborah reported ten minutes later.

"But it did happen, didn't it?" Jerry said.

"He's just a kid," she replied. "He doesn't really understand."

"Maybe he doesn't," her husband suggested. "But we do."

"Come on, let's not blow this out of proportion," she responded. "If we make a big deal of it, you know it's likely to make things worse for Matthew."

"We can't ignore it."

"I didn't say we should ignore it. I say we should let the school handle it. That's where it happened; that's where the appropriate action should be taken. You know the principal. You can talk to her and tell her how we feel, and then let her deal with it."

Deborah was a fourth-generation American who had never

been to Germany, hadn't lost any relatives in the Holocaust, and had learned everything she knew about the Gestapo and the Brown Shirts and the Hitler Youth through the filtered light of a classroom.

"You think some kids calling Matthew the 'son of a Jew bastard murderer' is just a school problem?" Jerry asked. "Let them take care of it and that's the end of it?"

"For now, yes," she reasoned. "In case you haven't noticed, there are bigots on this island. And what else is there for people like that to do around here besides giving vent to their fears and ignorance? But if what Rachel says is true, there are just a few of them, and I think we'd be playing right into their hands if we were to sink to their level." That was all she needed, Deborah thought, to have another messy situation in another community.

He looked at her, unconvinced. "Three bullies have targeted your son, and you seem to think it's nothing."

"I didn't say it was nothing," she told him. "But I believe in picking my battles, when I can. A few ten-year-olds calling Matthew names hurts, but it hardly warrants calling in the National Guard. I think he handled it brilliantly, all on his own, and I'd be very surprised if they bothered him again."

"This doesn't end with those kids and you know it," Jerry persisted. "How would they have known what to say if they didn't hear it at home?"

"They probably did," she conceded. "So, what do you want to do—go out and gun down the parents?"

"Of course not," he said. "But it may not be the passing thing you think it is. A couple of months ago, I came up against a student whose parents are apparently teaching revisionist history at home."

"You're kidding," she replied in surprise. "What did you do?"

"I told him to bring in his books and we'd study them along with the traditional texts, and let the class decide the truth about the Holocaust."

"What happened?"

Jerry shrugged. "He never brought the books. He never said another word about them. It became a nonissue, and we went on with the regular curriculum."

"Well, there, you see?" she said. "You didn't have to get down in the dirt and fight him, or make a big fuss about it, did you? A small humiliation in front of his peers was sufficient."

"That approach may have worked in that particular instance, but this is different," he reminded her. "In case you forgot, they called me a murderer, to my own son."

Now it was Deborah's turn to shrug. "The police are desperate to solve the Breckenridge case. In their zeal, they leaned on you a little too hard, and some people got the wrong idea. Maybe some of them were stupid enough to talk about it at the dinner table. You know better than I do that kids are like sponges. They soak stuff up and squeeze it out without any real comprehension. This is probably nothing more than that, and I wouldn't go out looking to find some great community conspiracy lurking in the shadows."

"Are you sure?" he asked.

"Yes, I'm sure," she assured him complacently. "You'll see. It'll all blow over. This'll turn out to be just an isolated incident."

2

So accustomed were the readers of the *Seward Sentinel* to seeing the big black-banded box that had appeared in the classified
section with daily repetition for more than a month that they re-
acted with alarm on the morning it was no longer there.

"What happened?" they wondered on Friday over double
lattes at The Pelican.

"Where is it?" they asked as they boarded the ferry.

"Why aren't they printing the Purdy ad anymore?"

"What does it mean?"

"Have the police caught the killer?"

"Who turned him in?"

"Who gets the reward?"

Telephone calls poured into Curtis House at the rate of two
dozen an hour.

"First they criticized us for printing the ad in the first
place," Iris Tanaka commented, "and now they berate us for can-
celing it."

"We didn't cancel it," Gail reminded her. "Malcolm Purdy
did."

Indeed, the ex-Marine had called late Wednesday, thanked them for their courtesy, and informed them that the notice would no longer be necessary.

"I understand that the police are close to an arrest," he said. "So I don't guess there's anything to be gained by running it any longer."

"An arrest?" Gail echoed, concealing her surprise. "I didn't know that was common knowledge." In fact, she had not even the slightest inkling from her latest conversation with Ginger that an arrest was imminent.

There was a pause at the other end of the telephone.

"Well, that's what I heard," Purdy told her.

"In that case," the editor inquired, "who gets the reward?"

"Too soon to say," he replied.

"My goodness, who are they arresting?" Iris wanted to know.

Gail shrugged. "The teacher, I assume."

"The teacher?" The editor's assistant was clearly bewildered. "They really think the teacher did it? I don't believe it."

"Why not?"

"I don't know. I guess because he seems like such a regular guy. My kid sister's in one of his classes, and she's always saying what a great teacher he is, how nice he is."

"Nice guys sometimes kill," Gail told her.

Iris frowned. "True. But I thought most of that stuff we were printing about him was just hype; you know, just for circulation."

An image of Alice Easton standing in an upstairs window flickered behind the editor's eyes and was gone. Maybe, she thought. "Maybe not," she said.

Ginger hummed the refrain of a current hit song while she ironed. Although this was normally a task she loathed, she had a whole week of work shirts crisply pressed before she realized it.

The secret, she decided, was in not thinking about what you were doing. And Ginger's mind was certainly not on ironing.

It was Sunday night. She had spent the day in Seattle with Ruben and Stacey, wandering through Pike Place Market, sampling the food, admiring the crafts, and laughing at the fishmongers who made a sideshow out of tossing their catch from one to another.

"Dungeness crab, already cooked," one of them encouraged Ruben. "Your missus won't have to cook tonight."

Ruben smiled. "Do you want crab for dinner?" he asked Ginger.

She looked at the price. "No," she said, wrinkling her nose. "I want pizza."

"Me, too," Stacey chimed in.

Ruben shrugged. "Sorry," he said to the fishmonger.

They read the names carved in the floor tiles of those who had contributed to saving the treasured landmark. They bought some fresh vegetables and flowers. And then, coming home on the ferry, they argued over what kind of pizza to have, just like any family.

Ginger had never been happier. She knew that the break they needed in the Breckenridge case was just around the corner, and it would not only save Ruben's job, but also save their developing relationship. Even the city council would find it unreasonable to argue with success.

The teacher was guilty. She knew it for certain. It wouldn't matter that it had taken them three months to zero in on him. There had been few clues, and he had been very clever, very elusive. What mattered was that she had finally seen through his boyish act of innocence and was about to nail him. That's what the people would care about, what the newspaper would report—what the council would have to acknowledge.

It had taken her twenty-eight years to find the man with whom she wanted to spend the rest of her life. While some might think them a strange match, there was no doubt in her mind that Ruben Martinez was totally right for her; so calm when she was wired, so thoughtful when she was impulsive, so wise, so caring, so sexy. She knew she would fight, if she had to, get down in the gutter, if it came to that, and do whatever was necessary to prevent anyone from taking him away from her.

Ginger finished pressing the last pair of work pants and hung them on a hanger on the back of her closet door so they would be handy in the morning. Then she turned off the iron, scrubbed her face, brushed her teeth, and climbed into bed. Twink jumped up and stretched out next to her, purring.

"Well, you're not exactly Ruben," she said, stroking his fur, and remembering with a sigh who had been beside her the night before, "but everything in its time."

She fell asleep with a smile on her face.

Charlie Pricker hated being sick. Even a cold made him irritable because it dulled his senses, and this was no cold.

"It's pneumonia, and there's nothing you can do but take your antibiotics and wait it out," Magnus Coop told him.

"Pneumonia?" echoed Charlie. "How the hell did I get that?"

"You tell me," the doctor retorted. "I told you a month ago to come in about that cough."

"It was nothing," groused Charlie.

"Well, it's not nothing anymore. You've got chills, a fever of a hundred and three, and bloody sputum. Now go home and stay there, or I'll put you in the hospital."

"I can't be out of the office for more than a day or two," Charlie protested. "I've got a stack of work higher than the Space Needle."

"I'll explain it to Ruben," Coop said. "And I'm going to tell Jane to take the phone out of your room," he added. "You're to have complete rest."

"I'll bring you some soup," Jane said when her husband arrived home fifteen minutes later. She had already talked to Coop;
the bedroom telephone was in her hand.

"I'll come down for it," Charlie said.

Jane shook her head. "I'll bring it up. I promised Magnus I'd
lock the bedroom door from the outside if you went one step further than the bathroom."

He didn't argue. Although he would never have admitted it,
Coop's diagnosis scared him. He had one relative who died of
pneumonia brought on by a boating accident, and another who
had succumbed after traveling in India. Weak lungs ran in his
family.

Charlie remained under Jane's house arrest for ten days,
until his fever was gone and he had stopped coughing up blood.
He returned to work on the third Thursday in January to find a
letter from the crime lab in the pile on his desk.

"Hey," he said to Ginger. "This must be the report on
Frankel's latents. Sure took them long enough. How long has it
been sitting here?"

She glanced over. "It came in late yesterday, I think."

"Why the hell didn't you open it?"

Ginger gave him a blank look. "We don't open each other's
mail," she reminded him.

"Weren't you curious?"

"Of course I was," she said. "And I would have called you
about it, but Jane said you'd be back to work this morning."

Charlie tore into the envelope and scanned the report.
Within seconds, a big grin spread across his face.

"We got him!" he cried. "The son of a bitch—we got him!"

On the basis of the fingerprint match, backed up by an array
of circumstantial evidence, Judge Irwin Jacobs was persuaded to
sign a search warrant for the person and property of Jeremy
Frankel.

Ruben, Ginger, Charlie, and Glen Dirksen arrived at the teacher's Larkspur Lane residence on Friday afternoon at five minutes past three. Frankel and his son were at home; his wife was not.

"I'm sorry, sir, but we have a warrant to search the premises," Ruben said, holding out the official, blue-jacketed document.

Jerry looked at it blankly. "What are you talking about?" he asked. "Search my house? Why? For what?"

"We are looking for evidence related to the Breckenridge case," Ginger said.

"I don't understand," he replied. "There isn't anything here."

"Perhaps not, sir," Charlie said. "But the warrant says we get to look."

"Am I supposed to call my lawyer?"

"That's up to you," Ruben told him. "However, we do have a legal right to be here. I doubt your attorney will tell you anything else. Now, may we come in?"

"You mean, right now?" Jerry asked.

"Yes, sir."

"But my wife's not home from work yet. Shouldn't she be here if strangers are going to go through her house?"

"We have no control over that," Ruben said.

Frankel looked at Ginger. "I don't know what to do," he said. "I have to think. Can you come back in a couple of hours?"

"No, I'm afraid not," she said.

"But my son is here. You can't do this in front of my son. He's only nine years old; he doesn't understand."

Ruben and Ginger exchanged glances.

"Perhaps your son could leave the house for a while," Ginger suggested. "Does he have a friend he can visit?"

Jerry seemed to think about that for a moment and then he nodded.

"Why don't you take a moment to arrange it," Ruben said.

As though in a daze, Jerry turned away from the door, and then immediately turned back. "What do I tell him?" he asked.

"Whatever you need to," Ginger replied.

"These people are going to be here with me for a while," the teacher told his son. "And it would be better if we were alone. I called Mrs. Hildress. She said you can come over and play with Billy until I'm finished."

Matthew took a long look at each of the police officers and then turned his dark eyes on his father. "Okay, I'll go," he agreed reluctantly. "But you call me if you need me."

"Count on it," Jerry said. He helped the boy put on his jacket and guided him to the door. "Stay at Billy's until I come for you," he said. "We'll go get pizza for dinner."

Ginger felt an unexpected catch in her throat. Just like any family, she thought.

The little boy walked down the front path, glancing back toward the house several times. Then he turned onto the street and was gone.

The search was thorough. The police tried to be neat, but within just a few moments, it was clear to Jerry that Deborah was going to know they had been there, and any thought he might have had to keep it from her vanished.

"No, you can't stop them," Scott confirmed from his office in Seattle in response to the urgent call. "What are they going to find?"

"Nothing," Jerry replied.

"So let them search."

The four police officers worked quickly and efficiently, spreading out into all the rooms, leaving nothing unchecked. The teacher followed after them like a lost puppy. An hour later, they met in the kitchen, having found nothing.

"There's still the garage," Ruben said. "And we might as well take a quick look around the outside before it gets too dark."

During the summer months, daylight in the Pacific North-west stretched until almost ten o'clock at night; during winter, it lasted barely past four-thirty.

It was Glen Dirksen who went inside the part of the back-yard that Jerry had fenced off for Chase. The retriever wriggled up to him, and Dirksen stooped down to pet him. Taking that as a sign that the stranger would play, Chase bounded off and re-turned a moment later with one of his favorite toys—a dirty gray sweatshirt, rolled up and knotted at two ends, that he and Matthew used for tug-of-war.

In the gathering dusk, Dirksen took up one of the ends. It was a full minute before he realized that the rag wasn't just dirty, but had dark stains on it. He untied one of the knots and unrolled the material. The stains were splattered all across the front of the sweatshirt.

His heart pounding, Dirksen hurried toward the garage. "Take a look at this," he cried. Ruben and Charlie stopped what they were doing and came over to see.

"It's just an old shirt the dog chews on," Jerry said.

Charlie examined the material. "These look like they could be bloodstains," he said.

"They are," Jerry confirmed. "I cut my thumb a while back and bled all over myself. The stains didn't come out when my wife washed the shirt, so we gave it to Chase."

"We'll have to check this out," Charlie said. He knew that, in addition to the blood, a number of unidentified light gray fibers had been found on Tara Breckenridge's body. He folded the sweatshirt and placed it in a paper bag. Then he stapled the bag shut and scribbled something across the outside with a black felt marker.

A matter of seconds later, Ginger came toward them with an expression on her face that was half disbelief and half exultation.

"Take a look at this," she said. In her hands was a piece of newspaper; inside lay a knife with a thick black handle and a six-inch curved blade.

"Where did you get that?" the teacher asked.

"From the hidden compartment in the back of your car," Ginger replied.

"My car? What was it doing there?"

"That's a good question, Mr. Frankel," Ruben said. "One I was just about to ask you."

"I have no idea," Jerry said, as he peered down at the object. "It's not mine. I've never owned a knife like that."

"We'll have to check this out, too," Charlie repeated, and everyone watched as he duplicated the procedure he had followed with the sweatshirt.

"Mr. Frankel," Ruben said. "I now have to ask you to accompany us down to the medical clinic, where a sample of your blood and hair can be taken for testing."

"The search warrant says you can do that?" Jerry asked.

"Yes, sir, it does."

"Will it take long?"

"Not very," the police chief told him. "You should be able to pick up your son by six at the latest."

The teacher sighed. "I'll get my coat."

Gail Brown knew about the search before it began. It was just the way things happened in small towns. She didn't have all the details, but she had enough to draw some reliable conclusions and get her ace reporter on the story.

"I'm holding a full column," she told him. "It's tomorrow's lead. You have an hour. Don't disappoint me."

He didn't. Fifty-nine minutes later, he handed her a cogent account of the conditions under which the search warrant had been granted, and an accurate description of who had participated in the search and how long it had taken. All it lacked was a specific accounting of what the police had found at the Frankel home, because Ruben was apparently not yet willing to release that information.

She scanned the paragraphs quickly, noting that no mention of the Holman Academy or Alice Easton appeared in the warrant particulars. Without knowing exactly why, Gail felt a strong sense of relief. Admittedly, she had gone to Scarsdale looking for information that would break the Seward Island case wide open, images of Pulitzers dancing before her eyes, but she was uncomfortable with what she had found—or more precisely, what she had not found. When she took the information to Ginger, it was with the hope that it would be used only to keep the police focused on the teacher long enough to uncover some concrete evidence of his complicity in the Breckenridge murder, should there be any.

Apparently, from what her reporter had learned, there was.

Unlike Eleanor Jewel, Mildred MacDonald, and a few others of similar ilk, Libby Hildress was not considered an Island gossip. She belonged to several community organizations and had a wide circle of acquaintances, which placed her in a position to gather numerous snippets of information, but the only person with whom she ever discussed any of the things she overheard was her husband.

"In the middle of the afternoon, he calls," she said as soon as Bud and Billy had been excused from the dinner table and sent off to do their homework. "Can Matthew come over to play for a while?"

"So?" Tom responded.

"So, Matthew tells Billy the police are over at his house, talking to his father."

"That again?"

"Tom, don't dismiss me. I tell you, it means something. Why would Matthew have to leave his house just because the police were there? Does that make any sense?"

"What are you getting at?" he asked.

"I don't think the police were there to talk. I've got a pretty good hunch they were there to search the house. I think they were looking for incriminating evidence. That's why Jerry sent the boy away."

"They have to have a search warrant for that," Tom told her. "And they need a lot more than a hunch to get it."

"My point exactly."

Tom looked at his wife. "You think he killed her, don't you?"

"I don't want to think that, but I don't know what else to think," Libby said. "This interest in him has been going on much too long. When he came to pick Matthew up, he was trying real hard to act normal, you know, but I could tell he was frazzled."

"Frazzled?"

"Well, you know what I mean," she said. "He looked wild-eyed and like he was sort of coming unglued. Well, I don't know how else to say it except to come right out and say it: he looked guilty."

3

Ruben and Ginger couldn't resist indulging in a little private celebration. They had uncovered the direct evidence they believed
was going to solve the Breckenridge case, and they were relish-
ing the moment over fish and chips and a pitcher of beer at the
Waterside Cafe.

"I knew once we got a search warrant, we'd find what we
needed," Ginger exulted, being careful to keep her voice down
because they were not yet ready for public disclosure.

"What's scary is to think we'd already cut him loose," Ruben
said.

"It was Gail who saved the day," Ginger acknowledged, giving the editor her due. "If she hadn't dug up that stuff at the Holman Academy, we wouldn't have had any other choice—we
wouldn't have anything at all."

"Maybe so," Ruben allowed, "but it was your brilliant water
glass maneuver that locked it up. Without that latent match, we
were dead in the water."

Ginger shrugged carelessly. "It doesn't matter how it happened," she said. "What's important is that we got the son of a

bitch, and now the city council is going to have to dance barefoot on broken glass to keep you."

Ruben chuckled. "Well, maybe nothing quite so drastic."

"Oh come on," she teased him. "You've got to make them crawl just a little."

"You know, I always credit good police work," he said thoughtfully. "But it's amazing how many times a case is cracked just because the suspect was careless."

"What do you mean?"

"Well, we searched Frankel's Taurus that first day we were out there, and we didn't find the knife."

"Yes, but we didn't have a search warrant then," she reminded him. "So I never opened that compartment in the back."

"But that's my point," Ruben said. "He's not a stupid man. He knew we suspected him. Why would he keep a murder weapon in his car?"

Ginger considered the question. "Because he didn't think we'd search there again?"

"No, I mean why would he keep it at all? There are plenty of places on this island where he could have gotten rid of a knife, places where we never would have found it, and he had three months to do it."

"Who knows," Ginger suggested. "Killers do stupid things. Maybe he thought he'd outsmarted us and was going to get away with it, so he figured he didn't need to throw away a good knife. Maybe he wanted a souvenir."

In twenty-five years, Ruben had dealt with his share of killers: smart ones, stupid ones, and smart ones who did stupid things. It had been his experience that, while some had been inclined to keep guns, they invariably got rid of knives.

"That's what I mean by being careless," he said. "It never makes sense."

"Does it matter?" she asked. "He did it—isn't that what counts?"

"You have a point," he conceded.

"I have to tell you," Ginger confided, "for a while there I was really afraid that he was going to get away with it, and that you were going to get fired, and Seward Island's first homicide was going to go unsolved. It's scary to think how close we came."

"Then let's not think about it," he suggested.

"Tell me, if you were in his place, would you try to run?" she asked.

"I don't know," Ruben replied. "Maybe, if I didn't have a family to consider. But he does, and besides, he's got one of the best criminal lawyers in the country."

"Well, just in case the idea occurs to him," she said, "I assigned Dirksen to watch him."

Ruben laughed appreciatively. "You're a damn good cop, you know that?" he told her. "You're thorough, you're professional, you cover all the bases, and you have a healthy distrust of all mankind."

"I'm so excited," Ginger said with a giggle. "I think I could jump off the top of Eagle Rock and fly. Frankly, I was devastated at the thought of having to break in a new police chief."

"I was rather concerned about having to leave here myself," Ruben conceded with a shy smile. "Although, I must admit, my concern wasn't entirely about the job."

Ginger grinned. "I should hope not," she said. Under the table, where no one could see, they clasped hands. "The *Sentinel* will probably run a story tomorrow about the search. When are you going to tell Albert what we found?"

"Charlie should have preliminary results on the knife and the sweatshirt by Monday," he said. "On the assumption that they'll go the way we think they will, we'll get the paperwork over to Van Pelt. Then I'll tell the mayor."

Harvey Van Pelt was the Puget County prosecutor. He

would determine if the case against Jerry Frankel was solid enough for an arrest. Ginger sighed contentedly. It would be the first step in nailing the bastard who had so mutilated Tara Breckenridge.

Deborah Frankel spent Friday night putting her house back in order: folding, arranging, replacing, rearranging. She felt totally violated at having had strangers paw through her possessions without her presence, her permission, or even her prior knowledge. She was outraged that this kind of thing could happen. And much as it appalled her to admit it, she was frightened—more frightened than she had ever been in her life—that the police might know something she hadn't yet allowed herself to consider.

"But how could they have gotten a search warrant?" she demanded when there was nothing left to rearrange, and Jerry was finally able to persuade her to come to bed. "On what grounds?"

"They said they matched my fingerprint to one they found on the cross the Breckenridge girl was wearing," he replied.

Deborah stared at her husband. "Is that possible?" she breathed.

His eyes slid past her shoulder. "I don't know how," he said, "but I suppose so."

It was then that the fear gripped her, like a cold fist in her stomach, and the unthinkable thought she had tried so hard to keep out of her mind crawled in. And with the thought came all the protective, maternal instincts she had been developing, without fulling realizing it, since the day so long ago when she first came to acknowledge that her husband needed a mother more than a wife.

"Let's take the weekend off," she suggested suddenly, recklessly, forgetting the packed briefcase that had accompanied her home. "Let's just get in the car and go someplace."

"Where?" he asked.

"I don't know—out to the coast, maybe. Or up to the mountains. Or we could even take the ferry over to Victoria. I don't care where. We just need to get away from here for a couple of days. I feel like the walls are closing in on me."

"I'm not sure we should do that," he said slowly.

"Why not?"

"All things considered, this may not be such a good time to leave the Island. It might look—funny."

"You mean, because somebody might get the wrong idea and think you're trying to run away?"

He shrugged. "Something like that."

She stared at him, the question she couldn't bring herself to ask filling the space between them. After a while, she turned off the light and pulled up the covers.

It was barely an hour later when the telephone rang, but the shrill sound jerked Jerry out of a deep, dreamless sleep. He groped for the receiver in the dark, wondering where he was and what time it was.

"Murderer!" a nameless, faceless voice cried. "We know you killed that poor defenseless girl, and you won't get away with it. Filthy Jew bastard murderer!"

Beside him, Deborah was fumbling for the switch on the bedside lamp. "Who would be calling us at this hour?" she demanded irritably. "For heaven's sake, it's one o'clock in the morning." Then she saw his face—drained of all color. "What is it?" she gasped. "Has something happened to Aaron?"

Jerry did not respond. He simply lay there with the receiver clutched in his hand. Deborah snatched it from him and put it to her ear, but heard only a dial tone.

"Tell me," she insisted.

"It wasn't about Aaron," he told her in a dead voice. "It wasn't about anything. It was just a crank call."

"A crank call?" she muttered in disgust. "You look like you've seen a ghost from the past."

A ghost from the past, he thought, that was not a ghost at all, nor from the past, but alive and well and living on Seward Island.

"It woke me up, that's all," he replied.

Deborah yawned. "With a little luck, maybe we can get back to sleep." She reached over and snapped off the light.

"Remember what you said about wanting to go someplace over the weekend?" he said into the dark. "Well, the hell with the timing; the hell with what anyone thinks. Let's go."

"Okay," she mumbled into her pillow. "It won't take more than a few minutes to throw some things into a suitcase. We can take the early ferry."

"Have you seen the morning *Sentinel*?" Rachel Cohen asked her husband at breakfast. News of the search was splashed across the newspaper's front page.

Scott nodded.

"I'm sorry, but I just can't believe that Jerry could have had anything to do with that girl's death."

The Cherub shrugged.

"I know you can't talk about a client," she said. "But these people are our friends . . . They're going to arrest him, aren't they?"

"It's possible," he conceded.

"This is terrible. That poor family."

"Have you spoken to Deborah?"

Rachel shook her head. "I called first thing, but the machine picked up. I can only imagine what she's going through. She puts up a good front, you know, but I think inside she's scared to death. She might have made light of that incident at school with Matthew, but I know it had to have upset her."

"What incident with Matthew?"

Rachel blinked. "Those bullies who beat up on him and called him anti-Semitic names. I'm sure I told you about it."

Scott frowned. "If you did, I don't remember. Tell me again."

As best she could, Rachel reconstructed what Deborah had told her. "I know there are certain elements here on Seward who feel that way, but as I told Deborah, they usually stay pretty much underground," she concluded. "I don't remember anything as blatant as that ever happening before."

"Anti-Semitism, eh?" he murmured.

Scott's hooded green eyes narrowed and his wife smiled. It was Saturday, the day of the week on which he officially did not work, but that had never kept him from thinking. Almost as though there had been an audible shifting of gears, she knew his mind was now fully engaged in its own kind of processing. She got up and began to clear away the breakfast dishes. There was no point in her saying another word; she knew her husband would not hear her.

The telephone in Ginger's apartment rang shortly before one o'clock on Saturday afternoon.

"I'm out at Ocean Shores," Glen Dirksen reported.

"What the hell are you doing there?"

"Following Frankel," the young officer replied. "You told me to watch him, didn't you? Well, they were up at dawn this morning, and on line for the early ferry—teacher, wife, kid, and dog. I didn't know what they had in mind, so I thought I'd better follow them."

He had sat a discreet half block from the Frankel house all night, dozing off only when the upstairs lights had gone out for good, and awakening every half hour or so until the lights went back on.

"What are they doing?" Ginger asked, suddenly alert.

"They checked into the Lighthouse Suites Inn, then they

went into town and ate lunch at the Dairy Queen, and now they're walking on the beach."

"What kind of luggage do they have?" Ginger asked.

"One small suitcase, weekend size."

"Do they know you're there?"

"I don't think so. I'm not in uniform and I'm driving my pickup. There aren't a heck of a lot of people out here this time of year, but I'm being careful."

"Get as close to them as you can," she instructed. "I don't care if they spot you. I want you to stick to them like glue."

"I can do that," he assured her.

"Do you have enough money for a room and food?"

"Yeah," he replied. "But it's my rent money, so I hope I can get reimbursed."

"Don't worry about that," she said. "Now listen, if they so much as glance in the direction of Canada, stop them. Arrest him, if you have to, on any pretext you can concoct. Otherwise, just keep me posted."

"You see, I was right," Libby Hildress declared, waving the *Sentinel* under her husband's nose. "That's why Matthew was sent over here—so he wouldn't be home when the police found the incriminating evidence."

"The newspaper didn't say anything about anyone finding any incriminating evidence," Tom reminded her. "It could all be much ado about nothing."

"If the police were able to get a search warrant, it isn't about nothing," Libby insisted. "We haven't heard about anyone else's home being searched, have we?"

Tom had to concede they hadn't. "Still, let's not be in such a hurry to tie a noose around his neck until we know something more specific," he suggested.

"I'm sorry," she said. "Matthew may be a nice enough boy, but I don't think we should let Billy have any more to do with that family. He's spent hours and hours over there when neither one of us really knew what was going on. I know I haven't said anything about it before, but I was never very comfortable about that friendship from the beginning."

"Why not?" Tom asked.

"Because we don't know how those kind of people think," she told him. "Or how they might have tried to influence an impressionable boy like Billy."

"Influence him about what?"

Libby shrugged. "I don't know," she said. "All sorts of things. Against Jesus, maybe."

"You're not serious?"

"Of course I am. Jews don't believe in Jesus. They might have tried to convert him."

"Libby, I think you're stretching. Billy's never said anything that would lead us to believe the Frankels ever talked to him about religion."

"Well, who knows what they might have said, or even what they practice?" she persisted. "For all we know, they could be members of one of those weird mind-control cults out there that parents have had to deprogram their kids from."

"Oh come on," Tom declared. "What would make you think they were into anything like that?"

"I don't know that they are. I'm just saying we should be careful," she replied. "After all, what do we really know about them?"

"They're people, just like us," he said.

"Oh no, they're not," Libby shot back. "They're not like us at all. They don't look like us. They don't think like us. They certainly don't believe in the same things we believe in. And with people like that—well, how do we know what they'd do?"

4

Including the night of the polygraph test, Stacey Martinez had been out with Danny Leo four times: on New Year's Eve, a second time to the movies, and once to a concert in Seattle. Tonight would be their fifth date, and they were going ice skating.

Because of the moderate winter climate, there was no natural ice on Seward Island. About fifteen years ago, the city fathers had been persuaded, by a majority vote of the population on a special bond issue, to build a covered outdoor rink. For a remote area, with little to occupy its youth, the project was promoted as a potential antidote to skyrocketing drug use.

The Ice Pavilion was located on a bluff that jutted out into Puget Sound, just north of town. It was maintained by the city parks department. A well-stocked snack bar helped to defray costs, as did the school district, which leased the facility during the winter for its hockey team. With its glass roof and three open sides, the rink afforded skaters a wonderful mural of the mainland at any time of the day. At night, they could watch Seattle's lights dance across the water as they glided and twirled to the music.

Three times a week, from November to March, Danny Leo trained at this rink. He knew every inch of it.

✵ ✵ ✵

"You're seeing quite a lot of this young man, aren't you?" Ruben observed as Stacey waited for her date. "Three weekends in a row."

"I like him," she said. "He's a whole lot more mature than most of the boys at school. He's really got his act together. Do you know he's got his whole life planned out already? He knows exactly what he wants to do."

Ruben looked at her. "It's my fault," he said sadly. "You had to grow up way before your time. Now you're too old in your head to think about parties and pretty clothes, like other girls, and boys your own age are too young for you."

Stacey came over and gave her father a hug. "I don't know why I am the way I am," she told him, "but right now I wouldn't want to be anyone else."

He couldn't remember ever loving her more than he did at that moment. Tears crowded his eyes. He blinked them aside and cleared his throat.

"You're—uh—not doing anything foolish with this boy, are you?" he asked.

Stacey giggled. "Nothing as foolish as you and Ginger, if that's what you're asking."

"It is, and I don't appreciate the comparison," he said, but he couldn't quite keep from smiling.

"Danny's a perfect gentleman," she assured him. "And since you taught me to be a perfect lady, you can put all those worries right out of your head." She gave him a mischievous look. "At least for a while anyway."

"How long a while?"

She screwed up her face in thought. "I guess until I get with someone who makes me feel the way Ginger makes you feel," she said.

"And Danny Leo doesn't?"

Stacey considered that. "Maybe he could," she replied with a toss of her silky blond hair. "If I gave him the chance."

"You're seeing an awful lot of this girl," Peter Leo remarked, standing in the bathroom doorway, watching his son shave, and wondering where the years had gone. "Is it such a good idea?"

Danny blinked at him through the mirror. "I can't see as it's hurting anyone," he said.

"She's young," Peter reminded him. "If anything should happen—if she should get herself in trouble—she's underage, you know. It would ruin you."

"Then I'll just have to make sure nothing happens," Danny replied with a trace of a smile.

"Don't be cocky," Peter retorted. "Sometimes, things can get out of control despite our best intentions."

"Stacey and I are friends, Dad," Danny assured him. "There's nothing more going on."

The evening was clear and unusually cold, even for January. A thousand stars smiled down through the glass roof, and the lights of Seattle glittered across Puget Sound. The ice was crowded, mostly with teenagers. The snack bar was doing a banner business in hot chocolate.

Danny was an excellent skater. There was no question that he would be playing hockey for Harvard next year. Stacey was graceful, but not nearly as comfortable on the ice.

"That's okay," he said easily. "Just hold on to me and you'll be fine."

He put his arm around her waist and guided her smoothly over the ice, in perfect time with the music. She felt as though she were floating.

"I've never skated almost outside before," she told him, used to the sterile, air-conditioned rinks of California. "I can't believe how different it is."

He looked up at the stars and out across the water. "This is the way it's supposed to be," he said, and whirled her around until she was dizzy and laughing.

"Are you two an item?" Bert Kriedler asked them when they stopped to catch their breath. "I mean, like officially together?"

Danny looked at Stacey and smiled. "We're officially friends," he said.

"What's your secret?" Melissa Senn wanted to know when she cornered Stacey in the rest room. "I could never get the high school hunk to look twice at me."

"I don't think I have any big secret," Stacey told her honestly. "We're just friends."

"Do you think she's putting out?" Melissa asked Jeannie Gemmetta. "Is that why he's interested?"

Jeannie shook her head. "Not Stacey. She's Catholic and cautious, and she knows her daddy would kill anyone who touched her. When she spreads her legs, it'll be for nothing less than a ring and a ceremony."

"Yeah, but remember," Melissa cautioned, "that's what we thought about Tara, too."

Two shots of Scotch, half a bottle of wine with dinner, several sips of his Kahlúa, and a warm fire had made Ruben uncharacteristically loquacious.

"I'm a simple man, with simple needs," he told Ginger as they lay curled up on her living room floor, Twink at their feet. "I never wanted a lot of money. I never wanted to be famous. I just wanted to do something worthwhile with my life, and have a crack at being happy."

"Well, it's for sure you don't have a lot of money," Ginger said with a chuckle, "and you aren't famous, and you do very worthwhile work. So all that's left is—are you happy?"

"I think so," he replied. "But you can ask me that again after we collar the teacher."

She reached over and poked him in the ribs. "You're such a romantic," she chided.

"It depends on your definition of romance," he told her, teasing. "I think miracles are romantic, and solving the Breckenridge case was nothing short of a miracle. Getting Frankel to drink out of that glass before his attorney showed up was more than just luck."

"Sometimes miracles happen," she said with a shrug.

Twink blinked.

"True," Ruben conceded. "But this one probably saved my job. And while I wouldn't admit it to anyone but you, I'm just a little bit happier about saving my job than I am about solving the case."

Ginger sighed a very self-satisfied sigh. "Me, too," she said.

Twink yawned.

"You know, I never cared that much about where I worked," Ruben went on. "As long as the schools were good and safe and the environment was healthy, a job was a job, and I was always ready to move on to the next one. But things are different now, and I admit I'm struck by the irony."

"Of what?"

"Let's face it, I don't fit in here. I'll never fit in. I'm about as outside as an outsider can get on Seward Island, and it's not likely that I'll ever be welcomed into the bosom of this community. And yet, this is where I want to be; these are the people I want to serve; this is the department I want to run; this is the staff I want to go on working with. This is where I want Stacey to finish high school and where I want her to come home to from college. This is where I'd like to grow old. I didn't realize how important the place had become to me until I thought I was going to have to leave it."

In response, Ginger put her arms around him and hugged him. She didn't want to tell him how frightened she had been at the thought of losing him.

Twink purred.

"And as long as I'm running on at the mouth here," Ruben added, "I guess I should tell you that I'm getting a little tired of spending all these wonderful evenings with you and then having to get up and go home. I think it's time for a change."

"Exactly what sort of change did you have in mind?" Ginger asked, pulling back to look at him.

"Well, that's just it, I'm not sure," he replied. "You see, I'm selfish enough to know that I want to marry you, but I'm also smart enough to know that a young girl shouldn't marry an old man."

"Last time I looked," she responded breathlessly, "I wasn't so young and you weren't so old."

"You know what I mean," he said. "When a woman like you marries for the first time, it should be about starting a brand-new life—not picking up in the middle of someone else's. And what about children? Every woman dreams of having children. I wouldn't want to rob you of that joy. But I'm old enough to be your father. If we had children, I'd be more like a grandfather to them."

"I don't think anything in life is ever perfect," she said slowly. "Even the best parts require some kind of accommodation. I'd be lying if I said I hadn't thought about having children someday. I guess it's natural for a woman to think about that. But I'd also be lying if I said having children was more important to me than you are."

"You may think that now," he cautioned. "But what about a year from now, or ten years from now, or twenty, when it would be too late?"

"I don't have any idea how I'll feel then," she told him honestly. "I only know how I feel now. And how I feel now is that I would be silly to give up what I *know* I want for some future perfection that might not even exist."

Ruben peered at her in the firelight. "You sound like you've already thought this all through."

"I have," she admitted, smiling softly. "The night of our second date. I've just been waiting for you to catch up."

He wondered if she would always be a step ahead of him, and decided he really wouldn't mind if she were. "Well then," he said, taking a deep breath, "will you marry me?"

Ginger took a moment to stare into the fire and let his words sink in. She wanted to be sure that she understood all the ramifications of what this would mean. She looked down the twenty-eight years of her past, at the path that had led her here. Then she looked at Ruben, her future, waiting for an answer.

"Yes," she said.

"I guess you can't do anything in this town without everyone trying to second-guess you," Danny said as he walked Stacey to her front door. "Everyone's sure we're getting it on."

"I don't care what they think," she replied. "We know we're just friends."

"Well, that's just it," he said, scuffing the tip of his shoe against the porch steps. "I'm beginning to think maybe we could be more than just friends."

She giggled. "Peer pressure getting to you, is it?"

"Not a chance," he replied with a grin. In fact, his friends were telling him he was crazy to spend so much time with a sophomore when he could just about have his choice of the senior class.

Stacey looked up at him through the moonlight. "I like you," she conceded. "Does that make us more than friends?"

"Well, I don't know," he said. "Why don't we find out?"

He leaned over and pressed his lips lightly against hers. They felt soft and warm and tingly. The world slipped a notch off center.

"How was that?" he asked.

"I don't know," she murmured breathlessly. Not for anything in the world would she tell him that this was her first real kiss and therefore she had nothing to compare it to.

"Well then, how about this?"

He brought his lips down to hers again, only this time they were slightly open and moist, and he seemed to want to suck the air right out of her. The world turned upside down.

"That was nice," she admitted skittishly, not sure where this was going and not sure she was ready to find out, "but I think maybe I'd better go inside now."

Danny chuckled. "That's okay," he whispered, touching her cheek with his hand. "There's no hurry."

5

"Three months ago, a terrible crime was committed in our midst," intoned the minister of the Eagle Rock Methodist Church at the Sunday morning service, "and it now appears as though a reckoning may finally be at hand. We are decent and law-abiding people with no animosity in our hearts. We were horrified by the thought that one of us might be guilty of this heinous act, and so we prayed to the Almighty to be merciful. It is with enormous relief that I am standing here today to tell you that our prayers have been answered. The monster who murdered Tara Breckenridge was not one of us."

Here the good reverend paused and several members of the congregation looked at one another and began to smile.

"But let this be a warning to you that we cannot relax our vigil," the minister continued. "Satan walks among us and he takes many forms. He may try to look like us and he may try to act like us, but he is not one of us, and we must always be on our guard, ready to ward off his evil whenever and wherever we encounter it, and protect ourselves and our loved ones from him. In the name of our lord, Jesus Christ, amen."

"Amen," said the congregation.

"You see?" Libby Hildress whispered to her husband sitting beside her in the second pew. "Isn't that just what I told you?"

"Ruben and I are going to be married," Ginger announced in the middle of Sunday dinner.

Verna Earley dropped her salad fork. "Married?" she gasped, although she had been steeling herself against this moment for over a month now. In fact, this was the first Sunday dinner since Christmas that the police chief and his daughter had not been in attendance.

"Married," Ginger confirmed.

"Hey, congratulations, Sis," her eldest brother said. Despite his mother, he didn't see anything so terribly wrong with Ruben. In fact, the police chief played a pretty decent game of pool.

"Yeah," echoed the others. "Congratulations."

"Have you set a date yet?" one sister-in-law asked.

Ginger shook her head. "Not yet. But sometime in the spring would be nice. I don't think either one of us is interested in a long engagement."

Jack Earley got up from the table and came around to give his daughter a hug.

"If this is what you want for yourself," he whispered, "then this is what I want for you."

"Thanks, Dad." She beamed. "Thanks, everyone." She looked pointedly at her mother.

"Well, I suppose this means a wedding," Verna said as brightly as she could, under the circumstances. "You're my only daughter, so this is going to be my only chance."

"A small affair, Mom," Ginger requested. "It's Ruben's second trip to the altar, you know. We don't want to make a big fuss; just the family, and maybe a few friends."

"That sounds fine," Verna assured her, relieved to have a legitimate reason to exclude certain members of her social set. "No one ever said that small weddings can't be every bit as elegant as big ones."

Ginger regarded her mother with surprise. "Thank you," she said. "I was afraid this was going to be a battle."

"It's your life," Verna told her. "Besides, now that you and Ruben are about to wrap up the Breckenridge case, I expect he's going to be a very popular man around town."

"It isn't wrapped up yet," Ginger said, cautious as always about what she revealed, but unable to keep a note of satisfaction from her voice. "But I wouldn't be surprised if it didn't take much longer."

"It'll be a small wedding," Ruben told Stacey. "Just something quiet and official."

"Gee, Dad, you're not committing a felony, you know," Stacey responded. "You're getting married. Make the most of it."

"You don't think it's a mistake?" he asked. "I mean, there are so many things against it."

"Do you love her?"

"Very much," came the immediate response.

"Do you think she loves you?"

"Yes, I do."

Stacey shrugged. "Then what are you worrying about?"

"For one thing, I'm concerned about the big difference in our ages," he said. "And for another thing, I'm concerned about what *you* think."

The teenager cocked her head as if in thought. "Yeah, I guess the age thing could be pretty sticky for you," she agreed. "But if you can handle having another daughter, I can handle having a big sister." And she quickly ducked out of his reach.

The maroon Taurus rolled off the late ferry and headed north with Jerry behind the wheel. In the back of the wagon, Matthew and Chase slept, one curled around the other. In the front passenger seat, Deborah was thinking that the two days they had spent at the shore had done wonders for all of them.

They had run and played and sucked in the ocean air as though they didn't have a worry in the world. And now, as they turned into their neighborhood, the Taurus's headlights flashing across a familiar house here, singling out a well-known tree there, she was ready to believe it was true.

"I'm glad we went," she said with a yawn. "This is the first time in I don't know how long that I've felt truly relaxed."

"Then we'll have to do it more often," Jerry suggested, making a right onto Larkspur Lane.

"But let's not plan it," Deborah replied. "I think it was the spontaneity that made it work. I never thought I'd hear myself say it, but I'm even glad to see our street."

"Then we're definitely going to be more spontaneous," he said with a chuckle.

"You know, maybe this isn't such a bad place, after all," she conceded. "Maybe we shouldn't let the attitudes of a few contaminate the whole."

Jerry swung left into the driveway. "I think you're right," he agreed.

And then they saw it, caught in the headlights as they pulled up in front of the garage—big and black and spray-painted across the double-wide door.

They sat there, disbelieving and believing.

"How could anyone . . . ?" Deborah sputtered. "Why would they . . . ? What did we ever . . . ?"

All of her questions had answers of a sort, but Jerry knew there was little point in providing them. He had heard about it from the time he was ten, learned about it in the classroom, and read about it in a dozen different books. But for the first time in his life, Jerry now knew what Aaron had known as a boy: the humiliation, the betrayal, the fear, and the overwhelming sense of helplessness.

First it was Matthew and the bullies on the playground, and he had let that pass. Then it was the telephone call, and he had allowed himself to dismiss it. Now it was this Nazi obscenity on his garage door. He knew it was the Breckenridge investigation that had triggered it all, but he wondered who was behind it, and how much further it would go, and whether he could keep his family safe.

He looked at his wife with a heavy heart. "Do you still think this is just an isolated incident?" he asked.

Officer Glen Dirksen was tired and hungry and glad to be home. He had seen the Frankels off the ferry, followed them until they turned onto Larkspur Lane, and then made a beeline for his own apartment, a roomy ground-floor unit in a recently renovated Victorian on Johansen Street, just three blocks south of the Village Green.

It was a far bigger place than he could ordinarily have afforded, but the landlord had given him a nice break on the rent because the other tenants liked the idea of having a policeman in residence. So far, his furniture consisted of two futons, one in the bedroom on which he slept and one in the living room on which he watched television, a big oak cabinet from a secondhand store that housed the television as well as a stereo system and an eclectic collection of CDs, and an old wooden dining table with two chairs that he had painted dark green enamel.

There wasn't much of anything in his refrigerator, so he contented himself with two peanut butter sandwiches and a bag of chocolate chip cookies, washing it all down with a glass of milk. He had eaten little during the past two days and slept in his truck, because he didn't want to let the Frankels out of his sight any more than he absolutely had to. He would never have been able to explain having them slip away in the dead of night while he was sound asleep in some comfortable motel bed.

His big adventure to the coast had turned out to be pretty routine. The family seemed content to eat fast food, take leisurely walks along the beach, and poke around the few local shops that were open at this time of year. They had made no move toward Canada, nor in any other direction, nor did they show any particular interest in the out-of-uniform policeman who followed them.

"The place was almost deserted," Dirksen reported to Ginger. "He couldn't help but see me, but I don't think he remembered who I was, because he smiled at me a few times; you know, like strangers do when they're away from home."

"Good work," Ginger told him. "Now get some sleep."

But sleep didn't come right away. Instead, Dirksen lay on his futon and thought about Jerry Frankel, and what he thought about most was that the history teacher had acted completely normal, and not like someone who had committed a brutal crime.

The young police officer had been trained to look for signs of guilt in a suspect's body language, in the way he made eye contact, in his basic demeanor and in his general attitude toward his surroundings, even when the suspect was unaware that he was being watched. But in two days of undetected observation, Dirksen had seen no clues at all, and he marveled at the man's ability to control himself. Which only goes to show, he decided, how cool some murderers could be. He would remember to tell Ginger that the teacher would not be likely to crack under pressure.

Jerry and Deborah lay open-eyed for the better part of the night, separated by their thoughts, neither dozing off until almost dawn. They forgot to set Deborah's alarm, and would likely have slept well into the morning had they not been awakened at seven-thirty by what sounded like a power washer.

"What the hell?" Jerry mumbled. He struggled into his

bathrobe and made his way to the front door. Sure enough, half a dozen of his neighbors stood in his drive, scrubbing down the garage door.

"This must have happened after dark yesterday," one of them said. "I came home at four o'clock and I'd have seen it if it was there then."

"We don't have that kind of neighborhood," said another. "We want you to know that this is an embarrassment to all of us."

"We know you, Jerry, and we like you and Deborah and Matthew," said a third. "You've been a fine addition to the block, and we're proud to call you friends."

"Thank you," Jerry said, but he was unable to tell them what it really was that he was thanking them for.

"We couldn't type the bloodstains on the sweatshirt," Charlie reported to Ruben and Ginger. "Too much bleach. The lab boys may have some luck with DNA, but I wouldn't hold my breath. However, the fibers are consistent with the ones we found on Tara Breckenridge's body. Of course, that might not be very helpful; the shirt is local—you can buy it in half a dozen stores around town."

"What about the knife?" Ginger asked.

"We had better luck there. Magnus says it's definitely the same kind and size of knife used in the killing, and we found a speck of blood right where the blade joins the hilt. It matches Tara's blood type. As it happens, it also matches half the rest of the population on the Island. So we'll need DNA to tell us for sure."

"That it's the victim's type is enough for now," Ruben said.

"And there's something else," Charlie added. "The newspaper we found the knife in—it was the wrap-up edition of the *Sentinel* for the second weekend in October."

"I'll be damned," murmured Ginger.

"Of course, it's still all circumstantial. Fingerprints on the knife would have been the clincher. But we couldn't get any clean ones."

"Well, it figures they'd have gotten smudged," Ginger said.

"What about the newspaper?" Ruben asked.

"Nothing clean there, either," Charlie told him. "But the important thing is," he added, "we've got what is in all likelihood the murder weapon."

"Okay," Ruben said. "Let's take it to Van Pelt."

Harvey Van Pelt was nearing the end of his professional life without ever having had that one headline-making, career-defining case that most attorneys dream of having.

Large and lanky, with a bushy head of salt-and-pepper hair, a bristly mustache, and a pleasant, smile-creased face that seemed reassuring to most people, Harvey had some years ago toyed with the idea of entering politics.

"If you want to get elected to something other than the prosecutor's office," he was told by a member of his party who was in the know, "get yourself a reputation."

"What kind of reputation?" he asked.

"On second thought," came the response, "you're probably better off staying where you are."

Van Pelt had stayed. He was now sixty-two and in his twenty-ninth year as Puget County prosecutor, having been re-elected every four years virtually unopposed. Although nobody except his wife yet knew it, this was his last term in office. The cancer that was slowly destroying his liver was not going to grant him another four years.

He wasn't bitter. All things considered, he'd had a good run for his money. The view of Gull Harbor from his office window was prime, his chair was comfortable, and his home was a mere ten minutes from the courthouse in one direction, and five minutes from the golf course in the other. He had a time-share on Maui, he drove a Lincoln, and he had put all four of his children through college and two through graduate school.

More than that, Van Pelt genuinely liked his job. It was interesting work, not overly demanding, and occasionally rewarding, and it gave him a degree of stature and respect in the community—a significant accomplishment on Seward Island for the son of a seamstress whose husband had abandoned her when the boy was only six months old. But the prosecutor was only human, and he would periodically reflect on the fact that, while his career in Puget County had been gratifying, it had provided him limited opportunity to shine.

At shortly past ten o'clock on the third Monday in January, however, all that changed. The case of a lifetime reached the desk of Harvey Van Pelt.

What could be more perfect, he thought, than to close out his career with the conviction of the bastard who had butchered poor little Tara Breckenridge? Here in front of him seemed to be motive, opportunity, intent, circumstantial evidence galore—and even the probable murder weapon. All that was missing were the DNA results, which would likely be icing on the cake for a jury who could accept them or not as it wished. In sophisticated legal terms—it was a slam dunk.

Well, almost a slam dunk. There was the small matter of Frankel's attorney. Van Pelt had never gone up against Scott Cohen in court, but he knew the attorney's reputation. He knew that, in more than twenty years of practice, the Cherub had never lost a murder case. And therein lay the challenge. What a victory it would be, he exulted, to convict a murderer and hand Cohen his first defeat in the same instance.

"It looks to me like you've done a good, thorough job of this," he told Ruben. "I can't see a reason to waste any more time. Go get him."

❂   ❂   ❂

The second lunch period had just begun at Seward High School. As usual, Melissa Senn and Jeannie Gemmetta were seated at a table with Hank Kriedler and Bill Graham. What was not so usual was that Stacey Martinez had been invited to join them.

"You and Danny Leo are the talk of the school," Jeannie informed her.

"We are?" Stacey replied. "Why?"

"Well, I guess because you've been seeing so much of each other."

"We're just friends," Stacey said automatically. She had no intention of sharing anything about her relationship with Danny with these people.

"Hey," Melissa said. "You've landed the neatest guy in school—enjoy it."

"Yeah, us sophomores aren't good enough for you anymore, are we?" Hank teased.

Stacey smiled benignly. Neither he nor his friends had ever shown any interest in her. In fact, they had pretty much ignored her. She was exactly the same person she had been before, but now, because of her relationship with Danny Leo, she had apparently gained some measure of value in their eyes.

"How would I know?" she told him. "None of you ever asked me out."

Hank and Bill exchanged leers. "I guess we'll have to do something about that," they joked.

"Guess what?" Jack Tannauer said, plunking down beside them. "I just saw your father, Stacey. He and Detective Earley were going into Huxley's office."

"Really?" breathed Melissa. "What do you think that means?"

"Do you think it means they're going to arrest Mr. Frankel?" Jeannie gasped. "The newspaper said they searched his house on Friday, remember? They must have found something."

Jack shrugged. "Maybe Stacey knows."

But Stacey shook her head. "Sorry to disappoint you," she told them, "but my dad doesn't tell me about his cases. I don't know any more about this than you do."

"Wouldn't that be a kick," Hank mused. "If the teacher did it, after all."

"Hey," said Bill, jumping up. "Why don't we go find out?"

Ruben and Ginger entered Jerry Frankel's fifth-period history class ten minutes before the bell sounded, leaving Jordan Huxley to hover in the corridor outside. The teacher was writing on the blackboard with his back to the door.

"Jeremy Frankel?" Ruben said, moving toward him.

Jerry whirled around, startled. "Yes?"

Ginger stood in front of the door, her gun drawn. Ruben stood less than two yards from him, one hand poised on his holster. "Jeremy Frankel, you are under arrest for the murder of Tara Breckenridge."

The teacher blinked. "What are you talking about?"

"May I ask you please to turn around and put your hands on the blackboard."

"Wait a minute, I don't understand. There must be some mistake."

"Turn around, please," Ruben repeated, "and put your hands on the blackboard."

"You have the right to remain silent," Ginger began to recite. "If you waive that right, anything you do say can and will be taken down and used against you in a court of law. You have the right to an attorney . . ."

In the hallway, Jordan Huxley was holding Jerry's fifth-period students at bay. "You can't go in there right now," he told them. "Just stand over here, against the wall, please."

It took less than a minute for Ruben to determine that the teacher was not carrying a weapon and only a few seconds to secure his hands behind his back.

"Is this really necessary?" Jerry asked. "I'm perfectly willing to go with you. Must you drag me out in handcuffs in front of the kids?"

"I'm sorry," Ruben replied. "Regulations."

Ginger opened the door, and positioning the teacher at her side, walked with Ruben down the hall, past a crowd of curious eyes, and out of the building.

6

"Rachel, I need you to go pick Matthew up from school," Scott Cohen instructed his wife less than an hour later. "Right now. Take him home with you and keep him inside, if you can. I've called Deborah. She'll be on the next ferry, and she'll come by to get him. I'll be on the next ferry, too, but I'm going over to the courthouse first."

"This is awful," Rachel said.

"It doesn't look good," her husband agreed.

The Puget County Courthouse was a three-story, gold-domed rectangle built of limestone that had survived half a century of ridicule for its pomposity. It sat on Seward Way, at the north end of town, in the middle of three landscaped acres that were meticulously maintained by the ladies of the Garden Club.

In addition to two fully appointed courtrooms, the larger one of which was almost never used, the building housed the spacious offices of Judge Irwin Jacobs and his associates, the more modest office of prosecutor Harvey Van Pelt, plus a score of others on a lesser level.

The third floor of the west wing contained the county jail, recognizable from the outside only by a row of iron-barred windows. It was here that Jerry Frankel was taken to be booked, fingerprinted, and photographed. His allotted telephone call had been to his attorney, and on the Cherub's advice, he had afterward declined to make any statement, or answer any questions.

Scott found him sitting on the edge of a bunk in a small cell, looking dazed.

"I don't understand what's happening," he said after they had been escorted to a room, just big enough to hold a table and two chairs, and left alone. "They can't have uncovered any evidence that links me to the Breckenridge murder."

Scott was flipping through the file he had demanded upon entering the courthouse. "They say otherwise," he reported. "They say they found your fingerprint on the cross the victim was wearing. They also say that a bloody sweatshirt having fibers similar to those found on the body was discovered in your backyard, and that a knife which the medical examiner has declared to be consistent with the murder weapon was found hidden in your car."

Jerry shook his head as though to clear it. "It was *my* blood on the sweatshirt. I cut myself on something in the shop. And I have no idea where that knife came from. I've never owned anything like it. I'm not a hunter—why would I have a hunting knife? Besides, even if I did kill that poor girl, do you really think I'd be stupid enough to keep the murder weapon lying around for anyone to walk right in and find?"

Scott looked intently at his client, the hooded green eyes missing nothing. "If you did hunt, we might be able to argue that the knife was a weapon of opportunity, not intent. That would be murder two, which would mean prison, but maybe not life," he said slowly, carefully. "However, if you don't hunt, then a good case could be made for premeditation with special circumstances, and Van Pelt would almost certainly seek the death penalty."

Jerry blinked. "If you're trying to scare me, you're doing a first-rate job of it."

"I'm trying to tell it like it is."

There was no mistaking the message, and Jerry took a long moment to stare back at his attorney. "I don't hunt," he said finally.

"All right, then," Scott said with a brief nod, "let's go to work."

"Ruben, let me be the first to congratulate you," boomed Albert Hoch, stalking into Graham Hall shortly after two o'clock, much as Ginger had predicted. "I knew you were the right man for the job, first time I met you. There was no doubt in my mind you were going to get that bastard."

"I'm glad we were successful," the police chief said, neither his face nor his voice revealing his thoughts.

"Now don't you worry about the city council and all that firing nonsense," Hoch went on. "Mark my words, when I get through with them, they're going to be begging you to stay on."

"I appreciate that, Mr. Mayor," Ruben said, making a supreme effort not to smile.

In her office down the hall, Ginger could barely keep from laughing out loud.

The parade began about four o'clock when, one by one, members of the city council, who somehow just happened to be in the neighborhood, dropped by to express their gratitude for the excellent work Ruben and his department had done, and to offer the hope that he would understand the tremendous pressure they had been under to see results.

"Of course I understand," Ruben told each of them in turn. "I was under the same pressure myself."

"I'm so glad everything worked out," Maxine Coopersmith confided. "I wasn't really in favor of replacing you."

"Well done, old man," declared Dale Egaard. "Among other things, you've saved us a lot of unnecessary headhunting."

"We behaved like a bunch of old farts," Ed Hingham admitted. "We hired you for the job; we should have had more faith in you doing it."

The only member of the city council who did not present himself was Jim Petrie.

"He's probably too busy down at the hardware store," joked Charlie, "returning all those dead bolts he won't be able to sell anymore."

Deborah couldn't seem to concentrate on anything. She went through the motions of getting on and off the ferry, of collecting Matthew from Rachel's house, of bringing him home and feeding him, but she couldn't have said what she fixed or whether he ate any of it. She brushed aside his worried questions because she didn't have any answers for him. She didn't have any for herself.

Scott came by about six and told her that Jerry was all right and had sent his love.

"When will they let him come home?" she asked.

The attorney shook his head. "We won't get bail," he said. "It's a capital offense."

"You mean he has to stay there?" she cried, horrified, picturing the kind of place and people she had seen only in movies.

"He isn't in prison," Scott assured her, as though reading her mind. "It's a county jail. He's in a cell all by himself. It's small, but it's clean and safe and the Waterside Cafe provides his food. He's only been accused of a crime; he hasn't been convicted of anything. No one is going to bother him."

As soon as Scott left, Deborah called Scarsdale and talked to her parents.

"No, don't come out now," she said, feeling so horribly ashamed when she told them what had happened. "Matthew and I are okay. There's no point. Maybe later."

Then she made herself call Cheltenham.

"I was afraid of something like this," Aaron said at once. "I've had a worry ever since you were here, ever since Matthew and I talked. My son's being used as a scapegoat."

"We have a really terrific attorney," Deborah told him. "He's also a good friend. Believe me, if Jerry is being set up, he'll find out, and then he'll make the whole thing go away."

"I want to come out," Aaron said.

"I know, but not yet. When the trial starts—if it comes to a trial, of course—that's when he'll need you, when we'll all need you." The last thing she wanted was to have to deal with his pain when she didn't know how she was going to deal with her own.

Around eight o'clock, the neighbors started to arrive, bringing with them cakes and pies and solemn faces as though it were the aftermath of a funeral. Deborah knew they were trying to be kind, but they only made things worse.

"I don't understand how this could be happening," she cried. "Jerry couldn't have done what they say he did."

"Sometimes the police make mistakes," they told her, although they weren't really certain anymore. But they didn't want to hold the woman and the boy responsible for something the husband might have done.

Somehow, she got through the condolences, got the dog fed, got the dishes done, got Matthew to bed. Much later, as though she actually thought she was going to sleep, she went into her bedroom and put on her nightclothes. Then, as she stood in the bathroom and began to wash off her makeup, she caught sight of her pale face and hollow eyes in the mirror.

"He didn't do it," she said to her reflection. *Are you so sure?* a little voice answered back.

And then the tears began to flow.

✻   ✻   ✻

"Teacher Charged in Breckenridge Case," screamed the headline in the morning *Sentinel*.

"Authorities arrested a popular Seward High School teacher yesterday in connection with the death of Tara Breckenridge.

"Jeremy Frankel, 35, was arrested in his classroom, concluding a three-month murder investigation. Breckenridge, 15, was stabbed to death at Madrona Point Park in October.

"Frankel, who has been a history teacher at Seward since last January, left his former teaching job in New York State under a 'possible cloud,' according to police detective Ginger Earley."

"Maybe it did take three months, Kyle, but we got him, didn't we?" Albert Hoch declared. "I know a lot of us were looking for an overnight solution, but like Ruben says, some things just don't happen before their time. In the end, it was patience and determination and damn good police work that did it. I know for a fact that the whole bunch of them down at Graham Hall never gave up, not for a minute."

"The case they've got against the teacher—is it really solid?" Breckenridge asked. "The bastard isn't going to slip through any legal cracks, is he?"

"Oh, I wouldn't worry about that," the mayor assured him. "Ruben is a very cautious man. He isn't sloppy, and he's not the kind who would spring a trap until he was sure he was going to snare the right prey."

"Martinez is a good man, after all," Breckenridge conceded. "I admit I had my doubts, but obviously I was wrong."

"Well, you were in good company," Hoch told him with a slight smile. "I've got a city council over at Graham Hall eating a lot of crow right now."

Breckenridge shrugged. "A little humility won't hurt them," he said.

Hoch inspected his fresh manicure. "You know," he commented, "it wouldn't be such a bad idea if you were to maybe drop by and say something to Ruben yourself."

"Coaching me, are you, Albert?"

The mayor flushed. "Just making a suggestion, Kyle, that's all."

"Don't worry," the bank president said. "I fully intend to make my own appearance at Graham Hall before the day is out."

Hoch smiled. "It'll mean a lot," he said.

"The important thing is that we can finally begin to put our lives back together," Breckenridge said with a long sigh. "It's been a dreadful three months; not only for me and my family, but for the entire island, I think. What we need now is a proper trial, a swift conviction, and justice. It'll be difficult for all of us, especially Mary, having to relive it again, but it's the only way for the healing to happen. I just hope there won't be any delays."

Mary Breckenridge spent the day in bed, with the lights out and the curtains drawn and her headache medicine on the night-stand.

She had come down to breakfast with her husband and daughter, as she did every morning, as she had when Tara was still there. In fact, she still insisted that the place to her left at the magnificent oval rosewood table be set for every meal, as though her elder daughter would claim it at any moment, a rather macabre ritual that Kyle and Tori did their best to ignore.

"Humor her, Mrs. Poole," Kyle instructed. "We all grieve in different ways."

On this morning, as always, the housekeeper brought Kyle his juice, his cereal, and the morning editions of the *Seattle Post-Intelligencer* and the *Wall Street Journal*. Then she brought Mary her coffee, her buttered toast, and the morning edition of the *Sentinel*.

One glance at the headline was all it took. The coffee spilled all over the table, a piece of toast got stuck in her throat, and without explanation, she fled upstairs.

The last thing Mary wanted to know was that someone had been arrested for killing her daughter, especially after all the effort it had taken to convince herself that Tara was not really dead, but simply not here. That was how she was dealing with the loss, the only way she could deal with it, as a temporary condition that would one day correct itself and make her world right again. Let everyone else think what they liked.

While the story had never really died down, the daily reports in the newspaper had been mostly speculative; perhaps this, maybe that—all vague enough to discount. An arrest was not vague, it was vivid, and it threatened to bring Mary face-to-face with the truth she had worked so very hard to ignore.

She waited for what seemed like hours, until she was sure that Kyle had left for the bank and Tori had gone off to school and Mrs. Poole was occupied somewhere else in the big house. Then, summoning a courage she hadn't realized she possessed, she picked up the telephone from the table that separated her bed from her husband's, and dialed the number at Graham Hall.

"Hello, I want to talk to Chief Martinez," she told the clerk who answered.

"I'm sorry, but he's not here at the moment," Helen Ballinger replied to the unidentified caller. "Can I connect you to someone else?"

"No," was the answer. "No one else. I want to talk directly to him."

"Then perhaps I can give him a message?"

Mary considered that for almost a minute. "Yes," she said finally. "Please give him a message. This is Mrs. Breckenridge calling. Will you tell Chief Martinez that the teacher he arrested didn't kill my daughter."

"I beg your pardon?" Helen replied, stunned.

"I said the teacher didn't kill her."

"How do you know that, Mrs. Breckenridge?" the clerk asked gently.

"I know because—because he's a fine teacher. Tara says he's the best teacher she's ever had. He's been helping her with her work, you know. He would never hurt her. You must tell Chief Martinez."

With that, Mary hung up, knowing she had done as much as she could do, and hoping it was enough to keep reality at bay, at least for a little while longer.

"That poor woman," Helen said later when she related the conversation to Ginger.

"She's in denial," Ginger said. "If we arrest someone for her daughter's murder, it forces her to admit that her daughter is really dead."

7

Word got out about the swastika having been painted on the Frankels' garage door, as it was bound to. It happened not so much out of maliciousness as out of disbelief. Most people simply couldn't accept it. It was inconceivable to them that a symbol of so much brutality and bigotry would ever be openly exhibited in their community, and in such a cowardly fashion—an anonymous somebody with a spray can under cover of darkness.

While the power washer had removed most of the paint, a recognizable impression still remained. Soon, those who could not help themselves were cruising slowly along Larkspur Lane, intent on getting a glimpse of the stigmata.

"I didn't believe it until I was standing right there in front of it," Paul Delaney, the *Sentinel* photographer, told Gail Brown. "This is my hometown, for God's sake. People here don't do things like that."

"Don't they?"

"Come on, I was born here, same as you," he replied. "And I've never seen anything like that before."

"Did you get a good shot of it?" the editor asked.

Delaney grinned. "You bet I did," he said.

"Under no circumstances do we support or condone the piece of graffiti recently put on public exhibit," half a dozen different religious leaders quickly stepped forward to avow. "Regardless of what may have instigated this open display of depravity, we are dismayed that such a thing could happen on our harmonious island."

"It's probably the first time those roosters have agreed on anything," Charlie Pricker observed.

"While freedom of expression is the bedrock of our nation," the city council said in a carefully worded release, "we condemn the crude example of ideology that has defaced a structure in our community. This sort of thing hurts us all, in our own eyes, as well as in the eyes of the world."

"Well, if those people hadn't come here in the first place," a devout Presbyterian wrote to the editor, "Tara Breckenridge would still be alive and no one would have had any reason to paint that garage door."

"What people is she talking about?" Rachel Cohen asked rhetorically. "Nathaniel Seward and his crew?"

"Anti-Semitism has reared its ugly head on a remote island in the Puget Sound," Peter Jennings began his report on the ABC evening news. "Someone has painted a swastika on the garage door of a Jewish teacher who has been charged with the murder of a local fifteen-year-old girl."

"Oh, terrific," Albert Hoch said in disgust. "Now the whole country is going to think this place is nothing but a hotbed of Nazis."

"Don't worry about it," Jim Petrie told him. "We'll have our fifteen minutes of fame and then it'll all be over, and we'll be forgotten again."

"Maybe," the mayor groused. "But if we had to be famous, I'd just as soon it was for something else."

It was a very somber group of residents who gathered in the apse of the Cedar Valley Unitarian Church. Called together at the last moment, they represented fifty-nine of the Island's seventy-three Jewish families.

"What are we going to do?" they asked one another.

"What does it mean?"

"We didn't know there were people who openly thought that way here."

"How are we supposed to react?"

"I can't believe this is happening."

"We've only been on the Island for a short time, but we've always felt so comfortable, so . . . unnoticed."

"Just because they think one of us murdered that girl, does that mean they have to condemn all of us? When one of them does something wrong, do we condemn all of them?"

"When it comes to us, one bad apple in the barrel, and we're all rotten. That's the way it works."

"All right everybody, let's sit down," said the leader, a well-respected cardiologist, "and see if we can make some sense of this."

"We've lived on the Island for close to ten years now," a local real estate broker began. "Aside from a letter to the editor every now and again, there's been no real problem that I know about."

"You mean the sort of drivel that came out at Christmas about Jewish retailers making all the money?" asked a tax accountant.

"Yeah, that sort of thing."

"And you don't think that means anything?"

The broker shrugged. "The people writing those letters are malcontents. They're anti-Semitic, anti-black, anti-gay, anti-everything but their own personal interpretation of the New Testament. They're fringe elements, they don't represent the mainstream. Look at me—I'm selling houses, my wife's boutique is selling *chachkas*, and my kids are friends with everyone."

"Well, my brother's nursery went under when the hardware store put in its fancy new gardening department," a computer consultant complained. "They undercut his prices so drastically he couldn't compete. And then the minute they closed him down, their prices shot up higher than his had ever been."

"That's not discrimination," someone said with a dry chuckle. "That's free enterprise."

"The truth is, we're a minority here," said the local chiropractor. "And like most minorities, if we offer a service that the majority wants, we're tolerated. Otherwise, we're ignored."

"Until now," the cardiologist said with a sigh. "Now we have a Jewish teacher accused of murdering a gentile teenager and somebody seems to want to make a statement about that. The question is, what are we going to do?"

"You mean, are we going to protest it?" a successful insurance agent asked. "How? Make a march down Commodore Street? Take out an ad in the *Sentinel*? Assure people that we're really good folk and don't deserve to be gassed?"

"Well, what do *you* suggest?" someone asked.

"I say, don't rock the boat. I think it's fair to assume that most of us live here because we like it. It's relatively safe, and it's a low-key kind of place where the overwhelming majority of the people are content to live and let live. If we start making waves, mark my words, it'll backfire on us."

Everyone looked at everyone else. "You mean, we should just pretend it never happened?"

"Why not? Let's be practical. We're talking about a teacher who's been arrested for murder. So somebody paints a swastika on his garage door. So that's his problem. It's not on any of our doors, is it?"

"Not yet," someone murmured.

"Wait a minute," someone else interjected. "The last time I looked, wasn't Jerry Frankel one of us?"

There was some foot scraping and seat shifting at that, and a number of eyes looked down at the floor.

"Of course he's one of us," the cardiologist took the opportunity to emphasize. "And putting that thing on his garage door is the same as putting it on all our garage doors."

"Oh no, it's not," said the real estate broker. "I didn't murder anyone."

"Is that what this is all about?" the tax accountant wondered. "Let us be the first to cast Jerry out so we won't be painted with his spray can?"

"Why not?" asked the insurance agent. "If he's guilty, he deserves to pay for his crime."

"You don't get it, do you?" the tax accountant said. "This isn't just about Jerry Frankel. This is about all of us. Someone is simply taking advantage of Jerry's misfortune to send us a very clear message."

"Rubbish," scoffed the real estate broker. "This is no time for hysteria. There's no ominous message here. There's no master plan behind that stupid swastika. It's ridiculous to think that sort of nonsense could ever happen on Seward Island, in practically the twenty-first century. It was just a prank, probably done by kids, and put up to it by one of our famous Northwest nut groups. I admit it wasn't in very good taste, but those people *have* no taste, so what do you expect?"

"You're absolutely right," agreed the insurance agent. "We're making a *tsimmes* out of nothing. And as long as it doesn't cost me any clients, I intend to stay well clear of it."

A murmur of assent rippled through the majority of the

group. Almost everyone looked relieved. The cardiologist and the tax accountant exchanged glances.

"So those of us who see something sinister in this are just being alarmists?" the cardiologist asked.

"Yes," said the insurance agent. "Come on, this is our home. We know these people. We live next door to them. We do business with them. I've even been invited to their country club. They haven't turned on us. Whatever happened, you'll see, it was nothing more than an isolated incident."

8

In the days that followed Jerry Frankel's arrest, the residents of Seward Island began to come out of their three-month, self-imposed seclusion. People stopped bolting their doors, locking up their children, and looking over their shoulders, and started to trust one another again.

"I invited my next-door neighbor in for coffee today," a homemaker wrote to the editor of the *Sentinel*. "It's the first time in months I've done that. It's the first time in months that I didn't have the thought in the back of my mind that her husband or her son might be a murderer."

"Our streets are once again safe, our daughters are safe," penned the local barber. "And we owe it all to Chief Ruben Martinez and his outstanding police department. On behalf of my wife and our three girls, I would like to take this opportunity to express my thanks for a job well done."

"Three cheers to Chief Ruben Martinez and Detective Ginger Earley," agreed the owner of Seward Island Stationers. "And to all the members of the police force who contributed to the investigation and apprehension of Tara Breckenridge's killer."

"When we make a decision, we don't always know for sure whether it will turn out to be the right one," wrote city councilwoman Maxine Coopersmith. "But it is clear now that our decision to hire Ruben Martinez as our chief of police was the right one."

Both Ruben and Ginger were overwhelmed by the Island's show of appreciation. Boxes of candy, baskets of fruit, and bouquets of flowers began arriving at Graham Hall, running the gamut from simple to downright extravagant. Cards were delivered by the dozens. Commendations were being proposed, ceremonies were being suggested.

"A week ago, they were clamoring for our heads," Ginger observed with a smile. "Now we're heroes."

"We were just doing our job," Ruben said with genuine modesty. "I don't know what all the fuss is about."

"For all these months, I've been so afraid that the murderer was one of us," the secretary of the Puget Sound Lutheran Church wrote to the editor. "I thank God that it wasn't."

"What does she mean by that?" Deborah asked Rachel. "Who is this 'us'?"

"Jerry Frankel's employment has been terminated," Jordan Huxley informed the *Sentinel* in the midst of all the furor. "On paper, I must say, he seemed ideal. There certainly was no indication of any aberrant behavior. I feel as though in part I'm to blame for Tara's death. But how could I have known?"

"I home-teach my three children," wrote the wife of an environmental engineer. "I always thought I was doing it because my husband and I wanted our kids to have a better education than we felt they could get in the public school system. But now I see it was really to protect them."

"There has to be a better screening process for hiring teachers in our community," wrote a parent whose daughter was a freshman at the high school. "We must find a way to safeguard our children from anything like this ever happening again."

"Why does everyone all of a sudden think we're so safe?" a forty-nine-year-old spinster who lived a life of caring for her invalid mother demanded to know. "Just because one of them is behind bars doesn't mean we're safe. What about the rest of them who've moved in on us and walk around as if they owned the place?"

"I say a jury trial's too good for someone who preys on little girls," wrote a man who was the product of an abusive family. "Especially someone in such a position of authority over children. Anyone care to join me at the old maple tree?"

This last was a reference to the giant first-growth maple that sat in the middle of the Village Green, and according to Island lore had, in bygone days, been used as a hanging tree.

"Freedom of the press is one thing," Scott Cohen sternly cautioned the editor of the *Sentinel*. "But publishing a letter that flat out calls for a public lynching is going too far."

"It's one man's opinion," Gail replied with a shrug. "But you might as well know, that opinion happens to be representative of more than half of the letters we've been receiving."

"My client is innocent until proven guilty," Scott told her. "And that's not an opinion—it's the law of our land. Be sure you tell your readers that."

Gail smiled brightly. "May I quote you?"

* * *

"They've already got me convicted, and now they can't wait to hang me," Jerry protested to his attorney.

"Sentiment doesn't seem to be running in our favor right now," Scott agreed.

"So what do we do?"

"We stay calm, we proceed with caution, and we don't rush into anything for which we are not fully prepared."

"Easy for you to say."

"Look, I know this isn't the nicest position you've ever been in, but bear with it. The preliminary hearing is coming up, and then we'll see what kind of a case Van Pelt thinks he has. I'm also going to move for a change of venue."

"Will we get it?"

Scott nodded. "I think so," he said. "The *Sentinel* seems to be doing everything it can to hand it to us on a silver platter."

Harvey Van Pelt was thrilled with the Frankel case. The deeper he got into it, the more convinced he became that this was indeed the big one—the one for which he had waited his entire career.

Ruben had seen to it that every bit of documentation had been laid out for the prosecutor as precisely as a road map to his own front door. There had been no mistakes made, either with the warrants or with the collection and handling of the evidence. Everything had been done by the book. All that was wanting were the scientific analyses and the DNA results. Van Pelt wondered how long it would take Scott Cohen to come looking for a plea bargain.

And go away empty-handed, he thought with an inner smile. Taxpayers' dollars notwithstanding, this was one case that was going to go all the way to the gallows. For the first time in his twenty-nine years in office, Van Pelt was glad that hanging was the state's primary method of execution. Barbaric though it was, it certainly suited the perpetrator of this crime.

The legal gamesmanship that generally marked the first stages of a trial had already begun. Motions had been filed, disclosure issues were being argued, schedules were being discussed. It was like a chess match, each side attempting to size up the other, second-guess the other, get one step ahead of the other. It was the part of a case that Van Pelt liked best. He was an excellent chess player.

Not that he didn't appreciate the actual trial itself. He did. In particular, he enjoyed the sound of his own voice resonating throughout the courtroom as he loomed over a jury and hammered home his points. He was a charter member of the local chapter of Toastmasters, and had always prided himself on being a good public speaker.

More than that, though, Harvey Van Pelt was a good public servant. In over a quarter of a century, no hint of corruption had ever attached itself to him or to his office. He was known as fair, honest, and totally dedicated to the principles of justice and the law.

Although his was an elected position, Van Pelt did not play politics, and never allowed himself to be swayed by outside influences of any kind. With an impartial eye, he evaluated every case that came across his desk on its own merits, and he never undertook a prosecution in which he didn't thoroughly believe. After a careful review of the Breckenridge file, he thoroughly believed in the guilt of Jerry Frankel.

"I rarely speculate about a pending matter, especially in the early stages," he told the *Sentinel* reporter who came for an interview. "There's always a real danger of poisoning the jury pool, you know. I believe in trying my cases in the courtroom, not in the media. All I'm prepared to say at this time is that I'm confident that justice will be done."

❊   ❊   ❊

"Van Pelt's a good man," Scott told Jerry. "And I think a much better lawyer than his record might indicate. So, at this time, I'm obliged to ask you if you would entertain any kind of plea?"

"What do you mean?"

"I mean I don't know what Van Pelt's thinking is at this point, or how confident he is about a conviction, but it's possible we could plead down to murder two."

Jerry blinked. "What does *that* mean?"

"It's saying that you killed her, but you didn't really intend to," Scott replied, his expression revealing nothing. "It was more or less a heat-of-the-moment kind of thing. You were arguing. Maybe the knife was only supposed to scare her. The argument got out of hand, you went a little crazy, and you didn't realize what you were doing. It would mean a long prison sentence, but it's better than the alternative."

"It's not better than an acquittal," the teacher said.

"No, it's not," the attorney agreed.

"I'm not pleading to anything," Jerry declared. "If Van Pelt thinks he has enough evidence to get a conviction, let him try."

"Perhaps I'd better tell you a little something about our court system," Scott said. "A conviction sometimes has a lot less to do with the evidence than with how the jury perceives the defendant, which in this case is you. If they see you as guilty, they'll tend to believe the evidence. If they see you as innocent, they'll make every effort to ignore the evidence."

"Wait a minute—I thought I was innocent until proven guilty."

"That's always the ideal," Scott said. "Unfortunately, it's not always the reality."

Jerry frowned thoughtfully. "It's obvious that folks around here want to lynch me, regardless of the evidence. Will a change of venue make a difference?"

"It might. But the murder of a pregnant fifteen-year-old girl might not sit too well with a lot of people, no matter where the case is heard."

"Are you recommending that I plead?"

"No," Scott told him. "The decision is yours. My job is to make sure that your decision is an informed one. Clearly, there was enough evidence to warrant an arrest. Van Pelt must feel he has enough to prosecute. But that doesn't automatically mean there's enough for a conviction."

There was a moment of silence then, while the teacher considered his options and the attorney waited.

"I think I can beat this," Jerry said. "They can't prove that was my knife, and even if they find Tara's blood on it, mine isn't, and neither are my fingerprints. So what's to say that the real murderer, who knew I was under suspicion, didn't plant it in my car? It wouldn't have been all that hard to do. My garage was never locked."

"That's certainly a point we would try to make," Scott confirmed.

"Also, I've been doing some reading about DNA while I've been stuck in here, and I say that it was *my* blood on the sweatshirt, and I don't think anyone's going to come up with any convincing evidence that it wasn't."

"You may be right."

"As for that partial fingerprint they say they found on her cross, who knows how it got there? It could have happened anytime. That day in the back hall, for example. There's certainly no proof it was left there on the night of the murder."

"That's true," Scott conceded.

"And you assured me that the Alice Easton incident is not going to be admissible in court."

"It isn't," the attorney confirmed.

"Then I think that adds up to reasonable doubt. I say we go to trial."

"Okay," declared Scott, "we go to trial."

Matthew Frankel had become a commuter. Two days after his father's arrest, the three bullies dragged him into the bathroom and stuck his head in a dirty toilet bowl, holding him there, thrashing and gagging, until the boy almost passed out. They might well have finished the job—they were having such a good time of it—but a sixth-grader walked in on them.

"What're you doing?" he asked.

"Nothing," they said.

The intruder took in the entire scene, studying the three fifth-graders through round eyeglasses, memorizing their faces.

"Get out," he told them.

The bullies fled, leaving the eleven-year-old to pull Matthew out of the toilet. He laid the boy on his stomach, turned his head to one side, and pumped until the fourth-grader threw up, and it was clear that he would be all right. Billy Hildress found his best friend on the bathroom floor five minutes later.

"Somebody pulled me out," Matthew related afterward, "but I couldn't see who it was."

"What's the matter with you people?" Deborah stormed at the principal. "He's only nine years old, for God's sake. He hasn't done anything to deserve this."

"I quite agree with you, and I'm most dreadfully sorry," the principal said solicitously, fearful that the outraged mother seated across the desk from her might be tempted to bring legal action. "And just as soon as we identify the boys who did this terrible thing to Matthew, they will be dealt with, I assure you."

"Why wasn't anyone paying attention?"

"I realize now, of course, that we should have been," the principal was forced to concede, "but the truth is, we don't have the personnel to watch every child every minute of the day."

"After two previous incidents involving *this* child, I think you should have found the personnel," Deborah retorted.

The principal swallowed her anger. What did you expect? she wanted to shout. Your husband murders someone else's child, and you think it isn't going to rub off on yours?

"We've never had this kind of situation before," she said instead. "If you'll just be a little patient, I'm sure we can come up with an appropriate solution."

But Deborah didn't wait. She contacted a private school on the mainland to arrange a transfer, and within a matter of days, mother and son could be seen riding the ferry to and from Seattle together five times a week.

Matthew didn't miss his old school very much. He liked his new teacher and got along well with his new classmates. Best of all, nobody seemed to know who he was, and he didn't have to be afraid to walk down the hallways or across the playground.

The worst of it, though, was that he and Billy didn't get to see each other every day anymore, only on Saturdays, when they would try to catch up for the whole week. Sometimes, Deborah would take them on excursions off the Island, or they would take Chase for a romp at Madrona Point Park, or go skating at the Ice Pavilion, or just hang around the house, playing video games. And if something came up that just couldn't wait until Saturday, they would call each other in between.

It was to Billy that Matthew confided his deepest fears about his father, in the dark days and weeks that followed the arrest.

"My dad couldn't hurt anyone," he told his best friend. "He's not like that. Why, he never even gets mad at anyone. My mom, she gets mad, but not my dad. He's always nice to everyone, and he's always willing to talk things over. He's really a lot like *your* dad."

Billy nodded. "That's exactly what I think," he replied. "Probably this whole thing is just a big mistake."

"But I'm so scared that nobody else besides us knows that."

"Don't you think Mr. Cohen knows?"

"I guess," Matthew conceded. "But if he can't convince the police, they might lock my dad away for the rest of his life for something he didn't do."

"I don't think that's the way it works," Billy said. "I think it's something called a jury that decides."

"What's a jury?"

"I don't know," Billy confessed. "But my dad says Mr. Cohen has to convince a jury not to lock up your dad if he didn't do anything wrong."

"Oh," Matthew said, feeling a little better, although not exactly sure why.

It was his lifeline, his friendship with Billy; someone he could talk to, someone he could trust to tell him the truth, someone he could count on to be there for him when things got really rough.

"I'm sorry, Matthew, but Billy's not here right now," Libby Hildress said into the telephone one Wednesday evening, while her younger son scowled at her from less than ten feet away.

"Oh?" came the puzzled reply. "He left a message for me to call him as soon as I got home. It sounded important."

"Well, I guess it wasn't so important, after all."

"I guess not."

"Or maybe he was calling to tell you that he won't be able to spend Saturdays with you anymore," she said.

There was a pause.

"He won't?" Matthew asked.

"No, I'm afraid he won't," she said firmly. "We've decided that Saturdays are going to be family days from now on. The four of us realize we haven't been spending nearly enough time together."

"Oh."

"I hope you understand that we have nothing against you personally, Matthew," Libby took the opportunity to add. "But under the circumstances, we feel it would probably be better all around if you didn't call again."

9

The preliminary hearing took place at the Puget County Courthouse on the second Monday in February, in the larger of the two courtrooms—the one that was almost never used.

It was an impressive space of high windows, gleaming wood paneling, ornately carved moldings, and oak flooring. By nine o'clock in the morning, the room was packed with as many spectators as could be crammed into the six rows of benches that rather closely resembled church pews.

The proceedings were separated from the gallery by a low wooden railing that extended the entire width of the room. Just inside, and accessible by a swinging gate at the center, were two long tables. Harvey Van Pelt and three members of his staff were seated at the table to the left of the aisle, while Jerry Frankel and Scott Cohen occupied the table to the right. The jury box, a raised platform set off by its own polished wood railing, ran beneath the row of windows on the left. It held fourteen armchairs that, for this particular event, would remain empty. On the right side of the room, at a small desk with a telephone on it, sat Jack Earley, dressed in his bailiff's uniform, his gun strapped to his hip.

Above everything loomed Judge Irwin Jacobs, a small, bald

man of sixty-six, with a prominent nose and thick dark eyebrows that appeared to run together in an unbroken line. Other than his head, his hands were all that could be seen of him; the rest seemed to be lost inside his black robe.

It took little more than three hours for a handful of people to be sworn in, take the witness chair, and offer their testimony.

Kristen Andersen was first, looking extremely nervous, her voice barely above a whisper.

"So three days before her death, you saw Mr. Frankel put his arms around Tara Breckenridge in what you considered to be an inappropriate embrace, is that correct?" summarized Harvey Van Pelt.

"Yes."

"Your witness," he said to the Cherub.

"Can you recall any time in your life when you were upset to the point of crying about something, and someone, let's say your father or some other adult male, put his arms around you?" asked Scott Cohen.

Kristen darted a look at her parents, who were seated in the second row of the gallery.

"I guess so," she mumbled.

"Can you give us any reason why he would do something like that?"

"Because he wanted to make me feel better."

"Precisely," Scott agreed. "So, can you now state, with absolute confidence, that what you saw take place in the back hall at the high school was inappropriate?"

"Well . . ."

"Is it even possible, Miss Andersen, that Mr. Frankel could have been trying to comfort Tara Breckenridge, much the same way your father would try to comfort you?"

Kristen thought about that for a long moment. "I guess it's possible," she said.

"Thank you."

*   *   *

"Can you tell us what time you saw the maroon Taurus wagon drive into Madrona Point Park?" the prosecutor asked Owen Petrie.

"About eleven," the teenager replied.

"What time did you leave?"

"About eleven-thirty."

"Was the Taurus still there when you left?"

"Yes."

"Your witness."

"Mr. Van Pelt just described the Taurus you say you saw drive into the park as maroon," the Cherub said. "Is that the way you described it to Chief Martinez?"

"Well, not exactly," Owen allowed. "I said it was a dark color, not black but maybe green or maroon or brown. I wasn't sure. I also said it could have been a Sable."

"Have you ever seen Mr. Frankel's car parked at the high school?"

"Sure. Every day."

"And when you saw the Taurus you've described in the park that night, did you automatically think to yourself—'There's Mr. Frankel's car'?"

Owen blinked at the Cherub several times before he answered. "No."

"Did you happen to see the license plate?"

"No."

"Well then, can you positively identify the car you saw at Madrona Point Park as my client's car?"

"No," he replied. "And I never said I could."

"Can you tell us exactly what you personally witnessed between the victim and the defendant during summer school?" Van Pelt asked Heidi Tannauer, who had made a special trip back from Northwestern for the hearing.

"I saw Tara and Mr. Frankel alone together several times after class."

"What were they doing?"

"Walking, talking, laughing together. Once I saw him sitting on one of the benches, and Tara came over and sat down beside him. Another time when I saw them, they were sharing an apple."

"Did you ever see Mr. Frankel walk and talk and laugh with any of his other students after class?"

"No."

"Your witness."

"The apple that you say you saw Mr. Frankel and Tara Breckenridge sharing," Scott inquired, "were they both eating from the same piece of fruit?"

"What do you mean?"

"Were they passing a whole piece of fruit back and forth to each other? Or did one hold the apple out to the other to take a bite?"

"No," Heidi replied. "They each had a half."

"In all the times you say you saw the two of them together during summer school—uh, I'm sorry, how many times was that?"

"Two or three."

"Yes, well, in all those two or three times, did you ever see Mr. Frankel touch Tara Breckenridge? Put his arms around her? Hold her hand? Caress her in any way?"

There was a pause. "No. Not that I remember."

"As a result of your autopsy, Dr. Coop, what did you determine was the cause of Tara Breckenridge's death?" the prosecutor inquired of the medical examiner.

"She died as a result of multiple stab wounds," the physician replied.

"Can you please describe the murder weapon to the court?"

"It was a hunting knife, with a curved blade about six inches in length and approximately one and one eighth inches at its widest point."

"Were all of the injuries that the victim sustained consistent with having been made by that weapon?"

"They were."

"And were you able to determine whether they were inflicted by a single perpetrator?"

"I believe they were."

"And from your thorough examination, have you determined anything else about the perpetrator?"

"From the nature and angle of the wounds, I estimated that he was between five feet ten inches and six feet two inches tall, and reasonably strong," Coop said.

"Do you happen to know how tall the defendant is?"

Coop squinted at Frankel. "As I recall, I measured him last August at five feet eleven and one half inches."

"Anything else?"

"It is my opinion, based on my analyses, that the killer is most probably left-handed."

"Do you happen to know, Doctor, whether the defendant is left-handed?"

"I happen to know that he is," said Coop.

"Your witness."

"Doctor, how many of your regular adult male patients would you say are between five feet ten and six feet two inches tall?" asked Scott.

Coop pursed his lips. "At least two hundred."

"And how many of them are left-handed?"

"Perhaps twenty."

"And without naming names, how many of those twenty would you say knew Tara Breckenridge?"

Coop eyed the attorney for a brief moment. "In all likelihood," he replied, "I'd say at least seventy percent of them."

"Now, Doctor," Scott went on. "The knife you described as the probable murder weapon—is it an uncommon kind of knife?"

"No."

"Well, if you were to rank it in popularity, say between one and ten, with one being the least, how common would you say it was?"

"Nine or ten," the medical examiner replied.

"And if you were to estimate how many such knives would be found, as a matter of course, in homes around the Island, what would your guess be?"

"Objection," Van Pelt cried. "Calls for speculation, Your Honor. How would the witness know how many knives there are on the Island?"

"There's no jury here, Mr. Van Pelt," Judge Jacobs said mildly. "And I believe I'm an experienced enough jurist to evaluate the testimony. I'll allow it."

Coop shrugged. "I'd say at least five hundred."

"One last question," Scott concluded smoothly. "Based on whatever personal knowledge you might have, how many of your twenty left-handed patients who are between five feet ten inches and six feet two inches tall currently own such a knife?"

"I personally know of eleven that do," the doctor replied.

After Magnus Coop left the stand, Ginger testified about the defendant's statement, and about the discovery of the knife in Jerry Frankel's car.

"Will you please describe that knife," prompted the prosecutor.

"It's a hunting knife," Ginger replied. "It has a black handle and a six-inch curved blade that measures an inch and an eighth at its widest point."

Next, Glen Dirksen took the stand to explain how he had happened to find the stained sweatshirt in Jerry Frankel's backyard.

"Was it buried?" asked Scott on cross-examination. "Did you have to dig it up?"

"No, sir."

"You mean, it was in plain sight, for God and everyone to see?"

"Yes, sir. The dog was playing with it."

At that, a nervous giggle rippled through the courtroom.

Charlie Pricker was the final witness, testifying to the match of Jerry Frankel's fingerprint with the partial print on Tara's cross, and the identification of the fibers on the victim's body as being consistent with the bloodstained shirt in the teacher's possession.

"We were unable to type the blood on the sweatshirt, but we are hoping for something from the DNA analysis," Charlie said.

"Did you find any blood on the knife?" Van Pelt asked.

"Yes," Charlie replied. "We were able to get a small sample of blood from the knife, and we determined that it's the same type as the victim's."

"Your witness."

"Tell me, Detective Pricker," Scott asked, "did you find any bloodstained pants in your search of the Frankel home?"

"No, sir."

"Did you find any bloodstained shoes, or socks?"

"No, sir."

"What do you think happened to them?"

"I'm sorry, sir?"

"Well, if my client was foolish enough to keep an incriminating sweatshirt around where you could so easily find it, what do you think he did with the rest of the clothing he was wearing that night?"

"I don't really know, sir," Charlie replied. "Maybe he disposed of it. Or maybe none of the rest of it had blood on it."

"Given the brutality of the crime," Scott prodded, "does that seem reasonable to you?"

"I just do my job, sir," the detective said. "I don't spend much time thinking about what should or shouldn't be."

At twelve minutes past noon, Jerry Frankel learned that he would be required to stand trial for the murder of Tara Breckenridge. There was no fanfare, no drumroll, just a crack of a gavel and an eleven-word ruling.

"I find sufficient cause to bind this defendant over for trial," Judge Jacobs declared in a throaty voice devoid of any inflection.

"Is that all there is to it?" the teacher asked his attorney as Jacobs stood up and left the room, and Jack Earley came over to escort him back to his cell.

"That's all there is to it," Scott told him. "What did you expect?"

"I don't know," Jerry said with a shrug. "This is my life that's being decided. I guess I expected more."

A magnum of champagne greeted Ginger, Charlie, and Glen Dirksen when they returned to Graham Hall.

"Good heavens, where did this come from?" Ginger asked.

Ruben grinned. "The city council," he replied.

"News sure does travel fast," Dirksen said. "It's only a ten-minute walk from the courthouse."

Ginger laughed. "Welcome to a small town."

"It may have taken only a couple of weeks to get to the preliminary hearing," an irate taxpayer wrote the editor of the *Sentinel*. "But I hear it could be at least a year before there's a trial. I can't afford to sit around reading books and watching television and eating three meals a day from the Waterside Cafe. Why should I have to pay through the nose so some bloody murderer can?"

"The wheels of justice turn too slowly in this country," wrote the manager of the Island Market. "Even if we get a conviction in the next year or so, it will take decades to wade through all the appeals that are sure to be mounted. Tara Breckenridge never saw her sixteenth birthday, but her killer might live another twenty years before he has to pay for his crime."

"We got the change of venue," Scott said two days later. "The case will be heard in Whatcom County."

"But that's only three hours away," Jerry said.

Scott shrugged. "It's the best Judge Jacobs would do. Van Pelt was chewing nails as it was."

"Too bad," Jerry said with a sigh. "I sort of had my heart set on Bucks County."

"We don't have a Bucks County in Washington," Scott told him.

"No," Jerry conceded. "It's in Pennsylvania."

The hooded green eyes blinked. "Well, at least you still have your sense of humor," the attorney said. "That's good."

"What difference does it make?" the teacher declared. "I sat at that hearing and listened to what those people were saying about me. And the truth is, if I didn't know I was innocent, I would have believed them. *I* would have thought I was guilty."

"That was only one side of the story," Scott reminded him.

"I know that," Jerry conceded. "But tell it to me straight— do we really have a chance? In any county? With any jury?"

"We always have a chance," Scott replied, looking his client in the eye. "There are a lot of loose ends in this case—ends Van Pelt is going to have to find a way to tie up if he wants a conviction."

"Four months ago, I had a life," Jerry said. "I had a family. I had a job doing something I thought was important. I was full of lofty ideals about making this a better world. Now all I want is to kiss my son good night again, hug my wife, and look out a window that isn't covered with steel bars."

"This case isn't over yet," Scott assured him. "Trust me, it hasn't even begun."

"What's wrong with this picture?" an outraged mother asked the editor. "Jerry Frankel butchers Tara Breckenridge right here on Seward Island, but he has his trial moved to Bellingham? Is this what happens when we let killers hire shyster lawyers to get them off?"

"I say it's *our* murder and it's *our* trial," wrote the owner of the auto parts store. "And the jury should be made up of people who knew and cared about Tara Breckenridge. That's all the impartiality this murderer deserves."

"I argued against a change of venue as vociferously as I could," Harvey Van Pelt defended himself on the steps of the courthouse. "But Judge Jacobs ordered it." There was the slightest of pauses. "I'm sure he had his reasons."

"Sure he did," someone muttered in disgust. "One Jew looking out for another."

Van Pelt, who was a good enough lawyer to know that the judge had made a legally appropriate ruling in this case—in fact, the only appropriate ruling, given the nature of the pretrial publicity—pretended not to hear.

10

It didn't make a bit of difference to Ginger where the trial was held. That was somebody else's responsibility. She had already done the job she was required to do. She had helped build the case that eventually caught a vicious murderer, and for her efforts, she had become something of a local heroine. She had also become engaged to be married. It was the happiest time of her life.

At two months before her twenty-ninth birthday, she felt as though the pieces of her life had finally come together in the right pattern—very much like those jigsaw puzzles she and her father had worried over during so many of her childhood evenings.

While Ruben might never be welcomed into the upper echelons of Seward society, he had at least been accepted as someone of stature in the community. It was some of her mother's friends who, surprisingly, were among the first to acknowledge him.

Verna had taken it upon herself to insert a small announcement of the engagement in the *Sentinel* soon after Jerry Frankel's arrest. In a matter of days, little handwritten notes on flowery, perfumed paper found their way to Graham Hall, congratulating Ruben and Ginger on a job well done, and taking the opportunity to remark rather favorably on the upcoming nuptials.

"What a pity the two of you have decided against a big wedding"—Verna pouted, riding the tide of her daughter's success, "when the whole island wants to help you celebrate. Why, it could be the social event of the decade."

"They tried so hard to hide it, didn't they?" Helen Ballinger cooed.

"Yep," Charlie Pricker agreed with a grin. "And they failed so miserably."

"Er, well, I guess you're going to be outgrowing that little house of yours," Albert Hoch boomed, shaking Ruben's hand so hard the arm almost came out of its socket. "I'm going to have a chat with Ed Hingham. He owns half the Island, and I happen to know he's got a real pretty place over on Somerset that Ginger might like. It has three bedrooms and two baths and a great view of the harbor. And we're going to want to renegotiate your contract, too. You know, to make sure we can keep you happy for the next five years or so. I'm going to get with the council on this as soon as possible, and I don't want you to worry about a thing."

"He may have a point," Ruben said to Ginger. "My house is awfully small."

"They're worried that you're going to jump ship because they treated you so badly," she told him. "I know the house on Somerset. It's a beauty. I say, let's take advantage of their generosity for the brief time it's being offered."

"I wouldn't really have thought of it, but they're so perfectly suited to each other, aren't they?" Maxine Coopersmith suggested to Dale Egaard.

"Of course they are," said Egaard. "I just wonder what took them so long to figure that out."

"Congratulations, Ruben," Keven Mahar said one Sunday when the police chief came to pick Stacey up after church. "You not only caught yourself a murderer, you seem to have caught yourself a wife in the bargain."

"Ginger is a very lucky girl," Doris O'Connor added with a genuine smile.

"Have the two of you set a date yet?" Lucy Mahar asked. "June is such a beautiful month on the Island, you know."

"In the aftermath of tragedy, comes healing and even love," Gail Brown began an editorial.

Ruben was embarrassed. "I wish they'd stop," he said. "I guess I don't mind the hullaballo over the Breckenridge case so much, but I'd really like our private lives to be just that."

Ginger was much too happy to care. In a few short weeks, Ruben had gone from scapegoat to savior, and she had helped to make it happen. Soon they were going to be married and live in a wonderful home. Forever linked with that was a history teacher who would be tried for murder and no doubt convicted of his crime, and she had helped make that happen, too. While it was all too true that one might well never have occurred if not for the other, she refused to let herself dwell on it.

If the Island wanted in on the celebration, Ginger had no objection. After all, occasions such as these were the public measuring sticks of a person's life; events that would be remembered, times that would be cherished, singular moments that would secure a past and define a future. If she lived to be a hundred, she knew it would not get any better than it was right now.

So why was it, she wondered, that she had lain in bed, tossing and turning, unable to sleep through a single night for the past six weeks?

Deborah Frankel also lay awake nights. A few short months ago, she had been in control of her life; her son thriving, her career moving forward, her marriage surviving. Now everything had been turned upside down. The boy barely smiled, she was falling woefully behind in her work while her colleagues at the office were whispering behind her back, and her relationship with her husband was being conducted in a visiting room, through a slit in a Plexiglas wall.

"How's Matthew?" Jerry asked at the beginning of every visit.

"He's doing as well as can be expected," Deborah lied. There was no point in telling him the truth—that she could hear his son crying himself to sleep every night. "He's adjusted very well to his new school, he's now an avid Sonics fan, and he and Chase have become inseparable."

"I miss him."

"He misses you, too. Maybe I could ask Scott to arrange a visit."

"No," Jerry said quickly. "I don't want him to see me in here. I don't want him to have to talk to me through a damn hole in a wall."

"Okay."

"Does he understand any of what's going on?"

"A little," she told him. Probably more than either of us realizes, she thought.

"And how are you?"

"I'm putting one foot in front of the other," she said truthfully. "It's the best I can do right now."

Deborah hated these visits. She didn't want to sit and make small talk with him, she wanted to scream. She wanted to pound her fists against the Plexiglas wall. She wanted to reach through that damned little hole and grab him by the throat and demand to know why he had done this to them. Then she would lie in bed at night and count the hours as they passed, and wonder if perhaps she couldn't blame it all on him; if perhaps she had played a part in the terrible tragedy unfolding around them.

"It takes one to make a bad marriage," her mother had always told her. "It takes two to make a good one."

Had she been too wrapped up in herself and her career? Had there been too little of her left for him? Had she not cared enough to recognize his needs? Was a nine-year-old boy the only thing that was keeping them together?

There had been any number of times that Deborah had thought about divorce. But it was a thought in the abstract only, as a convict might think about executing an impossible escape from a maximum security prison; it was more a mental exercise than a realistic possibility. And as quickly as the idea came, it was gone. Whatever had happened to their marriage, she would never leave her husband. Not because she didn't sometimes yearn for a different kind of relationship, but because she knew he would not survive it.

Aaron had raised his son to believe that there was nothing more important than family, nothing else you could count on, nothing else you could trust in. Then Emma had abandoned him in the cruelest possible way. Deborah could not even guess at the scars that her suicide must have left, because Jerry never spoke of her death. In fact, he rarely mentioned his mother at all, and then only in passing.

To the world, he was the outgoing, optimistic, dedicated visionary that had first captivated her as a junior at Byrn Mawr. But she had learned that he also had a dark side. She saw occasional glimpses of it when she would come upon him unexpectedly. Sometimes it was an expression, sometimes a gesture. Sometimes it was a mood that overtook him and drove him away from her and Matthew.

Everyone had a dark side, she knew, but Deborah could never really get a firm fix on the extent of Jerry's. All she understood was that it was mixed up in his fragility, his dependence, and his reluctance to deal openly with pain.

For ten years they had shared the same bed, and it had been a safe haven; a gentle place where they could put down the burdens of responsibility for a while; a neutral place where they could turn out the lights and confide in one another; a tender place of truce and comfort that, even if it didn't involve the kind of intimacy that it once had, was nonetheless satisfying.

Until Alice Easton. Then everything had changed.

Deborah had stood by his side through that whole sordid business; protecting him, defending him, holding her head high despite the invective, the censure, the mud. But it wasn't the same after that; they weren't the same. Even though he had repeatedly protested his innocence, nothing had been the same.

"I never touched that girl," he had proclaimed. "You do believe me, don't you?"

"It makes no difference what I believe," she replied wearily. "It's what everyone else believes that's going to count."

It was Deborah who had thwarted his attempt to stay and fight the charges. What was the point of staying in a place where his reputation was already ruined? she reasoned.

"Tucking my tail between my legs and running away is like saying I'm guilty," he argued. "I can't do that to my students. What will that teach them?"

"I don't care about them," she declared. "I care about us, and about Matthew. Even if you win, your job is lost anyway. Alice Easton's father will see to it that you never teach at Holman again. Or at any other school within a thousand-mile radius, for that matter. So what's the point? It'll be much better if we just go away and start over someplace else, someplace where nobody knows us, and we can put this all behind us. So take the deal they're offering you and let it go."

He had given in to her, of course; he always did. And the place she chose was as far away from Scarsdale, New York, as her company could send her. It just hadn't been far enough.

Now, lying alone in their bed, Deborah stared dry-eyed into the darkness, looking for an answer that wasn't there—the answer to a question that had dogged her like a shadow from one coast to the other. Had her maturity, her refusal to have more children, her commitment to her career, their slow alienation from one another helped to send him off some precarious edge?

The Jerry Frankel she knew, and had lived with all these years, could never have molested Alice Easton or murdered Tara Breckenridge. But what about the Jerry she didn't know?

Mary Breckenridge was another who waited for the hours of the night to pass.

She didn't want to think about Jerry Frankel, she didn't want to have to see his face or hear his name, but she couldn't help herself. Even in the sanctity of her bedroom, in the darkness, she could picture him—the straight brown hair, the intelligent eyes, the boyish looks, the set jaw. And in the silence, she could hear his name ringing in her ears, over and over and over again.

Her desperate attempt to convince Ruben Martinez had accomplished exactly nothing. The history teacher was still in jail, and every detail of his life was being endlessly dissected on the television, in the newspapers, across the front pages of the tabloids.

Every gruesome detail of the crime that had consumed the Island for so many months was now being played and replayed for a national audience. It seemed to be all anyone could talk about—or write about.

"CNN has finally discovered Seward Island," a nursery school teacher informed the editor of the *Sentinel*. "What a pity it had to be because of the one thing that makes us ashamed rather than the many things that make us proud."

*   *   *

"The next thing you know," wrote a conservative, "the liberal media will stick its noses and its cameras into our courtroom and try to direct the trial."

"Why do we need a trial at all?" asked a fisherman. "We know he did it. Why don't we just save the taxpayers a lot of time and money, and feed the bastard to the sharks. Now, that would be justice."

Mary couldn't stand it. Every word about him was an assault, every picture of him a defilement, and she felt them each as a thrust of a knife plunging deep into her very soul. Like Tara must have felt.

She knew she couldn't risk another call to Graham Hall for fear Kyle would find out and be furious with her. Or worse, send her away to some hospital for the mentally sick. But she had to do something. Something that would make it all go away. So she shut herself off from the television and the newspapers and the people she had known all her life, and retired to her room, to lie awake at night, to doze fitfully during the day. But each time she fell asleep for more than a few moments, it was Tara she saw, with tears overflowing her eyes, reaching out, silently begging for comfort and help. And the harder Mary tried to get to her daughter, the further away the girl slipped. Then the pain was so sharp it would jolt her awake in an agony that was becoming too much to bear. By the end of February, Mary Seward Breckenridge knew what hell was.

Gail Brown spent most of February closeted away in her office, creating five articles that she believed constituted the finest work of her career to date. She called the series *The Anatomy of a Tragedy*, and it chronicled the murder investigation in a fascinating and detailed step-by-step account that had her readers, a great many of whom thought they already knew everything there was to know about the Breckenridge case, riveted to their seats.

As soon as the fifth article, articulating all the legal maneuverings that surrounded the trial, had been published, Gail decided to add two more to the series: the sixth to be written when the case actually went to trial, and the seventh when the verdict was rendered. She had already scoped them out, with the intention of making the long round-trip to Bellingham herself each day to bear witness to every moment of the court proceedings.

"I decided to follow one case from beginning to end," she said about the series. "I wanted people to know what an honest-to-goodness, everyday criminal investigation is all about. And then I want them to know what really goes on during a trial—both inside and outside the courtroom. This seemed like the best way to do it."

Accolades were coming in from all over the country, calling her work powerful, insightful, masterful. The *Seattle Post-Intelligencer* asked for permission to rerun the entire series. Other major publications wanted excerpts. Television newsmagazines were requesting interviews.

"You're famous," Iris Tanaka declared when she took a telephone call from a producer of *Nightline*. "Even Ted Koppel wants you."

Gail grinned. "If that's what it takes to put Seward Island on the map, I guess I can suffer through it."

The skinny brunette thought about her current wardrobe, and wondered whether her bank account could withstand a trip to Seattle and a major spending spree at Nordstrom's.

Libby Hildress read Gail Brown's series in the *Sentinel* and felt vindicated. It seemed ordained that her husband would be the one to find Tara Breckenridge's body, and then that she would be among the first to consider the involvement of Jerry Frankel. She secretly wondered if, perhaps without realizing it, she had received a message from God. Just the thought was enough to buoy her spirits and strengthen her conviction.

"If you suspected him all along, why didn't you say something?" her friend Judy Parker whispered during choir practice.

"Because I'm a good Christian," Libby whispered back, "and I don't like to think ill of another person, even if he isn't one of us. But I guess, after a while, with everything that was going on, I knew that two and two just had to add up to four."

"And to think you let your Billy spend so much time with those people."

Libby sighed. "I have only the good Lord to thank for keeping him safe."

But Billy Hildress didn't realize how safe he was. All he realized was how lonely he was.

"Matthew's my best friend," he complained. "I don't understand why I can't play with him anymore."

"Because his father's done a very bad thing," Libby patiently explained to him.

"But Matthew didn't do anything bad. What does what his father did have to do with him?"

The apple doesn't fall far from the tree was the thought that came immediately to mind, but Libby knew she couldn't tell that to the boy because, for some unfathomable reason, he remained very loyal to his friend.

"You're just too young to understand," she took refuge in saying. "Someday, when you're older, I'll be able to explain it to you better."

Not satisfied with her evasion, the nine-year-old tried his father.

"I think maybe you'd better discuss it with your mother," Tom Hildress suggested. "She has it all worked out in her mind."

"She says I'm too young to understand," Billy said. "But I'm not. She thinks Mr. Frankel is guilty, and that somehow that makes Matthew guilty, too. But it doesn't, does it?"

Tom sighed. "No, it doesn't," he replied. "But I don't think that's exactly what she meant."

"If Matthew hasn't done anything wrong, why can't we be friends anymore?"

"Until the situation with his father is resolved, I think Mom feels you might not be safe at Matthew's house," Tom told him.

"But his dad isn't even *at* his house," Billy protested. "He's locked up in jail. And anyway, Matthew could come here."

Tom tried never to lie to his children. "Billy, we don't always know what other people will do, especially under stress. I think Mom feels it would be better to let things with the Frankels settle down a bit. In a few months, it all might be resolved happily, and then you and Matthew can start seeing each other again, the same as before."

"Dad, tell me honestly," the boy asked, "do you think Mr. Frankel murdered that girl?"

"Honestly?" Tom replied. "I don't know. It kind of looks that way right now, but I keep remembering that we're only hearing one side of the story so far."

"Mom seems pretty sure he did it," Billy said. "But is it okay if I wait with you to hear the other side?"

"I think that would be all right," Tom replied.

11

The case against Jerry Frankel began to unravel in the middle of March.

"We didn't get a match on the hair," Charlie Pricker said on the second Wednesday of the month. "Not one of the samples we took from Frankel is consistent with any of the hairs we found on the victim."

"That's odd," Ruben said with a frown. "You'd have thought there'd be at least one."

"Could he have worn a cap of some kind?" Ginger asked hopefully.

"There's no indication of that," Charlie said. "And we certainly didn't find any caps in the search. Of course, there's always the possibility that he *was* wearing a cap and he got rid of it with the rest of his clothes."

"Could whatever hairs he might have left on the body been dislodged when he rolled her in the rug?" Ruben inquired.

Charlie shrugged. "I suppose," he said. "But we didn't find any of his hairs on the rug, either."

❖   ❖   ❖

"What does that mean, no match on the hair?" Albert Hoch asked.

"It means that the lab didn't find any hairs, consistent with Frankel's hair, on Tara's body or on the rug," Ruben replied.

"No, I mean what does this do to our case against him?"

"Well, a match certainly would have helped," the police chief conceded. "Another forensic nail in the coffin, so to speak. But it doesn't necessarily hurt us that much. There are ways of explaining the absence of hair. He might have been wearing a cap. Or whatever hair he may have deposited on her body simply came off when he rolled her in the rug."

"You found other hairs on her, didn't you?"

Ruben nodded. "But they might have come from the rug itself."

The mayor rolled his eyes. "I can hear Scott Cohen gloating all the way from Seattle."

"We've got to go with what we've got," Ruben reminded him. "We can't manufacture what isn't there."

"But are you sure what you've got is enough?"

"I think we gave Van Pelt a very strong case," the police chief responded. "Granted most of it is based on circumstantial evidence, but I'd have no problem leaving it up to a jury."

"The sweatshirt came back from the lab," a dejected Charlie reported on Thursday. "No go on the DNA. We can't prove the blood was Tara's."

"What about the fibers?" Ginger asked.

"They're consistent, positively," he confirmed. "But we did a little checking, and we found three stores on the Island that have been selling the identical sweatshirt—same dye lot and everything—for at least the last six months."

"We didn't get much from the car," Charlie related the following Monday.

They had impounded Jerry Frankel's maroon Taurus on the day he was arrested. The crime lab in Seattle had then spent the better part of two months putting it through every test known to man.

"Let's have it," Ruben said.

"No fingerprints," Charlie told him.

"None at all?"

"None belonging to Tara."

"He wiped them off," Ginger said flatly.

"That's possible," Charlie conceded, "but there was also no hair—again. At least, none consistent with the victim. No skin traces, either."

"He vacuumed," Ginger declared. "Don't forget, we didn't get the car until three months after the fact. He had plenty of time to be very thorough."

"Is there any *good* news?" asked Ruben. "I find it very hard to believe, even after three months, that Tara could have ridden all the way from Southwynd up to Madrona Point without leaving some microscopic clue behind."

"Well, we may be in luck here, but then again," Charlie replied with a shrug. "The lab boys found some blue denim fibers lodged in the front passenger seat cushion, which are consistent with the skirt she was wearing that night."

"Does that do it?" Ginger asked anxiously.

"Not exactly," Charlie cautioned. "You see, they can't positively identify them as coming from that particular skirt. Just like the sweatshirt, turns out the skirt was one of the hot items on the racks last fall. In fact, there's a store here in town that purchased two dozen of them, again the same dye lot and everything, and sold them all."

"Okay, we've got no prints, no hair, and questionable fibers," Ruben said. "What about blood?"

"That's the biggest problem," Charlie said. "The car is clean."

Ginger looked stunned. "There must be some mistake," she cried, and now there was a definite note of desperation in her voice. "That's just not possible."

"That's what I told the boys at the lab," Charlie said. "But they told me the only substance they could identify in that car was a common household cleaning product."

"In other words," Ruben said with a heavy sigh, "the lab hasn't come up with one piece of conclusive evidence that Tara Breckenridge was ever in Jerry Frankel's car."

"That's about it," Charlie agreed. "We have a possible, maybe even a probable, but not a positive."

"Could it be that she was never in the car?" Ginger wondered aloud. "That she got to the park some other way and met him there?"

"That doesn't fit with everything else we have," Ruben reminded her.

"No," Charlie concurred. "The timing, the sequence of events—everything we have hinges on him picking her up near Southwynd sometime after ten o'clock and driving her up to Madrona Point at about eleven, when the Petrie kid said he saw the Taurus. And we did get some pieces of gravel from the tires that are totally consistent with the type they use in the parking lot. But of course, we can't prove that they got there on that night."

Ruben began to rub his temples with the tips of his fingers. "No conclusive evidence of the victim ever being in the car I can maybe live with," he mused. "But no blood? The job he did on her—he had to have been covered in it. Is it possible he could have gotten every single trace of it out of the car?"

"With enough time and enough cleaner?" Charlie replied. "The answer is . . . yes."

The police chief sighed. "First there's none of Frankel's hair on the victim, then we strike out with the sweatshirt, and now we've got next to nothing from the car—I'm not sure I like where this is going," he told them.

"What's happening, Ruben?" Albert Hoch bellowed over the telephone.

"I don't know," the police chief replied uncomfortably.

"Is this case about to blow up in our faces?"

There was a long pause. "Not yet," Ruben said finally. "There's still the DNA to come in, and we're pretty confident about that. In the meantime, we still have the knife, and we still have the fingerprint."

Ginger scrubbed her face and brushed her teeth and slipped into her pajamas. But she didn't even bother to look at her warm, inviting bed; she knew she would not be sleeping in it tonight. Instead, she pulled on her bathrobe and a pair of heavy socks, and padded out into the living room.

A fire crackled smartly; she had laid it the way Ruben had taught her. Twink was curled up on the dusty blue sofa, basking in its warmth. Ginger sat down beside him, and idly began to scratch him behind the ears.

Things were not going at all the way she had thought they would. Like a row of clay pigeons, every piece of evidence she had been so sure would point an irrefutable finger at Jerry Frankel was being shot down by their very own investigators.

The case she had helped to build, one excruciatingly small piece at a time, was now threatening to come crashing down around her. What had, just days ago, seemed to be unequivocal was now beginning to appear insufficient.

Ginger sighed. Two months earlier, she had made an agonizing decision—her little deal with the devil, as she thought of it. Although it had sent the investigation rolling in what she firmly believed was the right direction, she was now faced with having to undo that deal—and it was likely to destroy more than just the rest of the case against Jerry Frankel.

She stared into the fire most of the night, as though searching for an answer among the embers. Occasionally, she would get up and set another log to burn. Then she would sit back down again and pick up her thoughts. Every once in a while, almost as if he were reading her mind, Twink would slap his tail and whine.

While it might have been very much on Harvey Van Pelt's mind, Scott Cohen rarely thought about the fact that he had never lost a murder case. He preferred to concentrate on each case as it came before him, as though it were the only one that had ever come before him. Each situation was unique, with a series of defining circumstances that set it totally apart from any other. For that reason, no two cases could be prepared alike, or tried alike.

He had represented clients in whose innocence he had believed one hundred percent, and he had searched through the prosecution's case to find the one inevitable flaw that would result in an acquittal.

Similarly, he had defended clients in whose guilt he had believed one hundred percent, and he had searched through the prosecution's case to find the one obscure mistake that would create reasonable doubt.

Whichever way it went, Scott had no trouble sleeping at night, because he believed absolutely in the law. Imperfect though justice could sometimes be, his entire professional life was predicated on the single principle that, before a man could properly be found guilty of murder, the case against him must be solid enough to withstand a major assault from any direction.

In the hundred or more cases he had tried over the past quarter of a century, the Cherub had never lied to a jury, or misrepresented the facts of any matter, or put forth a theory he could not evidentially support. The secret behind his success lay in the fact that he was a superb strategist. He knew exactly where to look for the weak points in an argument, and then how to keep digging at them until they came apart, one by one, and the whole case collapsed in the prosecution's lap.

"I have nothing against the state," he said once in a *Seattle Times* interview. "But I wouldn't be willing to put my life into the hands of unchallenged civil servants. The same goes for my clients. We are fortunate to have an adversarial system in this country; many countries in the world do not. And it is this system, which holds the state accountable for the capability of its employees and the integrity of their work, that protects us all."

The case against Jerry Frankel perplexed him. While the individual pieces fit together in a nice neat little pattern, they did not appear to have been cut from the same cloth, but rather from various pieces of fabric that were then hastily sewn together, and were now beginning to fray.

The fingerprint on the cross; the sighting of the Taurus in the park; the bloody sweatshirt; the knife; the eyewitness accounts that placed the teacher and the student together—much of it was apparently being mitigated, if not out-and-out contradicted, by the scientific evidence. There were holes in that fabric through which the attorney knew he could drive a herd of buffalo.

Despite the fact that Jerry was a friend as well as a client, Scott had no clear certainty one way or the other about the teacher's guilt or innocence. On the surface, the man was a gentle philosopher, incapable of violence. But underneath, Scott had always sensed an unsettled soul. It didn't matter, really; it was not an issue with which he had to concern himself. All that mattered was that the state's case was falling apart.

"You've got nothing," he told Harvey Van Pelt on Tuesday. "Nothing that puts my client at the scene of the crime; nothing that puts my client in contact with the victim; nothing that conclusively puts the victim in my client's car. You don't even have positive identification that it *was* my client's car at Madrona Point. Your case is nothing but smoke and mirrors and wishful thinking."

"What are you talking about?" Van Pelt scoffed. "I still have motive and opportunity, I have the murder weapon found in his car, and I have the fingerprint on the cross. And any day now I'll have the DNA to corroborate."

"Are you so sure?" Scott asked softly.

"Of course I am," came the irate response.

"I'm sorry," said the Cherub. "I know how important it is to everyone on the Island to prosecute Tara Breckenridge's killer, but I'm afraid your people haven't done their job." He handed the prosecutor a blue-jacketed document. "I'm moving for a dismissal."

"Ruben," Van Pelt entreated, "I need your help on this. Cohen's going before Judge Jacobs in the morning. Do we have anything we can use to fight this?"

"I'll get back to you," the police chief replied.

They sat in the interview room, with Ruben and Charlie at either end of the metal table and Ginger in the middle. She was strangely quiet, her face pale, her eyes little more than dark holes.

"Are you okay?" Ruben asked, because she looked bad enough to worry him.

But she simply shrugged him off. "I didn't sleep very well," was all she said.

"I checked with the lab," Charlie reported. "The DNA analysis isn't complete yet, and they can't tell us anything concrete until it is. Without those results, and given what's happened to some of our other evidence, I don't know what you can say to Van Pelt."

"Maybe what all this means is that we weren't really meant to get him," Ginger said in an emotionless voice.

Ruben stared at her. "That's strange talk coming from you," he observed. "The Seward Island holdout for truth and justice."

"If we don't have the evidence," she said with a shrug, "Van Pelt isn't going to get a conviction."

Now both men stared at her.

"Wait a minute, what's going on here?" Charlie asked. "It was you who convinced the rest of us that Frankel did it. It's not like you to give up."

"I'm not giving up," Ginger replied with a sigh. "I'm just being realistic."

"But we have solid evidence," Charlie said. "Maybe the shirt and skirt fibers are a little iffy, but the knife was in his car."

"Yes," she said dully, clasping her hands until the knuckles turned white because she knew what was coming next.

"And his fingerprint was on her cross."

It was here, the moment she had been dreading, the moment that had kept her awake so many nights. And she realized, as though looking down a long tunnel, that it had been inevitable, right from the beginning.

"No," she whispered, so softly that neither of the men was sure he heard her right.

"I beg your pardon?" Ruben asked.

Ginger took a deep breath that came out as more of a shudder. "It wasn't his print," she said.

"Yes, it was," Charlie corrected her. "I saw the report."

"No," she said again. "You saw the *second* report."

The two men were clearly confused.

"I don't follow," Ruben said.

"The print we took off the glass Frankel used didn't match the latent we had from Tara's cross," she explained in the same flat voice. "I made up a new one and sent it to the lab."

"You did what?" Charlie asked in disbelief.

"I switched the latent to get a match," she said.

"Whatever possessed you to do a thing like that?" Ruben demanded.

"I knew he was guilty," Ginger replied. "And I knew the only way we were going to prove it was to get inside his house. All we needed was one piece of solid evidence for the warrant. I figured, if the search came up empty, no harm was done. But if we found what we were looking for, well then, the killer was caught. And I was right—we found the murder weapon."

A heavy silence descended on the windowless room.

Charlie twisted uncomfortably in his chair. "I've got to go do something," he mumbled finally and escaped.

Ruben just sat there. He didn't move, not even a muscle twitched, but Ginger could feel him pulling away, distancing himself from her. She had come so close to having it all, she thought, everything she had ever wanted. The brass ring had actually been in her grasp, and she had unceremoniously dropped it.

"They were going to fire you," she whispered, tears filling her eyes. "I'd just found you. I didn't want to lose you. I knew he was guilty."

He didn't know what to say to her, what to feel, what to do. The woman he had waited so long to find; the lovely, warm, witty, exciting woman he was planning to marry in three short months and spend the rest of his life with, had turned out to be someone he was suddenly afraid he didn't even know.

He had worked with cops before who had considered it acceptable to help evidence along in order to nail down a particularly elusive case, and it had always been done with the best of intentions—to put the guilty son of a bitch behind bars where he belonged. It didn't matter; Ruben had fired them all. The law was the law, and he had taken an oath to uphold it. More than that, he believed without exception that police officers who bent the law were no better than those who broke it.

"I have to call Van Pelt," he said at length.

Ginger nodded numbly.

Ruben got slowly to his feet and went to the door. "We'll have to sort all this out, of course, but not now," he said. "Why don't you take a couple of days off . . . Call in sick or something." And then he left the room without looking at her.

"Please, Your Honor," Van Pelt protested on Wednesday morning when Judge Jacobs did indeed dismiss the charges against Jerry Frankel. "We still have what is almost certainly the murder weapon, and we have the right defendant. The DNA results will nail him."

"If they do, you can always refile," the judge told him in a world-weary voice. "But this man has no priors, he appears to be an upstanding member of the community, and I'm not going to keep him in jail based on the current state of your case."

Van Pelt looked as though smoke and fire would burst from several of his orifices at any moment. He was embarrassed beyond words; not because Jacobs had summarily dismissed his case of a lifetime, but because he knew in his heart that the judge was right to do it.

"I should have dropped the charges myself, the moment Cohen showed up," he told his assistant. "I knew it was the right thing to do. Now I look like such a fool. I should have waited for the DNA before I filed. I was in too much of a hurry."

"What do you mean, I'm out of here?" Jerry asked.

"I mean, the judge has dismissed the charges against you for lack of evidence," Scott told him.

Jerry wasn't sure he had heard correctly. "I thought you said they had such a strong case."

The Cherub shrugged. "It seems to have fallen apart on them," he said.

"Fallen apart?" the teacher asked, dumbfounded. "You mean the DNA came back negative?"

"No, that's not in yet. But there isn't enough other evidence to hold you. Of course, they can always refile if the DNA goes their way."

The teacher began to giggle, a borderline hysterical sound. "You ever had the feeling you were tied to a train track?" he asked his attorney. "You see the train coming right at you, closer and closer, and you know it's going to hit you, pulverize you, but you can't get away? And then at the last moment, the train stops, just inches away from you, and you don't know why? That's how I feel right now."

"Give it a couple of hours to sink in," Scott told him. "Give me one more night to get all the formalities taken care of, and by tomorrow morning you'll be on your way home where you can kiss your son and hug your wife anytime you like."

"Okay, so Jacobs turns the teacher loose," Glen Dirksen said on Wednesday afternoon. "Then what happens when the DNA comes in?"

"If it nails him, Van Pelt will refile," Ruben replied. "If it doesn't, we reopen the investigation."

"Van Pelt won't get the chance to refile," the officer predicted, clearly upset. "I watched Frankel during the preliminary hearing; he knows what the DNA results will be, and he's not going to hang around for them. I wouldn't, if it was me. And once he's released, I could follow him to Timbuktu and it wouldn't matter. There's not a damn thing we can do to stop him."

"We did our best with what we had," Ruben responded. "We just didn't have enough."

"Well, look at the upside," Charlie Pricker said. "No one will blame us for not making the case. Everyone knows he did it. They'll blame his hotshot lawyer for getting him off."

"Jacobs is letting Frankel go?" Gail Brown exclaimed.
"That's what I heard," Iris Tanaka said.

"Unbelievable," the editor breathed, already beginning to figure how she could rework the sixth and seventh articles in her exemplary series to show how a diligent investigation could sometimes go awry. "Get someone on it right away and scratch tomorrow's editorial. I'll do a new one."

"After all that," Iris remarked. "To end up with the wrong man."

Gail sighed as an image of Alice Easton came into focus. She had never revealed the contents of the anonymous letter to anyone but Ginger, nor the results of her trip to Scarsdale.

"That's the trouble," she said now. "What if he's not the wrong man?"

It surprised Malcolm Purdy that he should have taken the death of Tara Breckenridge so personally. But he had, and as a result he had followed the official investigation every inch of the way, and had even gone to the trouble of running a private little investigation of his own, calling on a few well-placed sources around the country. He had, of course, reached the same conclusion as the authorities, only way ahead of them. It never ceased to amaze him how slow the police were to react, how laborious the process was, how far backward they had to bend not to trample the precious rights of a murdering piece of filth.

There was no doubt in the ex-Marine's mind that Jerry Frankel was guilty. The psychological abnormality of the man was obvious to Purdy: the classic symptoms of inadequacy, stemming from the background of a Holocaust-surviving father and an unbalanced mother, steering him into a profession where he could manipulate the minds of children, leading to the abuse of that position. Anyone with even limited intelligence could see it, anyone who had studied human behavior as he had . . . anyone with daughters.

After the preliminary hearing, Purdy had celebrated. Until then, he'd had little faith in the bleeding-heart liberal legal process. But the system had prevailed. The good guys had come out on top. Tara Breckenridge had won.

There was a young man with him at the time, and the two of them split a case of beer and a bottle of bourbon as they sat around a crackling fire well into the night, the woman trying to get them to eat something, and cleaning up after them.

"The motherfucker's gonna hang," Purdy predicted as he whirled the woman around the room in an off-balance version of a jig.

The night he learned that Frankel was going to be cut loose, he paced the floor until dawn. He felt betrayed. His reborn faith had been short-lived—the system had failed after all, and Tara Breckenridge was not going to have her day in court.

It didn't take a genius to figure out that the bastard wouldn't wait around for the DNA results to come in, but would take off at the first opportunity. Purdy spent the dark hours wondering if the police, crippled by their rules and red tape, would be able to stop him.

The nightmare was about to end, Deborah Frankel thought, having spoken briefly with Jerry and then at length with Scott. Or was it just beginning? When she faced herself in the mirror, she wasn't sure. At the very least, the case against her husband had been discredited; enough so that the judge had agreed to let him go. Well, for the time being anyway, until the fancy blood analysis was complete.

She found herself wondering what the DNA would show. Had Jerry had an affair with Tara Breckenridge . . . was he the father of her unborn baby . . . did she really want to know? He had denied both vehemently and repeatedly, and she had taken some measure of comfort from that, but in the uncompromising glare of the bathroom light, she wasn't sure she really believed him. In many ways, it would have been easier to let a jury tell her what was true.

For Matthew's sake, she was glad that Jerry was coming home. The boy adored his father, hung on his every word, and trusted him implicitly. How uncomplicated childhood was, she thought. For her, however, there were decisions that needed to be made. Whether the DNA would eventually prove Jerry guilty or innocent, she had to protect her son and herself, and if it came to that, her husband. For Matthew's sake.

Putting the house on the market was an obvious option. It was what she would have done had Jerry gone to trial and been convicted. It was what she should do now. Living on Seward Island had become pure hell for both her and her son, and Jerry would certainly never teach here again, so what was the point of staying on one moment longer than necessary? Deborah put a note on her calendar to call the real estate agency first thing in the morning.

She would quit her job, of course. That is, if the firm didn't fire her first. Given the renewed media coverage the Breckenridge case was getting, going into the office each day had become as difficult for her as it had been for Matthew to go to his former school. Deborah knew that, as good as she was at her job, she had become a public relations liability, and the company would be only too glad to be rid of her. But that was all right. They had some savings to tide them over, and she knew she would have little trouble hooking up with a different firm in another state. Her track record spoke for itself. All she had to do was contact one of the big head-hunting outfits, and then wait for the offers to come in.

Jerry, however, was another story. Even were he to be exonerated of Tara Breckenridge's murder, Deborah doubted that he would ever teach again. There would be no bargain this time, as there had been in Scarsdale, no deal with the school, no protection.

A charge had been filed, an arrest had been made, an indictment had been handed down. True or false, upheld or not, it was part of the record, and it would follow him wherever he went. Besides, she was certain he could not possibly have the stomach for teaching anymore.

But an idea had been turning around in her mind for a while now. There were so many different aspects of history that fascinated Jerry; he was always jotting little notes to himself, and promising that one day he would organize the notes into a book. That was something he could do—spend his life writing. Why not? It was a perfect way for him to stay in his field, and out of the classroom. And it wouldn't matter if he were published or not; they wouldn't really need the second income.

Deborah made a mental note to broach the idea when she and Matthew went down to the courthouse to collect him after his release.

12

For the first time since the day he had been arrested, Jerry Frankel slept the night through. No nightmares haunted him, no sense of panic jarred him into consciousness. The deputy who brought him his breakfast at seven-thirty Thursday morning had to wake him.

"I'd have thought you'd be up and ready to go by now," the officer said without a smile.

"Me, too," Jerry agreed with a sheepish grin.

He couldn't remember when coffee had tasted so good, or orange juice so fresh. He marveled at how crisp the bacon was, how perfectly the eggs had been scrambled, how the toast had just the right amount of butter melting into it. He knew that never again would he take the small pleasures of life for granted. He decided there was no narcotic as powerful as freedom.

Scott had brought him a fresh set of clothes: gray slacks, white shirt, blue sweater, underwear, socks. He changed into them as soon as he was finished eating, leaving the onerous orange uniform he had been forced to wear in a heap on the floor.

Sunlight filtered through the barred window of his cell. A new day, he thought, a new beginning. Deborah had said she would bring Matthew with her when she came to pick him up. Jerry hadn't seen his son for two months, and he couldn't wait to wrap his arms around the boy and promise never to leave him again.

A crowd began to gather on the courthouse plaza, made up of silent, somber people who had been drawn to this place to witness something, but were unsure of exactly what or why. They stood in little clusters that grew larger as the minutes ticked by, until there was just one large mass of bodies overrunning the sidewalk, the circular drive, and even the grassy slope that flanked the imposing building. Only some measure of timidity seemed to have kept them off the broad flight of steps that led up to the front entrance.

"This is unbelievable," Gail Brown murmured to Paul Delaney. "There must be a thousand people here."

They maneuvered themselves to the edge of the steps for a preferential view, only to find a dozen other reporters and photographers with the same idea. Ever since the swastika had been painted on Jerry Frankel's garage door, the case had been attracting a lot of attention.

"What are they all doing here?" Glen Dirksen wondered aloud from inside the lobby of the courthouse as he peered through the massive leaded glass entry doors.

"They've come to observe a travesty of justice, young man," Harvey Van Pelt, overhearing, replied. "That's what they're doing here."

"Why did the time of my client's release have to be publicized?" Scott Cohen asked.

"The people have a right to know, and a right to be here, if they so choose," the prosecutor reminded him. "Besides, the newspaper didn't ask our permission before printing the information. Maybe you'd feel more comfortable going out the back door."

"My client is guilty of no crime," the Cherub responded.

"He doesn't have to sneak out of here. He has every right to walk out the front door, a free man."

"I don't think there'll be a problem, Mr. Cohen," Jack Earley said. "They don't look like a lynching mob. I think they're just curiosity-seekers."

"Can you at least clear the drive so we can get the car in?" Scott asked.

It was ten minutes past one. The paperwork was done, the formalities and technicalities had been taken care of. All that remained was for Deborah Frankel to drive up to the courthouse and take her husband home.

"We can do that," Glen Dirksen said. He gestured to two other uniformed officers standing in the lobby and the three of them left the building, jogged down the steps, and began to make their way through the crowd, directing people to back off.

At twelve minutes past one, Deborah maneuvered the maroon Taurus wagon up the plaza drive and brought it to a stop at the bottom of the steps. A murmur rippled through the crowd at the sight of the car.

"Okay, let's go," Scott said.

Jack Earley escorted Jerry out of a small waiting room off the lobby, and with the Cherub on one side and the Puget County bailiff on the other, the three men walked through the front doors of the courthouse into the sunlight.

"Here he comes," Gail cried, directing her photographer. "Get everything."

Jerry never really saw the crowd. His eyes were fixed on the car, searching until he located his son in the rear seat. Then a broad smile spread across his face, and he started to run down the steps.

"Wait a minute, Mr. Frankel," Jack Earley called, but the history teacher paid no attention.

At exactly the same moment that Jerry broke from his escort, Matthew scrambled out the back door of the Taurus and started up to meet him. The boy could not remember ever having been so excited. It was such a special day that his mother had taken off from work and allowed him to skip school.

When the two were twenty steps apart, a cold chill, like a gust of Arctic air, swept over Scott Cohen. When they were fifteen steps apart, the attorney, acting on an instinct he would not later be able to explain, suddenly bolted after his client. When father and son were ten steps apart, Scott began to shout at Glen Dirksen and the uniformed policemen who were still among the crowd. When the man and the boy were but five steps apart, the Cherub heard the sound he had feared he would hear, like the distant backfire of a car, and saw Jerry Frankel collapse into his son's arms.

Few among the onlookers paid much attention to the sound, so intent were they on getting a view of the scene unfolding before them. At first, most thought they were witnessing a heart-wrenching reunion. Then those at the front of the crowd began to realize that something very different was taking place. They could see that the attorney was bending over his client, gesturing frantically, the bailiff was thundering down the steps, and the three policemen were closing in on the scene with their handguns drawn.

Jerry lay with his head in Matthew's lap, his eyes open, staring sightlessly at his son.

"Dad? What's the matter, Dad?" the boy cried, even as his jeans were being soaked by blood and brain matter.

He got no answer. A single bullet in the forehead, leaving a hole no bigger in diameter than a pencil, had blown off the back of his father's skull.

Inside the Taurus, Deborah couldn't seem to move. She had watched Jerry's descent, had seen his progress halted by a force that snapped his head backward and buckled his knees, and had grasped the reality of it immediately. She knew she had to get to Matthew, to shield him, to get him out of there. But she found herself unable to move, her hands frozen to the steering wheel, caught somewhere between a gasp of horror and a guilt-ridden cry of relief.

Outside the Taurus, the crowd pressed forward, finally comprehending what they had just witnessed, and erupted in a resounding cheer.

The entire event had taken twenty-six seconds.

They took the body over to Magnus Coop at the clinic. The coroner put it in the morgue, on the same table that had held Tara Breckenridge's remains, and covered it with a sheet.

"This is terrible," he muttered over and over again. "This is absolutely terrible."

"Get that stuff developed and on my desk as soon as you can," Gail instructed Paul Delaney as the two of them rushed back to Curtis House. "Clear the entire front page," she barked at her assistant. "We're going to have one hell of an issue tomorrow!"

"What happened?" Iris Tanaka demanded.

"Somebody assassinated Jerry Frankel as he was leaving the courthouse," Gail told her.

"Oh my God, who?"

"Don't know. Chances are, we'll never know. But get someone on it anyway."

"Did you actually see it?" Iris asked.

"Sure did," Gail said. "Peter and I were right up front. There must have been, oh, at least a thousand people there. And as soon as they realized what had happened, they went wild—cheering, dancing, singing in the streets. I've never seen anything like it."

"That's awful," Iris murmured.

"It wasn't pretty," Gail agreed. "And we got it all on film. Call the printer. Tell him to double tomorrow's run."

❈   ❈   ❈

Charlie Pricker was back in the office by three o'clock. It didn't take him very long to reconstruct the event. An evaluation of the angle of the entry wound and a survey of the buildings along the perimeter of the courthouse plaza brought him to the widow's walk of a three-story Victorian about four hundred yards away that was undergoing extensive remodeling to suit an assortment of trendy boutiques. The construction would have afforded a sniper unlimited roof access.

"Judging from the distance, I'd say the shooter used a hunting rifle with a scope," he said afterward. "Judging from the entry wound and the bone and shell fragments I found on the courthouse steps, he used some kind of varmint slug, not more than thirty-caliber. That thing exploded inside Frankel's head like a miniature hand grenade. The chances are slim to none we'll ever be able to trace it. Whoever this guy was, he knew what he was doing."

"Not exactly the way we wanted to close the case," Ruben observed with a sigh.

"But when you think about it," Glen Dirksen remarked, "it *is* justice, even if it's only poetic justice."

"I see your point," the police chief said tonelessly. "But that doesn't make it right."

"Maybe not," the officer agreed. "But he was this close to getting away with it." Dirksen held up his thumb and index finger, separated by a bare eighth of an inch. "And you know as well as I do that someday, somewhere, he was going to do it again. We might not like the method, but there's at least one teenage girl out there who'll appreciate the result."

"It's not our job to protect society from a crime that hasn't yet been committed," Ruben instructed him.

"Well, it's done," Dirksen replied, "and I can't say I'm very sorry about it."

Ruben sighed again. "I don't imagine there'll be any great

push for us to find the shooter," he said. "But we at least have to open a case file."

"Are you kidding?" Charlie declared. "This guy'll be the new town hero. Legends will grow up around him. 'The man who set Seward Island free,' they'll call him."

"He's still a murderer," the police chief declared, "and it's our job to get him if we can."

"Don't get me wrong," Charlie said. "I really feel for Frankel's wife and son. Especially the boy, to have something like that happen right in front of him. I can't imagine anything more horrifying than what they've just gone through. But I doubt anyone else will be grieving tonight. A murderer has been murdered—that's all anyone will think about."

"You may be right," Ruben conceded. "But just for the sake of argument, what if he didn't do it?"

Dirksen stared at him. "Are you saying you have any doubt?" he asked.

"I always have doubt," Ruben replied. "Our work is never perfect. That's why I rely on the system. It's what keeps us honest."

"But the system failed," the officer said. "The lawyer got him released."

Ruben shook his head sadly. "No," he said. "The system worked. It was lack of evidence that got him released."

"But he was guilty," Dirksen argued. "I don't care what happened with the evidence, I know he was guilty. So maybe the victim wasn't in his car, so what? Maybe he wasn't even driving his car that night."

"What about the Petrie kid?" Charlie asked.

"He could have been mistaken," the officer declared. "Maybe we got it all wrong, and they met at Madrona Point. Frankel lived less than a mile away, maybe he walked there. Either way, we found the bloody sweatshirt, didn't we? Even if we couldn't get it to test out. And we found the knife. And he had a motive, and he had the opportunity, and we know he'd done almost the same thing at least once before. As far as I'm concerned, he got what he deserved. And if that means I care more about justice being done than I do about the system working, well then—maybe I do."

At three-thirty-eight, Ginger walked resolutely through the doors of Graham Hall, down the corridor, and into Ruben's office, and dropped an envelope on his desk.

"My resignation," she said simply, and turned to go.

"Wait," he said. He had spent the better part of two nights thinking it through, staring at his bedroom ceiling, trying to find a way to hold on to what he believed in, and still make room for her in his life. In the end, he decided that, right or wrong, emotions could sometimes distort one's judgment. He rationalized that what she had done had been as much for him as for herself or the Breckenridge case, and that meant he had to accept some of the responsibility. "We need to talk."

She shook her head. "There's nothing to talk about," she told him. "I did what I did for what I thought were all the right reasons. But when I looked at it through your eyes, I realized how terribly wrong it was. I can't work here anymore. We both know that."

"You're a good cop," he said.

"I was," she conceded.

"We all make mistakes."

"Ruben, I falsified evidence in a homicide case."

"Yes," he agreed. "But only up to a certain point. You were willing to let a search warrant hang on that fingerprint—but you weren't willing to let the whole case hang on it. That's the difference."

"It seems a small point to me now," she said. "A man is dead."

"That isn't your fault."

"Of course it is," she cried. "He wouldn't have been in jail in the first place if it hadn't been for me."

"You don't know that," Ruben told her. "You don't know how the investigation might have gone. We might have come to him from a totally different direction."

She looked at him wearily. "We were at a dead end."

Ruben shrugged. "You believed he was guilty. You didn't want anyone else to get hurt."

"What I did violates every principle you live by," she said thoughtfully. "And here you are, trying to justify it. How can you do that?"

He considered his words very carefully before he spoke. "I'm not justifying it," he said. "But I can't ignore the fact that you're only human, and you were under a great deal of pressure. Yes, what you did was wrong. But when it came right down to it, even though you knew it would cost you your career, you came clean about it. If I can't cut you a little slack for that, well then, I'm not much of a police chief—or a man."

"I'm sorry I let you down," she said. "I'll have my desk cleaned out in half an hour."

Ruben had to accept her resignation—he had no choice, really. He was only grateful that she hadn't left it up to him, because he didn't know how he would have been able to fire her.

"I think it would be better all around if you give a month's notice," he said. "You can cite exhaustion, or a career reevaluation, or something along those lines as the reason. That way, we don't disrupt the department, and we keep speculation to a minimum."

She stared at him. He was offering her a graceful exit instead of the public humiliation she deserved. It was a straw and she desperately wanted to grab it.

"But what about Van Pelt?" she asked.

Ruben shifted a bit uneasily in his chair. "All I told him was that there was a mistake," he replied, "a mix-up with the lab, and that we only found out about it when we went back over everything."

Ginger stared at him. "You lied to him?"

He shrugged. "It wasn't exactly a lie. There was some truth to it."

She seemed to hesitate for a moment, and then she shook her head. "There's also Charlie," she said.

"I've already squared it with Charlie," he told her. "So what happened will stay right here between the three of us."

Ginger blinked. "You owe me nothing," she said. "I betrayed my oath, I betrayed your trust. I deserve to be kicked out of here in a city garbage truck. Why would you compromise yourself because of me? Why would you want me to stay on the job one more minute, much less a month?"

He smiled, a wistful little smile. Perhaps her image was a little tarnished in his eyes. Perhaps there might be an occasional moment during the next few weeks when he would find himself wondering whether he could ever trust her again. But perfection, he knew, was something that, while frequently sought, was rarely attained.

"Because I love you," he said. You don't stop loving someone, he thought, just because they disappoint you.

The Cohens took Deborah and Matthew home with them. Rachel gave Deborah a Valium and put her to bed in the guest room. She stripped the boy of his bloody clothes and put him into the bathtub, running the water as hot as she could to counter the shivers that had wracked his small body since the moment he realized what had actually taken place on the courthouse steps. She sent Daniel to fetch Chase. By the time the puppy arrived, Matthew was sitting in the kitchen, wrapped inside a terrycloth bathrobe, trying to eat a bowl of chicken noodle soup.

"We'll keep them here with us tonight, of course," Rachel told her husband. "This is no time for them to be alone. Deborah's parents are catching the red-eye; they'll be here first thing in the morning. Jerry's father is due in at noon."

Scott nodded. "This is a terrible day," he said. "A terrible day for the Frankels, and a terrible day for Seward Island."

After Matthew had swallowed all he could of his soup, Rachel gave him a Valium and tucked him into bed beside his mother. Chase curled up on the floor. Then she went into the living room and sat with Scott, saying little—for what was there to say?—until it grew dark and the friends and neighbors began to arrive.

"We never dreamed it would come to anything like this," they said.

"This is a civilized island. We can't believe that such a thing could happen here."

"Why?" someone asked. "We thought, when they dismissed the charges, it meant he was innocent."

"I guess somebody saw it differently," Scott replied.

"We're in total shock," a neighbor exclaimed. "People actually cheered?"

"Yes, a lot of them did," Scott confirmed.

"Do you think this was related, you know, to the other thing?" the cardiologist and the tax accountant wondered in private.

"It's hard to tell," Scott acknowledged.

"A couple of months ago, we brought you the story of a Jewish teacher who had been accused of murdering a teenage girl on a remote island in Washington State, and an incident of anti-Semitism connected with it," Peter Jennings reported on the evening news. "Now the story has taken a bizarre twist."

"Well, I certainly didn't want him to get murdered," Libby Hildress told her husband. "I just went down there to see what was going on."

"What did you think would happen?" Tom asked wearily. "The way this island was all riled up, it's a wonder they didn't fall on him and tear him to pieces right in front of the boy."

"You can't blame the Island," Libby declared. "If you want to blame someone, blame that lawyer of his."

"Why? Did the lawyer shoot him?"

"Oh, you know what I mean."

"And now I suppose you're going to tell me that you were one of those who celebrated?"

"Well, maybe a little bit," she confessed. "I couldn't help myself. None of us could. There was such a sense of—I don't know—relief. And well—everyone was doing it. Of course, now I wish I hadn't."

"Really?" Tom inquired. "Why?"

She bit her lower lip and looked up at him. "Because I realize it's going to get all distorted in the media, to a lot of people who don't even know us. It's going to make us look like we're a bunch of . . . of heathens."

The doorbell at the Martinez house rang at seven-thirty, and Stacey went to answer it. Danny Leo stood on the front porch.

"Hi," he said.

"Hi," she echoed.

"I heard about what happened today," he began. "I felt just awful, and I wanted to come talk to your dad about it. Is this a bad time?"

Stacey shook her head. "He's pretty upset," she told him. "But I don't think he'll mind."

They went into the living room where Ruben sat on the sofa, an untouched glass of Scotch in his hand, staring at empty space. Ginger had agreed to giving a month's notice, and they had put off the wedding.

"We both have things we need to work through," she told

him. "Maybe we can find a way back to each other with this between us, maybe not. Only time will tell."

She was right, of course. And he knew, probably better than
she, that their future together was uncertain at best. Rebuilding
their relationship would be a painstaking process, with no guarantee of success. At any moment, the most insignificant issue
could come along and topple it for good. The one thing they had
going for them was that they both still wanted it; they had established that much, at least. He looked down the months, if not
years, that now lay ahead, and the loneliness was almost overwhelming. It was the second lowest point of his life.

Danny cleared his throat to catch Ruben's attention.

"I wanted to say how sorry I am, sir," the boy began.

Ruben glanced over. "What is it you're sorry about, Danny?"
he asked softly.

"I'm sorry because this isn't the way it's supposed to happen," he replied. "For a while there, I know you thought maybe
I was the one who murdered Tara, but I had the chance to clear
myself. Mr. Frankel never got that chance, and now there'll always be a question. I think those people who celebrated out
there today were wrong. And those who think that whoever murdered Mr. Frankel is a hero are wrong, too." He stopped, a little
embarrassed by his monologue. "I just wanted you to know how
I felt," he said.

Ruben took a moment to study the boy. "I admit I wasn't exactly thrilled when you started dating my daughter," he said. "But
I've always trusted her judgment, and tonight, I think I can see a
little of what she sees in you."

Danny grinned. "That's good, sir," he said, "because I really
like Stacey a lot, and with your permission, I sure would like to
go on dating her."

How uncomplicated childhood was, Ruben reflected sadly.
Why did it all have to change when you grew up?

✦   ✦   ✦

As hard as she tried to shield herself from the world around her, Mary Breckenridge heard about the death of Jerry Frankel.

Irma Poole told her when she brought a tray of tea to Mary's bedroom. "It's over," the woman said firmly. "For better or worse, it's done with. God willing, we can put it behind us now, and go on."

Mary looked up at the housekeeper who had cared for her and her family for almost a quarter of a century.

"Is it?" she asked pathetically. "Can we?"

13

Curtis House was quickly flooded with letters about the killing of Jerry Frankel, and true to Charlie Pricker's prediction, they ran five to one in support of the assassin.

"If our mighty legal system couldn't take care of one murdering teacher," a garage mechanic told the editor, "it's lucky for us that someone else could."

"I don't ever want to know who pulled the trigger," a romance novelist wrote. "I'd much prefer to imagine him as a handsome crusader on a prancing white steed."

"Whoever he is, he did us all a favor," opined a local plumber. "We should applaud him, not prosecute him."

"Well, Ruben, you dodged a real bullet," Albert Hoch confided. "If that bastard had gotten away with it, there would've been hell to pay. This way, we can mark the case closed, and get on with other business."

"There's still the matter of the shooter."

The mayor shrugged. "Oh, I wouldn't spin too many wheels over that, if I were you," he said.

"It's my job," Ruben reminded him.

"Well, if it'll make you feel better," Hoch conceded with a broad wink, "you can spend a few hours rounding up the usual suspects."

"As long as I have your approval," Ruben said smoothly, "I may as well tell you that Kyle Breckenridge is at the top of that list. He had more motivation than anyone else I can think of to kill his daughter's killer."

The mayor's eyes bulged. "Well, you can take him right back off that list," he snapped. "It just so happens that Kyle and I were in a meeting together at exactly the moment Frankel was being shot."

"You'd testify to that?" Ruben asked. "Under oath, if necessary?"

Hoch didn't even blink. "Yes, I would," he replied. "And since you seem to be having some difficulty reading the climate of this community, let me strongly urge you to move along to something else."

"I wonder if it's occurred to anyone on this island that the only thing that makes our country work is that we live by a system of laws," Ruben said irritably.

"I think everyone is so relieved that it's finally over, they haven't gotten to that point yet," Ginger told him with a touch of irony. "Give them time."

"Time is something we don't control," he said, "and our esteemed mayor notwithstanding, we have an investigation to conduct."

"All right, then," she said affably because she was, after all, still on the job, "aside from Kyle Breckenridge, who else is on your list?"

*   *   *

Malcolm Purdy opened the electrified gate, and watched calmly as Ginger pulled her black-and-white to a stop in front of his ramshackle cabin.

"What took you so long?" he asked with a cynical grin.

"You were expecting me?" she parried.

"Yesterday."

"Good," she said. "Then you know why I'm here, and we don't have to waste any time with preliminaries."

"Hell, you can waste your time any way you like," he offered. "But it seems to me that someone has just saved the taxpayers a whole lot of money. If you find the guy, you ought to give him a medal."

"I'll certainly keep your suggestion in mind," Ginger replied.

Purdy chuckled. "I was here the entire day," he told her. "I have two witnesses, if I need them: a man who is staying with me for a few weeks, and the woman who works for me. Both of them were here with me the whole time."

"Do you mind if I take a look at your guns?"

"Do you have a search warrant?" he asked.

"Do I need one?" she countered.

He shrugged and led the way around to the back of the cabin where he unlocked the door to a converted wood shed, revealing a small arsenal that ran the gamut from assault weapons to target rifles to hunting rifles to shotguns, all of them freshly cleaned and oiled and standing in felt-lined racks. On a shelf above sat every kind and size of scope imaginable.

"You could wage quite a little war here, if the occasion ever arose," Ginger observed.

"My war days are over," he told her. "Now I just amuse myself."

The detective took her time scrutinizing the collection before reaching out to lift a Winchester rifle from its rack. It was a beauty. She ran her hand over the smooth wood stock and down the length of the blue steel barrel, observing the 270-caliber des-ignation stamped into it. She noted that the Winchester was fit-ted for a scope. Next, she pulled back the bolt, noting the fluid action, and smelled fresh oil in the firing chamber. Finally, she returned the rifle to its rack, and allowed Purdy to accompany her back around to the front of the cabin.

"I guess you're off the hook," she said as she was about to climb into her car.

"Am I?" he asked with a smile.

"For the reward," she clarified. "The hundred thousand dol-lars. That ad of yours was worded 'for the arrest and conviction,' wasn't it?"

He cocked his head. "Far as I'm concerned, the terms were met. And the way it looks right now, Detective, you're in line to collect."

"Me?"

"You're the one who came up with the first piece of real ev-idence, aren't you—the fingerprint match?"

"Sorry," she said abruptly, closing the car door and starting up the engine. "I'm not eligible. If you're determined to give your money away, you'll have to look somewhere else."

Purdy waited until he was certain there had been enough time for her to pass through the gate before he pressed the but-ton to close it. Then he went back behind the cabin to lock up the shed.

The woman was standing at the rear door. "You took a big chance," she said.

"No, I didn't," the ex-Marine assured her with a small smile. "She could have been holding it right in her hands, and would never have been able to prove it. She knew that."

"He has two witnesses who'll swear he was with them the entire time," Ginger reported to Ruben, "and a beauty of a Win-chester he knows we'll never be able to identify."

"Do you think he's our shooter?"

"I'm sure of it. We can investigate every other guy on the Island who owns a rifle capable of shooting a thirty-caliber or less varmint slug, but it would be a waste of time."

The police chief sighed. "All right, then," he said. "Let's not spin our wheels on it; put the investigation on an indefinite hold."

"And the Breckenridge case?"

Ruben shrugged. "As soon as the DNA results come in, close it."

Charlie Pricker stood in the doorway to Ruben's office. "Well, you're halfway there, then," he said.

"What do you mean?" Ginger asked.

He held up an envelope. "The DNA on the knife just came in," he replied. "It was Tara's blood, all right."

A big grin split Ginger's freckled face, and it was much more about relief than about joy. "I knew it," she cried. "I knew he did it. I knew the DNA would prove it!"

"It sure looks that way," Ruben said.

"The paternity report should show up sometime next week," Charlie said. "But that's just a technicality now."

"What a weight off my mind," Ginger exclaimed. "Oh my God, I was so afraid I might have been wrong—that I might have gotten an innocent man killed."

"Well, apparently, you didn't," the police chief was quick to concede.

"I feel like climbing to the top of Eagle Rock," she said exultantly, "and shouting at the top of my lungs—'Yes!'"

"Yes," Charlie echoed, "but will you settle for a normal voice and a plain old press conference? As soon as this gets out, we're going to be swamped. We didn't just make the local stations on prime time last night, you know, we made the networks."

"You do the interviews, Charlie," Ginger told him, sobering instantly. "You're much better at it than I am, and you can talk all that technical stuff that I don't know a thing about."

Glen Dirksen popped his head in the door. "I just got a call from one of the real estate agents here on the Island. He says he talked to Deborah Frankel at nine o'clock yesterday morning, and she told him to put her house on the market."

"What do you know about that," Charlie murmured.

"So I was right," Dirksen said. "She would have picked him up at the courthouse and never looked back. They'd probably still be going."

"Charlie," Ginger suggested. "I think you should let Officer Dirksen here do the press conference with you. Give him some experience."

"Really? Me on TV? Wow, wait'll I tell my folks!" Dirksen exclaimed and dashed out.

"He's got the makings of a good cop, that boy," Charlie said with a chuckle.

Ginger looked at him. They had been so close and shared so much. Next to Ruben, she knew she would miss him most. "The fact that Frankel turned out to be guilty doesn't erase what I did, and I know that," she told him. "I appreciate your willingness to keep it between us, and to let me leave on my own legs. But if the day comes, anytime in the next month, when you decide you can't live with it, I'm out of here—no explanations necessary. Are we absolutely clear on that?"

Charlie shrugged and then nodded. "Who knows," he said gently. "If I'd been wearing your shoes, I might have been tempted to do the same thing."

This time, the basement meeting was not really a meeting at all, but a boisterous celebration. There were cheers and laughter, and an ample quantity of champagne as the seven men sat around in the ambient candlelight, and congratulated themselves and each other. Everyone had at least one toast to make.

"To the fools who never knew what hit them," said Axel Tannauer, who managed the local movie theater.

"To us," said Tavis Andersen, the pharmacist.

"To the beginning," said Grant Kriedler, of the local Ford dealership. "Now that we know we can do it, no one can stop us."

"When you think about it," Andersen marveled, "it was all so ridiculously easy."

"Most of it," Tannauer agreed. "The stroke of genius was sending that letter to Gail Brown."

"It was pure luck that I happen to have a cousin living in Scarsdale," Jim Petrie, hardware store owner and city council member, confessed. "The genius was in knowing that Brown wouldn't quit until she found a way to dig the story out."

"What I can't get over was that swastika business," Barney Graham, the mortician, said, shaking his head.

"Why?" Anderson asked. "We didn't do it. That was somebody else."

"That's my point," Graham declared. "We started the ball rolling, and someone else got up and ran with it."

"It was perfect," Tannauer concurred. "It proves our effectiveness even more."

"It was a stupid thing to do, and it could have ruined everything for us," Kriedler said with a sharp edge to his voice. "I could tell right away that it made the Jew lawyer suspicious."

"You worry too much," Andersen said. "You're starting to sound like a Jew yourself."

The other men laughed and stamped their feet.

The noise ricocheted through the house and awakened the eleven-year-old boy who slept in the second-floor bedroom. Or perhaps he had not really been asleep at all, just waiting for an opportunity. He crept down the stairs in his pajamas, his feet bare so he would make no sound.

No one heard him as he opened the basement door a few inches. No one saw him as he crouched down beside it. His eyes squinted through his round spectacles to identify the men in the flickering light, to memorize their faces. His ears strained to hear their boasts and their claims, to catch a name, to attach it to a face, to store it away in his mind for another time, when he knew it would be important that he had been witness to this night.

He didn't understand a good deal of what he observed, but it was more than he needed to conclude that something was very wrong. He knew better than anyone that those fifth-grade bullies might have killed Matthew Frankel in the school bathroom that day, and now somebody had indeed killed Matthew's father . . . and for some inexplicable reason, these men were celebrating.

"Any of you have any idea who the shooter was?" the boy heard Petrie ask.

The men shrugged.

"I could make a pretty educated guess," Kriedler said, "about a certain ex-Marine who was so all fired anxious to give away his money."

"If that's the case, I say, we should elect him mayor," said Andersen.

The others chuckled.

"I expect now he'll probably figure he earned the reward himself," Tannauer said.

When they ran out of toasts and champagne, they declared the evening at an end and made their unsteady way out of the basement. The boy slipped off, unnoticed. He had seen and heard enough. Someday, when he was older, when he could find people who would listen, maybe he would tell.

The night was bright with stars, the air was crisp and buoyant and smelled of early spring. For no apparent reason, the men found themselves stopping on their way to their cars to look across the drive. The house next door was dark and still; no boy's voice broke the silence, no dog barked. The garage door had a fresh coat of paint. A "For Sale" sign had been impaled beside the front walk.

"One last toast," Tavis Andersen said as he waved an imaginary glass. "To improving the neighborhood."

Their host, Martin Keller, chuckled.

"Now that it's all over," Axel Tannauer wondered, "do you think he really did it?"

"Who knows?" replied Jim Petrie.

"Who cares?" asked Grant Kriedler.

"Does it matter?" questioned Keller.

"He must have done it," Graham said. "They found the knife in his car, didn't they? Although God knows why he kept it, the idiot."

The six of them looked at the seventh man, the quiet one, the leader.

"Of course he did it," Kyle Breckenridge said. "No doubt about it. All we did was make it a little easier for everyone else to figure it out."

14

It was just her eyes he saw. It was always that way. In the moonlight, they seemed to burn with a life of their own, as though they had no relation to the rest of her, as though there were no rest of her. Twist and turn though he might, he couldn't get away from them, or from the hideous indictment in them.

He covered his face with his hands so he wouldn't have to see. But even with his face covered, there were the eyes. Always the eyes. He tried to hide himself, as he invariably did, whimpering and cowering because he knew what was coming next. It always came next. He covered his ears, hoping to shut it out. But even with his ears covered, the wretched scream split the night in half as it denounced him to the world.

He awoke, soaked in sweat, his chest heaving, his head ready to burst. The nightmare had come again, to ruin his sleep, to jeopardize his health, to threaten his very sanity. To expose him for what he was.

Child molester! Murderer!

There was no escape.

Why now? he wondered, as he gasped for air. Now that it

was over, now that the teacher was dead and the case as good as closed, now that he was finally free?

, It wasn't fair. Not when he had orchestrated everything so brilliantly: devising the clues, planting the knife, manipulating the public, making sure that someone else, someone expendable, would pay the price—and no one had been the wiser.

Except for her.

But he had only done what anyone in his position would have done—he had protected himself. It was clearly self-defense. She had given him no other choice. Why couldn't she understand that? Why wouldn't she let him alone?

He pressed his hands against his head, willing the pain to pass, willing her to let go. But she remained. *How much more of this do you think I can take?* he screamed at her soundlessly.

It didn't matter now whether he was asleep or awake, she was always there to taunt him, to test him, to make his life a living hell. He was no longer able to think her away, no longer able to put reason between them, no longer able to fend her off with rationalization.

He couldn't bear the thought of living the rest of his life like this, in emotional isolation. He craved the comfort of another person; someone who would not judge him; someone who, without having to understand, would absolve him. But it couldn't be just anyone. He needed someone who trusted him implicitly and loved him unconditionally to put her arms around him and hold him and make the pain go away.

He got out of bed and stumbled blindly to the door, yanking it open, in too much agony to care about being quiet. He stood for a moment, blinking in the soft light that lit the hallway. Then he staggered forward, toward a room at the far end, a room directly across from the pink and yellow room where he used to find solace.

In total horror, Mary Breckenridge watched him go.